FIELDS OF

An Episode in th
between Good & Evil
by
Alex Ferguson

I heard a voice say, 'Whom shall I send?'
Then said I, 'Here am I. Send me.'

To my friend
Pat

Alex Ferguson

CHAPTER ONE

"I'm working up the Angry Viking look."

Two soldiers were sitting cross-legged either side of the 81 mm mortar; ammunition neatly stacked behind them. Both weapon and soldiers, skilfully crafted, grew from the brown clay to twenty inches in height. The soldier to one side of the mortar was reading a book. His comrade was peeling a banana. The white Cornish clay of the fruit shone against the earth brown.

Samuel Ericksen laid down the probe when the telephone began to ring. He pushed up the magnifying lenses and stretched his aching shoulders. He ignored the persistent telephone. The ringing ceased.
He said to the cat, "Anyone who knows me won't ring when I'm working."
The cat called Glaze said only the mentally disturbed talk to cats.
"People who live alone talk to anything."

From a corner of the glaze cupboard he extracted a bottle marked HIGHLY TOXIC and poured himself a draught. He sank into the shabby old chair by the window that looked out on the industrial yard; the studio was flanked by Tip Top Tyres, the Right Garage and The MOT

CERT Centre. He sipped his whisky. From the kiln shelf, Glaze looked upon him sternly.

"For my nerves," Sam said, "I'm a very nervous person."

The cat mewed disapproval.

When the telephone rang again, he rose from the chair without spilling a drop.

"Wardley Chinese Laundry. Who speaky, please?"

A familiar voice said, "You know it's me."

"I don't know any me but me."

"Hannah? Your ever-loving sister? Though God knows why."

"But I'm working."

"I couldn't wait."

"For what?"

"You're invited for dinner tonight. Then I'll tell you something that will surprise you."

"You phone me, to tell me, you will tell me something tonight, while eating a Chinese takeaway, that will surprise me?"

"Yes."

"You're pregnant?"

Hannah laughed.

"No."

"You've found a better takeaway?"

"No!"

"Then what? Tell me now."

The telephone went dead in his hand. Sam Ericksen finished his whisky and went back to work.

*

Emily Harrison closed the street door quietly because she didn't want her colleagues to see she was wet, angry and frustrated. Six fellow estate agents were at their desks immersed in their screens. Tom Fenwick was lounging in his chair, juggling a biro between his fingers, regarding her with amusement. Emily had fallen for him at first sight and longed for his attention. She had heard him refer to her as 'the kid', which hurt.

Emily sat down at her desk, despaired at her hair and repaired her face. Rain ran tears down the windows, mocking the display of properties. She had not closed a sale in three months. It was comforting of Maria to say they all suffered blank periods, but this was Emily's first year with Madison & Major. She had so far sold three properties. She knew she wasn't given the choicest prospects. Joanne held the first desk and shared out the sales.

Emily had begun to complete her daybook when the phone rang. She listened to a male voice. She made notes. When the conversation ended, she allowed herself the luxury of a heartfelt sigh.

Emily looked up to find Tom Fenwick at her desk offering a cup of coffee. Her heart bounced.

"You could do with this."
"Thank you!"
He pulled over a chair, saying, "That was some sigh."
"Not my best afternoon."
"Gee, but it's tough to be an estate agent. Everybody hates us and it's raining."

Emily laughed. It was perfect mimicry of the manager, Mr. Buchanan's Glaswegian tones. She sipped the coffee and regarded Fenwick. His appearance was as perfect as ever, but he needed a haircut.
She said, "You need a haircut" before she realised she had spoken aloud. Embarrassed, she added, "Sorry," before he responded, "I'm sure you're right."

She dared to say, "I guess you have manicures too."
"I'm selling houses. Biggest purchase people ever make."
"Well, I'm trying to sell houses. But nothing works."
She was aware he was studying her appearance.
"That's not fair. I've just walked from the Terrace in the rain."

"Buy an umbrella. Buy two. One for the client."
"Thanks for the tip."
It was offered as a go away line, but Fenwick didn't.

"What went wrong?"
"Twenty-seven Salisbury Grove."
"Needs some attention. Call it character."
"It's a rundown Victorian villa. I thought I'd sold it."
"And?"
"They had no intention of buying the property."
"How long did it take you to cotton on?"
"When the wife mentioned she'd been born in the master bedroom. A trip down memory lane."

"That was the solicitor, Mansfield, on the phone just now. The owner's decided not to let the apartment at Harbour Mount after all. Now he wants to sell it."
"Pity that house was ever broken up. Palatial Regency mansion above the harbour. Superb views. Definitely Nob Hill. How did you get it?"
"Because it was a let."
"Good practice for you."

Emily wasn't listening, her head in her notes on Harbour Mount.

"Would you believe Mansfield has arranged two viewings for tomorrow? While I have a viewing for a let."
"Not your fault."
"I'll have to go over there now and change the board. And check the apartment."
"I'll lend you an umbrella."

Before she could refuse, Fenwick went to his desk and returned with a furled umbrella. He shook it open to display MADISON & MAJOR Estate Agents of Choice.
"Pretty cool?"
Emily laughed.
"Could I ask a very big favour?"
"Sure."
"Would you come with me?"
"Why would I do that, Emily?"
Emily's heart sank.
"Last time I was there someone was rude to me?"
"Didn't the client say anything?"
"Oh, yes! I've changed my mind about the apartment."
They walked arm in arm under the umbrella to Emily's car.

*

Hannah answered the door.
"You're late, Sam."
"I got caught up."

"And it took an hour?"

There was no mistaking their shared
Scandinavian heritage. She hugged her brother
smiling, but chiding. Sam hung his coat on the
hall stand and glimpsed his face in the mirror.
Hannah said, "The beard suits you."
"I'm working up the Angry Viking look."
"More the petulant potter?"
"Where's my favourite niece?"
"Isla's gone to bed long time. You're late.

"Sam produced a ceramic rabbit. Caught head-
lifted, as if scenting a fox.
Hannah said, "How do those gorilla hands create
such perfection?"
"I wear gloves."
"Still not waking Isla. School tomorrow."
"Which is her school coat?"
"The raggy one."
Sam slipped the rabbit into a pocket.
"Come and meet Keira."

*

"Keira, this is my brother Sam. I've warned you
about him."
There was no mistaking Keira's Caribbean
heritage. Hair dark as a moonless night. Eyes as
green as the sea.
"Hi!" squeaked Sam, weakly.

He couldn't think of anything to say
."I've looked forward to meeting you. Hannah's told me all about you."
"I hope not."
They shook hands formally.

*

The rain began to slacken as they drove. Tom Fenwick looked through the particulars of Harbour Mount. Emily worried about her driving. She jumped when Tom spoke.
"You ever heard of the battle of Harbour Mount?"
Emily shook her head, keeping her eyes on the road. His presence in the car made her nervous. The last thing she wanted to hear from him was, "Should I drive?" Her father had said that once and she failed the test.

"On the Mount, there was a hamlet of fishermen's shielings. Cottages. The remains of a Viking enclave. I don't know if that's true, but they kept to themselves and looked to the sea, not the town. What's now the Marine Park was just a hill of sand and grass that ran down to the sea where they beached their cobles. There were no piers then."
"When was this?"
"Eighteen fifteen, Napoleon's beat. England's on the rise. The rich are richer. The ex-soldiers and seamen are destitute. An armaments

9

manufacturer who has made a great deal of money from the wars decides he needs a fine house in the best situation in the Borough of South Aranport."

He paused as they waited at the traffic lights.

"So the fisher cottages have to go. He brought in bullyboys from Dunston to pull them down. Chose their time well. They arrived when the cobles were at sea."
"Cobles?"
"Sea-going rowed boats. The eviction turned to a massacre. Seventeen old men and eight boys were killed defending the shielings. Sixteen women and nine children died fighting when they refused to leave their homes. The bully boys couldn't shift them so they set fire to the shielings."
"Oh, my God! Is this true?"
"Would I bother to tell you otherwise?"
"Sorry!"
The windscreen wipers waved admonitory fingers at Emily.
"Shall I go on?"

*

"Totally unreliable."
"True."

"Once was a soldier. Now pretends to be a potter."

"I am a potter. I have a certificate to prove it."

Keira and Hannah laughed at Sam's discomfort.

"You forgot to mention, I hate my sister."

The doorbell rang to rescue Sam. Hannah went to receive the takeaway, saying, "There's somebody who turns up on time."

Hannah vanished leaving Keira and Sam together.

"I'm sorry if we embarrassed you."

"No problem."

"You're on your own?"

"I was nearly married. But she decided she couldn't bear the prospect of me coming home in a box. Or with bits blown off."

Keira looked concerned, saying, "I'm sorry."

"No. Don't be. Sensible girl. A soldier's wife has it harder than her man. Soldier's children even worse."

"I have a daughter. I couldn't bear to think I wouldn't be there to see her grow up."

"What's her name?"

"It was supposed to be Sophia. But she's been very firm about that. She doesn't want to be So-phea. She's Soph-ee and she's eleven."

"Soph-ee. Sounds good to me."

Hannah appeared in the doorway.

"Dinner's ready."

Sam jibed, "You mean you opened the boxes?"

Hannah blew a raspberry and Keira laughed.

*

"When the cobles saw the smoke, they raced for the shore. The bullyboys now had a real fight on their hands. The fishermen killed the agent, his secretary and seven of the bullyboys. They would've killed them all, if the militia hadn't arrived. The fishermen pulled down three troopers and taking their sabres killed four troopers and mutilated seven horses. The militia finally drove them onto the beach where the survivors took to their cobles and fled to the sea. Men, women and a handful of children."
"How do you know all this?"
"One of the captured children was a Fenwick. Sent to the Orphanage. My great, great times great grandfather."
"Really?"
"The dead were buried in a mass grave somewhere here on the Mount the abandoned cobles were burnt. Fishing crossed the river to North Aranport."
"Where the fish quay is now?"
"And Harbour Mount was built."

They drove up Mount Road in silence. The fine double-fronted house appeared on their left, facing the sea. Four storeys and cellars below. Flight of steps leading to a black front door. Fanlight shining. Gold railings guarding the basement. A parade of gravel behind the ferocious railings. A glimpse of the communal garden behind the house. Complementary garages to the left of the house. She parked the car tidily at the pavement. Tom Fenwick didn't comment on her parking. The pedestrian gate opened smoothly. Emily wondered whether the dead had been buried under this prestigious mansion. There was a Madison & Major board inside the railing. *Third floor Apartment to Let.* Tom Fenwick took the gummed tape and pressed it onto the board: FOR SALE. They approached the front door.

CHAPTER TWO

"Don't even think it. I haven't laid a finger on her."

It was a thoroughly enjoyable evening. The candidates were inducted with due gravity, but once freed from ceremony, there was much celebration among friends and colleagues. The Chancellor gave a speech that was greeted with applause. Appropriately short, which may have occasioned the applause, but the sentiment was appreciated by old and young. He finished his oration as usual with a jest. Everyone laughed although the Bishop regarded it as in poor taste.

There was great excitement among the newly inducted when it came to the most solemn moment of the occasion. The old man was the cause of much amusement as he pleaded for his life. However, the members who mimicked his piteous cries earned a rebuke from the Chancellor. The old man's naked body with sagging belly and withered genitalia was indeed an amusing sight, but there is always the matter of decorum to consider.

*

Emily almost handed the keys to Tom Fenwick. She recovered herself and opened the door. The entrance hall was laid with Regency mosaic tiles. The doors to left and right were the front doors of Apartments B and C. The basement apartment she knew as Apartment A. Before them rose the shadowed staircase down which Mrs. Proudlyrich's maid would once have flounced to send Emily and Tom to the tradesmen's entrance. When Emily trod on the first step the staircase was illuminated, chasing away the shadows. The staircase was discreetly decorated with nineteenth century prints.

"Don't forget the service charge," Tom said, "It can come as a nasty shock."

On the landing were the front doors of Apartments, D and E.   The door to Apartment E opened a crack.
Tom Fenwick called cheerily, "Hello! Madison and Major."
The door closed.
"Which am I? Madison or Major."
The upper landing offered one door, Apartment F.
Tom said, "This must be the prime property."
A narrower staircase continued upwards to the final Apartment G.
"That way, servant country," Tom Fenwick offered.

*

There were envious glances cast upon the new inductee who had been chosen as the Anointed. He broke the old man's neck most competently and sliced open his belly with one clean stroke. With a flick of the blade, he sent the genitalia flying to be scrambled after by younger members as a souvenir; a revered tradition. Unfortunately, this provoked the old woman, his wife, to begin screaming. The Anointed silenced the good wife in the most humorous manner. He cut off the old man's right hand and stuffed it down his wife's throat. Screaming was replaced by laughter.

*

Emily found the key and they entered the apartment. From the oak-panelled hallway, the door to the sitting room stood open.
"Wow! It's July, nineteen fourteen. World War One will start any time now. The master, the mistress and the children have just departed to hear the Marsden Colliery Silver Band playing Military Marches from the bandstand in the park."

They walked through the apartment together. Although Emily had visited previously she was further impressed. The furnishings were immaculately Victorian. There were impressive mahogany bookcases in the sitting room and fine club chairs. Below the windows stood an elegant chaise longue. The fireplace was unused but displayed an enviable marble mantelpiece and mirrors. The dining room sported an enormous mirrored sideboard and an ambassadorial dining suite. The five bedrooms would not have disgraced Windsor Castle. The only exceptions in décor were the kitchen and the bathrooms. The kitchen door led out onto a metal balcony and fire escape that served all the apartments.

Emily asked, "Do you know who was the original owner?"
"William Henry Tull. Did very well out of the Napoleonic Wars."
As an afterthought, Tom said, "Would've been madness to let this apartment." "I wonder what he is going to do with the furniture."

Tom went to check the bedrooms against the let specification. Emily looked out over the harbour towards the open sea. She sensed movement behind her and turned, expecting Tom. She saw a dark shadow cross the room and vanish into the wall. Emily was suddenly afraid. What had formerly seemed welcoming felt oppressive. If she had been alone, she would have fled instantly. She knew there was something here that wasn't human. If she stayed it would harm her.

*

As the Anointed prepared the old man's body, colleagues helped the Anointed female to lift the woman onto the altar. Unfortunately, she had difficulty breaking the old woman's neck and required assistance. She also needed assistance to open the belly to expose the entrails. It was however considered excusable as the female Anointed is twelve years old; a favourite of the Chancellor. The Bishop recited the appropriate entreaties to Our Lord and the feast began. The barbecue was popular, but traditionalists favoured gobbling fresh raw titbits. Forgive the feeble jest.

*

She called, "Tom!"
He didn't answer and she found him in the smallest of the bedrooms.
"Don't quote these figures. They're way out."
"Tom, d'y'think you could do the viewings tomorrow?"
Tom regarded her soberly. She saw he was disappointed.
"Please?"
"Being an estate agent isn't a part-time job."
Emily pleaded, "I've made a mess of my appointments."

She desperately wished to tell him what she had seen and how she felt. Yet she feared being laughed at. Reluctantly, Tom Fenwick said, "We won't mention this in the office. I can do the morning. You'll have to deal with the afternoon." She was so relieved, she almost kissed him and was disappointed that he stepped away.

"Thank you! Can we go now?"
He'll sell it in the morning. I'm sure he will.
As she turned, closing the house door, she saw a shadow on the staircase watching her.

*

They drove back to the office in silence. Emily knew Fenwick was not pleased with her behaviour. She parked in the Terrace car park, turned off the engine, but didn't move. Tom Fenwick moved to exit.
"Tom?"
He sat down again.
"Did you feel anything?"
"Feel anything?"
"At the apartment? Atmosphere? Positive vibes? Negative vibes?"
Tom Fenwick regarded Emily soberly.
"We're estate agents. Atmosphere is not our problem unless it stinks. We don't have vibes, positive or negative."
"I just thought."
"You just thought what?"
"Nothing."

*

It was the happiest of occasions and every face and body was bloody with good eating. One suspected the Anointed was a butcher as he did excellent work on both offerings. The provision of doggy bags caused great amusement. I suspect the Bishop does not approve of breaking with tradition, but we must move with the times. When the neighbourhood kiddies came for trick or treat, Angus answered the door and they fled screaming. We found it delightful that the old customs were still respected. Angus is a shy, reclusive creature who doesn't venture out in daylight, but is a charming companion nevertheless. We ended the occasion with hymn & prayer and parted in good humour, leaving singly or in pairs from the house. Younger colleagues exited over the back garden fence. We do our best to avoid any neighbourly interest in our proceedings.

*

Emily climbed out in confusion. Tom Fenwick addressed her across the car.

"If I were in my first year with Madhouse and Melancholy, I'd grab every chance to show a property. I wouldn't want my hand held and I wouldn't hand over any viewing unless I were dying of cholera. You're going to have to make up your mind whether you want to be an estate agent, Emily."

"You don't understand."

"I'll do tomorrow morning for you. But no more."

Emily fled through the office. Surprised faces looked up at her from desk screens. She locked herself in the toilet cubicle. Then she wept silently. Tom Fenwick followed Emily into the office. Amused faces greeted him.
"Don't even think it. I haven't laid a finger on her."
He dropped into his chair, but swung around to say to Maria, "Have a word with that girl. I wonder if she wants to be an estate agent."
"Tell me more."
"Ask her."

Tom Fenwick completed his daybook and called up Harbour Mount on his screen. He began to read. Tom didn't lift his gaze as Emily returned to her desk, collected her coat and left the office.

*

I remained with the Bishop until all had departed and when he was safely away, I set fire to the house with the appropriate prayers and supplications to Our Lord. I admit I have always had a fascination with fire. From the comfort of my car, I watched the firemen at work. And so to bed, as dear Pepys would say, All in all, a most satisfactory day.
As recorded by Amanuensis.

CHAPTER THREE

"It's going to be alright, Sparky! I know it's going to be okay!"

Emily was met at the door by Sparky, curling around her ankles, even as she hung up her coat. She carried the cat with her as she checked there was no one in the flat, even opening the wardrobe doors. She was sufficiently surprised by her actions as to remark aloud, "God, I've never done this before!" Satisfied, she fed Sparky and found consolation in her presence.
"Oh, I love you, Sparky! You're the one who never lets me down."

There were no voices on the answer phone. Emily switched on the television and switched it off again. She decided not to have a shower, but ran a bath. While the bath was filling, she closed the curtains in her bedroom, switched on the bedside lamp and opened the bed. As an afterthought she switched on the machine that filled the bedroom with sounds of a gentle sea breaking upon a shingle shore. She slipped into the comforting bubbles. Her voice enhanced by the tiling, she said aloud, "Baths are really a return to the womb. Or more rationally, being marine apes by descent, we retreat into the water in times of danger."

*

"Compliments to the chef," Sam Ericksen announced as his sister Hannah cleared the remains of the takeaway from the table and dropped the boxes into the waste bin.

"Coffee?" offered Hannah.
"Please," said Keira.
"So what is this exciting news that I hastened over to hear?"
Hannah countered, "No, you didn't hasten. You were late and you
came to eat."
"Are you going to tell me?"
The two women exchanged glances.
"Keira and I are going into partnership."
"Excellent! You've always wanted someone to boss around."
"We won't be here."
"How'd'y'mean? You won't be here?"
"We're setting up in Newcastle."
Sam sat considering what his sister had said. Hannah went to the refrigerator and returned with ice cream.
"Not for me," said Keira, "Thank you."
Hannah piled strawberry ice cream into a bowl and placed it in front of her brother. Keira added a spoon. Sam ate a spoonful and stopped.
"What about Isla?"
"What about her?"

"You'll be taking her with you?"
Hannah looked to Keira and said, "Of course, I will! She's my daughter." "This is her home." "Where I am is her home."
Sam was silent in thought.

"Do you mean Newcastle-under-Lyme, Newcastle, Newry, Northern Ireland or Newcastle upon Tyne?"
Keira tried not to laugh, but failed.
"I'd like to know where you're going. Not very good on ferries. And I have no idea where Newcastle-under-Lyme is."
"Newcastle upon Tyne," Hannah confirmed, "You can get a coach."
"The loos stink."
Sam was silent.

He looked appealingly to Keira.
"You won't like it there.""Why not?"
"Cold. Rains all the time. You won't understand what they're saying. Football team is hopeless. And."
Keira said, "Have you ever been to Newcastle, Sam?"
"Ferry to Norway."
"Doesn't count."
Hannah said, "Promise me, Sam, you will never, ever repeat what you just said to any citizen of Newcastle."

"What about me?"

"What about you?" Hannah enquired.

"What do I do?"

"What did you do today?"

"Gave myself back ache."

Hannah offered, "Just keep doing that."

"But I like coming here to eat."

"I thought for a moment you were going to say. I like coming here to see my adorable sister, single mother of an angel child. Not because I have a good Chinese takeaway and yours is rubbish."

"Do like coming to see you. You and Isla.

"Keira suggested, "Come and see us in Newcastle."

"Not very good on coaches."

"Take a train."

"Too expensive."

"You could fly."

"Don't fly."

"Keira, don't bother to talk sense to him."

"You won't like living in Newcastle, Hannah."

Keira said, "We're not living in Newcastle, Sam."

"We'll be working there," Hannah explained, "But we're looking for somewhere quiet on the coast. Some quiet, peaceful spot."

"When're you going?"

"Lease on the office is first of next month."

"Can I have your halogen oven when you go? My microwave doesn't work anymore."

*

Keira drove Sam home. They were both quiet in the car. Sam struggled desperately to find something to say. Keira's mobile buzzed in her bag.

"D'y'want to answer that?"

"I don't answer the phone when I'm driving."

Sam was discomforted.

"No, of course, not. If I were driving, I wouldn't answer the phone."

He confessed, "I don't have a mobile anyway," and contradicted himself.

"That's not quite true. I did have a mobile. Actually, I still have a mobile. But people kept ringing me up."

"Isn't that what it's for?"

"I suppose so. But they always ring when I'm working."

"You could answer it when you're not working."

"Yes, you're right. I could do that. Yes, I'll get it out again. If I can find it. That's a very good idea."

In desperation, Sam struggled for his wallet. He found a creased business card.

"Pop my card in the glove compartment?"

Sam suited the action to the words.

"Why would you do that?"

Sam struggled for words. "You might want to phone me?"

"Why would I do that?"

Sam couldn't think of an answer.

Keira rescued him.

"If I did, you wouldn't answer."

"Yes, I would. You're right, I should answer the phone. You've given me a timely reminder. Thank you. I will start answering the phone."

Keira drove on in silence. Sam tried again.

"How did you meet my sister?"

"At a seminar."

Sam wasn't quite sure what a seminar was.

"You just hit it off? At this seminar?"

"We realised we were better together. Shared so much. Madness to compete when we could work together."

"In this gate," Sam directed.

Keira hesitated. "This where you live?"

"Yes."

Keira stopped the car in the yard, but didn't turn off the engine. She was looking at his neighbours.

"Which one is you? You're not Stan the Garage Man, are you? Tip Top Tyres?"

"No."

"MOT CERT? Whatever that is."

"No, I'm the big shed."

"Looks like someone's thrown paint all over the Village Hall!"

"I painted it. Wanted it to stand out."

"It certainly does that."

Sam was reluctant to leave the car, but he couldn't find any reason to remain. He wanted to be with this woman. Keira regarded him with amusement.

"Aren't you going to get out?"

"Oh, yes! Thanks. Very kind of you to give me a lift."

"My pleasure."

"Well, good night! Hope to see you again."

"I hope so too. Good night, Sam!"

Sam struggled from the car, stopping in the open door to say, "You think I'm a raving idiot, don't you?"

Keira said, "Yes."

Sam wanted to die.

Sam watched Keira's car until it vanished from sight. Then he closed and locked the gate.

*

When the alarm buzzed, Emily Harrison awoke from an uneasy sleep. As she moved to silence the alarm, the novel she had tried to read last night fell from the bed. She started at the sound. She had given up reading when she found she was staring at the page, listening to the noises of the night. Young voices and laughter echoed from the street. The clock in the sitting room chimed two. She lay staring into the darkness, trying not to believe someone or something was jimmying the lock on her front door. When someone scratched at the bedroom door she wanted to die. When Sparky called, she was immensely relieved. She moved the chair from under the handle and opened the door.

The creature of shadows was holding up her cat by the tail. Sparky was clawing at the hand that held her. Emily screamed and awoke from the nightmare. She lay in bed until the trembling faded and then went to find her cat. The flat was all in order and Sparky was sleeping in her own crab pot. Emily pulled out the puzzled feline and took her to bed, which was against the rules. They shared a restless sleep until the alarm buzzed and the book fell to the floor. Emily dragged herself to the bathroom and Sparky to the cat tray. Emily fed Sparky, but had no appetite for breakfast. She wished she had never given up smoking.

When the telephone rang she ignored it.
"That's too early for Fenwick," she told the cat, "The viewing's at eleven."
Because she felt guilty she went through every competing estate agent's site on her laptop,

noting prices. She couldn't ignore Madison & Major. Harbour Mount was no longer a let. She was surprised at the sale price.

"*Possible inclusion furniture.* He must really need the money. Tom'll sell it."

Emily felt relief. Tom Fenwick would be sure to close the sale. She wouldn't ever have to go back to Harbour Mount.
"Just to make sure," she said to Sparky who had no interest in property sales, "I'll see if I can drop the viewing."
She was becoming quite light-hearted. She dialled, but no one picked up the phone.
"What should I say? Sorry. An offer has been made? A sale has been agreed? Thought I'd save you the trip. And if Fenwick doesn't sell it? I know I'm a coward. You don't have to tell me."

Emily avoided Sparky's accusing eyes and dialled the client's number again. She rang several times, but no one answered. The more often it rang unanswered, the more fretful Emily became. She filled the dishwasher with oddments, started the washing machine with anything she could find, cleaned the bath, the shower and vacuumed the flat. Her nerves twanged like an out of tune guitar. She almost missed the phone ringing in the roar of the vacuum cleaner. She was praying when she picked up the phone. Her heart was galloping in a cavalry charge. She took a deep breath.

"Hello?"

A voice announced, "Have you considered how much a funeral costs? Do you want to leave your family the burden of."

Emily ended the call. When her mobile rang, Emily fumbled in her shoulder bag. Maria said, "Emily?"

"What can I do for you, Maria?"

"Sorry to bother you. But can you tell me, please, where you filed the Northcliffe papers? Now they're complaining about ground rent."

Emily gritted her teeth.

"If you don't have them, they must still be on my desk. Sorry!"

Emily ended the call.

She was trembling and struggled for calm.

"It's going to be alright, Sparky! I know it's going to be okay!"

The telephone rang. Emily let the cat down onto the couch.

"Cross your paws, Sparky!"

She took a deep breath and picked up the phone.

"Hello?"

"Sorry. No go."

Emily's heart stopped. Her knees failed and she sat down on the couch.

"I don't believe it."

"I'm having trouble myself. Nice couple. Middle-aged. They loved it. The fact he's willing to do a deal on the furniture was a winner. I was home and dry."
"What happened?"

"We were coming down the stairs. The deal was done. On the floor below, the door opens and this guy appears. I say, Good morning! He ignores me and says to the client, You interested in the apartment? The client says, Yes. This guy says, Don't. I said, Whoa, whoa! What's it to do with you? He ignores me and repeats to the client, Don't! They were both terrified. No sale."
"That's all he said? Don't?"
"He didn't threaten them. He didn't insult them. He said, Don't! That's all. And they were totally scared out of their wits."
"What was he like?"
"Young. Bald. In a suit. Pleasant face."
Emily couldn't find the words.
"Better luck this afternoon! Play up the offer of a deal on the furniture. Sorry I couldn't swing it for you.

CHAPTER FOUR

"Don't forget to zip up his flies. You forgot yesterday."

The manager of the Newcastle branch of the Northern Counties Bank, Mr. Peter McCracken, has recently been the subject of our discussions. Like so many of his kind, it wasn't difficult to encourage him to join Congregation. To put it bluntly, our Mr. McCracken has been stealing from accounts that were not active, accounts of elderly customers. He has also been stealing from the safe deposit boxes; principally gold and jewellery. He snivelled when he talked to me. He wept when he told me he had notice of a General Audit. He hugged me closely when he confessed how he feared going to prison. Most distasteful! I had snot and tears on my shoulder. He admitted he had considered suicide rather than face his wife and daughters who have benefited greatly from his betrayal of trust. I explained that we would take care of everything. All he had to do was to keep calm and carry on normally during the Audit.
Mr. McCracken worked through the weekend with Norma and Kevin to rectify the situation.
The thefts, of course, were discovered and a young man and woman were arrested, later

convicted and went to prison. The Audit was signed off and the manager commended.

The unfortunates' posts have been filled by Norma and Kevin. The safe deposit boxes are a welcome bonus. You may be surprised what secrets they contain, along with gold and jewellery. When we have no further need of Mr. McCracken, I will arrange the Audit to convict him. It is pleasing to see how active we are in Our Lord's work. Such was the commendation of our Lord Archbishop.

As recorded by Amanuensis.

*

Emily Harrison ate crackers and cottage cheese for lunch. She visited the bathroom for the third time, checked her shoulder bag, and skimmed the notes once more. Around her neck she hung a small silver crucifix on a chain. Then she poured a double vodka and swallowed it. She refilled Sparky's water bowl and watched as the cat drank.

"Wish me luck, Sparky. I must sell this wretched apartment."

She couldn't resist a further vodka, locked the flat and was disappointed to find her car had not been stolen. Emily parked outside Harbour Mount and exited the car into sunshine and a pleasant breeze off the sea. The stage was set for a successful viewing. An older Lexus drew up

and parked behind her. A middle-aged couple left the car and Emily asked brightly, "Mister and Missis Clifford?" The man replied, "Pam and Dennis."
Emily shook hands saying, "Emily Harrison. Madison and Major."

Mrs. Clifford was looking at the harbour. Emily offered, "Isn't it a lovely view? You can see it every morning at breakfast," and added, "Perhaps it's loveliest at evening."
To Mr. Clifford she said, "It's a wonderful house, isn't it? Listed building Grade Two. The finest in South Aranport. Shall we proceed?"

Emily opened the pedestrian gate. She was aware Mrs. Clifford was much impressed. Emily led the way up the steps and opened the front door. She stood aside to let the clients enter, knowing they would be impressed with the entrance hall. She heard Mrs. Clifford's sharp intake of breath.
"Shall I lead the way?"

The lighting on the stairs chased the shadows as they ascended. Emily left the clients to themselves and went out onto the landing. They hadn't hidden their enthusiasm and Tom Fenwick was right. The owner's offer to consider offers for the furniture lit both faces. The service charge was reasonable and maintenance standards high. Emily filled in the basic details of the couple on her tablet and prepared to suggest a first bid price. The lights went out automatically and left Emily in shadow, but when she moved, returned. She felt a certain relief. By her watch the Cliffords had been in conference twelve minutes before the door opened. She knew from Mrs. Clifford's reluctance to meet her gaze that they weren't going to buy.

Emily said brightly, "What do you think? Isn't it a wonderful apartment?"
Mr. Clifford was hesitant to speak.
"If it's the price? I think we could win some space from the seller?"
Mr. Clifford said, "It's not the apartment. It's the stairs."
His wife added apologetically, "We're in our fifties now. We're looking for somewhere to spend our retirement. Now the children have gone."
Mr. Clifford said, "How long would we manage the stairs? It would be different if there was a lift. I'm sorry, but we have to say no."
Emily almost said, *then why the hell, are we looking at a third floor apartment?*
She said, "I quite understand. To look ahead is very sensible."

She led the way downstairs and kept her temper as Mrs. Clifford chattered about Ainsley in Australia and daughter Chloe in Hong Kong. On the last long flight to the entrance hall, they met a tall thin man coming upstairs. He smiled and stood aside to let the visitors pass. As Emily was saying thank you, the stranger tripped her and she fell to break her neck on the magnificent hall tiles. Mr. Clifford was first to reach her, his wife trailing down the stairs, one hand on the banister. He asked, "Are you alright?"

He tried to raise Emily and cried out, "Oh, God, she's broken her neck!" Shocked, he dropped her. He fumbled for a pulse as his wife scrabbled in her purse for her mobile.

"No pulse. No heart beat."

"No signal!" Mrs. Clifford complained.

"Outside!" her husband ordered.

With his wife following, he marched out of the house, leaving the front door open. He phoned police and ambulance from the pavement. A distressed Mrs. Clifford went to sit in the car. Her husband waited on the pavement for whoever should first appear, police or ambulance.

*

Emily Harrison was sitting in her car, writing up the Clifford viewing when the policeman rapped on the glass. He was an older man. She wound down the window and apologised. "Sorry, officer! I'll move it."

The policeman asked, "Are you Emily Harrison? Estate agent?"

"Yes."

"Please step out of the car, miss."

A confused Emily closed the tablet and slipped out of the car.

Beyond the policeman were the clients, Mr. & Mrs. Clifford. A police car blinking blue stood at the kerb.

"What's this about?"

"This gentleman has reported you lying dead in the hallway of Harbour Mount."

Emily looked to the couple who took a step back. They were regarding her with a mixture of fear and amazement. Mrs. Clifford was clasping her husband's hand tightly.

"I don't understand."

"I swear, on my Mother's grave," Mr. Clifford exclaimed, "this woman fell down the stairs and broke her neck."

He turned to his wife.

"God's truth!" she assured the constable, "She was dead."

The policeman turned to Emily.

"I showed Mister and Missis Clifford the apartment. They decided against purchase. We came downstairs and said goodbye. I went to write up the viewing. I presumed the clients had gone. Then you tapped on my window."

"She's lying," accused Mrs. Clifford.

"Why would I?"

Mr. Clifford was silent because he knew something was very wrong and wanted no part of it.

"The front doors open," said the policeman.

"I have to go back and check everything's turned off."

"Come away, Pam," Mr. Clifford urged and to the policeman, "You don't need us for anything?"

"No, sir. Thank you for ringing. It could've been very serious."

Mr. Clifford regarded Emily with a mixture of fear and dislike.

"You were dead. I've seen enough."

Emily and the policeman watched the Cliffords' car drive away as the ambulance arrived.

The grey-haired constable smiled at Emily, saying, "Welcome to the Congregation."

Before she could gather her wits, he went to greet the paramedic. She waited until he had dispatched the ambulance and was sitting in the police car. She rapped on the glass and the constable wound down the window.

He smiled and said, "Yes, miss?"

"What did you say to me?"
"Not a lot."
"The last thing you said to me."
"Can't remember."
"Yes, you do."
He regarded her thoughtfully.

"You've had something of a rough afternoon, miss. You didn't sell the apartment because they're the wrong people. I know you're desperate to sell it. But you must sell it to the right people. They were the wrong people."
"You don't know what you're talking about."
"You've been dead and now you're alive, miss. I think we should leave it at that, don't you? Welcome to the Congregation, Emily Harrison."

He wound up the window, started the engine and without a backward glance, drove away. A confused Emily stood in the road watching the blue lights blink off. A car behind hooted and she turned to curse the driver. She was surprised at the foulness of her tongue. She gave the next car the finger before she returned to the pavement. She walked up and turned off the services. She flushed the toilet. So many clients took advantage. When she had worked weekends on a new estate someone had used the show house toilet that wasn't connected. Being 'the girl' Emily had cleaned up. She straightened the cushions where Mrs. Clifford had sat.

"I should put up a plaque. Prize-winning pig's arse squatted here."

She laughed and felt the room laugh with her. She replaced the vase Mr. Clifford had moved aside as he stood at the window. She paused at the sitting room door before she left. There was a comfortable, welcoming ambience that she was reluctant to quit.

*

She only went to the office to show her face and snub the inquisitive.

"What're you nosy cows staring at?"

Tom Fenwick looked astonished. She used the toilet and didn't flush it.

"Hot tip. Stay out of there for an hour."

Nobody laughed.

When Maria asked how the viewing went, she was surprised how rude she was. "Gave him a blow job. He still said no."

The office was scandalised. Tom Fenwick protested.

"God's sake, Emily!"

When she headed for the door, Maria asked, "Where're you going, Harrison?"

"That's my business."

"It's only half three."

"What's it to you, Grandma?"

Maria was hurt and surprised.

"I am the senior here. This is the first time we've seen you today. And you're wagging off mid-afternoon? I shall report your behaviour to Mister Buchanan." "Don't forget to zip up his flies. You forgot yesterday."

Emily blew a raspberry and departed. She retained the keys to Harbour Mount.

*

Emily hooted the learner driver trying to make up her mind to turn right at the traffic lights. Her instructor started to get out of the car and Emily opened her door. The instructor retreated. The light turned to red. Emily hit the horn almost constantly, opened the window and shouted. Her mood swooped from euphoric to a sullen anger to a sense of power she had never experienced before. The learner's car gave up trying to turn right and drove on. Emily turned right. She parked in her neighbour's space regardless. On the stairs she pushed past the old lady with the carrier bags and heard a handle snap. Her clumsiness with the keys had vanished and she opened the flat door with a flourish. She almost fell over a small cat that scratched her leg. Emily kicked it so hard the animal flew the length of the entrance hall and struck the kitchen door. It lay without moving and she carried it into the kitchen. When it stirred, she fed the creature into the waste disposal unit. It vanished very quickly. In the sitting room Emily poured herself a large vodka. She hesitated over the tonic and decided against. She swallowed the vodka quickly and went to start her bath. She found herself singing which surprised her. She seemed lately to have little to sing about, but now she felt consumed by happiness. When she tried to think why, there was no response. It was enough that she was happy. She retrieved the vodka, but not the glass from the sitting room and lay contented in the scented bubble bath, drinking from the bottle.

CHAPTER FIVE

"Everything's gone to pot, so I might as well."

The kiln was cold and the wheels turned not. The drying cupboard was full and the pug mill was silent. The kettle was neglected. Spotlights lit the shelves of finished work, colourful, original and unsold. Rain was falling on the skylights. Sam Ericksen worked at the long bench. The studio was so quiet you might hear his breathing. He was painting an alder tree. His tongue protruded as he concentrated on the fine detail. From time to time, he licked the paint brush or added colour. In his head, he was at the waterside, shaded by an alder, studying another alder across the stream. There was a knocking at the studio door and he was rudely wrenched back to reality. Sam cursed, but kept control of the brush.

The knocking resumed and someone called his name through the letter box. He dropped a cloth over the unfinished jug on his lazy susan. The bell rang as Sam opened the door to say, "I don't discuss religion at the door, but, yes, I believe in the imminent deity."
"You took your time," Hannah chided her brother, "It's raining!"
Sam had eyes only for Keira.
"Hi!"

Hannah said, "Come here, you," and hugged her brother.

To Keira she said, "He's a big, clumsy puppy, isn't he? The one that chews and breaks everything. And thinks he's adorable. Not!"

Keira said, "I think he was at the most delicate moment of throwing a pot, Hannah. That's the right word? Throwing?"

Sam nodded.

"His hands are clean," observed Hannah, "He was having a crafty nap."

"I was working," Sam offered to Keira who was already exploring the studio.

"Wow! But these are beautiful! Astonishing! Never seen anything like this!"

Keira turned an admiring glance upon Sam whose heart began to dance. Hannah dropped the dead pizza into the waste bin, filled the kettle and found three mugs.

"Isn't there an even cheaper coffee you could buy?"

Keira was standing before a shelf of seven large jugs, original in design, in a matt glaze. Sam came to join her.

"They're a special commission."

On each of the jugs was painted a different tree in leaf.

Sam recited, "Oak, ash, willow, horse chestnut, beech, poplar, rowan."

Keira applauded, "They're astonishing."

"I told you he wasn't just a pretty face."

"I'm not meant to be a pretty face."

Keira said, "And you always burn your nail clippings because you're afraid of witches."

"My grandmother was a simple peasant woman from Norway."

Hannah added, "Whereas he's just simple."

The kettle whistled and Hannah made coffee. Emboldened, Sam said, "You might like this."

He turned the jugs about and the women gasped as he revealed winter trees. They stood spectral against differing skies of rain, snow, frost and winter sunshine, midnight and morning.

Both Keira and Hannah were silent in wonder.

"You match the jugs to the season. In winter you display the bare trees. In summer you display trees in full canopy."

"I can't think of the right words," Keira offered, "They're astonishing."

"They take forever to do."

Sam went to his lazy susan and took away the cloth. He seated himself on his stool.

"Bring a stool."

When they were seated, sipping coffee, Sam picked up his brush, carefully applied a speck of colour and added a shadow to the alder.

"Alders grow by the riverside. Water is tricky stuff to paint." He licked the brush.

Hannah said, "One day you'll poison yourself."

"How I get my vitamins."

To Keira he said, "See what I did?"

She nodded and he handed her the brush.

Keira studied the image and carefully added to the shadow. Sam approved and Keira sighed with relief.

"Hannah?" she suggested, offering the brush.

Hannah shuddered. "He'd kill me if I botched his precious pot."

Sam didn't disagree, but commented, "You also have to remember the firing will change the colours."

Keira hesitated to ask, "I don't suppose I could buy one?"

Sam shook his head.

"Sorry. Sold. To be delivered when all twelve are completed."

Her disappointment dismayed Sam.

"But I will create a jug for you. Whatever tree. As a gift."

Keira protested, but Hannah brushed aside her protest.

"Take advantage of him. He's an old softy."

"Thank you for the offer of the jug. A sumac tree, please."

"A sumac tree?"

"Stag's Horn sumac. You'll find one in Kew Gardens."

There was laughter in Keira's eyes.

"Would you like to tell me why you're here?"
Hannah said, "We're moving to Newcastle tomorrow."
Sam looked to Keira in dismay.
"Tomorrow?"
"What time? I'll see you off!"
"We're flying.
"Oh!"
"Sam's not keen on flying."

When the Stinger entered the helicopter, Sam Ericksen was reaching to the floor to retrieve his mission map. He hadn't time to do anything. There wasn't anything to do. The missile exploded and the broken machine fell like a stone, following the gunner and his weapon. Sam knew Gobber and Salim, the interpreter, sitting in front of him were dead. Frog beside him was dead. There was silence behind him where Taff and Tipper were sitting.

When the wreckage hit the ground there was silence. Sam was still conscious. When he heard men approaching, Sam kept his mouth shut because they didn't sound right. They came into the wreckage. They took weapons and anything else they thought might be useful. They wiped their boots on the dead and Sam's teeth met in his lower lip. They laughed and chattered to one another.

When they departed, the silence was unbearable. Sam had drifted into unconsciousness when men who spoke English arrived to collect the dead.

Hannah said, "Are you with us, dozy?"

Sam fled Afghanistan and said, "Found somewhere to live?"

"Not yet."

"How'd'y'mean? Not yet?"

"We're going to sleep over the office."

"Can't do that to Isla! And Sophie!"

Keira explained, "They're staying with my mother 'til we find the right place."

"You're going tomorrow?"

"God's sake, you sound like Christopher Robin! I want you to wave us off with flags! Not drippy tears on the tarmac!"

Sam could only look to Keira.

"When we have found Nirvana-by-sea, you must come and visit us."

"Can I visit Isla? I don't know Sophie."

"My mother will be delighted to see you. I'll make sure to tell her."

"I'll ring before I go."

"Actually, it would be a help, Sam. A familiar face. Don't fill them full of cheese burgers, please?"

"Promise," lied Samuel Ericksen.

Driving Keira home, Hannah said, "It was all arranged. When Sam returned from Afghanistan, he and June would be married. They'd been childhood sweethearts. He adored her. Only girl I ever remember him being with. But when she saw the state he was in. The x-rays were horrendous. Assorted lumps of helicopter in his lungs and stomach. June cried off. I think she thought she was being lumbered with a lifelong liability. Would you believe I cried because I wasn't going to be a bridesmaid?"

Keira said, "I don't know whether to laugh or cry."

"Sam didn't cry. Sensible girl, he said. Only time I ever saw him cry was when the kindly red tab asked what he wanted to be. Sam said, a soldier. But they didn't want him anymore. He'd worked so hard to learn to walk again."

"I think," Keira deliberated, "I think that must've been worse than the injuries."

"They paid for the pottery course. Sam made the worst joke ever. He said, everything's gone to pot, so I might as well."

*

Emily Harrison had scarcely hung up her coat before Maria said acidly, "Mister Buchanan wants to see you now."

Emily continued to her desk and Maria noticed the skirt that once had covered Emily's knees had shrunk to show a length of thigh.

"I said he wants to see you now."

The atmosphere was arctic. Emily continued to check her face.

"Did you hear me, Harrison?"

"I'm going."

She stood up as Tom Fenwick bustled into the office.

"What's going on?"

Emily opened an extra button on her shirt as she passed Maria's desk and proceeded to Mr. Buchanan's office.

Maria said, "She was very rude to me yesterday."

"She didn't sell the apartment?"

"She hadn't the courtesy to say whether she had or not."

"Then she didn't."

Tom Fenwick sat down at his desk and opened up his screen.

"Pembroke Terrace completed?"

"Done and dusted," called Maria.

Emily Harrison knocked on the door stencilled J.D. BUCHANAN MANAGER.

"Come!" was the masterly command. Emily entered.   Mr. Buchanan, ginger head & moustache, stern glasses, pretended to study the papers before him. Emily settled into the chair before the desk, crossing her legs. She checked the spread of her shirt collar. When Mr. Buchanan decided he had spent enough time intimidating the young woman, he looked up at Emily. The manager forgot what he was about to say, struggling to take his eyes from silken legs and generous bosom. He found his voice.

"Miss Harrison."

"Yes, sir."

"I understand you had something of a disappointment yesterday?"

"Yes, sir. It was very upsetting."

She re-crossed her legs anxiously.

"I'm sorry if I upset Maria. I have apologised to her. She's been a good friend to me since I came to Madison and Major. More like a mother."

The reprimand Mr. Buchanan was prepared to deliver began to slip away. To tell such a sweet girl to buck up or ship out seemed too severe.

"I did try very hard yesterday, sir. They loved the apartment, but felt the stairs would become too much as they grew older. It was very disappointing."

Mr. Buchanan leaned farther across the desk, trying and failing to keep his eyes from her legs as the poor child anxiously crossed and re-crossed them.

"I can understand your disappointment, my dear. When I was a youngster, I didn't sell a single property in six months. But my manager was very understanding and encouraged me not to give up. But to try, try, try!"

"Oh, I will, sir, I will! I'm absolutely determined to succeed. Please don't give Harbour Mount to anyone else, sir! I will sell it! I just need to find the right people."

Mr. Buchanan was very impressed at the young woman's enthusiasm. Her bosom rose and fell with the tides of emotion.

"Please, sir! I won't let you down."

"I'm sure you won't, my dear. I have every confidence in you. Tell Maria to mark Harbour Mount down to you."

To his disappointment, Emily Harrison stood up as though dismissing him.

"Thank you, sir. Now I must get back to work."

She turned at the door and smiled at him when her manager offered, "Any time you need advice. Or you have a problem, come to me. My door is always open to you, Emily."

Emily smiled too and said, "You're very sweet, sir!"

Mr. Buchanan sat for some moments savouring the image of Emily's pert posterior. He tore up and binned the sheet from his pad that read *Get rid of Harrison???*

On the way home Emily made a detour to the watch repair shop in Frederick Street where she had a copy cut of the keys of Harbour Mount.

CHAPTER SIX

"That's never been scientifically calculated."

Serving Our Lord as we do, it is often deeply unpleasant to view the depravity of humankind. Given the least incentive, they will betray their nearest & dearest, their sacred oaths, the very country they have sworn to defend. Many when they find they have made a bad bargain complain so bitterly. It is a relief to shut the doors of Hell and hear them no more. But occasionally a matter arises that is the cause of great amusement among us. Let me share such with you. We needed the services of a young banker. In a drunken moment, he revealed that his penis was minute and a cause of great sorrow and frustration. We offered to increase the size of his penis if, from his desk at the revered Sutton & Crozier, he would adjust some figures of interest to us. He rang at nine a.m. to say the adjustment had been made and his penis had grown three inches overnight. He was overjoyed and the Bank of Columbia collapsed with associated banks in seventeen U.S. states threatened with Federal intervention.

He rang at noon somewhat agitated as his penis had reached his knee and showed no sign of stopping. We were convulsed with mirth. At five

he was begging for help as his penis had reached his ankle. I confess I was hysterical with laughter. We advised him to tie it around his waist. He burst into tears, sobbing that he had arranged a very special date at a very expensive restaurant with the love of his life. However, the Chancellor decided we might need his services again and his penis was reduced to a useful length. We were very disappointed with this decision. I have entertained many a dinner party with this story.
Recorded by Amanuensis

*

The bell rang as the door opened. A man stepped into the studio.
"D'y'mind if I look around?"
Sam said, "Feel free."
"Your OPEN sign is upside down."
"That tells you all you need to know."

Glaze, the pottery cat, jumped down from the kiln roof where he had been watching Sam feed the kiln. He ran towards the door and when the visitor bent to stroke him, snarled and spat. The visitor recoiled, saying, "Your cat dislikes me on sight. He smiled to say, "Yet I'm welcome at Clarence House." Glaze scratched at the door. The visitor moved to open it, but the cat turned to display teeth and open claws. Sam opened and closed the door for Glaze.

"Sorry! He's not the friendliest of cats."
The visitor said, "My wife is much the same."
Whether he was serious or jesting, Sam couldn't tell from the back of his head.

The visitor studied the shelves of finished pieces. When he turned, Sam regarded his visitor. Dark hair receding. Greying above the ears. Green eyes. Expensive suit. Smooth appearance. Hairless face you wouldn't distinguish in a host of his kind.
"May I handle the pieces?"
"You drop it, I wrap it."
Sam continued packing the kiln until he was interrupted.
"The trees?"
"I'm sorry. They're already sold."
There was silence until the visitor said, "There are no prices on any of these pieces."
Sam said, "I don't know the prices."
"I do," the visitor remarked.

He offered a crisp card to Sam. The card read simply Alan Winterton.
"Winterton. Alan Winterton."
"Sam Ericksen."
They shook hands formally.
"You don't know my name?"
"Should I?"
"You don't read the Guardian?"
"I prefer the Sun."

Winterton smiled at Sam who offered, "I believe people should earn a living, not indulge their children and no Methadone for addicts."
"Why refuse Methadone?"
"Because it legalises their addiction."

"You have a remarkable talent, Samuel Ericksen. Painter, potter, sculptor? Philosopher? Which are you?"
"Don't follow."
"The best nineteenth century ceramic painters were not potters. They were frustrated Turners, Landseers, Palmers, Madox Browns. So? Which are you?"
"A painter who likes to stand by a hot kiln on a cold day?"
Alan Winterton laughed; a thin sharp laugh.
"A truthful answer."
"I try."

"I love your figures. You see not inanimate clay, but life, startling, individual, frozen in movement. Such subtle colours! Every figure questions. Your unglazed military figures are astonishing. The soldiers. The stretcher bearers. The dying man and his friend. Very moving. Real men. No glory. Just truth. They rise from the clay."
"Thank you."
"But difficult to sell," suggested Winterton

"So much of contemporary pottery is unusable. This denies the very function of the craft. Your spinning tops are exhilarating. The swirl of colour excites. Yet they are bottles that one can use. Jugs are so pedestrian. Your pieces are a wonder. The flight of sparrows around this jug. The magpie and the mouse. The heron flying and fishing. Snapshots. Once seen and gone forever, but your brush captured them. The jugs are too big to be practical. But you wanted a canvas on which to paint."

Sam pondered this insight.
He suggested, "No one uses jugs nowadays for their primary purpose. The tweeny no longer skips along to the dairy with the jug and a basket for eggs. They're decorative pieces."

"Do you have a relationship with a gallery?"
"I have a stall at Brigham Park Sunday Market. I do local Antiques Markets occasionally. I'm listed under bric-a-brac. And the studio's open all week." "Working from here is fine. Good for the discerning customer, but it's no good to sell from."
Alan Winterton picked up the larger of two hedgehogs.
"Have you ever considered working in bronze?"
"Clay is cheaper."

The visitor offered a cigarette from a gold case.

Sam refused.

"You say, you don't know the price of anything?"

"I fail as a shopkeeper. When my sister is here, she can sell anything and the customer goes home enlightened and happy. I can't do that. I am a mute, inglorious potter."

"She's not here?"

"No."

"Then I shall cheat you. Two hundred pounds. Two large jugs. The mountains of Afghanistan."

Sam was surprised.

"I don't know anyone who would recognise them."

"No one who has seen them would fail to recognise their sullen, menacing shapes. Anyone who looks carefully will see in the foreground of this one a half-buried cartridge case. In this, a scrap of the cover of one of those disgusting meal packs. Two hundred pounds and I'm cheating you."

"Who did you serve with?"

"I wasn't a soldier. Alright! Two hundred and fifty pounds and I'm done."

Sam said slowly, "Two hundred and fifty pounds?"

"Cash! I'm not going to offer you proper value. I'm here to cheat you."

"Thank you. Two hundred and fifty it is."

"And we'll talk later about a gallery exhibition."

"We will?"

"And I want you to paint a portrait of my wife."

*

Hannah stood in the unfurnished office looking out onto busy Pilgrim Street, Newcastle. Keira came clattering down the spiral staircase.

"We can survive up there. Bedroom, bathroom, shower. We can fit up some sort of kitchen."

"We mustn't get too comfortable. I don't want to wake up ten years from now and find we're still living over the shop."

Keira said, "The two smaller offices? Any preference?"

"Not really. The conference room's somewhat dingy. Our predecessors? What did they do?"

"Mortgages on commercial properties. I don't suppose they used it often."

"Then we must make it sparkle. Clients approach Reception and accompanied by appropriately pretty young receptionist pass through a bustling front office where busy clerks are glued to computer screens."

"Who is paying these busy clerks glued to computer screens? And suitably pretty receptionist?"

"Worth every penny. An air of industry and success is essential! On to the conference room where you and I await the clients and business begins at the boardroom table."

Keira laughed to say, "Wake up, Cinderella! There isn't a chair in the place."

"We can hire the furniture. What we can't hire are the skills of Sullivan and Ericksen."

"Ericksen and Sullivan?"

"No," Hannah decided, "Sullivan and Ericksen. It sounds trustworthy."

"No going back?"

Keira offered. "Because we have nowhere to go back to."

They kissed and hugged one another.

Hannah looked around at the empty office and asked, "Do we really own this?"

"Yes. What we don't own any more are homes. Yours and mine."

"It's a shivery thought, isn't it?"

Keira promised, "We'll make it work."

"What time are we seeing the bank manager?"

Keira looked at her watch.

"You have time to nip to the loo. It's only two minutes away. Seventeen, Pilgrim Place."

Heading for the spiral staircase, Hannah asked, "What's the name of the bank manager?"

Keira consulted her notebook. "McCracken. Mister Peter McCracken."

"Scotch?"

"Sounded Scots. However tough he is, kiddo, we will mesmerise him."

Skipping up the stairs, Hannah called, "I'll unbutton my blouse, shall I?"

"No way! I want him to concentrate on real figures."

"I'll use my best Scots accent, begorrah."

"Please don't! We need office furniture and a bed."

As they locked the front door, Hannah said, "You don't think Brother Sam is standing outside number eighteen wondering whether we've been abducted by aliens?"

"I'm sure he is."

Linking arms, they progressed along busy Pilgrim Street to keep their appointment with Mr. McCracken.

*

Sam set the kiln timer. He cleared the pug mill and turned it off. From the refrigerator, he took milk and the half tin of cat food. He set out the cat's supper and from the studio door called for the cat. Glaze did not appear. Sam left the door open. In the washroom mirror he practised his Angry Viking glare and was disappointed.

"That is what you don't want when you're going to see the bank manager. Try the stoical Norse fisherman."

Sam combed his hair and chided himself, "You need a haircut. No, I don't! I'm an artist. A remarkable talent. I don't have to have my hair

63

cut. How otherwise would anyone know I am an artist of rare talent?"

He combed moustache and beard. Contemplating his familiar features, Sam said, "I suspect my remarkable talent is for growing hair."
He remembered to flush the toilet and found his jacket.
"Remember! The bank manager is not your enemy. He welcomes small businesses. However, minute."

Glaze was not in the studio. Sam went to the door and shouted. No sign of the cat. He went out into the yard he shared with Tony's Tip Top Tyres, Tommy's MOT CERT station and Stan's garage.

When he bought the studio, Sam painted the outside in all the colours of the rainbow. To which he added THE STUDIO. His neighbours came out to watch him. Sam took the opportunity to introduce himself and what he would be doing. They agreed Sam was mentally deranged, but it wouldn't turn away trade. They were right on both counts and Sam was accepted.

Sam checked his watch and started a quick search of the yard. Glaze was popular with everyone and did the rounds to extract tribute. He found his cat thrown into the weeds by the gate to Commercial Road. The tyre mark across the crushed body was cruelly apparent. The MOT station was the nearest. Sam carried Glaze into the workshop, the limp body slipping in his arms like a furry eel. Bruce was sitting by the stove reading a newspaper.

Sam said, "Somebody ran over Glaze. Did you hear anything?"
"Oh, God! Poor little bugger. No, Sam, I don't think so."
"He must've been going out. He wouldn't run over Glaze. Dump him in the weeds and carry on here, would he?"
"I had only three MOTs this morning. One early this afternoon. Nothing since."
Sam's heart ached at the bedraggled bundle in his arms.
"There was that BMW come in for you."
"No, not him. The least he would've done was tell me."
"Tony's been busy."

Sam went to Tip Top Tyres, but although Tony was sympathetic, he knew nothing. Sam borrowed a spade from Stan to dig a hole to bury Glaze. As he dug, a boy appeared whom Sam had seen occasionally in the garage.
The boy said, "You have to say some words."
Sam looked at the ten-year-old for the first time.

"You're right! Have you any words?"

The boy thought for a moment and then said, "Gentle Jesus, meek and mild, look upon a cat called Glaze. Many thanks. Amen!"

Sam said, "Amen!"

This seemed to satisfy them both.

Taking the spade back to the garage, Sam asked, "Stan your Dad?"

The boy nodded.

"Wha'd'y'fancy when you grow up?"

The boy smiled to say, "Run the garage?"

The boy stated, "That Beamer run over Glaze."

"Why d'y'think that?"

"That was a Beamer tyre."

When Sam stared at him, he continued, "That run over Glaze."

"How do you know?"

"I know about tyres."

Sam struggled with the nagging thought that Alan Winterton had killed his cat.

He was nearly an hour late for the appointment with the bank manager. He hadn't sounded very pleased when Sam rang to explain. He seemed not to believe his story of burying his cat. Sam wheeled his bike to the gate. There were three potholes of varying depth in the gateway that very soon would become one vast pothole.

"Whatever happens with the bank," Sam promised himself, "Hannah will give me supper. Maybe Keira will be there. They'll understand about Glaze."

Then he remembered, they were there no longer. He was surprised at how discouraged he felt.

*

The bank was as quiet as a church. Hannah and Keira meekly approached the first cashier. When she looked up, Hannah said, "We have an appointment with Mister McCracken?"

The cashier replied, "One moment," and slipped from her stool. She returned to say, "Mister McCracken will see you in a moment."

The friends withdrew from the counter. A customer entered the bank, completed a transaction and departed. Keira whispered, "How long is a moment?"

"That's never been scientifically calculated. But I'm beginning to feel old."

When it seemed time had stopped, the door at the end of the armoured counter opened. A bald man in a suit that would soon be too small for him appeared. Mr. McCracken called imperiously, "Miss Ericksen? Miss Sullivan?"

The friends obediently moved forward and the bank manager retreated. He made no apology for the delay. Hannah and Keira followed the manager along a corridor into a stale-smelling office. The manager gestured towards chairs and seated himself behind the desk. The chair protested. He opened a slim file that he studied for a long moment.

Keira could sense Hannah's irritation.
"You are partners in this venture?"
"Yes," Keira admitted.
"What exactly is your business?"
Keira looked to Hannah.
"We forwarded a business plan with our application. Don't you have it?"
Mr. McCracken fiddled with the few papers in his file.
"I don't seem to have it."
Keira forestalled Hannah's response.
"We are investment counsellors. Successful investment counsellors."
Hannah said, "You have our last two years' accounts?"
The manager looked deeper into his thin file.
"I don't seem to have them."

Keira kept patience with difficulty.
"I'll see they're repeated to you."
Mr. McCracken closed his file.
"That's not necessary. I see nothing to encourage me to invest in your venture."
Hannah said, "Then why have you," and stopped as the door behind her opened.

A younger voice said, "I'm sorry. I was delayed. Please, forgive me. Mister McCracken is not au fait with your situation."

A young man, sharp-featured, bald as an egg and dark of eye, neatly suited, stood by the desk. He smiled at Hannah whose first thought was that he was somewhat attractive.

"I'm sure Mister McCracken will excuse us. I'll use the smaller conference room, shall I, sir? I wouldn't want to drive you from your office."

The manager said, "Thank you, Oliver, most considerate."

"Follow me, ladies."

The thought was shared. *Who is in charge here?*

CHAPTER SEVEN

"Don't say anything stupid, Samuel. Think before you speak."

Once they were seated and coffee had been served, the young man introduced himself, handing a business card to each.
"My name is Oliver. Oliver De'ath."
Reading the card, Hannah said, "Death?"
Keira said, "It's not a name I've ever met before."
"My surname derives from a medieval metonymic occupational name for a gatherer or seller of kindling wood from the Middle English 'dethe', fuel, tinder, from the Old English 'dyth'."
"I suspect you've explained this a thousand times," Hannah apologised.
"We can only blame my parents who took a perverse pride in the name."
He smiled at Hannah.
"Please, call me Oliver."

"I'm the Business Development Manager and I'll be working with you so long as you need my support. I have funds to encourage investment in this area. I shall do my best to steer the best projects in your direction."

Hannah exclaimed, "I can't think of anything to say except, thank you."

"We must get you off to a good start. The Pilgrim Street premises need to be well furnished. Please leave that to me. You need to hit the ground running. I suggest we hire a competent secretary/receptionist and four clerks. Anyone entering the front office must see the machinery of success."

Hannah, surprised, said, "That's just what I said to Keira."

"We'll book you into the Marriott until the work is done."

Oliver smiled at Hannah.

"You can be tourists visiting our fair city. If I can be of any assistance, you need only ask."

They walked back to Pilgrim Street. Keira said, "Mister Death has taken a fancy to you, Hannah. He didn't share out the smiles."

Hannah laughed, "Nonsense! But maybe we've found our very own angel?" "Who will book Hannah and her friend. . . I forget her name. . into the Marriott. Whereas we would naturally book into that little hotel on Lonely Street, called Heartbreak Hotel."

"You're showing your age."

They linked arms and tried to keep their feet on the pavement.

*

Emily Harrison's desk was now in the most favourable situation. Her smile was the first to greet potential clients as they entered the office. She had borrowed a screwdriver from the cleaners' cupboard and removed the modesty board on her new desk. No one but Tom Fenwick seemed to notice her legs were on display. They caught the attention of male enquirers. Joanne Murray, top closer, had been most upset to exchange desks and wept bitterly. Maria had supported her protest, but as Mr. Buchanan declared, "We must give the lass the chance to show her mettle."

The irony passed unnoticed.

Mr. Buchanan's decision may have been influenced by the fact that Emily had sold five properties in two weeks. Joanne may be excused as her mother had died three weeks previously. Hit and run accident. She had fallen from her bicycle under the wheels of a car as she attempted to turn right. She was pronounced dead at the scene. The offending car was never discovered.

Joanne caught Emily in the washroom.
"I know what your game is. Don't think I don't!"
"My game is selling houses, Joanne. What's yours?"
Joanne's face was red and puffy from weeping. Her hair was neglected. For a moment, Emily felt sorry for her, but pushed the thought away.

"You're playing with Mister Buchanan. Poor man! That's what you're doing."
Emily laughed, saying, "You're right, Joanne. Wha'd'y'think I'm doing? Fondling his knob? I'm not sure I want him cumming in my hand. A shag on his chair? Squeak, squeak! Bent over the desk? Wha'd'y'think?"
"I think you're the most disgusting woman I've ever met! I hate you!"
"Hate away, Joanne! I'm selling houses."

When she returned to her desk, the atmosphere was icy. Secretly, Emily was jubilant. When her phone rang, she spoke loudly as she arranged a viewing for a desirable property on the riverside. She closed the call and recorded the details in her daybook. It seemed to Emily that somehow she had gained the magic touch and couldn't fail to sell houses.

"I was trying too hard. Perhaps I seemed desperate?"

When she looked up, Tom Fenwick had steered his chair to her desk.
"Talking to yourself. First sign of madness."
"Go away!"
"Millwall Football Club."
"I haven't the slightest interest in football."
"Millwall Football Club used to have a chant. Probably still do. *Nobody likes us, but we don't care.*"

Emily consulted her watch.
Tom Fenwick recited, "Nobody likes Emily, but Emily doesn't care."
"So?"
"These women are your colleagues. You're gonna need them one day."
"No, I won't. They're pathetic."

Tom Fenwick regarded her seriously.
"You've changed so much, Emily. So quickly. It's not good."
"Then why're you here?"
"Nobody else will speak to you."
"But you're speaking to me? How brave!"
"I'm a man. I don't count. What would you expect of a man? A moth to your flame. Out for what he can get."
"Are you? Out for what you can get?"

She caught the reproach in his eyes.

"Fancy coming around, seven thirty this evening? I don't think I have anything on."

"If I thought we were going to talk."

"Why would we do that?"

"You appeared to be a girl who wants to be an estate agent. Now I don't know who you are. Why did you take the front off your desk? You're not selling Emily Harrison. You're selling houses. The women won't like it."

"The men have the money. Anything else?"

"Don't mess with Buchanan. Joanne absolutely adores him. Though God knows why."

Emily laughed.

"I wouldn't touch that horrible little man with a long stick."

"Joanne's mother has died. Killed on her bicycle. She's grieving. Have you no sympathy?"

"I didn't run her over."

"But you took her desk."

"Her desk? You can't be serious!"

"It meant a lot to her. And she shared out the viewings."

Emily consulted her watch.

"I have to sell another house. Anything else?"

Hearing herself speak, she glimpsed something was wrong, but as she tried to hold the thought, it slipped away.

We take a great share of blame for the evil in this world that isn't always engineered by us. Sometimes at our Parish meetings, I hear complaints about blame being laid at Our Lord's door for tragedies in which we had no hand at all. To be truthful, they would've been better handled if we had made the arrangements. For our younger readers I offer the example of a particular catastrophe. This occurred when a young man, Princip Gavrilo, shot dead Franz Urban, the lover of his faithless wife. Princip arranged matters to interrupt the adulterers at breakfast. The righteous husband shot dead an innocent postman and from his terrified wife learned her lover had been called in early to collect a bigwig from the railway station and bring him to the City Hall. Princip caught up with the car and shot Franz Urban dead.

If the woman in the back seat hadn't started screaming that would've been the end of it. But her screaming so irritated Princip he shot her dead. The red-faced gentleman beside her struck Princip with his stick. So he shot him too. It was all a tragic mistake. Gavrilo had shot the heir to the throne of the Austro-Hungarian Empire, Archduke Franz Ferdinand and his wife Sophie, Duchess of Hohenberg.

Much simpler is the story of our associate, Christopher, who followed in his Mercedes an obstinate female cyclist on a country lane who wouldn't give way. When they came to the main road, Christopher crushed the stupid woman and her bicycle. That incident may simply make you chuckle and cry, 'Tally-ho, Christopher!' But its implications are more rewarding still. Well done, Christopher! I trust the Merc wasn't damaged?
As recorded by Amanuensis.

*

The interview with the bank manager wasn't as frightful as Sam Ericksen had anticipated. In desperation, Sam showed him Alan Winterton's card. He recounted the possibility of an exhibition. The manager was impressed and granted six months' grace in which to reduce his overdraft. He offered his hand as Sam left, saying, "Alan Winterton, eh?" He smiled which disturbed Sam, continuing with, "A fortunate meeting, Mister Ericksen." Sam mumbled something and escaped. Sam found an Internet cafe.

He googled Alan Winterton and discovered he was Ceramics Consultant to the Crown and had recently discovered in a neglected storeroom at Windsor Castle, Chinese porcelain worth many millions. The Chinese government had registered a claim for the return of pottery, stolen from the Imperial Palace. There were photographs of Alan Winterton and the heir to the throne, examining jugs and bowls, enjoying lunch together and smiling upon the world. Sam mused, "I should've asked him to increase the overdraft."

He investigated further. There were photographs of the ceramics and more photographs of Alan Winterton in the Royal box at Wimbledon and Epsom.

"Why don't I like this man? Am I jealous of success? Something doesn't click with me. He's almost anonymous. Which is why he carries cards printed with his name. Are you going to refuse his money? Do I look like Goofy?"

Sam realised his neighbour was eyeing him curiously.

"Well? Do I look like Goofy?"

The young man smiled, "Game of Thrones?"

Sam laughed and his neighbour returned to his screen. Sam had his answer. Alan Winterton looked like nobody. If he turned away, you would not remember his face.

*

The telephone was answered and a woman's voice said, "Hello!"

Sam said, "You don't know me. I'm Hannah Ericksen's brother. Sam? Hannah suggested I might come to see Isla. I've never met Sophie?"

"You'd be very welcome, Sam!   It would be good to meet you."
"If I've called at a difficult time?"
"No, no! If you'd like to come this evening? Seven thirty? I won't tell the girls. It'll be a nice surprise for Isla."
Sam wrote down the address on the lining of his jacket.

*

When he entered the studio, Glaze was sitting on the kiln apron enjoying the warmth.   Sam was shocked. He stood still listening to his heart race. When he approached, Glaze jumped down to vanish behind the kiln.
Sam said, "You are dead. I buried you. The kid said a prayer for you."

Sam began to suspect he was hallucinating until the cat moved restlessly behind the kiln.   He went to the refrigerator and prepared Glaze's supper. He put down the dish and a bowl of milk. Sam listened to the passing traffic on the main road.
"Goody good stuff, Glaze!" he called, "Goody good stuff!"

There was movement behind the kiln, but the cat did not emerge. Normally the cat would come at first call.

Sam went out to the tangle of grasses and spindly birches. The hair on the back of his neck stood up when he saw the grave was disturbed. Something had dug into or out of the grave. A chill passed through Sam. He knelt down to assure himself no tool had dug out the hole. Something had scrabbled upwards, forcing a hole big enough for a cat to squeeze through.

It was a perfectly normal evening in early July. A contrail melted where a jet liner had passed. Beyond the railings, traffic progressed briskly. Sam could hear voices. A child shouted and someone laughed. He remembered very clearly Glaze's limp body in his arms; the corpse slipping from his grasp because the normal tension was lost. But Sam stood now in a different universe where dead cats dug themselves from the grave.

Sam returned to the studio. Both the supper dish and the milk bowl were untouched. Glaze was sitting on the kiln shelf. When Sam entered, Glaze jumped down and began to eat and drink. It was as if he had awaited Sam's return. When food and milk were gone, Glaze lifted his head to regard Sam. He saw no tyre mark. Glaze regarded him with two differently coloured eyes, blue and green, clad in his normal military camouflage. Sam was sure this was Glaze, the studio cat. He didn't attempt to touch him.

Sam showered and changed his suit. He was more comfortable in the suit he treated himself to when he left the army. When he believed firms would be queueing up to hire him for his skills; how to assault a building without casualties, how to win a firefight in open terrain, how to assure a dying soldier he would be okay, when he wouldn't.

Into the mirror, Sam said, "Too much thinking isn't good for Samuel of little brain. Everything is normal. Remember that. God, I wish Hannah was here!"

He returned to the studio to find Glaze sitting in the warmth of the kiln. Sam chose a rabbit for Isla, a chick for Sophie and placed them in jacket pockets.
"I go, I come back. No loud parties. No moving the furniture about. And don't let too many bogles in. Okay?"

Glaze mewed reassuringly. Sam put out the lights and locked the door. He mounted his bicycle and pedalled off to visit his favourite niece and her friend. And Mrs. Victoria Sullivan whom he hoped one day would become his mother-in-law.
"Don't say anything stupid, Samuel. Think before   you   speak.

CHAPTER EIGHT

"Rule One: Strike first and put him down. Rule Two: Don't let him get up."

Emily blushed modestly. Mr. Buchanan gazed on her fondly. Her colleagues stared with barely concealed hatred. Tom Fenwick formed his fingers into a lens and clicked rapidly. Mr. Buchanan interrupted his paean of praise to ask, "What're you doing, Tom?"
"Taking photos, boss. This glorious occasion must not pass unrecorded."
Mr. Buchanan sniped, "Perhaps you should consider a career as a comedian," and continued, "There are those who say you can't sell houses at holiday peak, but our Emily has sold eight houses in the last three weeks."

He looked to his staff for applause. Tom Fenwick obligingly clapped. The hostile stares were transferred to Tom who protested, "Oh, come on! You may not like our Emily, but she's selling houses. And that's why we're here."
"Well said!" approved Mr. Buchanan, "Tom's right! We're here to sell houses. And if Emily keeps up the pace, she will be the winner of a luxury holiday in Blackpool for the Illuminations, at the expense of Madison and Major."

Emily gushed her delight, almost kissed Mr. Buchanan who departed flushed with the almost kiss. The staff returned to their desks with Joanne commenting, "Still not sold Harbour Mount?"

"I'm waiting for the right buyers."

Tom Fenwick wheeled his chair to Emily's desk. In sickly tones he asked, "Please tell me how you're so successful, Miss Harrison."

"Charm and integrity."

"Not lacy bras and short skirts?"

Emily laughed.

"Do you realise that's the first time I've heard you laugh in ages? You're so tense nowadays."

"To answer your question. Women choose houses. Men pay for them."

"That's not what you said before. You're learning."

"No idea why I'm selling so well. I show them the house and they buy it."

"Then you come back and upset everybody. Is that necessary?"

"I like upsetting those bitches."

"Those 'bitches' were a team of hardworking professional women. Not any more."

"Tough titty!"

"Worse is you're driving Joanne mad. Seriously mad."

Emily's telephone rang. She answered and Tom Fenwick rolled his chair away.

*

The evening passed very pleasantly. Sam didn't say anything stupid. Isla was delighted to see him and hugged him until he couldn't breathe. Sophie had stood by patiently to shake hands because she didn't hug men she didn't know. Sam approved of this. Sophie was the image of her mother and Mrs. Sullivan was the older image of both. Sam felt an ache in his heart. He was reassured that both mothers rang every evening. He resisted the temptation to ask if either had mentioned him. Instead he was reprimanded for only having rung twice. "I keep forgetting," he offered, "But I know they're doing fine!"

Three female faces gazed sternly at him.
"Promise," he said, but the gazes were unrelenting. What they ate, Sam couldn't remember, but he had two platefuls. He was even more determined to have Victoria Sullivan as his mother-in-law. The girls loved their presents. Mrs. Sullivan examined both rabbit and chicken.

She regarded Sam with awakened respect. "You made these?"
"It keeps me off the street."
"They're wonderful! They're really alive. You're very lucky girls."

Isla volunteered, "I have a collection of rabbits. When Sam has a lump of clay left over he says, should I drop it in the bin or make something for Isla?"

"Then I drop it in the bin."

Sophie determined, "I'm starting my collection today."

"Oh, no! Not another non-paying customer! The expense! D'you think clay is just lying around waiting to be dug up? You will beggar me."

Sophie looked startled until she realised Sam meant the very opposite.

"Now do we have a treat for your Uncle?" Mrs. Sullivan hinted.

Isla produced a guitar from behind the couch to join Sophie. Mrs. Sullivan said, "They sing very badly. Please pretend you are enjoying the caterwauling."

Sophie cried, "Grandma!"

Isla said, "We have learnt an old song from Newcastle for our Mums. We're going to sing it when we go there."

Isla struck the chords and they began to sing. They sang to send shivers up Sam's spine. He saw again Geordie's face above the guitar, cross-legged on a table in the mess tent, playing to a silent audience that grew as men drifted in from the darkness to listen. There was an almost palpable longing for home. Sam fought not to

weep. He struggled to find something to say to the children. Two bright faces looked to him for appreciation. He managed to say, "Thank you. That was wonderful. You nearly made me cry."
The girls laughed at the idea that a grown man should cry.

As the children went to bed, climbing the open staircase, Sam heard Sophie ask of Isla, "If he's your Uncle, why don't you call him Uncle?"
"He doesn't like it. Says it makes him sound old."
"He's not that old. It's all the hair on his face."

The adults waited politely until the girls passed from sight before Mrs. Sullivan said, "It seems Isla is prepared to share her Uncle."
She rose to pour two brandies.
"A nightcap before you go?"
"Thank you, Mrs. Sullivan."
"Please call me Vicky."
They sat down at the uncleared table. Sam said, "I want to tell you something because I have no one else to burden with this. And you won't believe me anyway."
"You'd be surprised what I believe."

"It's about a cat."
"A story about a cat," Vicky said and nodded.
"The studio cat. Part of the fittings. Glaze was run over and killed in the gateway to the studio."

"I'm sorry. People are so regardless of cats."
"I'm hoping whoever did it didn't mean to do so. But he was just thrown aside into the grass. As if he didn't matter."
"So what did you do?"
"I buried him behind the studio. My neighbour's son said a prayer over him. Then I went to keep an appointment with the bank manager. When I came back, Glaze had dug himself out of his grave and was sitting by the kiln. Alive."

"Please, don't be offended, Sam. But the cat was dead?"
"Glaze was dead."
They sat in silence until Victoria Sullivan spoke, "I accept you believe what you're telling me."
"Every word."
Victoria said, "You have an affection for your cat. I suggest you assumed he was dead. The fact that he dug himself out of his grave tells me he wasn't dead. Perhaps if you'd laid him somewhere warm you would've seen him start to recover."

She waited for the man to protest. Sam made no response. She continued, "I trust I haven't offended you. There is an old saying that a cat has nine lives. There may be some truth in the saying."
The woman regarded Sam.

"I cannot read your face, but my daughter said you are a sweet man."

"She doesn't know me well."

"You see Glaze eating and drinking?"

Sam reluctantly agreed.

"Why would a dead cat need to eat and drink?"

"To fool me."

Victoria Sullivan regarded the bear of a man thoughtfully.

"You believe you have a dead cat walking?"

"I saw him dead, his lungs crushed and I buried him."

"Accepting your truth, then we have the Devil taking an interest in you."

"I don't know if I believe in the Devil."

"Unfortunately, he believes in you. A cat returned from the grave has to have a purpose. Yet you don't seem to be frightened?"

Sam pondered the thought.

"What might that purpose be?"

Victoria smiled, "Ah, you think I'm a witch from Barbados? Sadly, no! I'm only a clinical psychiatrist from Los Angeles."

"Yet you believe in the Devil?"

"I have met him on a number of occasions."

Sam had no answer.

"I must come and see this living dead cat."

*

Sam was standing, one foot on the pedal, waiting for a bus to pass before turning into the yard, when he realised three men were harassing a young woman by the gate. He had seen the prostitute before. She had appeared to work a beat outside the yard when the Muslim community had driven the women from the estate. At close quarters he had been shocked to see how young she was. It was when he saw a man raise his arm and she cried out, Sam dropped the bicycle. They were dragging her away despite her fierce struggle when Sam grabbed his bicycle pump and ran towards the abduction. The pump was old and not made of plastic.

Sam shouted, "Let her go!"
The men froze as if astonished that anyone should interfere. One man held the girl. His friends came for Sam.
"Piss off!" said the big man.
"With pleasure. When you let her go."
The big man grinned at his younger companion.
"If we doesn't?"

They acted as if rehearsing a television drama, but they had not been where Sam had been and faced opponents that Sam had fought. They were still amused when the bicycle pump struck the big man twice in the face and Sam broke his left leg. Rule One: Strike first and put him down.

Rule Two: Don't let him get up. He fell screaming as blood flooded his face and Sam stamped on his right arm. He heard the bone snap. His comrade stood paralysed and looked to the man holding the girl. He had vanished.
"Get him out of here."
He indicated the moaning wretch on the ground. Sam wheeled his bicycle into the yard, avoiding the potholes. He was locking the gate when he realised the girl was still with him.
"Yes?"
"Is that it?"
"Are you hurt?"
"No."
"Then what more do you want me to do?"

In the silence of the night, Sam could hear the painful struggle of the injured man.
"I'd like to say thank you."
"Not my style."
"Could I beg a cup of coffee? Tea?"
"What's your name?"
"Kim. I know your name."

Sam re-attached the pump to the bicycle and wheeled it behind the studio where an optimist might believe it wouldn't be stolen. The girl followed dutifully. He tried not to look into the wilderness of grass and birches.

He unlocked the door to the studio and switched on the lights.

"Come on in."

Glaze came mewing across the floor to twine about his legs. Sam hesitated and then bent to stroke his head. The cat felt warm.

"Could I take a pee?"

"Next to the kitchen. Pull the handle down and up or it won't flush."

Sam went to the refrigerator and refilled the cat's milk bowl. They drank cold milk together. Sam returned the bottle to the refrigerator.

"Well, you look pretty much alive to me, old chum. Whatever's going on, I don't reckon it's any of your doing."

From the glaze cupboard he brought his Highly Toxic bottle and settled in his thinking chair. Two or three swallows soon soothed his troubled mind. He heard the toilet flush, but the girl didn't appear. He heard kitchen noises. The girl appeared at the door.

"I'm making coffee? Okay?"

"Please. One sugar."

The girl disappeared, lingeringly, smiling, looking back at him, reluctant to leave him.

All part of the act, but Sam Ericksen was back in Helmand, clearing the compound that turned out to be a school. The Taliban were retreating, herding the girls with them as a shield. The presence of the children was a surprise. Driven into the open, the madmen stood there, pointing their weapons at the children. The leader shouted to the patrol to go away or. Blakey opened fire without hesitation. A young girl was shot as a Taliban fell, discharging his weapon.

The girl died in Sam's arms, lingeringly, smiling, looking at him wonderingly, reluctant to leave him. Kim brought the coffee to him, found a wooden chair and joined him.

"I'm not good at chit-chat," Sam warned her.
"Thank you for what you did."
He studied her thin face and frame. The smudged makeup was the face of a sad clown.
"I'm going to turn you out when you've had coffee."

Sam came to the gate to unlock it for her.
"You don't need to bother. I can climb over."
"I don't want you climbing over."
He had often dropped his bicycle over and climbed himself, but he wanted to see the road was clear. He watched the slight figure trot away into the estate on absurdly high heels. When he re-locked the gate, he found Glaze had followed him out.

"Wha'd'y'think, Glaze? I'm easy fooled. I notice you didn't go fawning all over her."

He locked the studio door and settled down to work on the tenth tree jug. He knew he would be lost when the set was complete. Sometime after two, Sam went to bed to dream of walking with Keira on a solitary shore. In the distance they could see Hannah and the children. When Keira vanished and the children began to scream, Sam began to run. Something that might have been a bear was dragging Hannah away. The children were striking and kicking at the creature. Then Keira called to him and Sam stopped running. Her mother was pulling Keira away. Sam awoke wrestling with the duvet. He struggled with incomprehension.

Sam went into the studio and rang the Newcastle number. A century passed before the telephone was answered, but he persisted. A sleepy voice said, "Do you know what time it is, Sam?"
Sam glanced at the clock.
"Twenty past four."
"What's wrong?"
"Nothing's wrong."
"Then why did you drag me out of bed?"
"I wanted to know if you were alright."
He listened to muffled exasperation.

"Yes, I'm alright. Everything is going well."

"Is Keira alright?"

"You dragged me to the phone to ask about her?"

"Yes. But I asked about you first."

"Don't apologise."

"Listen, Hannah."

"I'm listening."

"Just suppose. Just suppose there was something bad and you had to choose between me and Keira."

"How much have you had to drink?"

"Just suppose. Who would you choose to save?"

"Put like that? Keira."

"Why would you do that?"

"Because she doesn't ring me up at four in the morning."

Sam found no answer.

"I'm sending the men in white coats today, Sam. Don't fight them. Just go with them, please."

The call ended before Sam could respond.

"She didn't say if Keira was alright."

*

They stood on the Pilgrim Street pavement and admired the office frontage. The plate glass windows shone in the morning sun. Emblazoned on both windows in gold was SULLIVAN & ERICKSEN Investment Consultants. Oliver had insisted the friends meet him at a coffee house in the Haymarket. Not until he had received a call did he allow them to walk to the office in Pilgrim Street. The sign writer wiped away an invisible smear and stepped from the window, smiling.

Hannah cried, "Wow!"
"Is that the best you can say?"
"It's just gobsmacking," Keira offered.
Hannah said, "Thank you. It's a dream come true."
Oliver smiled, "It says *we are successful. Would you like to share that success?* That's the message we're selling."

He stepped to the double doors and addressed Hannah.
"Would you like to enter your new premises?"
As Oliver opened one door, the second was opened by a smiling young woman. Hannah and Keira took hands and entered together. Four young women rose from their desks and applauded. Oliver introduced Hannah and Keira to the receptionist and the clerks. They looked to Hannah and Keira.
"Speech, Hannah!" called Oliver.

Hannah hesitated to say, "I'll keep it short. We're going to work hard to persuade people to invest in the North East. We will make commissions and you will share that success. But we do have a lot of hard work to do."

Everyone applauded and Oliver said, "The first appointment is eleven thirty. Correct, Angela?"

The receptionist said, "Correct, Mister De'ath. A Mister Harding who has a proposition to create a sheltered housing complex in his home village. He is seeking a partner in the project."
"An excellent start. Now I'll vanish and let you begin. Good luck, everyone!" Hannah thought for a moment, Oliver was going to embrace her, but then he walked away.

*

"You won't regret it," Emily Harrison assured her clients, "It's a charming house. The previous owners have done a great deal to improve it. And as you heard, they were generous enough to accommodate your budget."
The young couple were grateful for the speed with which she had contacted the owner and bargained on their behalf. The owner, after no offers in three months, was equally grateful.

Emily left the happy couple at their car. She gave them every assurance. They had bought 27, Salmon Street. It was withdrawn from the market. There would be no further viewings. Despite her success, Emily felt drained of energy. She returned to the house, poured herself a sherry from the previous owner's drinks cabinet and flopped into an armchair.

Her feet ached and she pushed off her shoes. Her feet were grateful for the respite. She noticed the nail of her left little toe was black. She touched it but it didn't hurt. She enjoyed a second glass of sherry and washed the glass.

When she returned to the office to write up the details of the sale, she found herself alone with Joanne who ignored her. Tom Fenwick's telephone rang and as Joanne didn't move, Emily went to answer it.
"Madison and Major. Tom Fenwick's desk."

She listened and took notes. When the conversation ended she said, "Thank you for choosing Madison and Major."
As she returned to her own desk, Joanne said, "My God, you steal from the only person in this office who cares whether you live or die. You're an utter disgrace."

Emily blew a raspberry at Joanne, but relenting, tore the sheet from her pad and placed it on Tom's keyboard. Anger, so savage it alarmed her, flared against Joanne, but she restrained herself. Emily returned to her desk and completed her mundane tasks. When she went to the washroom, Joanne ignored her, but on the way back, she spoke and Emily stopped.
"Do you know how much everyone hates you?"

Emily knew she should just walk away, but the demon awoke.

"I don't think I do. Please, enlighten me."

She smiled sweetly and Joanne half-rose from her chair. Emily tensed herself for violence. Joanne, sensing the danger, sat down again.

"They wish you were dead."

"No flowers, please. Friends and family only."

"You put this on my desk, didn't you? Don't bother to deny it."

Joanne held up a withered condom tied in a knot. Emily laughed and loosed the demon.

"We get so little time together, Joanne. Skirt up. Knickers down. Bend over the desk. Head on the blotter. And before I can say, *Ooh, Mister Buchanan, you're a big boy*, he's shot his lot and is having a heart attack in his chair. *Will there be anything further, Mister Buchanan?*"

"You are a hateful, disgusting, most loathsome creature! You have seduced a dear, sweet man!"

"Please, please, so many compliments. You embarrass me, Joanne! I think you're just jealous. That's it, isn't it? You're jealous. Why not give it a go yourself? He loves sticking his snout in my boobies. Try that. You might enjoy it."

Joanne began to cry. Emily brought her the tissue box from Claudia's desk and left her to it.

It had been a wonderful day. She laughed as she drove home.

Relaxing in her bath, Emily examined her little toe. The top joint of the toe was black too. She could find no wound. Squeezing the toe didn't hurt. In fact, there seemed to be no feeling in the toe.

CHAPTER NINE

"I'd call that a threat, wouldn't you?"

Tony of Tip Top Tyres said, "Can you pronounce the names of any of them that's playing for the Hammers now?"
Sam looked questioningly at Tony. They were sharing coffee and yesterday's doughnuts in what passed for an office at Tip Top Tyres. Sam had no idea who the Hammers were and less interest in football.
He found it safest to say, "Sign of the times, Tony."

"Long afore you come. When I was mending punctures for the old man, this was a respectable working yard. And not a haunt of dilly-tanties."
Sam looked duly penitent.
"I could recite the whole team. And subs. British through and through then.
But not now."
Sam asked, "Where'd'y'get your tyres, Tony?"
"Germany."
The irony was wasted.

"They're very tight on tyres. They fail tyres with twenty, twenty-five thou to go."

100

Sam was thinking he was just as happy not to be driving when the postman put his head in the office.

Tony said, "Bugger off! I've got enough bills."

The postman ignored the witticism.

"For him. You has to sign for it."

Sam received the envelope wonderingly. It was expensive paper, gold rimmed, impressive. He had no idea who had sent it.

Tony advised, "It'll be a summons. Give it back to him. You haven't signed for it. You haven't received it."

Before Sam could react the postman scribbled on his electronic pad and walked away.

"They're buggers like that," Tony sympathised.

Sam apologised, "I'll have to read this in private, Tony. I don't want you to see me weep. But thanks for the coffee and the rock buns."

"Just keep saying, no comment."

Sam settled in his thinking chair with Glaze in his lap before he opened the letter. The papyrus-like paper unfolded crisply. The heading read Alan Winterton Associates. The letter was to inform him that his work had been selected for a gallery exhibition at the Contemporary Ceramics Centre, Great Russell Street, Bloomsbury. The small print flowed beneath Sam Ericksen's astonished eyes.

The telephone rang in Hannah's office where the partners were enjoying a morning break with percolated coffee and fresh doughnuts. Hannah answered the telephone.

"Sullivan and Ericksen."

"It's me."

"I know it's you. I can hear you breathing. Like the rolling sea. What have you done now? Do the police know about it?"

Keira put down her doughnut and Hannah switched on the loudspeaker.

"Why should I've done anything?"

"I know you too well. You ring in the morning, you want taking somewhere. You ring in the evening, you're hungry."

Keira laughed.

"We're too far away to act as your taxi service and it's not supper time. Therefore, you're in trouble. Q.E.D. What've you done, Sam?"

"I haven't done anything."

"Then you've said something. You have to keep your opinions to yourself. The PC Gestapo are everywhere."

"I have a letter."

"Oh, no! That's worse!"

"It says my work has been selected for a gallery exhibition at the Contemporary Ceramics Centre, Great Russell Street, Bloomsbury."

Both women gasped with delight.

Keira cried, "That's absolutely wonderful, Sam!"
Hannah said, "Is the letter addressed to you?"
Sam went on to read aloud.
"It says each piece must be marked and how it must be packed.   No damaged or imperfect pieces. Etcetera, etcetera."
Hannah's scepticism faded.

"Congratulations, dear brother!   Wonderful news!   A breakthrough at last!   Who's your sponsor?"
"Alan Winterton. D'y'know him?"
"Never heard of him."
"Writes for the Guardian?   Told you he came to the studio."
"You must include your dinner service. The one where the fox hunt gallops across the plates, fat men falling off, skinny women ending up in hedges, until there's only one exhausted horse and rider and one hound.   And the fox is laughing at them."
"Too many pieces."
"They'd appreciate the satire."
Keira interrupted to say, "Choose what you like, Sam. I wish we could be there on Opening Day."

Afterwards, in the quiet of the office, Hannah said, "Everything's changing too fast. Do you realise in the last ten days we have accepted three million pounds of individual, corporate and bank

funds for investment?   Three million pounds!"
"And Oliver fancies you," concluded Keira.

*

When Emily walked into the office she found the atmosphere subdued. No one took any notice of her. She noted Joanne was missing. The women were quiet. When Julie rose as if to go to Mr. Buchanan's office, Maria shook her head at her. Tom Fenwick was busy at his screen. Emily hesitated and dialled Tom's desk.
"Madison and Major. Tom Fenwick. How can I help you?"
"By not acting surprised."
"It's you."
"It's me."
They regarded one another.

Emily said, "What's going on? It's like Death Row at Christmas."
"You don't want to know."
"Of course, I do! How am I to cause mischief if I'm out of the loop?"
"Joanne went into the boss's office and exposed herself. Buchanan sent her home until she learns to button her clothes. I suspect she won't come back."

Emily sat silent. Her little toe began to ache. Tom Fenwick said slowly, "My feeling is you engineered this mess. But you probably don't understand what you've done."

Emily went to collect her coat and stopped at Mr. Buchanan's door. She tapped and no one answered. She opened the door and Mr. Buchanan sat at his desk unmoving. He looked sad and bewildered.

"Just stopped to say I have a viewing for Harbour Mount, Mister Buchanan. Perhaps they'll be the right ones?"

The sad man behind the desk summoned up a smile.

"Well done, Emily! Thank you for telling me."

The words sounded empty; a muffled railway announcement. Emily Harrison closed the office door and went off jauntily to a viewing at Harbour Mount.

*

Sam was absorbed in creating the foliage of a sumac tree on a jug when the studio door opened and footsteps entered.

"Mister Ericksen? Samuel Ericksen?"

He put down the brush and looked up.

"What can I do for you?"

His visitors were a burly man in a tired suit, accompanied by a police constable.

"Mister Samuel Ericksen?"

"Sam. But, yes, Samuel Ericksen."

"I'm Detective Sergeant Curlew and this is Constable Thomas."

"My pleasure."

"Do you mind if I ask you a few questions, sir?"

"Not at all. I'll try to answer them truthfully."

"Where were you on the evening of the third?"
Sam thought for a moment.
"Had dinner with the lady I hope one day will be my mother-in-law. Is something wrong with Missis Sullivan?"
"Not that I'm aware. And when you returned home?"
Light dawned on Sam.
"Saw three men abducting a girl."
"So what did you do?"
"Told them to let her go."
"And they obliged?"
"No. Two of them warned me off."
"What did you do?"

"I hit the big man."
"When you say hit. Wha'd'y'mean, sir?"
"There were three of them."
"What did you do to him?"
"Hit him in the face, broke his leg and his arm."
Sam read the pain in the constable's face.

"They were going to rape that girl."
"What happened then?"
"She used the loo. Gave her a cup of coffee. Said good night."
"Did you avail yourself of her services?"
Sam looked with contempt upon the sergeant.
"I have to ask the questions, sir."

106

"Well, if you're charging me with assault, I'm guilty as charged."

"That's not why we're here."

"Then why?"

"I have to tell you the girl's dead. Beaten to death."

Sam was devastated.

"Oh, no! No! That poor kid! What happened?"

"She was found this morning in the children's playground by a dog walker." "Well, that's appropriate. She's only a kid."

Sam noticed the constable had begun an inspection of the studio. He vanished into the bedroom.

"Can he do that? Search without a warrant?"

"Have you any objection?"

Sam shrugged.

"You're a potter, sir?"

"Please don't touch anything."

The sergeant ran a finger around the rim of the jug.

"This your work?"

"Yes." The policeman looked about the studio.

"You're not making a fortune."

"No, I'm making pots."

"We all have to live."

"I manage."

"You work with a gallery?"

"I have work on exhibition."

"You get grants?"

The sergeant didn't approve of grants.

"No, I have a sponsor."

"Yes?"

"Private individual."

"Who would that be, sir?"

"If it's any of your business. Alan Winterton."

Silence clouded the studio.

"Excuse me one moment, sir."

D.S. Curlew walked out of the studio. A puzzled Sam watched him using his mobile in the yard. The conversation was short and the sergeant wasn't happy. The detective appeared in the studio doorway.

Sam asked, "Everything alright?"

"Very satisfactory, sir. Percival!"

The constable appeared in the bedroom doorway.

"Yes, sarge?"

"It appears our work here is done, Percival."

He looked to Sam with distaste.

"Forgive us disturbing you, sir."

Detective Sergeant Curlew vanished. The constable followed, saying, "My name's not Percival. That's his storm warning is Percival."

"I don't understand."

"Not for us plebs to understand. Your pal Winterton must be chums with the right people, sir. But I could've done with a cup of coffee."

"Next time? When I have the coffee machine working."

"I doubt that," said Constable Alun Thomas.

Sam heard a very angry Fiesta scatter the gravel as it left the yard. Stan was the first of the terrible trio to appear.

"That prossie got herself killed then?"

"Stan, that girl was somebody's daughter. Be a little kinder."

"Sorry. You're right. Thought we'd be next for interrogation, but they scarpered."

"D'y'know how to make coffee machines work?"

"I can make anything work. I could raise the dead if they was nuts and bolts."

*

They were a young couple, Mr. & Mrs. Montgomery. Too voluble to be trustworthy. The husband, Giles, had been promoted to the management of what Emily recognised as a betting shop in Newcastle. His wife, Coira, was hoping to find a teaching post. Emily disliked the couple from the moment Giles put an unwanted arm about her shoulder. The address, Talavera, Holly Wood, Killingworth was reassuring, but there was something wrong about the couple.

Standing on the pavement, their enthusiasm at the location and the age of the house seemed contrived. They were on first name terms by the time Emily opened the door. To Emily's surprise, the woman became less forthcoming as they progressed through the apartment.

Emily tried, "If you were contemplating starting a family, Coira, both primary schools have good reputations. And I have a niece," she lied, "at the local nursery. She loves it."

Coira cut her short with, "Why hasn't the furniture been cleared?"

"The owner was hoping to include the furniture at, in my opinion, a giveaway price."

She hoped she was mistaken that the young woman suppressed a shudder.

"You prefer a minimalist approach?"

"I certainly don't want to spend my life dusting antique furniture."

"The apartment would be cleared, if you were interested."

Emily knew she had lost the sale, if the possibility had ever existed.

The husband, Peter, went to stare out of the window at the harbour and the North Sea as if he had lost interest in the apartment.

Emily said, "If you'd like me to leave you alone to discuss."

She was interrupted by Coira who cried, "God, no!"

Emily sat down on the big sofa by Mrs. Montgomery.

"I'm sorry. I love coming here. I find it warm and friendly. I think of all the generations that have come and gone within the security of this house."

Mr. Montgomery came to stand by his wife.

"Do you want to say anything, sweetheart?"

The young woman hesitated. "I think it's the worst flat we've seen."

As Emily struggled to hide her growing anger, Coira responded, "I wouldn't want to be found dead in this museum, never mind, buy it!"

Emily struggled to say, "I quite understand. The house is almost two hundred years old. It won't suit everyone. It's a matter of taste."

Which was as close to being politely rude as she could contrive.

Peter Montgomery looked to his wife.

"Time to go, sweetheart."

Coira rose to take her husband's arm.

They stepped out of the house, down the steps, across the gravel, onto the pavement. Emily shook hands and lied she would find them the house of their dreams.

"I hope you won't give up on me."

I trust I never see you again.

"Not at all!"

"You have my card?"

Emily waited to wave the couple away and then went back into the house.

*

Stan the garage man and Sam were enjoying coffee and putting the world to rights in the studio.

"If they was," Stan enquired, "To send you back where you come from, where would that be, Sam?"

"Why would they send me anywhere?"

"Well, you're not a true Brit, are you?"

"Of course, I am."

"Where was you born?"

Sam hesitated.

"My father was a timber importer. We lived in Balham."

"But where was you born?"

"A place you wouldn't know. Ullevalseter. Norway."

"You was in the Army. Right?"

"Yes."

"What was you?"

"I was a cook."

"There yar! They didn't trust you with a gun."

Sam laughed.

"But yarra decent bloke, Sam. I wouldn't let them send you back to Elevator. You can count on that."

Stan was generous in his victory.

"My Norwegian father married a girl from Worcester Park. She was homesick the moment she landed in Norway. My mother only stopped long enough to give birth. I wasn't there more than ten minutes."

"Long enough. When I get something with foreign words on it, I know where to come."

"I should make you wash out your own mug," Sam threatened.

The BMW entered the yard followed by an immaculate black van.

"It's your posh mate. With a posh van. Contemptuous Ceramics Centre. That the nobs' bailiffs, is it?"

"Get out of here, you cheeky sod!"

"I go, I come back!"

Sam watched as Stan spoke to Alan Winterton as he emerged from the BMW. Four men in white overalls opened up the van and entered the studio carrying stacks of flat boxes and a large roll of bubble wrap. They greeted Sam politely. Alan Winterton entered.

"Good morning, Sam! Are we ready?"

"All ready to go."

Out of the corner of his eye, Sam noticed Glaze vanishing into his hidey-hole behind the kiln. He indicated the shelves on which he had placed the chosen items. The movers began work, making up boxes, wrapping pots & pieces.

"I have the paperwork here. Took me hours."

"Good! That's the discipline you need."

Winterton picked up the nearest pot and checked it was clearly marked.

Sam had found a nineteenth century seal on a Sunday Market that boldly stamped SE within a feather. He pressed it into the base of everything he worked on.

"I see you've included the hunting dinner set. Very bold."

Sam was reluctant to ask what that meant, but instead, asked, "I saw Stan speak to you at the car. What did he say?"

Alan Winterton looked up from the handwritten catalogue and smiled.

"He threatened me."

"He what?"

"If I recall correctly, he said, Sam's soft in the head. You don't treat him proper, you'll have me to deal with. I'd call that a threat, wouldn't you?"

Sam was embarrassed. "Sorry. Stan has a good heart."

"Then I must treat you properly," Alan Winterton said, smiling, "Would you like to meet my wife? Seeing as you're going to paint her portrait."

"I am?"

"She'll come to you. This is where you work, isn't it?"

Sam managed, "Yes. I suppose so."

"She wants to see the studio. Make no endeavour to tidy up. She wants to see the bear in all the foulness of his lair."

Sam tried to laugh.

"Now shall we make coffee for those who are actually doing the work?"

Alan Winterton opened the refrigerator and brought out the milk.

"We can sign the contract when the van's on its way. Insurance bumph. That we have accepted care of the items in good order. Something like that. D'y'want to read the small print?"

When the van drove away, Sam felt a keen sense of loss. Alan Winterton said, "You look like a child deprived of his toys."

"Something like that."

"Then let me be the ray of sunshine behind the dark clouds. What commissions do you have in hand?"

Sam shook his head.

"Splendid!" announced Alan Winterton.

"Splendid?"

"I have a commission for you. Have you heard I discovered a treasure trove of Chinese porcelain at Windsor? Vases, bowls, teapots?"

Sam nodded.

"The Chinese government has already put in a claim for their return. And doubtless, we'll comply."

"They were stolen from China."

"I want you to copy them, so we may display them after the originals are returned to China."

Sam hesitated.

"I will take you to see the items. You may take photographs, measurements, whatever. I will supply you with the official photographs. The challenge is to complete the blanks before the Chinese government retrieves its property. One thousand pounds for each piece I find acceptable. Would you like to see the treasure trove?"

CHAPTER TEN

"Nobody does perfect better than the Old Firm."

Emily Harrison was closing the door of the apartment when her mind signalled something amiss. It was only an echo; the slightest whisper. Emily was tired. Nowadays, she often found herself tired. She almost walked away and then turned back. She walked through the rooms without finding relief. She sat where the clients had sat. In the corner of the big sofa, Emily realised what was wrong. Two miniatures were missing from the side tables. Through the apartment there were photographs of long-dead people and a scattering of miniatures; portraits of a range of men, women and children. Emily recognised their value and had brought this to Mr. Buchanan's attention. He had assured Emily the photographs and miniatures were of little value; besides which clients were never left alone.

"Everyone leaves them alone for ten minutes. That's the moment you can close the sale before they change their minds."

Emily remembered one miniature was a portrait of a pretty girl child holding a doll. Under a watch glass on the reverse was a curl of blonde hair. Emily had shivered when first she saw the relic. The second missing item was a charming study of a young boy in midshipman's uniform of Nelson's time. A keepsake for his mother as he was accepted on his first ship. She was sure Mr. Montgomery had stolen the miniatures. Her first instinct was to phone. She decided not to do so. Emily would deal with those who would steal from. She almost used the words . . . my house.

*

It wasn't until the van carrying his work for the exhibition had departed, the contract had been signed and Alan Winterton had gone that Glaze emerged from hiding behind the kiln. Sam was sitting in his thinking chair, sipping his favourite toxin in celebration, when Glaze jumped up into his lap.

"I'm not sure whether you're my mortal enemy or my true friend. I always thought we were partners."
The cat mewed gently.
"To celebrate the upcoming exhibition, Glaze, you shall have a treat. I was saving a kipper fillet for my tea."
Sam rose from his throne to take the plastic packet from the refrigerator.
"I never read the best before dates and you can't, so."

Sam found a clean plate and slid the remaining fillet from the plastic. He refilled the milk bowl and placed the plate on the floor. Glaze sniffed the kipper, ignored the milk and retired to the kiln apron.

"Ungrateful Glaze!" Sam rebuked the cat.

He bent to the plate and the smell caught him. The kipper stank.

"What the hell?"

Holding it as far away as possible, Sam emptied the fillet into the bin. He started to wash the plate in the sink until a sudden thought stopped him. He returned to the refrigerator.

Three beef slices fresh from Cheapskate were slimy. The bacon packet contained small maggots and the sausages had changed colour. Sam moved the bin over to the refrigerator and cleared the shelf. He cracked an egg and dropped the putrid mass into the bin. He followed it with the egg box. He was closing the refrigerator door when he picked out the milk bottle. He tested it and spat. He emptied the glutinous mass into the sink and swilled it away. He washed Glaze's milk bowl. The freezer compartment smelt of wet cardboard. Both his curry treats were soft and smelt badly. He cleared everything. The refrigerator-freezer was working normally.

"Bacon, sausage and egg were alright at breakfast. The beef sandwich was okay at lunch. The milk was okay. I made coffee for Stan. Winterton and I made coffee for his posse. Everything was okay. Until."

He saw clearly Winterton's pale manicured hand returning the milk bottle to the refrigerator.
"No! Don't believe it. Can't believe it. He's fixing the exhibition for me. He's offering the commission of a lifetime. Why would he do that? No way!"

Sam turned to Glaze, ensconced on his favourite perch and called, "Did you do this, Glaze? If so, why did you do it? D'y'think it's funny?"
The cat paid no attention.
"Are you my cat or the Devil's?"

*

Emily Harrison found the nail from her little toe when she cleaned out her bath. She examined her foot. The little toe was black, malleable, but without feeling. She tested her right foot. The toes were warm and had feeling. She felt a certain sense of unease. She decided she would ring the surgery tomorrow morning. Emily wrapped the nail in a tissue and put it in the bathroom cabinet. She was comfortable in pyjamas and dressing gown, buried in her favourite chair, when the doorbell rang. She silenced the television and waited for someone to go away. The bell rang again.

If it's the big guy, Hector, I met last weekend at Nemo's, I will. Or maybe I won't.

She opened the flat door to Joanne.
"What the hell're you doing here?"
A wild-eyed Joanne answered the question by stabbing Emily twice in the breast with a long-bladed kitchen knife. Joanne couldn't pull out the knife from the second wound. They both stood staring at the knife deep in Emily's left breast until Joanne pushed Emily backwards into the flat. As Joanne forced Emily back, she was startled to feel no pain. When Joanne tried to push her down on the couch, Emily pushed back and saw the surprise in Joanne's eyes at her strength. The first wound was not bleeding.

In what she now believed to be a dream, Emily pulled out the knife from her breast. It came out so slowly, the bright blade shining under the ceiling light. There was no gush of blood. The lips of the wound almost closed. Joanne stared in horror.
"My God, that's not right!"

She turned to escape. In the dream, Emily stabbed Joanne in the back seven times and every time there was blood. Joanne half-turned as if to

121

plead for her life and Emily stabbed her in the throat. There was a flood of blood and Joanne fell down. The last Emily saw in Joanne's eyes was disbelief. Then Emily woke up and dropped the knife.

Her hand was dripping Joanne's blood. Her dressing gown and pyjamas were covered in blood. She was about to scream when she saw a young woman in the doorway of her flat.
The stranger said, "Oh my word, you've got quite a mess here, haven't you, sweetie?"
"I suppose I have," Emily answered politely.
Joanne lay dead on the floor, drenched in blood, so ugly in death, so precise in life. The young woman stepped over the corpse to approach Emily.

Emily said, "Do I know you?"
The petite red-haired woman, nose bridged with freckles, smiled to say, "Jacqueline."
"Emily."
They shook hands, smearing the stranger's hand with blood. It didn't seem to concern her.
"We should've met earlier. You must forgive me."
Emily was confused, but didn't ask the question why.
"I think it's best if I take charge, don't you, sweetie? I suspect you're somewhat shocked?"
Her impish face looked up to Emily, smiling.

"Shouldn't we ring the police?"

Jacqueline laughed; a pure childish laugh. "Oh, my word, you're a regular comic! Just do what I ask you to do, please, there's a sweetie."

"If you say so."

"Everything off, please. Quickety quick!"

Emily stood bewildered until the little minx pulled at her dressing gown cord.

"Should I do it for you, sweetie?"

Emily took off her dressing gown and looked around for somewhere to put it.

"Just drop it."

Emily dropped everything to stand naked. Jacqueline said, "Well, sweetie, you certainly have everything in the right place."

"I'm not doing this for your amusement!"

"Ooh, touchy! Hop across the hallway. Into my place."

When Emily hesitated, the tone became brisker.

"Do you want to go to prison?"

Emily shook her head.

"Then off we go, sweetie!"

As Emily scampered across the landing, the lift doors opened and four men in white overalls stepped out. They carried tool boxes and large bundles. They ignored Emily. Jacqueline's flat was a surprise. It was an older person's flat, cluttered with worn furniture; the walls and shelving crowded with family photographs and porcelain figurines of implausible ladies.

Jacqueline ordered, "Go and take a bath, sweetie."
"I've just had a bath."
"You've just killed a woman. Go and have a bath. Don't lock the door."

Filling the bath, Emily heard Jacqueline on the telephone. When she was beginning to relax, the pixie entered without knocking and sat on the toilet seat, tipping ash from her cigarette into the bath.
"Don't worry, sweetie. I haven't come to fiddle your bits."
"What about Joanne?"
"It's all sorted. Forget her. Just one of those things. It's not supposed to happen, but it did."
Emily said, "Why don't I feel anything?"
"Do you want to feel something? Poor Joanne. Sob, sob, sob! My heart bleeds for her."
"My wounds don't bleed."
"I'll dress them when you're dry, sweetie."
"They don't bleed."
"Lucky you! You saw the mess Joanne made."

Jacqueline stood up and quit the bathroom. She returned carrying clean pyjamas and Emily's old dressing gown.
"They've nearly finished over there."

She kissed Emily on the mouth before she could stop her.

"I'll twiddle your bits another time, sweetie. You'll never bother with another man. Always a disappointment."

It was after midnight before Emily returned home. The flat smelt vaguely of summer flowers. Everything was as it had been before Joanne's unfortunate death. Jacqueline offered a glass of liquor that Emily gratefully swallowed. It lifted her spirits.

"Wha'd'y'think, sweetie? Did they do a good job?"

"Absolutely perfect."

"Nobody does perfect better than the Old Firm."

Emily allowed herself to be kissed and embraced longer than expected, but would've admitted it wasn't an unpleasant experience.

"Why didn't my wounds bleed?"

"I'll explain another time. But not now. Sleep tight, sweetie. Don't let the bed bugs bite."

Jacqueline exited and Emily was alone. She wished she'd asked the freckled pixie who the Old Firm were.

*

Next morning Emily Harrison rose refreshed and relaxed. She stopped at the door across the hall to thank Jacqueline. The door was opened by an older woman. Emily smiled, "Good morning! May I speak to Jacqueline, please."

The woman looked blank.

"No Jacqueline here, pet. Have yi got the right number?"

A bewildered Emily said, "But I."

The woman smiled and said, "I've been here twenty-three years. I think I'd know if I had a Jacqueline. Wrong number, pet."

"Sorry to trouble you."

"No bother. I hope yi find her."

*

Emily sat in her car until a neighbour tapped on the glass.

"Are you alright, Emily?"

"Yes. I think so."

"It's just you've been sitting there such a long time."

"I was thinking."

"Don't! It's bad for your brain."

She watched the woman walk to her car and drive away. When she had taken LSD with Dennis she had endured the most appalling experience. In the nightmare, she decapitated Dennis.

"But I know I killed Joanne. It was real. Then a woman called Jacqueline arranged for the body to be disposed of and the flat cleaned. That is the truth."

She unbuttoned her blouse and moved her bra to squint at the Elastoplast patches that covered her wounds.

"Why am I not dead?"

Winterton parked the car in what to Sam resembled a builders' yard. He noted Sam's surprise.

"This is Windsor Castle as the tourist doesn't see it."

Sam said, "Nobody stopped us. Nobody took any notice. Anybody could drive in."

Exiting the car, Winterton said, "Don't you believe it."

They crossed the yard to an unobtrusive door. It opened to Winterton's knock. They stepped into a guardroom.

"Good morning, sir," the large policeman announced cheerily to which Winterton responded.

"Mister Ericksen, if you'll sign here, please?"

A confused Sam scribbled his name and was rewarded with a beribboned badge.

The farther door was opened and Sam found himself with Winterton in a corridor painted a bilious green. At the second door, Winterton stopped, produced a key, opened the door and switched on the light. The windowless room had been painted a hundred years ago and was lined with forgotten boxes. The table in the centre was covered with an old tasselled table cloth.

"Are you ready?" Sam nodded and Winterton lifted away the table cloth.

Sam was stunned at what he saw.

"Well?"

"I don't know what to say."

"Can you copy them?"

"I'll die trying."

*

When Emily Harrison walked into the office, she half-expected Joanne to be at her desk. No one but Tom Fenwick took any notice of her. He looked up from his screen and smiled. Emily hung up her coat and as she returned, noted Joanne's screen was dark and her name plate missing from the desk. She lit her own monitor and began to check e-mails when she heard Mr. Buchanan's voice.

"If you'll be so good as to give me your attention for a moment, ladies and gent?"

The manager appeared supplicant rather than demanding: a clawless grizzly bear. Everyone gave attention.

"Thank you. I regret to inform you that our Joanne will not be returning to us."

There was a sigh of sympathy from the women.

"A valued colleague has taken early retirement. I know Joanne is irreplaceable, but I trust you will welcome a fresh face."

Mr. Buchanan's ponderous bulk stepped aside to reveal a figure familiar to Emily. It was the freckle-faced pixie, Jacqueline, who smiled at the assembled company.

"Please, welcome Jacqueline Prescott."

The women responded, cooed, hugged the newcomer and introduced themselves. Emily sat frozen.

"Oh, please, call me Jacquie!"

Tom Fenwick smiled, introduced himself and shook her hand.

"If I have a problem should I come to you?" flirted the pixie on the toadstool. Mr. Buchanan announced, "Emily is our top sales. I'm sure she'll set you straight on routine."

Emily gathered her wits and embraced the pixie who kissed her ear and whispered, "Our little secret is safe with me, sweetie."

"Will you see to stationery and what not, Emily?"

"My pleasure, Mister Buchanan."

Emily took Jacqueline to the stationery cupboard and found her a tablet and supplies. While she was standing on the ladder stool, Jacqueline stroked her legs. Emily protested, "I'd rather you didn't do that."

The freckled pixie pouted and said, "But we are going to be chums, aren't we, sweetie?"
Emily kicked at her and almost fell from the stool.

CHAPTER ELEVEN

"As a gift for a friend, I'm sure a cattle prod would be welcomed."

Hiding in the toilet, Emily Harrison avoided Jacqueline until she was sure the freckled pixie had left the office. She knew when Maria came into the washroom, saying, "My God, Gloria, does she never stop talking, sweetie?" Gloria countered with, "Be fair, sweetie, she's excited. It'll wear off, sweetie."

In the car, Emily set her smart new satnav for the address the Montgomery couple had given in Killingworth. The address was within an environmentally protected area: an expensive community of Listed Buildings.

Emily parked outside Grimm's Cottage. Coira Montgomery answered the door. She stared at Emily as at a stranger.
"Yes?"
"It's Emily Harrison? The estate agent?"
"God, you must be desperate."
Coira hesitated and suggested, "I suppose you should come in."
Emily stepped into the hallway.
Coira led her reluctantly into the sitting room.

"I suppose you've found the house of our dreams?"

"No. Is this your family home or your husband's?"

"My parents' home. If it's any of your business. It's not for sale."

She lit a cigarette without offering the courtesy to Emily.

"Is your husband here?"

"He's gone into town. I'm sure I can speak for him.   No, we don't want to buy anything you have to offer."

Emily struggled to keep patience.

"I trust your parents are well?"

"Do you care a bugger?"

"I've worried about you since you visited Harbour Mount."

Coira laughed.

"Why would we be any concern to you?"

"Because your husband, Peter, is a thief. He stole two valuable miniatures from Harbour Mount. I don't think this is the first time he's done so."

"That's an outrageous thing to suggest."

"One of the miniatures is standing on the sideboard behind you."

"Peter bought me that miniature."

"I have photographs of that miniature on display at Harbour Mount."

"You are mistaken. My husband bought me that miniature for my last birthday." Emily said, "You have no idea who you are dealing with, have you, Coira?"
"A vulgar little estate agent?"

Emily grabbed Coira by the hair and taking the cigarette from her hand, applied the glowing end to the woman's neck and pressed firmly. Coira screamed with pain and shock. She struggled, but Emily held her hair tightly and rapped her head on the cocktail cabinet.
"You've never in your shabby, little, thieving life ever met anyone like me, have you, Coira?"

Emily drew on the cigarette, nipped off the filter and pushed the burning end up Coira's nose. The woman screamed in agony.
"Oh, my God! Oh, my God!"
"That's painful, isn't it? The nasal tissues are most delicate. If I shut your mouth."
Emily clasped Coira's mouth.
"See? You have to breathe and that draws the pain deeper."

Emily released her frantic victim and Coira fell to the floor, sobbing. She struggled vainly to free the cigarette from her nose. Emily reached down and slapped her victim sharply on both cheeks. The cigarette freed itself in snot and blood.

"Give me the miniatures. Two minutes! Or I'll give you a kicking you'll never forget."

Coira returned with the miniatures. Her nose was bleeding. Emily checked they were undamaged.
"You're wrong. Peter bought them as presents for me."
"Such a loving husband! Has he given you many presents like these?"
"He won't be happy about this!"
"You have my card."

As she drove home to Aranport, Emily said aloud, "Where the hell did I learn to behave like that?"
She laughed and shared the joke with her face in the mirror.
"I wonder if a fag up the nose would work with clients?"

*

Sam Ericksen lifted his first Chinese teapot from the kiln in an old towel. He cleaned the foot and placed the vase on his lazy susan. He straightened up to admire his work. A woman spoke from behind him.
"My God, but that's astonishing!"
Angered, Sam turned to say, "Don't you bother to knock?"
He would've said more, but he stopped short.

The stranger had walked out of a fashion magazine. She was blue-eyed, blonde, fragile, with the face of an angel. The silk trouser suit and neckerchief needed no designer label. Sam was dazzled.

"I'm sorry. I didn't."

"I didn't want you to drop the teapot."

Her attention was on the porcelain. Not Sam. Somehow he felt diminished.

She turned the modelling board slowly, scrutinising the imagery.

"I wouldn't have believed you could do it. You did do this, didn't you?"

"Yes."

"Is this the first?"

"Yes."

The blonde vision regarded him with the same intensity she had given to the vase.

"I never expected them to be as good as this. It would fool anyone."

"Any expert worth his-her salt would find my initials. Although they're well hidden."

She looked at Sam again.

"Yes, you're a man who would do that. Did you ever play cricket?"

"No. I played chess."

"This is number three. Why didn't you start with number one?"

"The decoration is particularly difficult to copy."
"And you like that? Difficulty?"
"I suppose so."
The blonde vision in the silk trouser suit nodded.
"Yes. Alan said you would be."

She stopped and Sam said, "He said what?"
"You would be. Different."
"Is that a compliment?"
"I don't think so, do you?"
She removed her glove and offered her hand.
"Holly Winterton. And you are?"
"Sam Ericksen."
They shook hands. A cool slim hand that Sam
wanted to retain.

"To be honest, I didn't want you to paint my
portrait. I wanted a name."
"I have a name."
"You know what I mean."
"Neither was I keen to paint you."
"Why not?"
The young woman was visibly offended. Sam
amended his answer.
"I've never painted a portrait before."
"But now you will paint my portrait."
"I will?"
"Yes."
"Why would I do that?"

"Because you put your initials on the Chinese teapot."

"Is that important?"

"Alan wouldn't like it. Everybody does what Alan wants. I've never met anyone before who didn't. Do you have coffee?"

"It says coffee on the jar."

While Sam boiled the kettle, washed two mugs and made coffee, the vision of rare delight prowled the studio.

*

Keira said, "Do you realise we can begin to pay ourselves a salary?"

"Really?"

"We're doing well. It's down to Oliver pointing clients in our direction. But there's nothing wrong in that."

"Then I propose we start paying salaries to Ms Keira Sullivan and Ms Hannah Ericksen from the first of the month. Agreed?"

"Agreed."

They were sharing breakfast upstairs from the offices when Hannah's mobile rang.

"Sullivan and Ericksen. Good morning, Oliver!"

She listened and offered, "Ten thirty?"

She looked to Keira who nodded.

"Ten thirty it is!"

Hannah closed the call and looked to her friend.

"He always asks for me. Does that bother you?"

"No. It's not racist."

"How d'y'know?"

"Practice. He only has eyes for you."

They laughed together.

They walked to Pilgrim Square where the marble portico and stained glass of the Northern Counties Bank assured the world of its probity. They had begun to feel at home in Newcastle. The opening of the firm had figured in a two-page spread in the Chronicle. Its mission statement to initiate investment in the North East was approved and applauded.

Hannah said, "Now that we're in employment, the schools are closed, why don't we invite your Mum and the girls up for a really determined search for our little spot of Paradise by the sea?"

"I'll vote for that!"

They were met in the lobby by a young clerk who escorted them to Mr. McCracken's office. He knocked on the door, was answered and retreated. Oliver De'ath opened the door.

"Hannah! Keira! Punctual as ever! I trust I didn't disturb your morning. But this is a unique occasion."

Mr. McCracken sat behind his desk. A teenage clerk stood at his elbow. Hannah and Keira said good morning.

Mr. McCracken said, "Good morning, ladies. How can I help you?"

Oliver De'ath slid in to say, "It's all been arranged, sir. D'you remember? The Mathieson matter?"

"Yes, of course, I remember. The Mathieson matter."

The young clerk beside Mr. McCracken placed a folder before the bank manager.

"The Mathieson matter, sir," she smiled and laid a hand on his shoulder. He looked up to return the smile.

Oliver said, "All has been arranged, sir. It needs your signature to complete the transaction. Angel will show you where to sign."

Angel opened the file and pointed to where the signature was required, her young breast nudging his shoulder. To Hannah it seemed a little more intimate than necessary. Mr. McCracken signed the document. Angel took time blotting the signature.

"Splendid! Well done, sir!"

Oliver turned to the partners.

"Now, ladies, if you will sign the agreement?"

Hannah took up the pen offered by Angel. She signed where directed and noted the teenager was not wearing a bra. Keira signed reluctantly and asked, "What are we signing?"

Oliver said, "The Mathieson matter," and announced, "Ladies, if you would shake hands with Mister McCracken, our manager, to formalise the agreement?"

The partners shook the flabby hand. Mr. McCracken betrayed very little interest. Angel supported him in the ceremony. Unexpected flashes signified Oliver was recording the event.

"If you will follow me, ladies?"

As they left the office Keira caught a glimpse of Angel sitting in Mr. McCracken's lap and kissing his brow. The hand they had shaken to formalise the agreement was exploring Angel's shirt. They proceeded down a flight of stairs the partners had not noticed before.

As they progressed, Oliver said, "Perhaps I should explain? It's really a matter of pensions. And lump sums. A shame to be so near and yet to have the cup dashed from one's lips. We're all doing our best to carry the chief through to retirement. His wife is a lovely person and his daughters do him credit. I trust you understand?"

Keira said, "Don't you think Angel is too young to be his secretary?"

"Angel doesn't engage in anything complex. She's there to keep our chief happy. He thinks of her as his daughter."

The partners exchanged glances. From a bleak hallway, Oliver led the way into the vault. A young clerk was awaiting them. Oliver said, "The Mathieson matter, please."

"Certainly, sir."

From a wheeled trolley, the clerk brought two aluminium suitcases to the table. He stood aside as Oliver unlocked the cases.

Both were filled with bank notes packed in Northern Counties' wrappers.

Hannah cried, "Good God!"

Oliver smiled upon her. Keira lifted and replaced packages of notes in disbelief. Oliver's camera recorded her with packages of bank notes in each hand.

Hannah said, "How much is here?"

"Two million pounds."

"Is this legal?" Keira asked.

Oliver laughed. "This is the Northern Counties Bank. You shall have copies of the documentation. Mister Mathieson is somewhat eccentric. He mistrusts electronic banking."

Hannah asked, "What're we to do with it?"

"Invest it. I have some suggestions for you."

Keira asked, "Why can't it stay here?"

"We have too much cash on the premises. Our insurance covers a certain amount and no more."

"So you want to put two million into the safe at S & E?"

"You are insured for five."

Oliver closed the cases and locked them. He handed the keys to Hannah.

Keira said, "Before we take this money away, I want the cases bound and sealed, please."

The procedure was photographed.

The partners regarded the aluminium cases in the Pilgrim Street safe, bound by red ribbon and secured with sealing wax.

Hannah said, "I would never have thought we'd ever be holding two million pounds in cash."

Keira commented, "I'll be happier when we're not."

*

The Diocesan Magazine

We all do our very best to create as much terror, pain, distress, heartbreak and torment as we can. Seeking by our modest efforts to create Hell on Earth. To raise Our Lord to His true dominion. But there are moments when we must look to the general community; to be more light-hearted in our approach and share a jolly afternoon with our neighbours. With this thought in mind, the Chancellor decided to hold an Old Folk's Outing and entertain the residents of a local Care Home. This was not difficult to arrange as we have Congregation members among carers and staff. Our revered senior citizens were bussed to a local parish hall we hired for the occasion.

There, they were entertained by our members with food and drink. We were well advised that port and Guinness, sausage rolls and pork pies would be in great demand. They drank and gobbled enough to fill a ditch. The feasting was followed by, what I understand was called, a 'disco.' We played the raucous music of their younger days. It was a great success. Somewhat to my surprise, they were up and prancing about like billy-ho. There was little need for the cattle prods. There were tears in many an ancient eye as we played their favourite melodies: The Funky Chicken, Twist and Shout, Ring of Fire, My Girl, Stop in the Name of Love. The most appalling row ever!

We turned up the volume so that even the deaf might enjoy the favourites of their youth. I understand slates fell from the roof. We kept them dancing, twisting the afternoon away. Even when they cried to stop, we insisted they keep on prancing. We snatched the chairs from under those who believed themselves to be exhausted and drove them on. It's surprising what a simple whip can do to encourage physical activity. The doors were locked, of course, so no one could escape. As good hosts, we insisted they enjoyed themselves to the utmost.

Two of the older men died of heart attacks. We put them to rest in the games cupboard. Old ladies were weeping with exhaustion, but a tap with a cattle prod produced some remarkable pas de deux, that Nijinsky would have envied. It's some time since I passed a more agreeable afternoon. However, all good things must come to an end and reluctantly, we bade our guests farewell.

Everyone had enjoyed the jolliest of times.
Bewitched, buggered and bewildered, clutching their goody bags, their ears ringing from the calamitous cacophony, they struggled aboard the coach encouraged by the cattle prods. I won't spoil the surprise by telling you what was in their goody bags, but I can assure you there were some rare surprises awaiting them. The manager of the Care Home said to me, it was obvious everyone had thoroughly enjoyed themselves as she had never seen her charges so tired before. We helped them all to bed.

Those of considerable weight whom we had to drag up the stairs, we took care not to bang their heads on every step. The two deceased gentlemen were not discovered in the games cupboard for eight weeks. The smell became more oppressive than sweaty feet. Unfortunately, the captain of one of the badminton teams suffered a heart attack at the discovery and the match had to be postponed. I was surprised no one questioned that we returned two short.

Four of the ladies passed away some days later, which shows you disco fever can be fatal. So, if you think your itinerary is looking a little jaded, I suggest you spare a thought for our senior citizens. Their days pass in monotony; breakfast, bullying, beating and bedtime. I jest, of course. Sometimes, we should think of the neglected, the lonely, the loveless, the good, kindly people who have found out too late that they were wrong. Only fools play by the rules. If you are considering a gift for a friend, I'm sure a cattle prod would be most welcome. May Our Lord reward your wickedness, as you strive to inflict suffering and death upon the righteous. Pax vobiscum!

The above is taken from the Archbishop's Address to the People's Conference last month. Copyright must be acknowledged, but please, do employ the Archbishop's words to motivate your followers.

CHAPTER TWELVE

"I don't want a picture of a dopey bird sucking a lemon."

Sam Ericksen, tongue sticking out, was working with a one-hair brush copying a fold of clothing on a Chinese vase. Glaze jumped down from the cool kiln and broke Sam's concentration. The cat mewed at the door.
"I'm not opening the door for you."
Someone tapped and Glaze backed away.
"Okay, clever clogs!"
Someone tapped again and Sam laid down the brush.

Standing outside were Victoria Sullivan and the girls, Isla and Sophie. "Surprise, surprise!" cried the girls.
Mrs. Sullivan apologised, "I hope we're not interrupting your work. Keira said you."
"Welcome! Come on in! I welcome any intrusion," he lied
Isla hugged her Uncle and Sophie shook hands.
Victoria Sullivan watched, amused.
She said, "Do I merit a hug? Or a handshake?"
Sam gladly hugged his hoped-for-to-be-mother-in-law.
"I offered them dinosaurs, the Eye and penguins, but they said, no, they wanted Sam."

The girls agreed and Sam suggested, "I rated above the penguins? There's a backhanded compliment."

Isla said, "But where's all the lovely pots gone? That's what I wanted Sophie to see."

The display shelves were largely empty.

"They're now, as my friend Stan the Garage man says, on display at the Contemptuous Ceramics Centre, Bloomsbury."

"Is that a good thing?" asked Sophie.

Her grandmother said, "Isla's Uncle's work is at the Gallery so rich people can pay proper prices." When Sam protested, she went on to say, "Keira has told me. You sell wonderful pieces at ridiculous prices. You undersell yourself every time."

Isla offered, "Now he can sell them at enormously ridiculous prices!"

"Your friend Stan," Sophie said, "didn't mean contemptuous. He meant contemporary."

"Well done! Sharp kid!" Sam applauded.

Sophie's smile lit the room.

"Is the exhibition going well?"

"It's been amazing. So good it's been retained for a further two weeks."

Isla asked, "Did you have champagne?"

"I haven't been to the Exhibition."

"Why not?" his visitors chorused.

"Not my thing."

Sophie said, "But you should be there."

"I'm not very good with crowds."

Sam remembered the noise and smell when the rocket exploded in the crowded tent called, prophetically, The Last Saloon. Sam had stepped out because it was hot and noisy. It was the first time Camp Bastion had been penetrated.

"And are they selling?"

"So I understand. But the buyers can't take their pieces until the exhibition closes."

"So what're you doing now?"

"I'm forging antique Chinese pottery worth millions of pounds."

"You're not! Or I hope you're not."

Sam led his visitors to the bench where the unfinished vase stood. They stood in silence until Sophie breathed wonder.

"It's so beautiful."

"Did you do that, Sam?" asked Isla.

With a photograph of the original in one hand, Sam turned his lazy susan.

Victoria said, admiringly, "To be able to create something like this."

Sam smiled, "I'm not creating. Only copying. Alan Winterton found the originals in a storeroom at Windsor Castle. Dusty and forgotten. Vases, bowls and teapots. The Chinese government want them returned."

"Don't they belong to us?" Sophie asked.

"They were taken from the Imperial Palace in Peking during a war in the nineteenth century.
"Isla said, "So they were stolen?"
"Yes. The government will return them. It's a friendly gesture. So I'm copying them. For us to keep and display."
Victoria said, "But is that legal?"
"My copies are marked with my initials. I wouldn't do it otherwise."

It wasn't difficult to engage the girls in making their own pots. Sam provided over-size aprons and showed them how to build a ribbon pot, coil upon coil.

Glaze was in his favourite spot on the cool kiln from whence he could survey his kingdom. As they approached, he regarded Victoria Sullivan with an unfriendly stare. Sam tried to coax the cat to come into his arms, but was ignored.
"He isn't any different," Sam confessed.
"Dead cats don't breathe. Is he eating, drinking?"
"Waits 'til I come in to eat so I see him."
"Will he let you pet him?"
Sam stretched out a hand and stroked his cat. Glaze purred happily.

Victoria addressed the cat, saying, "What a beautiful old cat he is! A fine cat! A beautiful cat is Glaze!"

She reached out a hand. Glaze raked the back of her hand, driving the claws deep. Startled, she cried out. Victoria sucked her bleeding hand, shocked by the speed of the cat's response.

"Are you alright, Grandma?" asked Sophie.

"Just a scratch, darling. My fault. Stay away from the cat, please, girls. He doesn't know us. We're strangers."

To Sam, she said, "Painful though it may be, that's how a live cat behaves to nosy strangers."

In the bathroom, Sam cleaned the wounds.

"You've done this before."

Sam smelt the dust and heat of Afghanistan and felt the abruptly amputated lower leg of Corporal Charlton strike his shoulder. For a moment he struggled with the image.

"Once or twice, "Sam said.

"I can drive you. Get the bus back. No problem."

She shook her head.

"Only a scratch. I'll be fine."

To the girls, Sam said, "Enjoy your visit to Newcastle. I know two Mums who are dying to see you."

They parted regretfully.

*

Glaze watched as Sam cleaned off the girls' coil pots with a damp sponge, added rims and tweaked where tweaking was necessary. Aware of his scrutiny, Sam asked, "Why did you hurt Missis Sullivan?"

Glaze failed to meet his eye. Sam added the girls' names in slip.

"It's not cheating. They've made two sound pots. I'd like to think in years to come they'll still have their pencils in their first pots."

Glaze mewed scornfully.

"Yes, I know. Sentimental twaddle. But that's me. I am a sentimental twaddler."

He moved the pots to a board and carried them to the drying cupboard.

He returned to regard Glaze.

"Keira's mother's wrong. You're dead. If you don't know it, I do. Dead is dead."

To the empty air of the studio, Sam declared, "Well, Mister Devil, Satan, Beelzebub, whoever you are, why did you do this to my good friend Glaze? Does he know he's dead?"

Sam stopped as the terrifying implication struck him.

"My God, but that's frightful! To know you're dead, but still walking about. That is the ultimate punishment! You shit, you utter shit, Satan! What did Glaze ever do to deserve such a punishment?"

151

The question echoed in his head.

"What did Glaze do?" With startling clarity, the scene played out in his head.

Glaze ran towards the door and when the visitor bent to stroke him, snarled and spat. The visitor recoiled, saying, "Your cat dislikes me on sight." He smiled to say, "Yet I'm welcome at Clarence House." Glaze scratched at the door to exit. The visitor moved to open it, but the cat turned to display teeth and open claws.

Sam apologised, "Sorry! He's not the friendliest of cats."

"But that's not true. Maybe a dozen strangers wander in that door every day and Glaze takes no notice."

Sam returned to work on the current Chinese piece. He was learning to paint Chinese; to be patient; to learn from his mistakes. He realised he never previously learned from mistakes, but hid them; the Western way. To his surprise, he was beginning to paint the image before picking up the brush. But the nagging thought persisted. Glaze took a dislike to Winterton. The cat is at the gate to see off the interloper. A chum of Royalty, Sam's benefactor, runs over Glaze and throws him into the weeds. Sam said aloud, "It doesn't make sense unless." The black thought

persisted and Sam gave it voice. "Who would disturb a dead cat from his grave?"
He found it difficult to avoid the answer.
"Only the Devil."

*

Tony of Tip Top Tyres was seeking Sam's help with his choice of horses to back. He'd suffered a very bad week. Stan and Bruce had suffered accordingly. "I know nothing about racing, Tony."
"That's what I want. A know-nothing. Did Columbus know anything about America? Well, did he?"
"I suppose not."
"Exactly nothing. Like you. And what happened? He got lucky!"
"He could hardly miss America! But what if I pick all the wrong horses?"
"You won't. You're lucky. Like Columbus."
"How'd'y'make that out?"
"Stan says bloke walked in and you've got your stuff on show up West. Sheer luck! And the only Beamer that's ever come into this yard come to you. That's what I call lucky!"

Tony looked at Sam with the pleading eyes of a middle-aged spaniel.
"Show me what you want me to do."
"I've ringed the races."
Sam sat down at the bench, Tip Top biro in hand.

"Can I keep the biro?"

"You can keep the biro."

So I choose one horse in every race?"

"You've got it!"

"But just this one time only? You promise?"

"On my mother's grave."

"You never had a mother, Tony."

Tony studied the almost bare shelves as Sam struggled with the names of horses. Reluctantly he marked a horse in every race.

"Don't blame me."

"Cheers, Sam! Any time you want tyres."

"I haven't got a car."

Tony opened the studio door and closed it again.

"There is a top bird getting out of a Maserati Quattroporte out there! Who says you're not lucky?"

Someone knocked on the door.

"Open the door, Tony."

He opened the door to Holly Winterton, an absolute goddess in gold top and minimum skirt.

"Hi, Sam! Am I interrupting something?"

"No, you're very welcome!"

Holly turned to a mesmerised Tony to say,

"Would you be so kind as to bring in the packages from the car, please?"

Tony vanished.

Sam said, "I know you're doing this deliberately."

"Doing what?"

"Disturbing the nation's health. But this isn't the place to do it. We are simple peasants. Our heads are easily turned."

Tony returned with packages and vanished again.

"Aren't you glad to see me?"

"Of course, I am. You bring sunshine wherever you tread."

"Why, Sam, how kind!"

Tony returned with more packages.

"That's the lot."

Holly looked to Sam.

"This is Tony, a good friend."

Holly said, "Thank you, Tony. You're very sweet."

Tony smiled modestly.

Sam said, "Weren't you going to ring your trainer?"

"Oh, yeah! Right. Cheers!"

Tony returned to reality and vanished, clutching his newspaper.

Sam gestured at the packages. "Forgotten it was Christmas. Afraid I haven't got you anything."

"When I didn't hear from you."

"Your husband's been keeping me busy.

"Then it's time for a break."

"What's this? A paint by numbers Mona Lisa kit?"

"I hope not. I don't want a picture of a dopey bird sucking a lemon."

Sam set to work to erect the easel.

"You make me nervous. Watching me."

"I like watching you. You're very. I don't know. Competent? You know what you're doing. You make me feel safe."

Sam began to open the packages and whistled his astonishment.

"This is very expensive gear. Nothing cheapo here. That fresh smell is the scent of money."

He added, chidingly, "D'y'know how much all this cost?"

"No. Money's just pieces of printed paper."

Sam stopped to unbend his back and looked at the young woman.

"Do you know how much a single canvas this size costs? And we have a dozen! Thousands of people are expected to live on less than that for a week." "Don't talk about money, Sam. Money is very boring. Besides I'm worth it, don't you think?"

"A dozen canvases, the biggest palate in the world? A rainbow of oil paints? Not counting brushes? I don't think so."

"Why are you so unkind to me? I'm not unkind to you."

Sam was surprised to see Holly was genuinely hurt.

"Sorry."

"I keep thinking you're different."

"I can be different."

Holly smiled, saying, "You are different.

Glaze scratched outside the door and Sam went to open it. The cat stared at the visitor and then at Sam.

"Oh, how sweet! What's his name?"

"Glaze."

"I want Glaze at my feet in my picture."

"I don't think," apologised Sam and stopped. Glaze settled at Holly Winterton's feet.

"What don't you think?"

""That's it. I don't think. Rots the brain."

Glaze remained at Holly's feet for the afternoon as Sam started to work up a canvas.

*

Keira and Hannah were sitting on a bench outside St. Thomas's Church. They were enjoying the summer sunshine, seeking refuge from the busy world that pressed upon them. An older man sat down on the bench. He was thin and unshaven. His hair was dirty and disordered. He wore an old teeshirt promoting Busch Gardens, Florida. His jeans were faded and stained. He wore leather shoes, but no socks. When he moved along the bench, Keira would have protested, but Hannah tugged her to give way. When he shuffled closer still, Keira protested, "Please move away. We have a right not to be disturbed."

The man yielded bench space.

"Please. I must talk to you."

Hannah said, "We don't want to talk to you."

"Please. I mean no harm."

"Then leave us alone."

"I need to warn you."

Keira said, "What about?"

"I've seen you at the Northern Counties Bank."

"You've been spying on us?"

"I know who you are. You have the offices in Pilgrim Street."

Hannah took out her mobile.

"Go away before I phone the police."

The man moved as if to leave and then said, "If I tell you the Northern Counties Bank has been taken over by the Devil, would you believe me?"

The stranger stood up and limped away, vanishing into the lunchtime crowd.

"Why would he say that?" asked Keira.

Hannah offered, "Loonies home in on me."

Keira rose, pulling Hannah to her feet.

"Come on! I want to hear why."

They caught up with him in Northumberland Street. The lunchtime frenzy in McDonald's had passed. They found a quiet corner and sat patiently while the man ate ravenously. Hannah bought the meal. When he had eaten the last crumb and swallowed the last drop of coffee, he said, "Thank you. That was very kind."

Keira said, "We're not being kind. We want to know why you'd try to frighten us. Not a nice thing to do."
She sat back and waited for an answer.
"You won't believe me, so why should I bother?"
"Hannah bought your lunch."

Without preamble, the man said, "My name is Ronald Whitley. I was a solicitor, mostly family concerns. I looked after my clients and they trusted me. Once I had a home, a loving wife and three wonderful children. Now I live on the street." He stopped as a teenager came to clear the table. Hannah rose to buy fresh coffee. Keira took out her tablet.

"Ronald Whitley," she typed aloud and the stranger rose in alarm.
"Please don't write anything down!"
Keira persisted,
"Then how can I check what you say?"
The man was pale and agitated.
"They will kill me."
Keira closed the tablet, saying, "I'm not impressed."
Ronald Whitley sat down again.
Keira held up her phone to say, "I'm only phoning the office to say we're held up."
She noted the stranger never stopped moving: leg, arm, head or hand would continue to beat a

nervous rhythm.   Hannah returned with the coffee.

"Thank you," said Ronald Whitley.

As Hannah settled into her seat, Keira warned her, "We mustn't write anything down. And we mustn't check anything."

Hannah sipped her coffee and asked, "Why not?"

Keira responded, "Because they'll kill him."

Ronald Whitley moved to speak and then gestured surrender.

"I'm wasting my time."

Keira stated, "Wrong again. You're wasting our time. What I really must impress upon you, is not to slander the Northern Counties Bank.   They will take action against you."

She looked to Hannah and they both rose from the table.

"They killed my baby boy. Robert. Robbie."

The   partners   sat   down   again.

CHAPTER THIRTEEN

"Desolation Row. Hello!"

Sam couldn't find his bicycle. He marched up
and down behind the studio as if he were
suddenly going to espy his precious mount
somewhere amidst the neglected grasses. Finally,
Sam came to the obvious conclusion.
"Some poxy bugger's stolen my bike! Shit, shit,
shit, shit, shit! Excuse my French, Mother, but I
will rip the little sod's head off his manky body!
I will, I swear I will!"

He took to kicking at the grass and then in
desperation to search the iron railings that
bordered the industrial yard. In the hope that
some kindly person had leaned the machine up
against the railings to save it going rusty when
the wind had blown it over into the grass. The
bicycle was gone. When Sam came to accept his
loss, he stood in silent prayer looking hopefully
up at the heavens. No bicycle descended. Sam
went to bemoan his fate at Stan's garage, being
the nearest.

The three caballeros were sitting together
drinking mugs of coffee and munching
doughnuts.

"You won't believe this, guys, but some cretinous, loose-jawed, brainless Neanderthal has stolen my bike."

They rose with mournful faces and Tony said, "Even when our Samuel is in deep shit he never swears proply, does he?"

Sam was outraged.

"Did you hear what I said? Some shitty bastard has nicked my bike. Somebody could say, there, there, never mind!"

"How'd'y'know it's nicked?" asked Stan.

"Because it's not there! Where I leave it."

Bruce said, "Have you searched everywhere, Sam?"

Then he saw his precious mount was leaning up against the puncture bench. Sam cried, "What the!" They stepped back because he looked so fierce.

"This some sort of joke?"

"Calm down, Sam, calm down!" Stan implored.

"It'd better be good."

"Tell him, Tony!"

Tony declaimed, "Six out of seven, Sam! Six out of bliddy seven!"

Then Sam was fighting off their hugs and back-slapping. Three glowing faces shone on Sam.

"What six out of seven?"

Tony explained, "Six winners out of seven. Number seven was third."

The three men danced around him, singing raucously, "Six out of seven, six out of seven!"
"Horses?" said Sam.
They nodded agreement.
"So why steal my bike?" Sam growled, anger rising.

"Take a look," Stan invited, "Top tyres, all-weather mudguards, sandal pedals, new handlebars, top pro comfort saddle, digital brakes."
"An electric motor for when your old legs start wobbling."
"And little lamps that blink like a Christmas tree," added Bruce.
"We have a pink basket. But that's optional," Tony offered.
For one blinding moment Sam was close to tears. He hid his confusion, examining the bicycle.
"Thank you. Thank you very much. Very kind."
No bother," he was assured, "Don't bring your money to the Monkey tonight." "Just one thing missing," Sam said.
"Yeah?"
"Where's my bike?"

*

Holly Winterton said, "My bum's gone dead sitting on this chair."
Sam said, "Then we should take a break."
He flexed tired fingers.

"I shall make coffee."

"No, I will. I know how to make coffee."

Holly vanished into the kitchen as Sam stretched and shook cramp from his legs. He had become totally absorbed. There was nothing yet to suggest it was a portrait of a human being but Sam's head was buzzing. Perhaps Alan Winterton was right? Victorian ceramic painters were artists denied the privilege of canvas.

Holly appeared in the kitchen doorway to say, "I can't find the coffee machine."

"In my humble abode, there is no coffee machine."

"Then how do you," but Sam interrupted to say, "You are the coffee machine." Holly smiled, not comprehending.

"Fill the kettle half-full. Light the gas stove. Matches supplied. Rinse the two cleanest mugs. Find the bottle that says, Best Cheapskate's Instant Coffee. Put a spoonful in each mug. Pour boiling water into the mugs. Add milk and sugar to taste."

Holly looked downcast, saying, "You think I'm a dumbo, don't you?"

"No. You like playing the dumbo. But I suspect you're as sharp as a razor."

Holly smiled and vanished. Sam continued cleaning brushes. Holly appeared with two mugs of coffee.

"Let me see! Let me see!" "There's nothing to see."

Holly stared at the canvas, disappointed.

"It's a mess."

"And out of that mess will emerge a painting of Holly Winterton. Not a Marilyn Monroe poster, but a portrait of a real woman."

"If it's horrid, I shall cry."

"So shall I."

The young woman returned to the rickety chair to sip her coffee and Sam took photographs. When she threw a pose, Sam chided, "Don't act the dumbo. Just be Holly talking to a friend."

"What should I say?"

Sam hesitated to offer, "Tell me what you do."

Holly thought for a moment. "I don't do anything."

"Of course, you do!"

"I go places with Alan."

"D'y'like cooking?"

Holly laughed.

"Real cooking?"

"You have a kitchen, don't you?"

"I know how to use the coffee machine."

"Then you could learn to make a bacon sandwich."

"Why? If someone else will make it for me."

Holly laughed again. Sam decided he liked her laughter.

"We go out to eat. If Alan is having a dinner party, there's people who come in to do that."
"Horse riding?"
"We go to the races. But that's becoming somewhat tawdry, Alan says."
"The theatre?"
"If Alan's writing the review, we go. Mostly it's just boring."
"Cinema?"
"Leicester Square premieres. And sometimes in the States. Sun Dance. It's a film festival."

Sam bent to his camera to avoid meeting that innocent gaze. This child actually did do nothing. She appeared at the side of the august Alan Winterton as required.
"That should do," Sam decided.
"My turn."
Sam surrendered the camera. Holly walked around him, taking photographs. She laughed as she spun her web of enchantment.
"When did you last go to your exhibition?"
Sam confessed, "I've never been."
"Never?"
"Your husband is selling me as reclusive."
"He doesn't like to share the limelight."
"I'm not keen to go. Not good with people. Or criticism."

"I will take you to your Exhibition on Saturday. We'll be Mister Incognito and Lady Friend. No one will notice us."
"I very much doubt that."

Sam flicked through the photographs.
"You have a good eye for a photograph."
When he looked up, Holly was pointing a pistol at him with a steady two-handed grip. Sam recognised the Glock 21.45 ACP. Magazine holding thirteen rounds plus one.
"Where'd you get that?" Sam asked casually, while working out how to get close enough to disarm her.
"I could ask you the same."
"A remarkable American friend. He didn't need it anymore."

Sam could see the American clearly. Blakey held up the pistol for caution just before the grenade rolled into the crowded room. Terrified women and children had returned to the room because of threatening gunfire. Without hesitation, Blakey dived onto the grenade.

"Where'd'you find it, Holly?"
"In the cabinet under the sink. Alan says, always check the kitchen."
Sam nodded casually. Ignoring the pistol, gesturing with the camera, he said, "There's a particularly good shot of you and Glaze."

He moved forward to show it to the girl.

Holly smiled, "Not good enough," and pulled the trigger.

*

Ronald Whitley said, "It all started with a friend. A family friend, I would've trusted with my life. He revealed he was a member of a small group that was running a very successful algorithm that was making a great deal of money on the stock markets."

Keira said, "A computer program that buys and sells for you. You just feed it money."

Hannah commented, "I've heard of it."

Ronald Whitley said, "Until I saw the bank statements, I didn't believe it."

He suddenly started. "I must go. There's a man watching me."

He rose and fled to the street.

From a farther table, a short man left his coffee and hurried from the restaurant. They lost sight of Whitley and his follower until stopping for breath they caught sight of the pair in the back lane by the cinema complex. The man was speaking earnestly to Whitley. The friends ran to the pair. Hannah pulled the man away and Whitley fled. Keira accused him.

"Wha'd'y'think you're doing? The man's mentally ill."

"My dear ladies, I was trying to persuade the poor fellow to come to our Fellowship where we can offer a meal and a bed for the night. I saw your kindness towards him. You bought him a meal. I thought I would seize the opportunity. Do you know the chap?"

Keira shook her head and Hannah said, "We'd just met him."

The man produced a card. They glimpsed a clerical collar.

"St. Andrew's Refuge, Kielder Gate. I do apologise for any misunderstanding." The reverend gentleman hurried away.

Keira said, "Describe him to me, Hannah."

Hannah hesitated to say, "Short. Dark hair? Sorry. Best I can do."

"Anonymous," Keira stated, "Standing in front of us and he's invisible."

"Clergyman?"

"So he says."

Walking back to the office, Keira mused, "Could the Devil take over a bank?" Hannah said, "I don't believe in the Devil. I believe in a rational universe."

"But if he did exist. And I'm not sure he doesn't. Then he might take over all the banks."

*

We betook ourselves on an afternoon outing into the country to pay off an old debt. We were feeling jaded and matters had been somewhat pedestrian of late. Our destination was a delightfully ancient cottage built on the labours of others, which I most applaud. We coaxed home the errant husband, a persistent thief, to attempt reconciliation with his wife. We whispered in his ear that she was about to come into a very great deal of money. This quickened his desire for reconciliation. How foolish these creatures are! The family much enjoyed the opportunity to express their true feelings. The wife and her father despised the husband who had brought calamity upon them. The mother, struggling with her dementia, contributed little but anecdotes of affairs, which had sustained her through a dreary marriage. It was as we expected, a normal family bound together by mutual hatred. So, we set the husband and father-in-law to fight with kitchen knives. Most thrilling! Somewhat to our surprise, the husband killed his father-in-law. The older man tripped and his son-in-law did what one would expect a dutiful son-in-law to do. He stabbed him in the back. We strung the old lady up to a beam with her toes almost touching the floor. We set her daughter to hold her up to prevent strangulation. I would suggest older ladies should watch their weight. What an Herculean contest! Her daughter held her up for fifteen minutes and twenty-three seconds. An achievement we rightly applauded.

Her husband had refused to help, despite her pleas, blubbering behind the couch about a prolapsed intervertebral disc. So we strung up his wife and dragged him out to support her. A spiritless performance! The poor woman died in less than four minutes. The Chancellor reminded the graceless creature that he had once signed an agreement with our Congregation to avoid punishment and disgrace for theft. He denied us, of course, saying it had all been a joke. The Chancellor explained that stealing from Our Lord was a matter we took seriously. The worthless creature begged us to kill him, but tiring of the whole affair we made our excuses and left. He now resides in Broadmoor for the murder of his wife and in-laws.
As recorded by Amanuensis.

*

Holly pulled the trigger and the gun clicked. She looked at it as if the pistol had betrayed her. Sam took it from her hand.
"Why did you do that?"
Holly shrugged, saying, "I wanted to."
Sam struggled to suppress his anger.
"If I were so foolish as to leave a full magazine in the pistol, you would've killed me. D'y'realise that?"

"I suppose so."
"So why did you do it?"
"I just wanted to."
"You wanted to kill me?"

Holly giggled.
"I wanted to see what happened."
"What happened would be, I'd be dead."
"They do it all the time in the movies."
"That's just silly! You know the difference between real and pretend. In the movies they're pretending. If you had shot me, I'd stay dead."
Holly shrugged her elegant shoulders.
"Are you on some drug?"
"No."
"You wouldn't tell me anyway, would you?"
"Yes, I would. I don't tell lies."
"I don't know what to make of you, Holly. I should be angry, but I'm not."

Holly blossomed as an inner light brightened.
"Then you'll paint my portrait?"
"If you promise not to shoot me while I'm painting."
"Promise. And you'll come on Saturday?"
"If you promise to allow me to come home in one piece."

Holly laughed; a deliciously childish laugh.
"Promise."

She took a card from her purse, wrote upon it with a gold pen and gave it to Sam. In true Winterton fashion, it said simply *Holly Winterton.* When he turned it over he saw a mobile number.

"Ring me. If you want to. I'll collect you at one."

Holly stopped to stroke Glaze who purred and twined about her legs.

"I've never seen a cat before with such mixed-up fur. You can't say what colour he is."

Glaze escorted the visitor to the door. Holly blew a kiss and departed.

"You have me puzzled, dead cat of mine. If you are my cat. You hate the husband. Who, incidentally, is the Devil. But you already know that. Yet you've fallen for his missis. What am I to make of it all?"

Glaze said nothing. Sam went to the refrigerator and prepared a meal and milk. He watched Glaze eat.

"So remember not to bite the hand that feeds you."

Glaze retired to the kiln shelf.

For a long time after Holly had gone, Sam sat deep in thought. The telephone rang.

"Desolation Row. Hello!"

The familiar voice said, "Sounds everything is going well. Vicky and the girls are coming up on Saturday. Why don't you come with them?"

CHAPTER FOURTEEN

"He always goes for the eyes. Never the hands or the face."

The now familiar clock struck nine as Hannah carried a bin bag down the back yard. Beyond the circle of the security light, she sensed movement, but didn't react. She dropped the bag into the bin and returned to the back door of the offices. She locked the door, before going to find Keira who was still at her screen.

"There's someone in the yard."
Keira stood up.
"Is the security light working?"
"We need a better one."
Keira took a torch from her desk drawer.
"Come on!"
"What're we going to do?"
"We're not going to be intimidated. That's what we're not going to be."

They walked out into the backyard together.
"We know you're there. Come out into the light before we ring the police." There was silence until Ronald Whitley stepped into the torchlight.
Keira swore, "Shit! Not again!"
Hannah cried, "What the hell're you playing at?"

"I'm ringing the police."

"Please don't! I must talk to you!"

"Why would we listen?"

"They're going to kill me."

"You said that before."

"They know I've been talking to you."

Hannah decided, "Come inside."

She could see Keira didn't agree.

The man followed them into the conference room.

Keira demanded, "How did you get in the yard?"

"I climbed over the wall."

"Liar! We have roller barbs."

"My coat's up there."

"You never thought to walk in the front door?"

"I know you don't believe me. But they will kill me as they killed Robbie."

"I looked him up. Coronary occlusion. Unusual in a child of four."

"You never told me," Hannah observed.

"So how did he get his artery blocked? Too many pork sausages?"

Ronald Whitley sat silent.

"That was a bit harsh," Hannah commented. "Go on, tell us something we can believe."

The man started to rise and sat down again.

"I thought you might be the right people to talk to. But I was wrong. They'll kill me, so I'll tell you what you won't believe and then I'll go."

Hannah said, "I'd like to hear."
She looked to Keira who added, "Tell us about the magic algorithm."

"I was foolish enough to invite family and friends to join us. The returns were fantastic and the more we put in the greater were the returns. It was almost too good to be true, but the bank statements said otherwise. The only injunctions were that nothing could be withdrawn for six months and five per cent would be payable to the owners of the algorithm."
"And then?"
"The expected statements for the sixth month did not arrive. Everything had vanished. There was nothing. The bank denied the validity of the statements. It was as if it was all a bad dream. Except that I had ruined everybody. My trusted friend who let me into the scam committed suicide. When I protested Robbie died. My friend Alan protested and his family died in a road traffic accident. The message was plain. The Devil has taken over the Northern Counties Bank. What other branches may be corrupted, I don't know. When I'm dead, remember I told you."

Keira let Ronald Whitley out into the darkness of the back lane.
"You don't believe me, do you?"

Keira said, "No, I don't. I think you need help, Mister Whitley."

She locked and bolted the yard door. Hannah stood on the bin to poke his coat free of the spikes.

*

When Sam Ericksen put down the phone he felt sick. He was repulsed by his betrayal.

"I have to go. I don't have any choice. Alan Winterton made that clear. It's the last weekend of the Exhibition. I suppose Alan wants to make something of a fuss. Not my sort of thing. I hate crowds and I hate people saying nice things about me. Not that they often do. What I really want to do is come up and freeze to death eating pasties."

There was silence and then Keira said, "We understand, Sam. There will be other times. Good luck with the Exhibition."

"Thank you."

Hannah took the phone and said, "Shame we ordered all those pasties. But the girls will be okay with Vicky. And they can stuff down all the pasties."

"I feel I've let you down."

"Well, you have, you great oaf, but you can't help it. It would've been fun to go house-hunting together."

When he put the phone down, Sam picked it up again and started to re-dial. Then he stopped. He felt physically sick and went to sit in his thinking chair. Glaze came from the kiln to stare at him, unblinkingly.

"I'm a liar and a coward, Glaze. Did you hear me? Disgusting. Alan Winterton? He doesn't know I'm going to the Exhibition. I want to spend the day with his wife. Absolutely totally crazy. Madness! But I can't resist it. I want to be in that car with her. I want to walk around the Exhibition with her. Total madness."

Glaze mewed reproachfully and walked away to scratch at the door. Sam opened it for him.

"You don't like me much, do you?"

Without a word, Glaze reproached him, saying, "Not when you behave like this."

The cat exited, tail waving in disgust. Sam returned to his chair via the glaze cupboard. He didn't bother with a glass, but drank from the bottle.

"First time I've lied to Keira. I feel like shit. Second time will be easier? Third will be routine? Let's see how the truth works."

Sam took a long draught from the bottle. He sat in silence while the liquor burnt its way down to his stomach.

"My dear Keira, I choose to spend Saturday afternoon with Holly Winterton rather than you, because she has me totally bewitched. She tried to shoot me. To see what would happen. I suppose I want to see what will happen."

Sam drained the bottle. From the kitchen, he returned with the sherry bottle. When Stan switched off the grinder, he thought he heard someone shouting. He stepped out of the garage. He recognised the voice and went to listen at the studio door. Sam was singing. Stan called to Bruce who came to join him. Tony joined them out of curiosity.

Sam, obligingly, sang again. *"How could you believe me when I said I loved you when you know I've been a liar all my life. I've had that reputation since I was a youth, you must've been insane to think I'd tell you the truth."*

"Sad," mourned Stan, "Very sad. He'll have me crying next."
"That's what women does to you," Tony added, "Blondes is the worst."
Bruce offered, "Fred Astaire sung that song in the musical Royal Wedding. Nineteen fifty-one, I think it was. Burton Lane did the music. Alan Jay Lerner wrote the words."
"Alright, professor! Give it a rest!" Stan chided him.

"Here! Try this," offered Tony, "Who was the Formula One driver what was dead but still become Champion that season?"

*

Emily ate lunch in her car on the Terrace car park. She didn't eat at her desk now. To be ignored only provoked her to retaliate against laughter that might not always be aimed at her. She wasn't hungry and dropped the half-eaten sandwich back into the paper bag. Gloria was the only one who seemed reluctant to join in with the coven. Emily gave Gloria good properties. When someone tapped on the window, she spilt her sports drink down her shirt. It was Tom Fenwick. Emily wound down the window.

"Look what you made me do!"
"Sorry! Can I sit in?"
Emily nodded, regarding a wet shirt. Tom walked around the car to the passenger door. He sat down saying, "Would you like me to rub it dry for you?" He offered a large white handkerchief, which Emily snatched, from his hand. "If I have to go home and change that's down to you."
Tom said, "That's what I'd like to see you do. Change."
Emily glared at him.
"Cut the schoolboy smut or bugger off."

She was still surprised how coarse her language had become.

"You've become most unpleasant, Emily. If you'd started out like that. But you didn't. You were a really sweet kid."

Emily stopped wiping.

"What's it to you?"

"Well, I keep hoping it's all a front. I'd be happy to work with an Emily who found it hard to sell houses, but was willing to learn. She's my kind of girl."

They sat in silence. Emily wanted to switch on the ignition, but she didn't. "They were a happy little bunch at M & M. You taught them to be bitchy. Why favour Gloria?"

"What's wrong with that?"

"You're putting her in an impossible position."

"Before you say it, I did nothing to Buchanan."

"That's strange because he rarely ventures from his office now. And Joanne's gone. Her house is sold. Private sale. No forwarding address. For no reason I can think of, you ruined her life."

He waited for the explanation that wasn't forthcoming.

"Will you do that to Gloria?"

Tom Fenwick said, "I've driven past the office nine o'clock and later. And you're still there. If I stopped, would it be Lemon Drop Lizzy?"

"I want to sell houses."

"Why don't we steal an hour and go for a drink? Just Sweet Emily Rose and me? No Lemon Drop Lizzy."
"I have to go."
Emily switched on the ignition.
"Thanks for the sermon."
Reluctantly Tom Fenwick eased out of the car.

As she drove away, Emily Harrison fought the temptation to stop the car. A small voice from the darkness within her cried out to be loved by Tom Fenwick and never to be alone again.

*

The satnav took her out to Godly Vale, a village beyond Ryton she'd never visited, but loved the name. It had once been a colliery village, but only the older inhabitants remembered the history. Most of the pit houses were now occupied by young commuters. Emily found Managers' Row and parked outside Hazeldene. The garden gate screeched and Emily saw the net curtain twitch.

"Cheaper than a dog, I suppose."
She tapped on the door, which opened on the chain.
"Yes?"
It was an older voice
"I'm looking for Mister McDonald."
"Why d'y'think he lives here?"

Emily hesitated.

"He doesn't live here?"

"That's not what I said."

"Mansfield, the solicitor, gave me the address."

"Who are you?"

"Emily Harrison. I work for Madison and Major. I'm in the process of selling your apartment at Harbour Mount, South Aranport."

The chain was released and the door opened.

"I suppose you should come in."

"Thank you."

There was no hallway. Emily stepped straight into the sitting room that smelt of tobacco and was crowded with furniture. The ceiling was yellow with nicotine. Mr. McDonald was very old, thin and short of stature. His spectacles had been mended with tape. His moustache and beard were yellow with nicotine. Emily decided he looked like an ancient boy. Mr. McDonald studied Emily carefully.

"What did you say your name was?"

"Emily. Emily Harrison."

"Best you sit down."

She sat on the shabby couch and the old man sat opposite in a chair apparently built of cushions. The ashtray at his elbow was empty. A white cat crouched on the back of his chair. Emily became aware the cat and its owner were studying her.

She pressed her knees together and sat straight-backed on the unstable couch.

Struggling to find something to say, Emily offered, "Your cat's very," but was interrupted.

"He's a very good judge of folk. But you'll have to speak up. He's deaf. Did you know many white cats are deaf?"

"No, I didn't know that."

Emily found herself speaking more loudly. The cat seemed to approve.

"If he thought you'd come to kill me, he'd have attacked. He always goes for the eyes. Never the hands or the face. Just the eyes. So you're warned."

Emily protested, "I haven't come to kill you."

"Good! They're servicing the boiler tomorrow."

"Have you sold my apartment?"

"Not yet."

"You must be sure the right people buy it."

"How will I know the right people?"

The old man looked at her as if she were stupid.

"Because everyone else will be wrong."

Emily nodded.

"Why did you leave?"

"It became very difficult."

Emily was going to ask what was the difficulty, but the old man continued,"So you haven't sold it yet?"

"No," said Emily. There seemed little else to say.

"Your spectacles?"

"What about them?"

"Is the screw still there? Sometimes when the spectacles part, the screw is still there, but has just come free. May I take a look?"

Reluctantly, the old man surrendered his spectacles. Without them he looked totally forlorn.

"You won't bugger them up, will you? I cannot see much as it is."

The tiny screw was stuck to the tape. She fished out the leather tool kit her father had given her. *Be prepared*, he had recited endlessly. She replaced and tightened the screw. She checked and tightened the other screw, cleaned the lenses and returned the spectacles to the old man.

"Thank you."

"All part of the service."

She saw in the watery eyes something of amazement.

"Don't get up. I'll see myself out."

"You haven't a fag, have you?"

As she rooted in her shoulder bag, he continued, "We used to call them tabs. God knows why."

Ignoring the old man's chatter, Emily offered a fat spliff.

"A roll-up any good?"

"Bless you!   Cannot do it anymore. The artheritis."
Emily gave the spliff to Mr. McDonald.
"Enjoy!"
"You can come again," agreed the old man.

*

Emily set the satnav for home and locked her seat belt.
"Mend his specs? Why the hell did I do that?
She felt ashamed of herself.
"A regular Pollyanna. He hadn't had a wash for months. Disgusting! And a manky cat. I need a bath."
On the drive home, she squashed a squirrel and felt better.

Old Mr. McDonald enjoyed the toxic mix for only a matter of minutes before the demon arrived to open his scrawny chest with a long fingernail. He pulled out his heart and lungs to waggle before his dying eyes. The demon tried on the old man's spectacles before crushing them underfoot. The lenses were crystal clear. He flung the corpse to the floor and settled into the chair to enjoy an early tea. The cat came down to feed from the old man too, but the demon kicked it away. There are certain decencies to observe. Eating the hand that fed you is unacceptable even to the lowest of the low. The best one can say is that Mr. McDonald was free at last.

CHAPTER FIFTEEN

"Get Geordie-size mates. I've just carried a gorilla."

On Saturday morning Sam was aroused from an uneasy sleep by a persistent telephone. The studio clock read eight fifteen.

"Hello?"

"Sam, it's Vicky."

"Hi, Vicky! What's up?"

"I'm at Euston with the girls. I feel really terrible, Sam. My arm. It's bad." "I'm on my way."

He put the phone down on Victoria's voice.

Stan was opening up when Sam tumbled into the garage. "Stan, I have to beg a favour. Emergency. Can I borrow a car, please?"

Stan hesitated for a moment.

"Yeah. Sure. Don't break it. Going far?"

"Euston and back."

Stan was openly relieved.

"He won't be here 'til five anyway."

"Who won't?"

"The owner."

Victoria was seated on a bench on the concourse. She looked drained. The girls were anxious.

"What's happened?"

"Where Glaze scratched me. It's been difficult, but the infection."
She opened the dressing.
"I can't bear it fastened." Sam was shocked.
The hand and forearm were twice the normal size, oozing pus and almost purple.

Sam was back under the hot canvas with the clamour of aero engines in his ears. The nurse was wiping the Afridi's arm free of pus. Sam looked to Bridger who almost imperceptively, shook his head.

"You can't go anywhere, Vicky. You need medical help now."
Turning to Isla and Sophie, Sam said, "Sorry, girls, nobody's going to Newcastle today. Your Grandmother has to see a doctor."
Victoria interrupted, saying, "This gentleman has kindly agreed to chaperone the girls to Newcastle."
Sam hadn't noticed the tubby man standing by the bench. He offered his hand to Sam and said something. Sam didn't catch his name, but caught a glimpse of a clerical collar.
"I assure you the children will come to no harm with me, sir. If you will contact their mothers, I will meet them with the children under the clock on Newcastle Central Station at twelve seventeen. If the train is on time. If they have a

mobile, they can speak to their mothers from the train."

Isla held up her mobile. "We'll be okay," agreed Sophie.

The tubby man offered Sam a card that he glanced at briefly. *St. Andrew's Refuge, Kielder Gate, Newcastle upon Tyne.*

"Let them go, Sam!"

Victoria Sullivan and Sam watched as the girls and their escort hurried towards the platforms. Sophie and Isla waved as they disappeared. Sam realised Victoria was weeping and sat down beside her.

"They're safe with the vicar. Now let's get you some help."

"I don't think I can walk."

Sam picked up his-hoped-for-future-mother-in-law and carried her to the car. He was surprised how little she weighed.

*

Emily Harrison opened the curtains and began to strip the bed. Saturday morning, she allowed her brain to sleep longer while she did the necessaries that required no effort of the little grey cells. She saw it when she whipped away the duvet, but didn't recognise what was lying on the sheet. Using a tissue, Emily picked up what she suddenly realised was the little toe from her left foot. She dropped it to the carpet and sat down on the bed. The toe lay beside the tissue, a discarded stub of cocktail sausage. She fought rising hysteria. She shook off her slippers. The remaining toes were firmly attached. Where the little toe was missing was dry and painless, as if a dead twig had parted from a tree. There were five toes on her right foot. Stepping over the tissue, Emily went to the kitchen. She returned with a small plastic bag, picked up the toe and dropped it into the bag. She felt an urgent need to urinate and retired to the bathroom, taking the plastic bag with her. She took from the cabinet the toe nail previously discarded.

In the sitting room, she photographed nail, toe and both her feet. Emily poured a large vodka with no tonic and drank it in one swallow.
She said aloud, "Leprosy."
The flat swallowed the sound.
She tried again. "How the hell, did I get leprosy?"
She typed leprosy into the computer. When the first pictures appeared, she switched off. Emily dialled the surgery. A voice apologised that there was no weekend surgery. *In the event of an emergency, please.* Emily scribbled down the number and dialled. The telephone was answered promptly by a young man.
"Target Emergency. My name is Derek. What is your name?"
Emily surrendered her particulars.

"What is the exact nature of your emergency?"
"I believe I have leprosy."
The silence was broken by indistinct voices.
"How do you know this?"
"The little toe on my left foot has come off."
"Your toe has come off?"
"The nail turned black and came off first."
"Please wait a moment."

Emily waited. A woman's voice said, "If you are amusing your friends, you should be ashamed."
"I assure you I am not."
"Then I have to inform you, leprosy is not listed as an emergency. Please contact your surgery within working hours."
The call ended.
"Leprosy is not an emergency? How much more has to drop off?"
Emily poured another deep vodka and dialled Tom Fenwick. She was met by voice mail.
"Couldn't you be there just once when I need you?"
She fought for calm and into the silence declared, "Sorry, Tom. It's not an emergency."

*

As the traffic light turned to red, Sam glanced at Victoria Sullivan. She was lapsing into unconsciousness. He put his foot to the pedal and shot across the intersection to a chorus of protesting brakes.

She rallied enough to ask, "Where we going?"
"A doctor who knows this stuff. Colin Bridger. Private practice. Small hospital."
Victoria nodded agreement. Her eyes fluttered and closed.
"Don't fall asleep on me, Vicky! Vicky! You have to stay awake!"

Sam ignored the next traffic lights and breathed relief as he burnt rubber into Cadogan Gardens. He eased Victoria from the car and ran up the steps to crash into Reception. As the receptionist rose from her chair, Sam said, "Get Doctor Bridger now. Tell him it's Sam Ericksen. Or this woman's going to die right here."
From the phone, the receptionist said, "He's coming. You are his Sam Ericksen, aren't you?"
Sam nodded and sat down nursing Victoria's limp form.
She stirred to say, "Are we there?"
"We are. Everything's going to be alright now."

Doctor Bridger arrived without flurry.
"Sam! Wherever you are, there's trouble."
But his eyes were upon Victoria. He opened the dressing.
"Let's hope we're in time."
Colin Bridger was as tall as Sam, strongly built with a mop of black curly hair, sprinkled with grey. The mild green eyes behind the spectacles on a rugby player's face seemed out of place.

"Bring her through."

To the receptionist, he said "You know what to cancel."

In the corridor he asked, "How did this happen?"

"My cat scratched her."

"And she dabbed it with Kleraspot?"

"Something like that, I guess."

"A cat is a tiger only smaller. Why does nobody understand that?"

Sitting in the waiting room calmed by subdued classical music, Sam rang Hannah.

"So the girls are travelling by themselves?"

"No. They have a vicar as an escort. A nice man. They're safe. Isla has her mobile. The vicar will remind them to phone you."

"Okay. If you say so."

Hannah didn't seem too convinced.

"Would y'rather they didn't come? They'd've been very disappointed."

There was silence.

Keira said, "I don't understand about Mum. What's wrong?"

Sam experienced the sinking feeling he had felt too often: to tell the right mixture of truth and lies.

"Sam? You there?"

"Yes. It's all my fault. My cat Glaze scratched her hand. I washed it and dressed it, but

194

somehow it became infected. She wanted to bring the girls to you, but it was just too much. Very painful."

"So?"

"I took her for treatment."

"To a hospital?"

"To the Cadogan."

"A private hospital?"

"Yes."

"Why'd you do that?"

Sam was grateful for the entry of a young woman with a cup of coffee.

"Was that the doctor?"

"No. A cup of coffee. And a biscuit."

"Some hospital."

Sam could've said, your mother would be dead before she could be treated in a crowded, understaffed A&E.

"I took her to the Cadogan because an old friend works here."

"A porter?"

"No, the director. Believe me, she's in good hands. They cleaned the wound, pumped her full of stuff and she's sleeping."

"Sorry, Sam, I was panicking. I should know better. Will they keep her overnight?"

"I assume so."

"I'll ring the Cadogan tonight."

Hannah pushed in to say, "Enjoy your Exhibition, brother dear. You deserve it." Hannah ended the call as Keira said, "Bye, Sam!"

*

Sam found Colin in his office, signing a flock of papers put before him by a motherly secretary. When she departed, Colin said, "Sadly, this is where I spend too much time. What would I give to relive the good old days?"
Sam laughed ruefully.
"God forbid! Too much mud, blood and bullets for my taste!"
"But we believed we were immortal, didn't we?
Sam agreed.
"We learned the hard way."

As Sam leapt over the broken wall, he saw the explosion had torn away Colin Bridger's left leg. He was lying protectively over the Afghan policeman who was staring blindly into the pale moon. Colin's medic lay dead with his hands in his supply bag. Sam took a tourniquet from the bag and addressed the bleeding stump. Blakey led the team forward and cleared the checkpoint. No casualties. The Afghan police had retreated discreetly.

Blakey clicked back-off and Sam picked up Doc Bridger who cursed loudly. He staggered under

Colin's weight. Frog picked up the medic. Taff hoisted the dead policeman and Tinker picked up the Doc's escort who was still breathing. With Blakey and Gobber bringing up the rear, they trotted to the helicopter and Geordie's welcoming grin. The Doc's escort died in the helicopter. Clinging together like tired monkeys, they clattered their way homeward.

Blakey said, "Did we learn anything today, Sam?"

"Get Geordie-size mates? I've just carried a gorilla."

Sam blinked back to reality when Colin Bridger said, "Jane took me to your Exhibition."

"You went to my Exhibition?"

Sam was deeply embarrassed.

"Without the name, I would've known it was you. But I never knew you could paint like that. Jane was very impressed. But your squaddies sent a shiver down my spine. My God, you had them growing from the mud to which they would return."

They sat in silence together, remembering. Sam recited, "Ashes to ashes, dust to dust, if the clap don't get you, the Taliban must."

Colin Bridger grimaced. "You always had poor taste, Sam."

The secretary returned to put her head in the door and say, "Eleven forty-two."

Sam, though reluctant to leave, said, "Great to see you again, Colin. I'm glad you're safe behind that desk. Thank you for saving Vicky's life."

He rose, putting his card on the desk.
"Send me the bill."
Colin Bridger shook his head.
"Returning the favour."
Sam said, "I'm going to the Exhibition today. I'll take another look at those squaddies."
Colin Bridger rose from his chair. "You must come to dinner, Sam. I've always told Jane you were a bloodthirsty barbarian."
"Thanks, Colin. Remember, I eat the meat raw."

At the door, Colin said, "One odd thing about Victoria Sullivan."
"Hopefully, my future mother-in-law."
"She died on the table."
Sam protested, "But she's."
"Charlie was tidying up. His stitching these days is better than mine. Then without warning, everything switched off. She died. Big disappointment."
Sam sought to speak but Colin silenced him with a movement of the hand.
"You resuscitated her?" "I promise you, we did our utmost. We hate to lose. Time of death recorded. Charlie finished his needlework. Anaesthetist departed. We tidied up. I always wait for the mortuary to sign off."

"I looked at that calm black face and I said, 'I'm sorry, my dear. I fear we've let you down badly.' And your future-mother-in-law opened her eyes to say, 'No need to apologise, doctor. I feel fine.'"

"Sometimes the heart is stopped for two, three minutes. I think six is the record. Victoria Sullivan was dead for twenty-nine minutes, thirty-eight seconds."
"I don't know what to say."
"I'll let you know when the patient may be discharged."

*

Oddly enough, the clergy of all churches are the easiest to corrupt. One would believe these gentlemen, through training and experience, would resist temptation to the death. Sex, alcohol and money are their weaknesses. I have had too many priests on their knees who have offered as excuse that having denied themselves so much in life, surely they may be offered some latitude. They whine, 'I have raised so much money for charity, abusing a teenage boy to the point of suicide is surely excusable?' It is entertaining to debate with these creatures. 'If I were a champion racing driver with a following of millions, surely it's understandable under such stress, I may unfortunately, strangle a young girl who refuses me?' They are so easy to corrupt. 'To heat this ghastly house, surely borrowing from church funds can't be wrong? In a loveless life, surely I deserve the love of an innocent child? Falling in love cannot be a sin. And did not Our Lord say take a little wine for thy stomach's sake? And more is always better when one finds one's faith has evaporated.' We make good use of these creatures, as you know well.

Recently, in a village church with a congregation of a handful, I was fortunate to return to the church to question a Biblical reference, whereupon I found the old scoundrel pocketing the only bank notes in the plate. I assured him, in the circumstances, it was quite in order to make use of the widow's mite. I pressed twenty pounds into his greedy hand. He was very useful in the prosecution of an innocent doctor who was found guilty, imprisoned and struck off. His wife and family lost everything. But who would doubt the sworn word of the admirable vicar? In contrast, we have a worthy opponent in an Innocent who will not yield. Innocents are rare. His faith in truth is steadfast. He is not yet aware whom he faces. His presence is formidable. Very few of our company can meet his gaze. If you have an answer to this irritant, I would be glad to know of it.

However, we have disposed of a lesser irritant. I am sure some of you will groan if I mention Ronald Whitley. Groan no longer! Last Saturday night, he set himself ablaze on the Tyne Bridge. He succeeded in incinerating himself despite the best efforts of a policeman and a passing gentleman. The bridge was closed overnight causing great inconvenience. It would've been easier to induce a heart attack, but we decided he should go out in a blaze of glory to warn other malcontents. The policeman and the passing gentleman were both commended for their behaviour. Apparently, no one realised they were not tackling the flames, but setting him alight.

As recorded by Amanuensis.

CHAPTER SIXTEEN

"Much to your delight, I have agreed to go out with you.
Could you look a little more delighted?"

"You're panicking," said Keira, "We'll be running next."
She grabbed Hannah's arm and slowed her pace. The busy street buzzed about them.
"We're not running to a fire. We're going to collect our daughters from the train station. They've been looked after on the journey by a kindly vicar."
"We don't know the man."
"Nothing has happened to the girls. You heard them. They said they were fine. Isla said he was a nice man. He wasn't sitting beside them. They were sitting across the table from him."
"He could've been making them say that."
"In a carriage full of people?"

Hannah slowed to a stop.
"Isla is the most important person in the world to me."
Keira smiled, "I'm quite fond of Sophie, though she can be a stubborn pig." "You know what I mean."

"If something was wrong, Hannah, any woman in that carriage would interfere." Keira saw Hannah's acceptance.

"We have to relax and not cause alarm to our girls."

They started to walk again. Keira saw Hannah begin to calm down.

"We say thank you to the vicar. Hope they weren't too much trouble. Slip him a tenner for the poor box and take the angels for ice cream."

When the grey majesty of Central Station appeared before them, Keira had to restrain her friend from committing suicide under the busy traffic.

"Am I supposed to say, sorry, Isla, but your Mum got run over outside the station?"

They crossed the road, hand in hand and entered beneath John Dobson's magnificent portico. Hannah tugged like a terrier as they scanned the crowd below the clock. There was a shout of joy and the two girls came hurtling towards them. The hugs were joyful, long and grateful. Happiness was complete. As embraces reluctantly slackened, Sophie said, "Why're you crying, Hannah?"

"She likes crying," replied Isla, "Mum cries at anything."

"I do not."

"What about when my Teddy's arm came off?"

Keira said, "Where's your vicar?"

"Oh, he had to hurry off for his train to Carlisle. He left you his apologies." Sophie said, "And a note."
Keira pushed the envelope into her shoulder bag.

As they walked in happiness from the station, Hannah asked, "Was he alright, the vicar?"
"He was no bother."
"Wha'd'y'mean?"
"He didn't ask us questions about the Bible. When they come into school, that's what they do."
"He didn't ask anything much. He said, I know what it's like travelling with a stranger. I'll try not to be a nuisance. Just tell me if something's wrong."

"What did you do?"
"We played games on Isla's tablet."
"Cyril. That's his name. Had a snooze most of the way. He woke up in Durham and said, 'That must be the Cathedral.' We thought that was very funny." "Why?"
"It's really very big."
"He was very kind and didn't bother us."
"When a man who didn't look particularly nice came to sit with us."
"With Cyril really."
"He said, 'My lucky day. Sitting with two angels.'"

"Cyril said, 'I'm responsible for these children. Please go away and sit somewhere else.'"

"He didn't!"

"He did."

"And?"

"He was a lot bigger than Cyril, but he did what Cyril said."

Keira said to Hannah, "Gold star for our Cyril."

At the end of a joyous evening, when the Chinese takeaway had been devoured and the girls settled to chatter in their makeshift bedroom, Keira remembered the note from the vicar. Hannah was downstairs in the office. Keira opened the envelope.

The note was quite short. In an educated hand it read . . .. *Dear Hannah and Keira, What a pleasant journey I have spent with your daughters! But it might all have ended differently. Forget you ever heard the name, Ronald Whitley. Yours sincerely, Your obedient servant, Cyril Alston.*

Keira felt the room chill. The notepaper trembled in her hand. She read the letter heading. St. Andrew's Refuge, Kielder Gate, Newcastle upon Tyne NE8 2UQ. She felt sick.

She was standing again in the back lane by the cinema complex. She heard herself say,

"Describe him to me, Hannah." "Short. Dark hair? Sorry. Best I can do." "Anonymous. Standing in front of us and he's invisible." "Clergyman?" "So he said."

Keira refolded the note into the envelope. When Hannah came upstairs, she didn't read it to her and Hannah never asked. Unable to sleep, Keira rose to go to the security carrel. All the locks answered positively. She trolled through the cameras. Pilgrim Street was dark and empty. The backyard was well illuminated with the new lamps. There were no dark corners. Everything was secure. She watched a young couple entwined, pass along the farther pavement. She jumped when Hannah put a hand on her shoulder.

"What you doing?"
"Spying on that young couple."
"No. What're you doing?"
"Checking the security."
"You've never done that before."
Keira caught the whisper of anxiety in her voice.
"We should. With the girls here."
She sensed the easing of tension.
Hannah said, "We'll take turns."
Keira left security on automatic and rose.
She struggled with a thought that would keep her from sleep. That man threatened the girls. She found the thought frightening.

*

The Rolls Royce Phantom stopped outside the Studio at one o'clock precisely. The immaculate chauffeur opened the passenger door and Holly Winterton stepped out, carrying a cardboard box. Holly wriggled her fingers in greeting to Stan, Tony and Bruce. She vanished into the Studio. The traumatised trio shook their heads in envy and returned to work. Sam opened the door and Glaze ran to greet Holly. She put the cardboard box down on the work bench.

"I've brought you a present."
"I wish you wouldn't."
"For health reasons. Your coffee tastes like old piss."
"You would know, would you?"
"And a packet of real coffee."
Holly picked up the cat to stroke him. Glaze purred with pleasure.
"At least someone knows how to greet a lady."
Sam tried to explain, "I've never been one for gushing, hugging and kissing. It seems so false to me."
He was embarrassed.
"You see how he treats me, Glaze? So unkind! Now I am gushing and false! I think I'll go home. He doesn't deserve me, does he, darling? Would you like to come home with me, little cat?"

Sam waited, defeated, until Holly said, "Are you not going to apologise, you horrible man?"

"Holly, you defeat me every time. I apologise for whatever I have failed to do. I am a very stupid man."

The young woman pouted and protested,

"Even a stupid man should see how beautiful I am."

The sunlight bathed the young woman in a surfeit of light that exploited the simple lines of the summer dress of flowers, the delicate tracery in her hair; the peasant sandals that graced her feet; that Sam Ericksen might well have mistaken her for a supernatural presence.

"I have never seen anyone more beautiful. You take my breath away and befuddle my brain. Today I should be in Newcastle."

He stopped and continued, "I find it difficult to believe you are actually here. What on earth are you doing in this clay pit with a hairy potter?"

Holly laughed. "I've come to find out who you are."

"I thought we were going."

The young woman put a finger to his lips to silence him. She walked around him. "We are not going anywhere with you dressed like this."

Sam protested.

"This is my best rig-out!"

"You look like a bank clerk. I'm not spending my afternoon with a bank clerk. I'm surprised you haven't three biros in the top pocket."

"I'm sorry, but this is the best I can do."

For answer Holly marched off to his bedroom and Sam followed. "What're you doing?"

The young woman ignored him and rifled through his scanty wardrobe. She flung his old leather bomber jacket on the bed. She found a pair of tired jeans and clean white teeshirt. Burrowing like a terrier, she found an old pair of desert boots.

"You're joking?"

"Wrong. You as a bank clerk is the joke. I'll give you five minutes to change and do something with your hair. In ten minutes, I'll be gone and you'll never see me again."

When he emerged from the bathroom, Holly barely glanced at him.

"Where's my portrait?"

"Safely locked away. Maybe I'm not quite so stupid."

"When can I see it?"

"Maybe next week."

Holly looked him up and down. "You'll do."

The chauffeur opened the passenger door and Sam followed Holly into the luxurious interior. The door closed with a gentle hiss. The chauffeur took his post and the privacy screen rose between driver and passengers. The Phantom purred from the yard. Sam said, "I confess I'm looking forward to the Exhibition."

"Then you'll be disappointed. The Exhibition was packed up last night and is on its way to Edinburgh."

A puzzled Sam looked to the young woman.

"Then what're we doing?"

"We're playing a game. The rules are simple. I am sixteen. I've just finished my exams. You're eighteen. I would never go out with someone of my own age. You have never passed an exam in your life. Much to your delight, I have agreed to go out with you. Could you look a little more delighted?"

"I am beyond delight. But couldn't I have a C plus in woodwork?"

"You're not stupid. I wouldn't go out with a dead brain. You're a free thinker. You see exams as the imprisonment of the spirit. One day you will write books that people will clamour to read. But today I want you to myself."

"I'm honoured."

Holly smiled.

"Truly honoured. You're an extraordinary woman, Holly."

"I want to have the afternoon I didn't have at sixteen with the boy in the bomber jacket. An afternoon just for me. Not what somebody else wants for me."

She was silent and then said, "My Mum says, I have to be back by ten. My Dad doesn't like you. Where're you taking me?"

*

Emily Harrison parted from the clients with a sense of relief. They were a young couple with an adopted Thai baby, carried in a sling on the adoptive father's chest. Emily had chosen to show them Harbour Mount because they seemed ideal; Pierre, ruby earrings, flowing hair, linen suit and his wife, Mitla, the woman with the thinnest legs and shortest skirt, Emily had ever seen. Emily was not sorry to say goodbye, smiling gamely, assuring the clients that next time. She went back upstairs to flop into the couch and snap open her energy drink.

"I seem to be living on these."

She felt the apartment was her confidante and comfort. She had already sold a holiday home on Sunday; a flat from the butchered Pilot House overlooking the river, but felt no sense of gratification.

"Did they sense my dislike of them?"

She sipped from the can and heard footsteps in the hallway.

"Oh, shit! What now?"

The footsteps stopped and Emily prayed the intruder couldn't hear the beating of her heart. She prepared her phone at one press to ring 999 and stood up. A door opened and closed. Then the handle of the sitting room door turned. The door opened. Emily threw her phone at Tom Fenwick who adeptly caught it. "What the hell're you doing here, Tom?"
She found herself both angry and relieved.

"I saw you with your clients."
"You're spying on me."
"I had a viewing at Mason's Court."
"Give me my phone back."
Tom threw it and Emily muffed it.
"Sorry!"

Emily sat down on the couch and closed the phone. Tom came to sit beside her. She glared at him and he shuffled away.
"So every time I turn around you'll be there?"
"Not every time. I have to sleep."
Tom smiled, but Emily didn't.
"What went wrong?"
"Everything. Awful people."
"And they weren't right for your precious apartment?"
Emily had no answer.

On impulse, she said. "I went to the doctor because I thought I had leprosy." Tom said cautiously, "Like in the Bible?"

"Did you know leprosy is not categorised as an emergency?"

"What did the doctor say?"

"He said he didn't know. But it didn't have the characteristics of leprosy. Isn't that a wonderful phrase? The characteristics of."

Emily realised she was frightened and near to tears.

"I don't know why I said that."

Tom said gently, "What made you go to the doctor?"

"My little toe fell off."

Tom Fenwick didn't smile.

"The nail fell off and then my toe."

"May I see?"

Emily slipped off her shoe.

Tom got down on his knees to look at the foot.

"May I hold your foot?"

Emily nodded.

He held the foot gently and examined the clean dry joint from which the toe had parted.

"It isn't gangrene, but then the doctor would've spotted that immediately."

Tom Fenwick recited, suiting actions to the words

"This little piggy went to market, This little piggy stayed at home, This little piggy had roast beef, This little piggy had none. And this little piggy fell off the wagon."

Tom Fenwick kissed and released her foot.

"Forgive the liberty. But despite the lack of a toe, you are still Emily Harrison. If you lose them all, you can lean on me."

The surge of anger boiling inside her lost its way and Emily laughed.

"You're the daftest man I know."

"You see? The real Emily is in there after all. Would you come to the Edinburgh Festival with me?"

"So I can provide you with late evening entertainment?"

Tom sat very still and then stood up.

"It's not a doctor you need to see.

CHAPTER SEVENTEEN

"A pregnant teenage model ain't worth dick."

Holly and Sam stood, hand in hand, in their observation capsule. All London spread below them as the Eye slowly revolved.

The Phantom had delivered them to the Eye where they were met by a young man who recognised Holly or thought she was somebody else. He escorted them to the capsule. They didn't join the queue. They didn't show a ticket. They were treated as celebrities and members of the public took photographs that Holly gladly posed for: much to Sam's amusement. It was an idyllic afternoon.

Holly said, "Do you know you're supposed to be able to see Windsor Castle on a clear day?"

"This is a clear day."

They scanned the far horizon and finally decided the larger smudge at the end of the world was Windsor Castle.

"Shall we wave to the Queen?" suggested Holly.

They agreed and dutifully waved.

"I like the Queen. She's a game old bird."

"I think Her Majesty would be happy with that description."

"But Charlie is totally loopy."

"Shush! They have a big microphone aimed at the Eye."

"I don't care. Alan says he just repeats what the last person said to him."

"I hope it's not Alan."

"You worry Alan would cheat you?"

"He never mentioned about the Exhibition going to Edinburgh."

"He doesn't care about money. You must check your bank account some time. You may be surprised."

They sat in silence gazing upon the dizzying panorama below.

"I'm the Empress of the world, aren't I?"

"If you so wish."

"I wish I wasn't. I would like to be a real person."

Sam stumbled over a sudden surge of concern for the child.

"But you are a real person, Holly. A delightful young woman. Full of surprises."

"No, I'm not."

"Why do you think that?"

"Have you brought the gun with you?"

"I didn't think I'd shoot anybody today."

"Next time you must bring it with you."

The capsule slowly descended and regretfully they returned to common earth. "Thank you for taking me," said Holly.

"Was it your first time?"
"Everything is my first time."

*

Hannah smiled to say, "We have an appointment with Mister McCracken." "Ms Sullivan and Ms Ericksen?"
The cashier vanished and returned.
"The manager will be with you in a moment."
The formality passed unnoticed. A young man appeared at the open door.
"If you will follow me, ladies."
They followed him to the now familiar door. He tapped respectfully. A voice called and the young man opened the door.
"Your three o'clock appointment, Mister De'ath."
Oliver rose from behind the desk as the partners entered.

"Hannah! Keira! How good to see you!"
To Hannah's embarrassment, Oliver embraced her.
"Please, sit down. I understand your daughters are with you now?"
"Yes, they came on Saturday."
"I must meet them soon. Will they be staying with you?"
"If we can find the right property. We're going house hunting this weekend." Oliver beamed upon them earnestly.

"How can I help you? Although I suspect you're capable of helping yourselves. Your accounts are admirable."

He smiled at Hannah and then remembered to smile at Keira.

"How can I help you?"

Hannah said, "We're becoming somewhat concerned that we have almost four million pounds in what is now, our strong room."

Oliver laughed, "You'd be surprised how many businesses would wish to be in your position."

"We've never been in this position before. It's scary."

"Hannah, you have no cause for concern. The Bank bears the ultimate responsibility. Everything is sealed, as you wished. In many transactions, the actual money is never actually transferred. You have my suggestions for where the money should be invested?"

"Yes. We're negotiating with Tarquin Bros."

"You're playing with the big boys now, Hannah. The glass ceiling is broken. You have no reason for concern. The Northern Counties Bank and Sullivan and Ericksen Investment Counsellors are a good match. Is there anything else I can do for you?"

Keira commented, "Is Mister McCracken well? I suppose we expected to see him."

Oliver regarded the friends soberly.

"I'm afraid Mister McCracken is no longer with us."

Hannah interrupted to say, "Then I hope he enjoys his retirement. I know how you were all helping him through."

"Sadly that was not to be."

Oliver De'ath regarded the partners sombrely.

"Mister and Missis McCracken took a short holiday break in a Spanish villa. Grandparents and grandchildren died of monoxide poisoning."

Hannah and Keira were shocked.

"How dreadful!" Keira asked, "How did this happen?"

"Ventilation was inadequate. I understand there is an enquiry underway as to the responsibility of the landlord. A terrible tragedy."

Hannah asked, "Has a new manager been appointed?"

"I have the honour of becoming the manager," declared Oliver De'ath and smiled.

*

Emily Harrison drove onto the Terrace car park. Tom Fenwick was already parked, foraging in his boot. She heard him slam it shut and they walked to the office without exchanging a word. Tom held the door for Emily, but she ignored him and pushed the other door open, leaving him stranded. Nobody noticed. All the women were standing around Maria's desk.

"Tom!"

Maria beckoned Tom Fenwick to join the women. A curious Emily followed. Maria said, "Nobody's been able to speak to Mister Buchanan since lunch." "Have you tried?"

"The door's locked."

"What if he's ill?" asked Gloria.

"What if he's asleep as he was last time?"

"The door wasn't locked then."

Tom looked at the concerned faces. "You want me to break it down?"

Emily went to the office door and knelt down.

Maria called, "Don't interfere, Harrison!"

Emily opened her tool kit and selected two probes. When they moved to join her, she pleaded, "Let me have some light."

Tom said, "D'y'know what you're doing?"

"My father was a locksmith. This is a Mickey Mouse lock anyway."

With no difficulty, Emily unlocked the door. She rose and stood aside.

"Who's going to wake him?"

Emily noted the women looked to Tom. He opened the door and entered. The silence was broken when Tom cried, "Oh, my God!" He came to the door. "Ring for an ambulance. Now!"

He looked at the fearful faces and said to Emily, "You think you're so tough?" Tom caught her by

220

the arm, pulled her into the office and shut the door. Mr. Buchanan was hanging from the ceiling fan that no one had ever seen in use. Emily's knees buckled and she turned to escape. Tom Fenwick said quietly, "You did this. You're not running away now."

The fan was slowly revolving. The corpse grinned its deathly grin. Hello! Goodbye! Hello! Goodbye!

Tom planted a chair firmly and said, "Get ready to take his weight as I cut him free. Don't let him fall!"

Emily, numbed of thought, hugged the dead man's thighs. She discovered Mr. Buchanan had soiled himself.

"I don't want to do this."

"You've already done it."

Emily clung to the corpse and Tom cut it free. Emily gasped as she took the full weight and let the body slide to the floor. She found she couldn't take her eyes from the dead man's face.

She heard Tom say, "There's a note. It should be addressed to you."

He hesitated and read, "Forgive me. I have tried but I cannot live without Joanne."

Emily burst into tears and fled to the toilet. She heard Tom Fenwick speaking to the women. Then the weeping began.

They stood in the warmth of the butterfly house.
As they had approached, Holly had cried, "It's a
big caterpillar!"
She was entranced, turning to Sam with a smile
that rendered him dizzy. "That's where
butterflies begin."
Holly tugged at his hand.
"Let's go!"
Within the house, she laughed, danced and
pirouetted with butterflies on her hands, arms,
nose and hair.
"They think I'm a flower," she declared.

Children came to dance with her. There was a
simple joy about Holly that brought together
everyone in the butterfly kingdom. Sam worked
his camera as fast as it would function. He knew
he was seeing the real Holly: a child deprived of
the wonder of the world by too much money that
bought so little of value. They sat together on a
bench, amid the gentle greenery and watched the
languorous flight of these ethereal creatures.
Holly held out a hand and an almost fluorescent
yellow lace butterfly alighted.

"They're like angels. Perhaps they are angels."
Her butterfly was joined by another.
"Do you think they know who we are?"
"You mean Holly and Sam?"
"No, silly. That we're visitors come to see them."

"They seem to enjoy our presence."

Holly nodded thoughtfully. "Why have I never been here before?"

Sam shrugged. "You've been everywhere else."

"Not really."

A small blue butterfly alighted on her nose and she laughed.

"Is this what real people do?"

Sam hesitated to say, "Yes, it's one of the things they do. But they have to do a lot of unpleasant shit too."

"Do you know I have never walked in the rain?"

"I don't believe you."

"Whenever I want to feel the rain on my skin, my face, somebody rushes to hold an umbrella over me."

Whenever she has tried to enter life, someone has shut the door.

"What're you thinking, Sam?"

"Hoping it rains. We don't have an umbrella."

As they walked through the Gardens, Holly reached up to kiss Sam. He protested, "We don't do that."

He was aware of the cameras that were raised everywhere.

"Today we do. It's my day."

"That's alright then," said Sam, without conviction.

"I'm going to get Alan to buy me a butterfly house."

"Don't do that!"

Sam felt anger rising.

"Why not?"

"Unless he builds it with his own two hands, it's worthless. He doesn't care a toss for butterflies. That's why not."

Holly was silent. She took Sam's hand and they walked together.

*

Some of our younger members who are easily bored and would happily break open the crust of the earth to torment a handful of the righteous, regardless of the consequences, decided to test some of the old clichés. I grieve for this generation. It seems to have little of the spirit we shared in our younger days. Would they ever have thought of giving small pox blankets to the original inhabitants of North America? They walked away, wrapping their precious babies in the unwashed blankets in which small pox victims had died, giving thanks for our generosity. And the Jewish Holocaust? Would they have ever thought of offering hot showers to the tired, hungry people coming off the trains, bearing them to a new life in the East? They happily entered the shower blocks while we laughed our socks off as the Zyklon B poured from the shower nozzles. No, they show a complete lack of imagination.

Why does a chicken cross the road? Apparently, only if you dip its tail in petrol and apply a match. Creaking gates hang longest. They unscrewed the gates on an estate and seventeen old men and women broke their legs or hips. Or both. Childish behaviour.

A bull in a china shop? Fortunately, we had a collector of china to whom we have permitted some latitude and deserved a reprimand. His superb collection was housed in a Elizabethan long gallery in his historic mansion: a most astonishing display of antique and contemporary ceramics. Into this haven of culture, our bright sparks introduced a bull with disappointing results. The bored creature wandered about, excreted large mounds of shit and mooed incessantly.

It was only when they set fire to the bull that there was any action. Unfortunately, the bull set fire to the gallery, which set fire to the house. It was a national tragedy to lose both a world-acclaimed ceramics collection and a jewel of Elizabethan architecture. And the bull. Unfortunately, the owner attempted to enter the house to salvage what he could and never emerged. It was an uproarious lark for which we congratulate our young people, but it wasn't what was intended.

Recorded by Amanuensis.

*

"So I'm standing on a line that runs right around the world?" Holly asked. Hesitantly, Sam suggested, "In a sense, you are standing at the world's point zero, yes."

"That suits me. Zero."

"In October, eighteen eighty-four, the Greenwich Meridian was chosen to be the common zero of longitude and standard of time reckoning throughout the world."

"How do you know all this?"

"It says so in the brochure."

"That's cheating."

"In simple words, this is where you check your watch and from where you navigate your ship safely. Greenwich Mean Time."

"So if I step this way?"

"You're going West."

"And here?"

"East."

"And here?"

Holly moved to present herself to Sam.

"You're embarrassing me."

Holly laughed, "Then I navigated right? You are easy to embarrass."

She looked about her with childish awe.

"Why has no one ever shown me this?"

Throughout the display in the planetarium, Holly was silent, absorbed. Sam gazed upon her perfect profile; the lips echoing the commentary, the eyes wide open as the spaceship carried her to visit our neighbours in the solar system. When the audience dispersed, Holly didn't move.
"I'm going to ask Alan to."
Sam interrupted, "Let me see the real world."
"He never will."

As they walked to the car, Sam asked, "Did you never go to school?"
"We don't need no education. I was a model."
Sam was astonished, but not surprised.
"Children's clothes. Toys. But clothes mainly."
"When did this begin?"
"I was four. I remember having my birthday cake at a photo shoot."
"What was that like?"
"We had cake. Billy and the crew had champagne. Billy wanted me to have champagne, but my Mum stopped him. Then we went back to work."
"So you never had a childhood?"

The chauffeur held open the door for Holly and Sam said, thank you, as he slid into his seat.
"You really should smile and say thank you to more people, Holly."

"Why?"

"Because they're people."

"The Russian girls I worked with taught me smiling is a sign of weakness. Be sullen and they will always say, yes."

As the Mercedes glided into traffic, Sam asked, "You're a child model. What next?"

"I was given this drug to delay puberty."

"My God, why would anybody do that to you?"

"I was going to go to America. That would be really big, Billy said. But it made me ill. I nearly died. The contract was cancelled. It was my fault."

"Billy said that?"

"He was my director. And my Mum agreed."

"What about your Dad?"

"I never seen my Dad."

They dined at the transport café Sam had been introduced to by the terrible trio. It provided excellent food. The drivers were delighted to have Holly in their midst and were remarkably polite. Sam insisted the chauffeur ate too. He went to join some drivers who welcomed him. Sam ordered fish and chips; real haddock in a crispy, golden beer batter. And two pints of Guinness.

"When you recovered, what happened?"

"I became a teenage model. The clothes were better, but the hours awful. The director, Terry, kept us supplied with happy pills so we never noticed. The dragon, Doreen, kept the boys out. A pregnant teenage model ain't worth dick."

"Sounds like Dickens' boot blacking factory."

"Didn't you ever want to be famous?"

Sam shook his head. "I don't think so. To get drunk, yes. To win a teenage model, yes, but I don't think famous."

"So what did happen?"

"I thought I was interrogating you."

Holly was silent, waiting.

"Not a lot. When I was sixteen, I became a boy soldier."

Holly interrupted, "Sixteen? You're only a kid."

"I wasn't allowed to kill anyone until I was eighteen."

"Then you did?"

"I became a good soldier. Then they didn't want me anymore."

"Why?"

"Carrying too much metal."

"So now you're a successful teenage model. What happened?"

"Alan Winterton bought a number of models."

"You were one of them?"

They were both silent. Finally, Sam said, "If I get my hands on that Billy, I'll break his neck."

"He's dead. Died of an overdose. Like my Mum. But Alan's still alive."

"So?"

"Kill   him   for   me.   Please?"

CHAPTER EIGHTEEN

"You're probably going to get the boot."

The partners were in Hannah's office when the girls came in. Isla said, "Angela said it was okay. You didn't have anybody with you."
The girls knew to enter the offices quietly and never to interrupt anyone working. They were firm favourites with the office staff.
"Are we interrupting anything?"
Hannah said, "Where would you like to live?"

On the desk lay a map of coast and country.
"We've drawn a circle centring on Newcastle. That's the farthest we're prepared to drive every day."
Isla and Sophie studied the map.
"That's a long way."
"And you've got to come back."
"So we want to find somewhere as near as possible."
Hannah offered, "Seaside or green fields?"
"Seaside!"
"The country's really boring."

Hannah suggested, "So we're looking at a small town on the coast, right?" "Where we can run down to the beach!"

"Oliver's sent some estate agents' bumph. He doesn't recommend Blyth or Seahouses. Within easy reach, he suggests we look at North and South Aranport. Mouth of the River Aran."

The laptop was open to photographs of Aranport. Keira turned the screen to the girls.

"Pretty harbour. Piers and lighthouses. Easy access to Newcastle. Good schools, but I don't know how much Oliver knows about schools."

Hannah asked, "Who wants to go house-hunting this week?"

The vote was unanimous.

"Where've you been?" asked Hannah.

"The Eldon Centre."

"D'y'never go anywhere else?"

"The covered market?"

"Oh, nearly forgot," said Sophie, "We saw Cyril."

Keira said, "Wouldn't have thought the Eldon Centre was his sort of thing?" "No, we were coming home."

"Did you speak to him?"

"Yes."

"Wha'did he say?"

"Have you forgotten me."

"We said, no, we hadn't."

"He asked after you."

"Remembered your names."

"Sent his best regards." Isla continued, "Asked if we were enjoying Newcastle."

"Then we said, bye."

"And he went off, waving his umbrella."

Hannah said, "You wouldn't go off anywhere with him?"

"Why would we?"

When the girls had gone upstairs, Keira asked, "What have you got against the vicar?"

"I knew a vicar once who seemed great, but he wasn't."

*

The Mercedes purred through the wonderland that is London by night.

"Remember you promised my Dad you would see me home by ten."

Sam laughed.

"Don't you dare laugh! He's ever so strict. If I'm late, he'll beat you up. I'm his princess. His only daughter. He worships me."

"You said you'd never seen your Dad."

Holly hesitated. "If I had a Dad, that's the Dad I'd have."

"Have you had the day you wanted?"

"Yes, thank you. It's been my best day ever. In all my life."

"Then I wish every day to be your best."

"That's lovely, Sam. Thank you. But now I shall take you safely home, the boy with too much metal."

The Mercedes turned into the yard and stopped, headlights illuminating the rainbow studio.

Holly said, "That's the most awful shed I've ever seen."

"Thank you. Don't get out. Thank you for choosing me as the boy who shared your Saturday."

"My best Saturday."

"I'll ring you when the portrait's fit to be seen."

Holly caught his arm.

"I need you to shoot Alan."

He wanted to laugh, but her eyes were afraid.

"Please? For me?"

"Why would I do that, Holly?"

"Because he's the Devil."

*

Sam called, "I'm home!" to an invisible Glaze.

"Okay, be like that! See if I care."

On the bench stood the box Holly Winterton had brought. Out of curiosity Sam opened it to reveal a coffee machine.

"Wow! This is a posh piece of kit. I'll have to vote Tory now."

Sam set about preparing Glaze's supper.

"Does that mean I have to learn how to use it? It's much easier with a jar and a spoon."

Sam put down the dishes and called for Glaze.

"Goody, goody grub, Glaze!"

Glaze didn't appear.

"Now what's upset you? Is it Holly? But you like Holly, don't you? No, I didn't kiss her. No, she's not coming to live here. I'm just part of her fantasy life. She wants me to shoot her husband. That should tell you how sane she is."

He tried again, calling, "Goody, goody grub, Glaze!"

"I'm not going to chase after you."

Sam moved around the studio looking into the cat's private places. Glaze was not on the kiln. Glaze was under the kiln, which was unusual. Sam got down on his hands and knees. The cat was lying still, but his stomach was moving. Sam was relieved.

"Least you're breathing. What's up, old friend?"

He crawled under the kiln and called him again.

The cat didn't respond.

"Something's wrong."

Sam forced his way under the kiln to Glaze and took him by the tail.

"Sorry. Needs must."

He pulled Glaze out from under the kiln. The stink assaulted his nose. There was movement in the body. Maggots tumbled from the cat's mouth.

"Maggots!"

Sam stared in disbelief. When the shock subsided, he brought a stout carrier bag and laid Glaze within. His hand trembled as he sealed the bag. He was desolated. Sam retired to his thinking chair with the carrier bag at his feet. He drank half of his Highly Toxic bottle. To the empty studio, he said, "At least, now I know."
Before he retired for the night he rang the Cadogan.

"Are you a family member, sir?"

"Yes. I'm going to be her mother-in-law."

Silence.

"Have you been drinking, sir?"

"Yes. Sorry. I mean."

"Missis Sullivan is sleeping peacefully. Perhaps you should go to bed, sir?" The call was ended.

"You wouldn't get that with the NHS."

*

Emily Harrison bought four bottles of vodka. The girl behind the counter smiled to say, "Having a party?"

"Yes. Special occasion."

I can't say I'm going to get so blasted my brain dies.

"Mixers?" said the girl, smiling.

She's really trying. She should be an estate agent.

"Let's make it a dozen."

The girl returned with the soft drink packs.

"You've been promoted?"

Emily shook her head.

"Mister Creepy got fired?"

"Even better. The boss hung himself from the ceiling fan in his office."

The silence was icy. Everyone in the shop stopped breathing. The girl stopped smiling and pushed the carrier bags across the counter to Emily.

"It was my fault he did it. He left me a note."

Emily paid the girl who recited, "Congratulations! You qualify for free entry to our Drink Responsibly Lottery. Your tickets are in the carrier bag. You could win twenty thousand pounds and a wonderful Caribbean holiday. Please drink responsibly."

"Thank you."

Emily left the shop, steering between the icebergs. She heard the noise from her flat in the corridor. She put the key into the lock and braced herself. When she opened the door, the full blast struck her. Jacqueline, the malignant pixie, was dancing on the coffee table. Emily switched off the music.

"What're you doing here?"

"Is that any way to greet me, sweetie?"

"Do you know what sort of day I've had?"

"I had a great day. Sold Ravensbourne Terrace. And the clients are thinking over Chudleigh

Close. I'll ring them tomorrow to say there's another offer in. They'll buy."
"Buchanan hung himself. In his office."
"I heard about that. Good, eh? Another one bites the dust."

Emily stared at the intruder.
"My God, you're not joking!"
"Be honest. Do you care whether he hung himself or got eaten by a hamster?" Emily shook her head.
"Then I'm here at the right time, sweetie. You've had a bad day. We'll order a takeaway."
"No, we won't."
"My treat."
"I just want you to piss off."
"Then we'll retire to your boudoir with its soothing lights and murmurous sound."
"You've been in my bedroom?"
"It's awesome! You'll have multiple organisations and tomorrow morning, you'll be fresh and invigorated to take on the world anew."
"Lay a finger on me and I'll break it."
"Oh, you like the rough stuff, do you? Bring it on, tiger!"
Emily picked up the vodka and headed for her bedroom.
"Stay away from me!"

Emily drank vodka like a thirsty camel and wept because she didn't understand what was happening to her. She was sucking the second bottle when Jacqueline got into bed with her. She welcomed her embrace.

"How kind you are, Jacquie! Nobody else cares."

Jacquie blew into her ear and Emily giggled.

"What's wrong with me, Jacquie? Nothing is right any more. I don't feel anything. I hate everyone. I only feel good when things go wrong. When people die. When people are hurt. I rejoice."

"That's because you're dead, Emily."

Emily giggled disbelief. "I'm dead? I don't feel dead. Do I look dead? Dead people are buried." She giggled and added, "They'd have to catch me first."

"Lots of people are dead and don't know it. They feel nothing. They just go on eating, drinking, shitting and shagging. All meaningless. But they're useful to us."

"Who's us?""

"All you need to know is you're not alone. Everything is top shit. Don't worry." Emily found Jacquie's hands on her body and relaxed. Nothing meant anything any more.

"I'm not worried," she announced and sucked on the vodka bottle, "I never worry."

"That's my girl!"

"Tell you something though."

"What's that?"

"I'm going to be nicer to Tom Fenwick."
"Then I'll pretend I'm Tom Fenwick.
Would you like that?"

*

The freckled pixie was rummaging through Emily's bureau when the bell rang. "Shit!" said the elegant Jacqueline.

The bell rang again. Reluctantly she went to open the door.

Tom Fenwick said, "What the hell're you doing here?"

"I might as well ask the same."

Tom was staring at the nightdress.

"I want to see Emily."
"You can't. She's asleep."
"I just want to see she's alright."
"She's alright. She's asleep."
"You know Buchanan killed himself?"
"Yes."
"I just want to see Emily is okay."
"And I keep telling you she's asleep."
Tom Fenwick hesitated. "Good night, Mister Fenwick. See you tomorrow." Jacquie moved to shut the door, but Tom prevented her.

"This is Emily's flat?"
"Yes, but I don't want you disturbing her."
The freckled pixie was taken by surprise as Tom Fenwick forced the door inwards and pushed her

aside. The bedroom stank of alcohol. Jacqueline switched on the light. Emily was lying on the bed.

"Now will you leave her alone?"
Tom Fenwick stroked the girl's brow, pushing back her hair.
"She's not breathing!"
He fumbled for a pulse.
"No heart beat!"
He let go of her lifeless arm that fell to the bed.
"What've you done to her!"
"She's not dead. She's asleep."

Jacqueline pushed Fenwick aside to repeatedly slap Emily's face.
"She had a drink. Mebbes a little too much."
Emily began to revive, protesting at the slapping.
"Stop it! You're hurting me!"
Surfacing, Emily recognised Tom.
"What're you doing here?"
"You see? She's alive. She was sleeping."
"She was dead."
"She was asleep!"
Tom Fenwick shook his head.
"Anything happens to her," he threatened.
Tom exited the bedroom.
"Why's Tom here? I don't understand what's going on."
"Don't worry, sweetie. He's a man. You don't have to understand them."

*

Stan was busy so Sam took the spade without asking. He chose a clear space between two birches and began to dig. He dug a grave twice as deep as before. When he looked up, the boy was watching.

"I have to make sure Glaze isn't disturbed again."

The boy nodded his head in agreement.

Out of curiosity, Sam asked, "Does it bother you?" He indicated the second grave. The boy said, "It's not supposed to happen, but it did."

Sam was surprised, repeating aloud, "Yes, you're right. It's not supposed to happen, but it did."

Sam placed the carrier bag in the bottom of the grave and began to fill it. The boy vanished. When Sam was patting down the disturbed earth, the boy reappeared struggling with a concrete slab. Sam relieved him of it.

"Thought we'd make sure." Sam agreed.

They placed the concrete on the fresh earth and pressed it down.

"Any words?"

"Dear God, let Glaze be safe and lie quiet. Thank you."

"Amen to that," agreed Sam.

The boy ran off and Sam walked back to return the spade. As he walked a thought began to grow in Sam's head as he remembered what Victoria Sullivan had said.

A cat returned from the grave has to have a purpose.

*

When Emily walked into the office she found everyone at their desks, apparently too busy to notice her entry. She sat down at her desk. She checked her face and in her mirror caught Tom Fenwick lounging in his chair, practising his irritating trick of balancing four biros on the fingers of one hand, without a care in the world. She rang his desk and he answered, still balancing the biros.

"Tom Fenwick, Madison and Major."
"What's going on? It feels like death row at Christmas."
"The new manager's in with Maria. You're probably going to get the boot."
"I thought you were my friend."
"I'd like to be."

Maria came out of the inner office and announced, "Mister Tennyson will see us individually. Natalie, would you like to go first?"

Whether by coincidence or deliberately, Emily waited an hour before Tom came out and announced, "You're up, Emily."

As he passed her, he said, "Just play it straight."
Mr. Tennyson appeared to be an amicable middle-aged man in a middle-aged suit and rumpled hair, balding, bespectacled and floundering under the deluge of staff files Maria had provided for him. Emily waited to be seated while the new manager pretended to read the last file.

He said, "My name is Mister Tennyson. I am not Mike or boss. I'm not your friend. I'm your manager. But I try to be fair. Understood?"
"Yes."
"Take a pew."
Emily sat down. Mr. Tennyson said, "You have few friends out there, Emily." "I'm not here to make friends. I'm paid to sell houses."
"The young man, Fenwick, is the only one who didn't advise me to let you go. Is he your boyfriend?"
Emily laughed.
"No such luck."
There was a long silence.

Mr. Tennyson offered, "Do you like working here?"
"I like selling houses."
"How did you get on with the last manager?"
"I didn't have much to do with him."
"You didn't take advantage of an older man?"
"They think I did, but I didn't."

Silence prevailed until Emily said, "I'll clear my desk. My daybook's up to date."

She started to rise and the new manager said, "I'm not making you redundant. Go back to work."

"Thank you, sir."

She closed the office door and walked through a gauntlet of triumphant faces to her desk. Mr. Tennyson came to his office door to call Maria. Five minutes later she returned to whisper to Janice who burst into tears and fled to the toilet.

*

We are but a small part of an unholy empire. You might say a franchise whose business is chaos. Big Burger's mission is to create fat people. Our mission is to create hell on Earth. We reap our parish, causing pain and distress. Every child that is born with a head full of hope, it is our business to obliterate that joyous presumption and teach cruelty, greed, malice, violence and loveless sex. In a rational universe, there is no place for us so we must strive to bring darkness. Whether it's a corner shop or a supermarket chain, a naive innocent or an organisation preaching love & peace, each is a worthy target for our attention. As the jobbing gardener advertises, no job is too small or too big. And, of course, there is a bill to pay. There is the old saying: *there was all Hell to pay.* And, indeed, there always is. I say this, so you may understand the simple story I relate.

Our member appointed to be the caretaker of his local primary school reported that a particular teacher was a great inspiration to her children. She taught them to value one another, to cherish hope, to work to claim the future, to love the world about them. They came happily to school every day. All pernicious nonsense that we fight so hard to extinguish. I hasten to say, she also taught them to read, write and count which is dangerous for children to learn. How can we build a spiteful, vengeful, illiterate society if the potential members are literate & numerate? Our member dealt with the problem.

Being a helpful chap, he often corrected minor faults with the staff's cars. He simply frayed the brake cable on this outstanding teacher's car. You may say what is so applause-worthy in killing a schoolteacher? He extinguished an evil influence in thirty children's lives. And in the lives of all the children who would have come under her pernicious influence and swallowed her nonsense. How many classes of children had she previously infected? Multum in parvo! Much in little. If you will permit me a simple jest? The caretaker took care of it.
From a recent seminar as recorded by Amanuensis.

CHAPTER NINETEEN

"It's not supposed to happen, but it did."

They stood outside the window in the early twilight. There was a young man in the office.

"One more try? Then we head home?"

Hannah held open the door. Keira and the girls headed for the young man's desk. He looked up and smiled to say, "How can I help you?"

The girls were instantly smitten with this handsome man.

Hannah said, "We know what we want, so don't try to sell us what we don't want."

Tom Fenwick said, "Okay! Tell me what you want."

"We want an old property."

"Overlooking the sea."

"Where we can run down to the beach."

"A minimum of five bedrooms."

"Lighthouses that shine in the window at night."

"A building of character."

"It can be an apartment, but with wonderful views of the sea."

"And a garden."

"It would be even better if it had some history."

"Somewhere we would never want to leave."

There was silence until the young man said, "Wow! You don't want much, do you?"

*

Sam locked the studio door and entered a different world. There were moments when he paused to ease aching shoulders and was disappointed to find himself back in the familiar studio. Sam was working on the last Chinese teapot, wielding a single hair as his predecessor had done centuries before. At first he had been hesitant, but slowly he had begun to understand the Chinese masters. He paused to regard the teapot. It bore scenes of village life. When he revolved his lazy susan all passed before his eyes. The patron in his rickshaw. The shopkeepers at their stalls. Passing villagers bearing enormous burdens. Children chasing a dog. Young women gossiping about young men. An old woman reprimanding her grandson. A mother with a crying baby. Sam smelt wood smoke, heard the baby's cries, saw the flight of cranes and enjoyed the kaleidoscope of village life.

Someone turned the studio door handle. Someone knocked on the door. Sam called, "Go away!" The knocking was repeated and ignored. The knocking persisted. Sam surrendered. He opened the door to Alan Winterton.
"Couldn't you ring first?"
"You don't answer the phone."
Sam gave ground and Winterton approached the bench to examine the teapot.

"Astonishing! Absolutely astonishing."

"Just don't touch."

"I gather from your enthusiastic welcome that you're pleased to see me?" "No."

"Why would that be?"

"Why didn't you consult me before the Exhibition went to Edinburgh?"

"You would've refused the opportunity?"

Winterton took a stool, found his gold case and offered a cigarette to Sam who refused. "What's your problem, Samuel? I'm making you famous and a rich man to boot."

"When the Edinburgh Exhibition closes, I want my work back, please."

"No can do, old chum. It's booked for Amsterdam."

"You had no right to do that."

"Yes, I do. I've bought your work. I can do with it whatever I wish. If we're lucky, it'll go to New York. Your soldier pieces have hit a nerve. There are big commissions to come, Sam."

Sam was dumbfounded.

"You're a very fortunate man. Check your bank balance."

"But the tree jugs! They were a special commission. What do I say to him?" "Sadly, the buyer has lost interest in ceramics."

"How did that happen?"

"There was a fire at his home and he didn't survive."

"So you sent your wife to distract me as the exhibition went to Edinburgh?" "Holly had a lovely day. Thank you very much, Sam. It's so difficult to entertain her."
Sam struggled with growing anger. Winterton revolved the lazy susan.

"This is piece eleven."
"Sadly the last teapot."
"May I see the collection?"
"No."
Winterton didn't hide his surprise.
"Why not?"
"Compared with the originals, my copies look new."
"So?"
"I've buried them."
"Is that not risky?"

"I'll finish your wife's portrait. But I don't want your money. Whatever you've transferred to my bank account, I'll return. And you will return my work to me. When I deliver the Chinese copies, we're done, Mister Winterton. I want nothing more to do with you."

Alan Winterton was silent. He drew deeply on his cigarette and rising, crushed the butt underfoot.

"Don't react too hastily, Sam. We must remain good friends. You have a rare talent that I will help you develop. You are free now from financial restraint. How many men can say that at your age? But you do work for me."

"How'd'y'make that out?"

"You signed the contract."

"What contract?"

"When I collected the exhibition."

"But I didn't know."

"Read the small print, Sam. You'll find I have exclusive use of your services." Sam had no answer.

Winterton checked his watch.

"I must be about my father's business."

Sam was silent.

On the way to the door, Winterton stopped. "I bought the exhibition because everybody wanted it. Now I have the first work of Samuel Ericksen who will one day be as renowned as Bernard Leach. We must strive to be good friends, Sam."

Alan Winterton smiled, "Lovers' tiff, old chum. Tell me when I can see the Chinese collection."

Sam watched him walk across to the Porsche that Stan was admiring. They exchanged words and Stan stood back as the car moved off. Sam noticed the boy, Stan's son, was standing by the gate. The Porsche slipped through the potholes and vanished. Sam rang the bank. The balance in his current account was beyond belief.

*

When Emily awoke she found she had only three toes remaining; the big toe on each foot and a middle toe on the right foot. She sat on the edge of her bed to fight the overwhelming panic. She whispered to the empty room, "What if I lose my fingers?"

There was a dead toe in the bed. Emily flushed it down the toilet. She enjoyed a long shower that did little to improve her mood. She made toast and binned it. She was tempted to go back to bed. When the phone rang, she ignored it. A man's voice left a message. She drank her coffee slowly.

Emily was suddenly aware of the appointment. "Shit!"

The appointment was for ten thirty.

"What will they have to say they didn't say last time? Bits keep dropping off you, my dear, but we don't know why?"

Emily regarded herself in the mirror and fretted at her hair.

"Please, God, not my fingers."

As the Town Hall clock struck ten, Emily switched on the ignition and drove to St. Hild's Infirmary. She was sitting in the reception area when her mobile rang. The receptionist gave her a stern glance. Emily returned a raspberry.

"Emily Harrison. How can I help you?"
Tom Fenwick said, "It's me!"
"Who else would it be?"
"You have an eleven o'clock viewing at Harbour Mount."
"When did this happen?"
"They walked in as I was clearing up last night. Two Mums and two young daughters. Where are you?"
"The Infirmary."
"Something wrong?"
"Mind your own business."
"You're right, I should. Maria will send someone."
"Don't you dare do that!"

Emily snapped the phone shut. A nurse entered to say, "Ms Harrison, please?" She smiled when Emily rose from her chair.
"Professor Spengler will see you now."
Emily ignored her and walked out to the car park. She threw the penalty ticket to the ground and drove away.

*

There was silence until the bank manager said, "Did I hear you correctly, Mister Ericksen?"
Sam repeated, "I want you to return the last deposit in my account to Alan Winterton."
"Forgive me, sir, but have you been drinking?"
"I don't want Mister Winterton's money."
In the silence Sam could hear the man breathing.
"Mister Winterton has no connection to this money."
"No? Who then?"
"The source is an international foundation, but I cannot confirm that."
"Who transferred the money to my account?"
"That would be the Northern Counties Bank on instructions from the foundation, but they would have no attribution."
"What you're telling me is, it's dodgy money?"

The bank manager was shocked.
"Mister Ericksen!"
"Sorry, sorry!"
"You must understand, sir, when large sums of money. This is not a particularly large sum of money. But when large sums of money are transferred, security is paramount."
"Can you return the money or not?"
"You must deal directly with Mister Winterton."
"But you've just told me, Mister Winterton has no connection to this money!" "There is no need to shout, sir!"

Sam replaced the phone. The explosion in the yard shocked him from his thoughts.

*

When Emily saw a black woman and child exit the car, she complained aloud. "Aw, piss! Just what I need! Darkies!"

Her mood wasn't improved when a blonde woman and child followed. The children were enthralled by the harbour and the beach below the park. Emily presented herself to the two women.

She said to the blonde woman, "Emily Harrison, Madison and Major!"

The black woman responded, "Keira Sullivan. This is my business partner, Hannah Ericksen."

The black woman smiled to offer a slim hand. Emily took it reluctantly.   "Welcome to Aranport!"

Their eyes were on the house.

"Listed building Grade Two. Now redesigned as seven luxury apartments. The apartment we'll visit is the finest."

The girls were already in favour, unable to stand still.

"This is where we want to live, please!" begged the blonde child.

"It's wicked, mum," the black girl pleaded. The black woman smiled at Emily and said to the child, "We haven't been inside yet, Sophie!"

As they approached the house, Emily recited, "There is a garage for each apartment. A communal garden with a professional gardener." Looking at the children, she added, "Her work must be respected, but there is a barbecue and entertainment area."

As she opened the front door, Emily wondered why she was bothering to give information. She recited further as they ascended while her mind fumed. When she ushered her clients into the apartment they fell silent. The children's chatter stopped abruptly. Emily felt triumphant. She knew the apartment would defeat them. To have these people here!

The black woman said, "I don't know what to say."

The blonde woman cried, "God, Keira! Look at the furniture!"

Emily said, "Please explore the apartment."

Then we'll look at some cardboard semis. More your style.

When the clients moved off hesitantly to explore, Emily sat down on the sofa. A young man she had never seen before sat down beside her. He silenced her by raising a finger.

"Well done, Emily! At last, you have the right people for the apartment. Your efforts will not be forgotten."

Emily protested and was silenced.

"They will buy the apartment. Don't antagonise them. Ms Sullivan is well aware you're a bigot. Congratulations! Your task is completed!"
The young man smiled and rose to walk through the wall. In the silence, Emily heard the children's happy voices. She waited twelve minutes for her clients to join her.

When the car, with rejoicing children aboard, drove away, Emily returned to the apartment. She flopped onto the sofa and pushed off her shoes to ease her aching feet. She had one hand at her ankle before she realised she had lost all her toes. Emily cried aloud in fear. The apartment was suddenly oppressive. She tipped the dead toes from her shoes onto the carpet.

Congratulations! Your task is completed!

The apartment seemed dark and alien. A terrible foreboding settled on her and she began to weep. She wept as she gathered the cold toes and flushed them away. Her shoes didn't fit and she filled the toe space with toilet tissue.

*

Stan's garage was burning savagely with a thick black column of smoke ascending. The sirens of the fire engines wailed. A bewildered Sam ran to Tony and Bruce who were watching the inferno. "What happened?"

Bruce said, "No idea."

Tony offered, "Just blew up."

"Where's Stan?"

Neither looked at him.

"He hadn't a chance, Sam."

"We couldn't get near."

"And his son?"

Bruce hesitated and Tony said, "Gavin was with his Dad."

"Has anyone phoned his wife?"

"Stan was divorced years back."

The first fire tender crashed into the yard and the crew began their fight to subdue the blaze. Within the heat of the flames, Sam heard the boy's voice say, "It's not supposed to happen, but it did."

*

Colin Bridger took Victoria Sullivan's left foot in two hands. To the nurse he said, "You dressed Missis Sullivan's arm this morning?"

"Yes, doctor. It's clean. No further suppuration. The wound is healing nicely." Colin nodded as he manipulated Victoria's foot. He saw no indication of pain in the patient's face.

"Any discomfort?"

Victoria shook her head.

"Feels fine."

Colin took hold of the right foot. He manipulated the ankle and examined each toe.

When he released the foot, he said, "I don't understand what has happened, but I won't release you until I do."

In the corridor, Doctor Bridger said to the nurse, "Again, please. Every detail." "I settled Missis Sullivan in the Day Room with her newspaper. When I came back the maid reported Missis Sullivan had soiled the bed. I took a wipe and picked up the turd. But it wasn't. It was the patient's big toe from her left foot."

*

"We're home!" the girls chorused as Isla slammed the front door.
"Take your shoes off in the hall!" Keira called, "We have enough sand, thank you!"
When they were packing up the antique items to be stored in the smaller dressing room, Keira had joked, "Am I'm packing or unpacking? We seem to have at this forever."
Hannah had ignored her, intent on one particular photograph. She offered the frame to Keira saying, "Who do you know in this lot?"
It was a Victorian family group in a heavy silver frame; grandparents, parents, young people, children. Keira studied the faces.
"God, yes! That's Oliver!"
They peered at the photograph together. The resemblance was uncanny. Oliver De'ath stood

among the young men, eggshell bald, stiff in bow tie and celluloid collar.

"I'd say it's Victoria's Jubilee, eighteen ninety-seven?"

"How's it feel to be courted by a Victorian gentleman? He'll be asking you out to walk the promenade. I'll tag along as your chaperone."

Hannah ignored the teasing. "We'll keep this one. We can surprise him some time."

Hannah enclosed the silver frame in bubble wrap and slipped it into the bureau drawer. What neither noticed was how much the tallest of the three girls in the photograph resembled Hannah.

CHAPTER TWENTY

"It's all in a day's work, sweetie."

The girls tumbled into the sitting room, bringing a scent of salt water and sunshine.
"Do you two ever go anywhere but the beach?"
Both thought the remark very funny.
"What's so funny?"
"Why would we go anywhere else?"
"What're you going to do now?"
"We're going to put out more of our things."
"Are you comfortable sharing a room?"
The girls grinned at one another.
"We like to be together."
"Like sisters."
"And we want to have rooms for Grandma and Sam."
"Besides it's a humongous room!"
The girls vanished and the intercom buzzed.

"How have we become her best, best friends?"
Keira answered the buzz.
"Emily! We're just about to have coffee. Come on up!"
Keira pressed the door release and grimaced at Hannah.
"How long do we have to go on being polite?"

*

It rained at the funeral because it always rains at funerals. Sam remembered his father saying, it was a sin to have a funeral on a sunny day; a reminder how wonderful life is. Stan and Gavin's deaths were duly recorded as misadventure. A gas cylinder had exploded. They were dead before the fire began. Sam could find no connection between the events, but the coroner seemed satisfied.

Including the priest, there were four people standing in the rain; Sam, Tony, Bruce and the parson. Everyone wished the burial service would end quickly, but the priest was a stoic. Sam, Tony and Bruce went for a drink together. Sam glimpsed how close they had been, the three musketeers of the yard, helping one another out, backing each other up. Sam's arrival must've been a surprise. Bruce said, "That wasn't right, y'know. A gas cylinder exploding?"
Tony added, "Then the fire starts?"
Sam wanted them to say more, but they didn't. They conversed without words.

Sam returned to the yard to find a crew clearing the site where Stan's garage had stood. Later he was informed that Stanley George Mason had left his earthly possessions to his good friend, Samuel Ericksen. They were composed of an empty space in the yard and eighteen hundred pounds. Sam read the letter and wept. He spent the money on a good headstone for Stanley George Mason and his son, Gavin. In the darkness of his mind he knew these deaths were wrong.

*

Sam was examining the last Chinese piece. It was a superb bowl that seemed to float in his hands. It was the finest of the entire Chinese hoard. He had kept it back for his own personal enjoyment. Now that it didn't need him any more he felt curiously saddened. Within the bowl, in exquisite detail, was a Chinese city bustling with life. The city was under siege. Around the outside of the bowl paraded an army. It was a most magnificent display; general and officers, cavalry, archers, foot soldiers, pack waggons and all the necessary tail of servants, craftsmen, whores and traders. When he had seen the original, it had taken his breath away. He had determined to match the vibrant life that radiated from the bowl.

"Bliss to work on these pots. Stan, Gavin and Glaze the price so far? That's the irony of it, isn't it, Samuel of little brain?"

He returned the bowl to its companion pieces and went to wash his hands. Someone knocked at the studio door.

Sam shouted, "Bugger off!"

The knocking persisted. Sam dried his hands and returned to the studio.

He opened the door to Holly Winterton.

"Am I not welcome?"

Holly stood on the threshold, a goddess in an Islamic scarlet dress with gold emblazoning and dancing scarf. Sam struggled to retain his anger.

"It was a set-up, wasn't it?"

"What was, Sam?"

"Saturday. Making sure, I didn't see the Exhibition dismantled for Edinburgh." "Is that what he said?"

"Yes."

"And you believe him?"

"Yes."

"He is a very cruel man. He knows how to hurt people."

When Sam stood unmoving, she continued, "I would never do that to you. You know how much Saturday meant to me."

Sam stood aside and Holly entered the studio.

"I'm sorry. I'm easily fooled."

"Then you see, he makes fools of us both?"

She stood close to Sam and took his hands.

"You are most dear to me. My very gallant knight."

"Wrong! I am your dim hairy potter you twist about your little finger."

Holly laughed and shook her head.

"You are my only true friend, Sam."

"Who you wish to kill your husband."

"Would you, please? Then we will escape together to be happy forever and ever."
"Until you meet some gorgeous young man and I'll be left in an airport lounge without a ticket."
Holly laughed.

"But seriously, Sam, please shoot Alan. For me? It is such a little thing."
"I should confess, there is a woman that,"
Holly released his hands.
"You have a girlfriend?"
"She's not my girlfriend. She's my sister's friend."
"She's not your girlfriend."
"No."
"Have you slept with her?"
"No!"
"You haven't slept with her. Have you kissed her?"
"No."
"Have you held hands?"
"No."
"Have you spoken to her?"
"Yes."
"Saying what?"
"Hello. Goodbye."

Holly regained Sam's hands.
"Have you ever taken her to the London Eye?"
"No."
"The Butterfly House?"

"No."

"Greenwich?"

"No."

"The Planetarium?"

"No."

"Our secret restaurant?"

"No."

"Good! Then I need not be jealous," Holly announced with the utmost self-assurance.

*

Perhaps, I am sometimes hard on our younger members? I accuse them of being unimaginative, but I must relate the antics of Clifford and Sonia who with a couple of pals set up a tent for Mental Health at the County Fair. It advertised free sessions of consultation with Professors Mackenzie [Clifford] and Trelawney [Sonia]. Their pals fronted the tent, distributing literature. They presented themselves as DIRECT, a philosophy that urges the stressed to admit to their stress and thereby shed the load. To begin, consultations were few, but the first successful resolution was Mrs. Tomlinson's problem. Mrs. Tomlinson simply couldn't stand her neighbours.

One can imagine how she rejoiced to return home to find her neighbours dead in a house fire that unfortunately, also rendered the Tomlinson family homeless. Business improved throughout the afternoon and problems were investigated with sympathy.

One couple had grown to hate the lady's father suffering from Dementia. They recounted his obsession with talking up the sitting room chimney to Santa Claus. In the middle of the night, they would wake to his ravings echoing from the bedroom fireplace. As the husband comically phrased it, he was often tempted to stuff the old goat up the chimney and set fire to his trousers. One can only imagine how they laughed to return home to a chimney fire that consisted mostly of the old gentleman.

There are many other rib-tickling episodes I could recite, but I shall leave that to Clifford and Sonia who are self-publishing a modest volume of hilarious happenings. I will end by suggesting you do not complain as Mrs. Thornycliffe did of her dear Quentin. His behaviour was vile, but did he deserve his wife's desire to roast the pig with an apple in his mouth? I leave you laughing.
As recorded by Amanuensis.

*

"Come clean, Holly," Sam suggested, "What did Winterton send you to find out?"
Holly pouted over her coffee cup.
"Why are you so beastly to me? I adore you, Sam. Don't you adore me?"

"Let me guess. He wants to know if the Chinese copies are ready."

"He is so eager to possess them."

"So he sent you to ask."

Holly sat back in Sam's thinking chair.

"Do you think I'd be allowed to come otherwise?"

Sam made no response.

"The Chinese pots are finished. Presently I'm ageing them. They look too new."

"He said you had buried them. That worries him. Is it true?"

Sam laughed.

"I didn't know he had feelings."

"He's worried they may be damaged."

"You mean when I'm digging them up with my spade. Like so many turnips?" Holly's eyes opened wide in horror.

"You don't, do you?" Sam extended a hand. "Come and see for yourself."

*

It took Hannah and Keira fifty-eight minutes to be rid of Emily Harrison. Keira had run out of anything to say. She could sense Hannah's impatience. The girls looked in and retreated politely. It was Hannah's inspiration to call, "You can start running the bath."

Isla looked baffled, but Sophie picked up the cue. "We need our hair done too!"

268

Hannah rose, saying, "Duty calls!"

They escorted Emily to the stair head and watched her descend. They waited to hear the front door close and returned to the apartment.
"Once I can understand," Keira pondered, "But three times?"
"She feels some sort of attachment to the apartment."
They mimicked her interrogative tone.
"Do you find it welcoming?"
"How do the children cope? It must be such a change from where they were?" "Are you happy with the furniture?"
"You don't feel you're living in a museum?"
"If only she understood how we felt after a long day to come home to this paradise."
"Why was she asking what we'd done with the miniatures and photographs? I was tempted to tell her we'd given them to charity."

The girls entered and dived into the big sofa.
"Don't worry. We didn't run the bath."
Keira asked, "Are you happy here?"
"We wouldn't live anywhere else!"
"Total magic!"
"The old furniture doesn't bother you?"
"We're the Bastables of Lewisham Road."
When Hannah hesitated, Isla said, "Nesbit? The Treasure Seekers?"
"I'm Alice," said Isla.

"I'm Dora."

"But we don't have an Oswald."

*

When Emily approached, she saw Jacqueline was in the passenger seat.

"How the hell!"

As she slid into the car she couldn't hide her anger.

"What d'y'want?"

"What else but you, sweetie?"

"Has anyone ever told you how irritating it is to be called sweetie?"

"No, sweetie. Most are glad of an occasional endearment, sweetie."

"Don't call me sweetie."

"You didn't get the photographs?"

"Everything's gone."

"It's unusual for him to make a mistake like that."

"I wouldn't think they'd bother to look at them."

"Ever the optimist, sweetie!"

*

When the girls had retired to bed, Hannah brought out the photograph from the bureau. Keira dug out the Northern Counties bumph sheet introducing the new manager. They sat together on the small sofa with the two images before them on an occasional table.

"It's uncanny," offered Hannah. "Unless they're related somehow?"

The Bank flyer bore a photograph of a smiling Oliver De'ath.

"If you match them against the backgrounds of sideboard and bank counter, they're much the same height."

Keira suggested limply, "It's a pretty ordinary face."

Hannah scrutinised the photographs with the magnifying glass.

"You might want to take a look at this."

She gave the glass to Keira who gazed into the photographs and started with surprise.

"They're both wearing the same ring!"

"That's either the weirdest coincidence or."

"Two photographs of the same man."

"A hundred and twenty years apart."

Hannah looked again. It was a heavy ring with a central red stone.

"It is the same ring."

Keira shook her head in disbelief.

Hannah said, "I don't want to think about it."

"That Harrison woman was pretty persistent. What did she say about ownership of the photographs?"

"She really annoyed me. I told her we bought the apartment and its contents. That includes the photographs and the miniatures. She wasn't happy."

Hannah fingered the two photographs of a man who shouldn't have been in both.

"What do we do about this?"

"Nothing. We'll only frighten the girls."

Hannah shut the photographs into the bureau drawer and returned to the sofa.

"If the girls were ever in danger who would you save first?"

"What an odd question to ask."

Keira pondered. "A mother's instinct is to grab her child and run."

"Then you would leave Isla?"

"No! That's the dilemma. I couldn't leave Isla. Sophie would never be Sophie again without Isla. D'y'understand what I mean?"

Hannah said, "Isla would never forgive me if I left Sophie."

"Then it's all of us."

"Or none of us."

"When I've tried to talk seriously to Sam, and believe me, he's hard to talk to seriously, I've asked about when things go wrong. About the wounded and the dead. He assured me he has never left a man behind, wounded or dead. Ask him why and he hasn't got an answer. He won't admit he loved them more than anyone in the world."

*

Jacqueline said, "Leave these people alone. Others will decide what will be done."

"I enjoy being in the apartment."

"Then we'll break in when they're out."

"We'll do no such thing!"

"Suit yourself, sweetie! I'd enjoy eating your tits on that Persian rug."

"You disgust me!"

"And excite you, sweetie!"

"Oh, by the way, don't worry about Fenwick anymore."

"I don't worry about him."

"He's gone."

"On holiday. He'll be back."

"No, he won't."

"I helped him book. I know where he is."

"Do you know where he is now?"

To humour her, Emily asked, "Where is he then?"

"He's in the boot."

The freckled imp opened the passenger door saying, "How the hell did I ever got mixed up with you, sweetie?"

A dazed Emily followed Jacqueline.

"Voila!"

A naked man and woman lay in a tangle of arms and legs. The stink repulsed Emily.

"Satisfied?"

Emily said slowly, "Don't know the girl, but that's not Tom."

"Oh, shite!"

"You've killed the wrong people, sweetie."

Suddenly the girl moved, opened her eyes and began to whimper; a high-pitched wail of sheer terror.

Emily was frozen. Jacqueline pressed both hands over nose and mouth, leaning her weight upon the face. The girl squirmed feebly, struggling to breathe. Emily awoke to the nightmare and without thought, struck Jacqueline on the head with her rolled umbrella. Jacqueline fell to the ground. The girl cried out again.

"What the hell you doing?" Jacqueline demanded.

"This is murder!"

Scrambling to her feet, Jacqueline cried, "It has to be finished, you stupid bitch!"

Before Emily could intervene, the freckled pixie stabbed the helpless girl several times in´ the breast. She bubbled blood and died. Blood flooded into the boot.

A dazed Emily said, "I don't know what to say."

Jacqueline grinned, "It's all in a day's work, sweetie."

An older couple were approaching along the pavement. Jacqueline slammed down the boot lid. They got into the car and sat silent as the older couple walked past.

"Do I need to remind you who killed Joanne?"

"She attacked me."

Emily felt strangely calm.

"What now?" "

Well, I could do with a drink, sweetie. How about you?"

Emily nodded and started the engine.

CHAPTER TWENTY-ONE

"Do you know if she's ever been bitten by a red squirrel?"

A puzzled Holly followed Sam into the store room. There was a row of black plastic bins and a stack of plastic sacks of clay. The shelves housed bottles and boxes.

"I've been led astray before, but never into a room like this. You're irresistible, Sam."

"Winterton wants to know where the pots are buried? Yes?"

"You don't have to tell me."

Sam took the lid from one of the bins. The room stank of wet earth. Holly approached cautiously.

"The bins are filled with real Irish peat. Very expensive. Three pots are buried in warm, wet peat in each bin. They're ageing rapidly."

Holly clapped her hands. "Wicked! But then you are so clever! I shall tell him you've told me you've buried them behind the studio."

"Is that wise? He won't believe you."

"You think he'll hurt me?"

Reluctantly Sam agreed.

"Yes."

"What would you do if he did?"

"I'd kill the bastard."

Holly looked at him with such longing that Sam was overwhelmed. They stood in silence, not daring to breathe.

Holly said, "We should've met a long time ago, Sam."

"But he won't hurt you?"

"He'll think of something more painful."

"Such as?"

"Killing you."

Sam tried to laugh.

"It's all too late," said Holly Winterton.

*

Sam was dozing in his thinking chair when the phone rang. It was almost midnight. He had emptied his toxic tincture. Colin Bridger said, "Sam, I'm putting Victoria Sullivan into isolation."

"Why?"

"Her hand and arm are healing well. But she has lost a toe from each foot."

Sam was suddenly awake.

"I don't understand."

"Two toes have parted company from her feet. No pain. No bleeding. No visible infection. The toe buds dry and clean. She didn't know she'd lost them."

Sam was silent and Colin asked, "You still with me, Sam?"

"I think so."

"Victoria's not in any distress. But I must isolate her until we know what we're dealing with."

"Could it be leprosy?"

"Top man in tropical diseases, Norman Hamilton, has agreed to see her tomorrow."

"Have you spoken to her daughter, Keira?"

"Victoria insists she doesn't want her troubled at the present time. She's starting a business up North?"

"Yes. Am I supposed to know?"

"You're her honey chile, Sam-uel. Will we see you tomorrow?"

*

It was dark when they left the pub. Jacqueline drove. Emily knew they were in the industrial estate off Commercial Road, but exactly where she knew not. "Where are we?"

"You don't need to know."

"Why not?"

"Because it's safer for you not to know."

"Wha'does that mean?"

Jacqueline ignored her.

Emily had only closed her eyes for a moment to find they were driving into a commercial yard. Jacqueline parked between two lorries.

"Wakey, wakey, sweetie!"

The door to the factory building was unlocked. Emily followed the freckles into a shabby waiting room.

"Just stay here, sweetie! Okay?"

Emily sat down. It was a featureless room. The pixie was gone for an eternity. Emily became bored. She tried the second door in the room. It was unlocked. She opened it a trifle and listened to a clatter of machinery. Emboldened, she opened the door and entered an abattoir. The air was chill.

There was a ceiling tramway system supporting four lines of skinned & eviscerated beasts moving slowly towards the rubber curtains of the butchery department. Emily's first thought was that she was hallucinating when she realised one line carried disembowelled human corpses. She cried out in horror as Mr. Buchanan's flabby form slipped between the rubber curtains and vanished.

"I told you to wait there!"

Jacqueline's hand pulled a mesmerised Emily away from this vision of hell. "They're going to clean the car. So we can go home and I can take advantage of your drunken state."

Emily made no protest. Out in the yard, a limousine welcomed them aboard. Emily was grateful for the whisky the mischievous pixie poured for her.

"That wasn't real, was it, Jacquie?"

"No, sweetie, that was a film set."

Emily began to weep, not knowing why. Jacqueline poured her another large whisky.

*

Emily said, "Is there anyone would like Broderick Street? The better end?" None of the women acknowledged her offer. No one had spoken a word to her since she had come into the office. No one ever spoke to her.

"One careless owner. Name of Frankenstein."

No one responded. She typed the details on a yellow sheet and walked the length of the office to put the note into Maria's in-tray. On her way back, the street door opened and Tom Fenwick entered. Emily's heart exploded and she rushed to throw herself into his arms. He struggled to control her impetus.

"Oh, Tom, you don't know how glad I am to see you!"

He released her, saying, "Believe me, I think I do!"

Tom was then swamped by the women embracing him and Emily was pushed aside. She stood back and watched their affection sweep over Tom. She noted Jacqueline hanging around his neck. She returned to her desk and pretended to check rival estate agency websites while listening to Tom's protests. The excited clamour wound down as Tom cried, "Whoa! My mother said there'd be Monday mornings like this. But I didn't believe her." The women laughed as no one had laughed in that office for a long time.

"Now, if you'll sit yourselves down, you shall have your expensive presents." Emily itched to turn about to see what Tom was presenting at each desk. The office resounded with laughter. Emily was beginning to think she wasn't to have a gift; *Don't want anything anyway*; when she felt Tom at her shoulder. Her heart sang. She turned to glimpse her colleagues admiring bright teeshirts. "Would I leave you out?"
Emily found herself grasping a teeshirt from Busch Gardens, bearing the image of a crocodile. Turning around,
she saw all the shirts bore images of animals and birds. Her shirt was the only one flaunting an angry crocodile.
Emily said, "How thoughtful!" Her anger faded when she met that irresistible smile.
"Thank you, Tom!"
"That is not all," Tom declaimed, "I have for each, an estate agent's trusty weapon. A ball-point pen!"
Silence greeted his words.
"That writes in black or red at the touch of a button!"
Cries of wonder filled the office that brought Mr. Tennyson out from his office.

"Good to see you back, Tom. Place has been like a bear garden."

"Good to be back, sir."

They shook hands and Tom presented him with a large bottle of Kentucky Bourbon.

"A little tincture in times of stress?"

"By God, but I need it with this lot!"

The women laughed. Emily felt excluded.

"And a ball-point pen."

The manager retreated with his presents. Tom's presence relaxed the atmosphere. He related his encounter with Mickey Mouse in a downtown bar in Orlando and the women listened happily to his lies. Emily was ignored. No one noticed when she left the office.

*

Sam ate another grape from the basket he had brought Victoria who said, "Did you know hospital visitors eat more grapes than the patients?"

Sam said, "I'm not very good with compliments, but you look very well." "Except that my toes are dropping off. I dread to think of losing my fingers." Sam found himself looking at the elegant hands in Victoria's lap. He found nothing consoling to say.

"I'm finding it very difficult not to say anything to Hannah and Keira when I call."

"Would it help?"

"I suppose not."

"They have a business to grow. They must put their minds to that."

"What has Doctor Bridger said?"

Victoria smiled, "We must take more tests."

*

Colin Bridger admitted, "It's the most baffling case I've ever faced. I'd like to say it isn't infectious, but I can't. Her toes are dying and dropping off an otherwise healthy body. We need to know why."

"She's worried about her fingers."

"Her hands are fine. Circulation good. Joints normal. Nail growth normal. Do you know if she's ever been bitten by a red squirrel?"

Sam ignored the question to say, "I've come into a lot of money I don't want. I'm leaving you a cheque for fifty thousand pounds."

*

Sam sat in his thinking chair for a long time before he went to the telephone. He rang the bank.

"I'm afraid Mister Cuthbert is in a meeting."

"Tell him, Mister Samuel Ericksen is closing his account."

Sam ended the call and returned to his thinking chair. He had hardly taken two sips before the phone rang. Sam didn't hurry to the phone.

"Wardley Lunatic Asylum. Governor speaking."

Mr. Cuthbert said, "You have my attention, Mister Ericksen."

"Thank you for returning my call so promptly. I have issued a cheque to the Imperial Cadogan Hospital. Please honour it. Then close the account and send the balance to the Great Ormond Street Hospital."

The silence was loud. Sam could hear the man breathing.

"Is there anything you don't understand?"

"I would advise you not to disburse the balance and close the account."

"Why not?"

"It is not rational behaviour. I would advise you to take time to consider the matter."

"You've given me to understand the money is mine. Is that correct?"

The bank manager was silent.

"Is that correct?"

"If you persist in this foolishness, you will offend Mister Winterton. That is a most unwise thing to do."

"Mister Winterton has offended me. A most unwise thing to do. He has attempted to buy me and I will not be bought. Do you understand my instructions?"

"Yes."

Sam closed the call.

The Treasure Seekers tapped their way around the walls of their bedroom in vain. Isla said, "In the movies they find the secret panel in five minutes."
Sophie stopped tapping.
"Maybe, we're not doing this right?"
Isla blew away straying hair to say, "We tap and listen for it sounding hollow. What's not right about that?"
"In the films, they're tapping and listening and they don't notice a panel has swung open behind them."
They gazed hopefully about the room. Every wall was intact.
Sophie said, "If a teacher asked for an example of wishful thinking, that would be it."
The intercom beeped. Isla hit the button.
"Her ladyship is not to be disturbed."
A familiar voice called, "Tell her ladyship, dinner's ready!"

In the dining room, Hannah heard a scurry of feet and the slamming of the bedroom door.
"Do they always have to slam the door?"

In the silence of the bedroom, a sound no louder than a mouse signalled the opening of a large panel at floor level next to Sophie's bed. The panel swung open smoothly, although it had not been triggered in more than a century.

*

It was seventeen minutes past two when they came. Sam heard them climbing over the gate. He slipped out of the darkened studio and locked the door. He waited a moment for the night sight glasses to adjust. He recognised two of the men from the night they had attempted to abduct the girl, Kim. The leader was a stranger. He was a different fish. He wore a smart overcoat and cap. One of the thugs carried a heavy jerrican. The supervisor carried nothing. The cigarette in the shorter man's mouth flared, momentarily blinding Sam. The leader cursed and plucked the cigarette from his mouth. He ground it into the gravel.

"I forget sometimes how stupid you are."

Suddenly, Sam smelt and heard familiar scents and sounds. Gobber and Blakey were on the roof, covering the compound. Sam, Taff and Frog were crouched behind the low wall. Blakey clicked and Sam saw the three men enter the compound. The tall man carried nothing. The menials carried jerricans. They were coming to exact justice on an Afghan interpreter by burning alive his grandparents, wife, daughter, son and baby daughter. Gobber killed the supervisor. His two assistants stood petrified long enough for Taff and Frog to silence them. Sam picked off the jerricans with a flare and a bonfire roared as the bodies burned. No one came out of the houses. In the stillness of the night, broken only by the crackle of the bonfire, Blakey, Sam, Gobber and the twins vanished as if they had never been there.

The supervisor gestured and the thugs moved forward with the jerrican. Sam heard the cocking of the pistol. When he burst from the burning studio, Sam was to be shot and his body returned to the flames. It was neatly contrived. Sam struck the supervisor from behind with the baseball bat and he fell without a sound. When he approached the thugs, they were having trouble opening the jerrican.

"Can I give you a hand with that, mate?"

They stared up into the darkness with open mouths. Sam struck one as he crouched and the other as he rose. Using his sack trolley, Sam moved his would-be murderers out of the yard half a mile to prop them up against the railway wall. He drenched all three in petrol, cleaned the jerrican handle and dropped it over the wall. The short man began to stir.

"Have a fag. You'll feel better," Sam advised.

Sam retired to the yard, locked the gate, parked the trolley and returned to the studio. He broke up and burned the baseball bat. When he was satisfied with the ashes, he retired to bed with his toxic tincture and slept soundly.

When Sam quit the scene, the rear door of a parked BMW opened and a man stepped out. He approached the three figures against the wall. The short man said something, but the man from the BMW ignored his pleading. From his fingers dropped a spark and the petroleum vapour ignited. All three figures were enveloped in flames. All three writhed in agony. The short man struggled to stand and failed. The man from the BMW watched the men die and then returned to the car.

CHAPTER TWENTY-TWO

"I've been doing the Devil's work. But I didn't know I was."

A bored Victoria Sullivan was staring at page one hundred and seventy of a paperback thriller when a nurse appeared in the open doorway to say, "A gentleman to see you, Victoria?"
"Mister Ericksen?"
"No. I haven't seen him before."
"A mystery man? Even better! How do I look?"
"Most presentable."
The nurse smiled and vanished.

As Victoria scanned her face in a hand mirror, a young man appeared in the doorway, wearing a surgical mask over nose & mouth. His hands were enclosed in blue plastic gloves.
"Do I know you?" Victoria asked.
The visitor ripped off gloves and mask and dropped them into her waste bin. "No. My name is Oliver. I've come to visit you."
He was a pleasant young man with a generous smile. His skin changed colour from white, through shades to black. An illusion of light and shadow. A pleasant young black man stood before her.

"You shouldn't have taken off the mask and gloves. I'm in isolation. Please put them back on."

Oliver laughed.

"Simple superstition! I know what's wrong with you."

"Oh, yes?"

The young man didn't look dangerous. Her panic button was close at hand. "What is wrong with me?"

The young man smiled. "You're bored. Terminally bored. So I've come to see you."

"Do you do this a lot? Unboring patients?"

Her visitor looked concerned.

"Oh, no! I'm your Guardian Angel Oliver."

Victoria sat silent in the bed. The situation was perfectly normal. Bored patient is visited in hospital by her guardian angel.

"Except I don't believe in guardian angels."

"But you do believe in the Devil?"

"Oh, yes, I've met him in different guises."

"And yet you will not believe in angels?"

Victoria said, "I'm going to press this button and ask that you be excluded from the hospital."

"Please, give me one moment. What can I do to convince you otherwise?"

Victoria shot up against the bed head as he suddenly sprouted enormous black wings that darkened the small room.

"Oh, my God!"
The wings vanished as quickly as they appeared. Victoria was paralysed. Oliver shook his head.
"No! Any conjuror could do that!"
Before Victoria could move, the young man threw aside the single sheet and seized her feet with their missing toes.

"Oh, Victoria! How awful! Such charming feet! The feet of a ballerina."
Strong hands massaged her feet. To her amazement, she found herself saying, "When I was a child I attended ballet lessons. Just to please my Mom. In the audience, watching her duckling failing to be a swan. Her face, so full of pride. I was the first to go to University. My mother's grandmother worked the cotton fields. My mother in a factory for Whitey. I was the realisation of all her hopes. All the way from the cotton fields to John Hopkins. But still they didn't want me."

Victoria became aware Oliver had released her feet.
He said, "Ballet dancer's feet."
Victoria reached for her foot and counted. Her feet were complete. She looked up at Oliver, in gratitude.
"Thank you! I don't know what else to say. Thank you."

"Then you acknowledge Our Lord as your Master? When He calls upon you, will you obey?"

The phrasing sounded old-fashioned to Victoria, but she eagerly agreed.

Then she woke up and lived moments of utter despair, until she looked to her feet and found five toes on each foot.

*

Emily awoke in Tom's car when he unlocked the driver's door.

"What the Henry Higgins, are you doing here?"

He didn't wait for an answer, but continued, "How did you get in?"

Emily said, "What time is it?"

"I'm going to lunch."

"I must've fallen asleep. I thought you were never coming."

Tom settled into the driving seat.

"Let's start again. What're you doing here?"

"Waiting for you."

"How'd'y'get in?"

"I wanted to talk to you."

"Do I want to talk to you?"

"Please?"

Tom felt his anger subsiding.

"You are the craziest woman I've ever met."

"You need to get away from Aranport now!"

"Why?"

"They're going to kill you, Tom."

"What're you on, Emily?"

"You would be dead now, if you hadn't been on holiday."

"Who wants to kill me?"

"You loaned your flat to a friend while you were away, yes?"

"I told Ralph he could use the flat."

"They found a man and woman there. They killed them both, thinking it was you."

"How do you know this?"

"I saw the bodies."

Tom dialled his home number and switched it to loudspeaker. A young woman's voice chirped. "Hi, everyone! Maybe you don't know me?"

A young man's voice interrupted to say, "That's Lesley!"

There was laughter and the young woman's voice piped, "That's Ralph."

Both voices sounded tipsy.

"We've decided to quit the rat race," Ralph's voice announced.

"He means, we're running away. No more nine to five!"

"We may be in Thailand!"

"Vietnam?"

"The Philippines?"

"Definitely, not Spain! Too many gangsters!"

The young man's voice took on a serious tone.

"Thanks a heap for the flat, Tom. None of this would've happened otherwise. I owe you one!"
The message ended in laughter.
Tom said, "Does that sound dead to you?"

*

As the nurse gathered the tea tray, Victoria asked, "We've become friends, haven't we, Helen?"
"I hope so."
"Then I'll tell you a secret. I'll burst if I don't tell someone. But you mustn't tell Doctor Bridger."
"If it's a secret, I can't tell doctor," the nurse lied.
She sat on the bedside chair, holding the tray.

"The Angel Oliver came to see me."
Behind the clinical mask, Helen fought to control her voice.
"How nice!"
"He's my guardian angel. We all have one. Have you ever met yours?"
"Not yet. What does Oliver look like?"
"He's black. Which I suppose, you might expect. He gave me a shock when he opened his wings. Filled the room."
"Was there any particular reason why he came? Just visiting?"
"Prepare yourself for a surprise!"
Helen hesitated and said, "Ready as I'll ever be."
"Take a look for yourself."

Victoria pulled aside the sheet to display her feet. "You see?"

Helen inspected the mutilated feet, lacking seven toes.

"You see? The Angel Oliver has given me back my toes. Isn't that wonderful?" Helen's training asserted itself.

"Truly wonderful!"

"A miracle!"

"As you say, a miracle. And the angel did this?"

Victoria's face was flushed with happiness.

"In return I have to prepare myself to undertake a task for Our Lord."

Helen asked, "Did he say what you have to do?"

"I'm sure Oliver will tell me when I need to know."

Helen covered Victoria's legs. "If you don't mind, Vicky, I'll take your necessaries as I'm here."

*

The flat was spotless. Emily said, "This doesn't tally with a couple making whoopee."

"How not?"

"It's too clean."

"The cleaner might've been in since they left."

In Emily's head echoed the malicious pixie's words. *Nobody does perfect better than the Old Firm.*

"Who wants to kill me, Emily?"

"If I tell you the truth, will you try to believe me?"

Tom Fenwick sat on the couch. Emily joined him.

"They'll kill me too."

"Why would they do that?"

"I've done what they asked me to do."

"Which was?"

"Sell Harbour Mount to the right people."

"Who's that?"

"Two women. Partners in an investment business in Newcastle. Two kids," and as an afterthought, "I've made copies of the keys of Harbour Mount."

"What has that to do with somebody threatening me?"

"That was Jacqueline."

"Freckles and five foot nothing sweetie?"

Emily suddenly found herself near to tears.

"You don't understand."

"I'm trying to."

"They will kill us both."

"Who will?"

"The Old Firm."

"What the hell is that?"

"They cleaned up when I killed Joanne."

Tom Fenwick was stunned to silence.

"She attacked me."

Tom said slowly, "What, in God's name, are you mixed up with?"

"The Devil."

"Oh, sure, the Devil!"

"I've been doing the Devil's work. But I didn't know I was."

Emily began to weep.

"We must have a word with Sweetie."

*

Colin Bridger completed his notes and looked to the nurse.

"Everything you've told me, Helen, is as Missis Sullivan said? She was visited by her guardian angel, Oliver. A black angel. With black wings. He restored her toes and Jesus wants her to do something in return."

"She didn't actually say Jesus. She said, Our Lord. Though I suppose, there's no difference."

"Has she been visited by any young black man?"

"No."

"May I see your log?"

Helen waited while he perused the pages. Satisfied, he returned the book. "While you were with her, you decided to take pulse, temperature and blood pressure?"

"Yes."

The nurse handed Colin Bridger the chart.

"Good thinking! No. Nothing out of order. All fine. Anything else?"

Helen hesitated to speak.

"Go on! Tell me whatever!"

"Missis Sullivan is a highly educated woman. Very interesting to talk to. She just didn't sound quite herself. Childish might be the word. It's only because I work with her every day. Otherwise I wouldn't notice. Just not quite her style." The doctor added her thoughts to his notes.

"I presume there is no change to the condition of her feet?"

"No. Only three toes remaining."

"Then we must not disabuse the patient that there has been no miracle. We must play along and see what transpires."

*

Isla was scrubbing her teeth when Sophie returned to the bathroom.

"You won't believe this."

Through toothpaste and brush, Isla offered, "If you say so."

Sophie sat down on the toilet seat.

"There's a secret door opened in the wall of our bedroom."

"Really?"

"Beside my bed."

Isla rinsed her mouth and returned the toothbrush.

"You do know, if you are winding me up, I will kill you?"

The girls stared at the open door and the darkness within, trying to hide their excitement. Sophie said, in awe, "We're real Treasure Hunters now, Isla."
"I wonder where it goes?"
"It's not a secret passage. It's a cupboard. I tried it."
"Without waiting for me?"

Sophie took the torch from her bed and knelt down. Isla joined her. Sophie directed the beam into the darkness. It was a large cupboard.
Sophie reported, "It may not be a secret passage, but I spy treasure!"
The torch beam illuminated a number of dusty cardboard boxes. They read growing excitement in one another's eyes.
"I wonder what's in the boxes?"
"Maybe jewels?"
"In cardboard boxes?"
"Big jewels. Crowns and sceptres and tiaras."
"Or mouldy old clothes?"
"Worth a fortune on the Antiques Roadshow."

Sophie moved to enter, but Isla countered, "My turn."

Isla crawled into the cupboard and began to pass out the boxes to Sophie who said, "If we ever need to hide, this is our secret hidey-hole."

*

Sam was on the telephone with Colin Bridger when the visitors walked in, unannounced.

"Her Majesty's Constabulary have just walked in, Colin. If they don't arrest me, I'll be with you as soon as I can."

Sam ended the call.

"What a pleasant surprise, sergeant! Haven't you anything better to do?"

His visitors were a burly man in a tired suit accompanied by a police constable. "Good morning, Mister Ericksen!"

"What can I do for you, sergeant?"

"We have three incinerated bodies five minutes' walk from here."

"And you assume I set fire to them?"

"I did not say that."

"I assure you, I have set fire to no one."

The constable brought out his notebook and began scribbling.

Sam advised, "Ericksen is spelt s e n."

"We've identified one man as being involved in your last fracas."

"These are violent men. Perhaps they had a fracas with someone of their own ilk. I repeat, I have set fire to no one."

"One corpse has been identified as a respected local solicitor. His car was parked too near your gate for my liking."

"A solicitor? In dishonest company? Most unlikely."

"Where were you on the night of the sixteenth-seventeenth, Mister Ericksen?" Sam pondered for a moment.

"In the morning, I visited a wholesaler. In the afternoon, I had a chat with my bank manager. Always up for a laugh is Mister Cuthbert. Then I worked until sometime about six. Had my supper. Watched telly and went to bed. Sorry it's not more exciting."

"And you never left this hut?"

"The studio? Sadly, my social diary was empty."

The sergeant glared at Sam.

"Always the smart remark, Mister Ericksen. s e n."

Sam hesitated before he responded. "I know you don't like me, sergeant. Why, I know not. When I rescued that poor girl from that slimy trio, who have since murdered her, I told you exactly what I did. So I will say yet again, I have set fire to no one."

The detective sergeant walked out without another word. The constable lingered to gesture at the clay figure on the bench.

"Been there, done that. Bewitched, buggered and bewildered!"

Sam laughed. "I know the feeling."

When the constable departed, Sam sat on his stool to examine the work. The figure was two feet tall. It depicted a young soldier sitting on a rock, Bergen on his back, his weapon across his knees. He looked totally exhausted, his helmet at his side. But the viewer knew, at the word, he would stand and fight. "Because that's what we do," Sam said aloud.

He locked the studio and found his bicycle. Sam wiped the night's rain from the saddle and set out for the Cadogan, pedalling steadily.

CHAPTER TWENTY-THREE

"Don't poke your snout where you're not wanted."

The boxes were wrapped in brown paper, bound with string and sealed with red sealing wax. Sophie said, "These were put away, never to be opened again." They chose a big heavy box to open. It was a German toy steam engine, complete with carriages, a station, a bridge, sigmals and a multitude of railway lines. There were a number of male and female figures with moustaches or bonnets.
"It's a real steam engine. Their father must've played with them."

They chose the next biggest box, hoping for something more interesting. The box contained everything necessary to play cricket. Everything was boy-size; bats, gloves & pads, stumps & bails, score pads, balls, all unused.
Sophie commented. "There must've been boys living here."

The next boxes contained dolls that rendered them speechless. They were unmarked, wrapped in tissue paper as if they had never been opened. The ladies were dressed in early Victorian style; blue eyes in angelic faces blinking in the light: as pristine as the day they were bought. The outside of the doll boxes was printed in German. There were two dolls in each box.

"A soldier and his lady!" cried Isla amazed.
"A doctor and a nurse!"
"A sailor and his girl!"
"A gentleman and his lady!"
"A nursemaid and a child!"

Sophie and Isla looked to one another.
"These were never played with."
"D'y'think they were ever allowed to take them from the boxes?"
"Perhaps to set them out on a wet Sunday afternoon?"
The last box of the series contained a toy china tea set.

The largest box contained wooden pieces to build a fort big enough for two children. The instruction sheets were in German. The fort had never been built. There were eight boxes of lead soldiers in glorious uniforms, paint fresh: four boxes of cavalry with prancing horses and threatening lances. The soldiers were German. They were still restrained in their boxes by elastic threads.
"Something happened to these children."

Two large boxes contained wood & canvas perambulators waiting still to be constructed. There were twin baby dolls waiting for their perambulators. The necessaries for the babies were still in packets and boxes.

"There were two girls," Isla stated, "Two baby dolls, two girls."

"Too much stuff for one boy."

"Four children lived here nearly two hundred years ago."

"I wonder what happened to them?"

The last box contained nineteenth century board games, complete with dice and pieces. Ludo, Snakes & Ladders, Beat the Drum, Fox & Hounds, The Chimney Sweeps Derby and card games about birds and flowers. The last out of the box was a Ouija board.

*

Colin Bridger waited until his secretary served coffee and retired before talking to Sam.

"Missis Sullivan's situation has changed."

"I thought her hand and arm were healing well?"

"That's not the problem. Nor is the loss of her toes. Distressing though that may be."

Colin hesitated.

Sam said, "Colin, whatever it is, tell me."

"Missis Sullivan told her nurse she had been visited by her guardian angel. The Angel Oliver."

"Is that all?"

Sam was much relieved.

"As a reward for accepting to undertake some task for Our Lord, the angel replaced her missing toes."

"You're not serious?"

"Missis Sullivan believes it to be true."

"Has she got her toes back?"

"No. But we are presently conspiring with the Angel Oliver."

"Why?"

"Would it help to disillusion her?"

"I suppose not."

"With her daughter's consent, Missis Sullivan could be sanctioned and spend six weeks under observation in a psychiatric ward."

Sam interrupted to cry, "God, no!"

"Or she stays here. I'll be interested to hear what our psychiatrist says about a fellow psychiatrist."

Gloved and masked, Sam followed Colin into Victoria's sanctuary. She flung herself into his arms, her face alight with happiness.

"You won't believe what has happened!"

Without waiting for his response, she cried, "I've been visited by my guardian angel, the Angel Oliver! And what do you think?"

She freed herself from Sam's embrace and pirouetted on her mutilated feet. "Oliver has restored my toes! Isn't that a miracle?"

*

Tom squeezed out of the rain into Emily's Megane.

"It's not on the books. Which is odd. But her pad says 3, Wellington Terrace. Let's give it a go."

Emily started the engine and manoeuvred her way cautiously off a crowded Terrace car park. She was determined to give Tom no cause to criticise her driving.

She was startled when Tom said, "When you killed Joanne, if you did, what did you use to kill her?"

"She attacked me."

"But you killed her with what?"

"I took the knife from her."

"Joanne is, was, no wimp. I wouldn't enjoy tackling her with a knife in her hand."

"What's all this, is, was, if?"

Tom hesitated to say, "I'm having trouble believing you killed Joanne."

"I didn't take pictures."

"I don't want to accuse Jacqueline, pain in the arse though she is, with planning to murder me if you had a bad trip with some 'recreational' shit. Do you use drugs?"

"No, I don't!"

"You've already had me believing you were dead. Remember?"

Emily parked the car badly and turned off the engine.

"Jacqueline took me to an abattoir. Among the cattle hanging from the hooks was Mister Buchanan. Joanne will have passed through that hell hole. Ralph and his girl will be hanging there now. I have done what they wanted me to do. I'm redundant. I'll end up hanging there. And so will you. Unless you wake up. The Devil is here in Aran."

Tom was silent, struggling to untangle his confusion. When Emily was about to speak, Tom stated, "There is no Devil. There's only us. No God. No Devil. Just us, screwing up our lives."

"I was stabbed twice in the chest. Neither wound bled. They healed without a scar."

"That's remarkable, but there is no Devil."

The silence seemed to last forever.

Emily said, "Two people died. Mistaken for you. I don't think you should confront Jacqueline. You don't know what they're like. But you won't listen." "You think you're telling me the truth."

"I am telling you the truth."

"Then we're going to talk to Sweetie. Nobody is going to threaten you. Anybody has to come through me."

"Would you like to drive?"

*

Sam pushed up the magnifying lenses when somebody knocked on the door. "It's not locked."

Tony and Bruce walked in.

"What've I done to deserve the honour of your company?"

They didn't grin, so Sam said, "Don't break anything and I'll see what's in the coffee machine."

When Sam returned, the pair were studying the Chinese vases, bowls and teapots set out where the natural light illuminated their beauty.

"Two minutes."

Bruce asked, "Did you make these, Sam?"

"I decorated the blanks."

"God, man, they're bloody wonderful!"

"Thank you!"

"But the squaddie's your work? Right?"

"Right," said Sam, "A lad I knew. Name of Ginger."

"He'd love that."

Tony said, "The detail! You must have the patience of a saint. But I really love the way he sorta grows out of the rock. Colour of the clay helps, but somehow, Sam, you feel you know him. There's a lad two doors from us."

"They're always the lad two doors from us. We never notice them 'til they're gone."

Sam retired and returned with three coffees.
"This is better than you deadheads deserve. Straight out of the arse of some rodent or other."
"You're kidding?"
"I hope so."
They sipped coffee until Sam said, "Okay! Tell me the bad news."
"Not bad news. No way." Tony said, "We've both had offers."
"For the businesses?"
"Then you hasn't?"
Sam shook his head. Tony and Bruce exchanged glances.
Bruce said, "Offers hard to refuse."
Tony said, "They're offering four times what the business is worth."
"Who's they?"
"A Spanish firm. Fomento something."
"The solicitor has checked them out."
Silence fell.

Tony tried, "We was hoping you'd had an offer."
"This shed's worth nothing."
"But the ground it stands on has a value."
"So what did the solicitor say?"
Bruce said, "Don't hesitate. Take the money and run."
"Then that's what you must do."

They both protested, but Sam brushed it aside.
"You both have families. This is your big chance.
Your life-changing chance. The solicitor's right.
Grab it and run!"

Tony said, "No hard feelings, Sam?"
Sam laughed.
"Why would there be any? Congratulations,
guys!"
"What about you?"
"They'll have to make some offer."
Unless they try again to burn the studio down.
At that, they parted in friendship, Tony and
Bruce much relieved. Sam sat in his thinking
chair, hugging his toxic tincture.

*

Sam worked with Bruce and Tony to load the
lorries that carried away the equipment from both
businesses. Tony was the last to leave.
"No offer?"
"No."
"You should think of getting out, Sam."
"I like it here."
Tony looked around the empty yard.
"They'll be coming in to clear the site."
"And I won't have no more malarkey from you
monkeys."
Tony shifted uncomfortably.
"None of this seems right, y'know."
"Have they paid you?"

"On the dot. No problems. Cash in the bank."
"Then that's fine."
Tony shuffled about and gave Sam a piece of paper.

"Phone numbers. Me and Bruce. You ever need a hand."
When Sam found an answer, Tony was waving from his car. Sam followed the car out and locked the gate. He listened to his footsteps as he returned to the studio. The yard was silent.

*

Keira, Hannah and the girls stood on the steps of the Historical Museum & Literary Institute of South Aranport to be photographed and thanked yet again for their most generous donation of the Victorian toys. It was most embarrassing. Passers-by stopped to watch, but aware of the presence of the cameras, no one picked their nose. They had been thanked profusely inside what was once been The Mechanics Institute.

The young man had been somewhat dismissive when they had informed him at the desk that they wished to make a donation of Victorian toys. It was only when the removals men carried in the boxes that the young man's mouth fell open and he ran off to find Mrs. Doughtie who appeared irritated at being dragged away from her coffee and Bourbon biscuit. It was a transformation wonderful to behold, to see Mrs. Doubting become Mrs. Flabbergasted.

It had been agreed that a side gallery would be set up to display the donations with due acknowledgement to the donors. Mrs. Doughtie promised to research the background of the children of Harbour Mount for Isla and Sophie. The Aranport Chronicle ran a double-page spread of the gallery displaying the toys, the games, the fort and the perambulators now constructed. No one knew how to play Beat the Drum.

Isla and Sophie endured an embarrassing visit to the Victorian Toy Gallery with their class in company with local BBC cameras. Even more embarrassing, the unanimous opinion of their classmates was, they were right muzzas to give the toys away. Keira and Hannah had agreed the girls could keep the Ouija board under strict admonition that it was not to be played with. The Ouija board and planchett in the box were displayed on a small table in the girls' room.

*

On Monday morning, Sam opened the gate to a demolition firm. When they started to clear what had been Tip Top Tyres, Sam brought a stool out to watch. Demolition gangs may sometimes be too enthusiastic in their work. It took two weeks to clear the yard, leaving Sam's bizarrely painted studio standing alone. Two of the gang were ex-soldiers. The gang and Sam became good friends. They called the studio, Camp Bastard. They were punctual for coffee and respectful of his work. From the contractor, Sam learned much about who commissioned the clearance and much about the international consortium who were going to create an expensive Paradise on the yard. When they were gone Sam was alone. He realised he had never been alone before.

*

Jacqueline's Smart car stood outside 3, Wellington Terrace. A couple closed the gate to cross the road to their car. The woman was chattering happily. Tom said, "Another scalp on Freckles' belt!" They waited another five minutes, but Jacqueline didn't appear.
"Raiding the drinks cabinet?" Emily suggested.
Tom pressed the bell twice.
"Once is tentative, twice is serious."

Jacqueline opened the door, smiling and tried to close it again. Tom forced the door open, saying, "We need to talk to you, sweetie."
Jacqueline wasn't strong enough to keep the door and surrendered. Tom and Emily pushed their way into the sitting room. They stood frozen. Behind them, the freckled pixie laughed, "You shouldn't stick your snout where you're not wanted."

A middle-aged man and woman were sitting on the sofa. On the lap of each, a large cobra, hood extended, was swaying, jaws open to display needle fangs. The man and woman were rigid with fear.

Tom began, "What in the name of God!"

Emily, with a sudden insight, interrupted to say, "This is how she sells houses." "Smart cookie," complimented Jacqueline, "You like a certain house, I persuade the owners to sell. So simple, sweetie!"

Tom started forward angrily. The cobra slid from the man's lap and moved towards Tom who retreated.

"A sensible move, sweetie. You don't know whether the snake is real or an illusion."

The snake returned to the man's lap. The man emitted a low whimper. Emily noted with distaste he had wetted himself. His wife smiled at Tom.

"I'm afraid you're just too late, young man. We've sold the house to a very nice couple."

"Don't bother to answer," Jacqueline advised.

Tom sat down, but looked surprised.

"See? I made you sit down. If I wished, we could watch you cut your own throat."

"God's sake, Jacquie! Please, please, don't!"

"Similarly, Mister Fenwick, I can take your sweet Emily to bed and do whatever I like with her."

Tom didn't answer because he was staring at the cobra on his knees. Emily found she could not move. Jacqueline sighed and the cobra vanished.
"It's no fun if you're frizz."
Tom said, shakily, "I'm sorry, Emily."
"What is it you're sorry for, sweetie?"
"I didn't believe her."
"And what is it, you didn't believe?"
"I didn't believe in the Devil."

The freckled pixie laughed. "Now you do, you will learn to fear Him, sweetie." Jacqueline stroked Tom's cheek.
"You do know she's dead, don't you, sweetie? Best rut between her legs before she rots."
The pixie looked around the room.
"Such a pleasant house. Let this be a lesson to you both. Don't poke your snout where you're not wanted."
Flame dripped from a finger.
"Tis pity, but needs must when the Devil drives."
The carpet burst into flame and began to eat the furniture.
"Time to go!"
Jacqueline vanished. Tom and Emily fled. In a backward glance, Tom saw the couple on the

sofa unmoving as the flames roared to consume them.

CHAPTER TWENTY-FOUR

"Because where there is darkness will also be light."

Hannah and Keira arose in alarm from the breakfast table when Isla and Sophie arrived in tears.
"What on earth is the matter?"
"Are you hurt?"
"No."
The girls subsided into chairs as their mothers tried to calm them.
"Whatever it is, it can't be that bad!"
"We have a letter from Missis Doughtie."
"The Museum lady?"
"It's awful, Mum, truly awful!"
"What is?"
"Cholera."
"They all died of cholera."
"You mean the children who owned the toys?"
"And the maids and the housekeeper."
"The whole family except the Father."
Hannah said, "Let me see."

She took the letter from Isla's hand and began to read.
Keira said, "Read it out."
"She apologises for having such sad news."

She began to quote. "Cholera is spread mostly by unsafe water and unsafe food containing the bacteria."

Before the girls could phrase the question, Keira offered, "The Victorians were unaware of bacteria until the eighteen eighties."

"At that time cholera was considered a poor people's disease. Upper and middle classes were rarely afflicted. This makes the tragedy at Harbour Mount most unusual."

Hannah paused to say, "This was the finest, the richest house in Aranport."

She continued, "The children were taken ill first. Oswald."

Isla cried, "They had an Oswald!"

"The children were taken ill first. Oswald, Reginald, Matilda and Mabel. Then their Mother and the Governess. They all died within weeks despite the doctor's best efforts."

Sophie said, "They never played with their Christmas presents."

Isla began to weep afresh and Hannah comforted her daughter. Keira took the letter and continued. "Following upon the slaughter of the Crimean War, Sir Reginald Tull had decided to turn his back on his father's manufacture of armaments. He said, I quote; *it is time to turn our swords to ploughshares.* It was not the most popular view.

Within the year, the poor man had taken his own life."

There was silence in the dining room.
"He put all their toys away."
"He must've used the Ouija board to try to reach his wife and children."

*

Sam heard the Mercedes drive into the yard and stop. A second vehicle followed. He didn't raise his head from the figure of the soldier. The studio door opened. Alan Winterton said, "You're not short of parking now."
"The Chinese pieces are ready to go."
He heard Winterton moving along by the shelf.
"You break it, you've lost it. I'm not doing it again."

Holly Winterton said, "They're wonderful, Sam."

Sam checked the scalpel and saved the figure. Holly was smiling at him as Winterton was examining every item. Sam's heart stopped beating. She wore the simplest tunic and trousers, but she looked radiant. Sam knew he had never seen anyone more beautiful and more dangerous. The rearward light illuminated the halo of her hair. His heart started beating again.

"Aren't you speaking to me?"

The voice of a sad child.

"You surprised me."

"A nice surprise?"

"You know so."

Winterton said, "When you star-crossed lovers have finished billing and cooing, I have to tell you, Sam, these pieces are extraordinary. Everything about them is right. You do not know how good they are."

He was holding the bowl that displayed the besieged city and the besieging army. He turned it over and examined the base.

"I see you've displayed your customary modesty. No Samuel Ericksen fecit. But I have no intention of passing them off as the originals."

"How could I doubt your integrity?"

Winterton stood assessing the potter, fingering the bowl.

"I wish we could be friends, old chum. Perhaps it's not too late?"

He moved to the door and called to two men by a white van.

"Perhaps we could have coffee while the chaps wrap the pots?"

Holly moved, but Sam forestalled her.

"I've learnt to use the machine."

Sam and Holly sat to drink coffee while Winterton ignored his mug to watch the men as they wrapped the pieces and added them to boxes of bubble wrap.

"Are these coffee beans really excreted by some tropical rat?"

Holly laughed, saying, "I hope so. They certainly cost enough. Do you miss Stan and the boys?"

Sam decided not to lie.

"Yes, I do. They were more than three guys struggling to make a living."

"How were they more than?"

"They were honest. And that's rare."

"Yet they sold out?"

"What else could they do? Wait to be burnt out?"

Holly's face was troubled, but the shadow passed.

"Alan has his Chinese pieces. You promised me a portrait."

"I keep my promises."

Holly glowed with excitement.

"Where is it? May I see it? Can I take it home?"

"Let your husband see his pots safely aboard."

They sat in silence as Winterton watched the men seal the boxes. He held the door open for them and followed out to the van.

In the silence, Holly asked, "Do you mean I'm not honest?"

"No. The part you play is written by the author. You're not responsible for his dishonesty."

"Why did you give his money away?"

"Oh, it was his money, was it? The bank manager was so cagey."

"Why did you? You're not a rich man."

She gestured around the studio.

"If he had offered an honest price, I would've accepted it."

Holly persisted, "Think what you could do with the money!"

"Let me think. Oh, yes! I could buy drugs, alcohol, women, friends. But you might ask why your husband would bother with me."

"You want me to ask?"

They heard the van engine start.

Holly asked, "Do you love me?"

"Why do you ask?"

"No one else loves me."

Winterton returned to the studio. Sam wished he had answered Holly.

"You've been talking about me, haven't you? Go on! Admit it. I'm a popular chap and often talked about."

"Did you send those creatures to burn me in my bed?"

Winterton laughed.

"What an outrageous idea!"

Holly said, "You didn't, did you, Alan?"

Instinctively she rose to stand with Sam.

"May I ask? Have you finished my wife's portrait?"

From the bedroom window the girls watched the storm batter the beach. Clouds fled from the moon. Branches of the park trees were dancing wildly. Yet the lighthouses, north & south, green & red, probed the dark rain without flinching.

Sophie said, "What must've it been like a hundred, two hundred years ago, to be on a sailing ship on a night like this?"

"D'y'see that red light blinking? Across the harbour? Below the cliff?"

"Just about."

"There's a reef there. Hundreds of sailing ships ended up on that reef. It's called Hell's Door. They just call it the Door in Aran. They don't say Aranport. They just say Aran."

"Who told you all this?"

"Phoebe. She knows everything."

After the agency disaster, Oliver De'ath had found an admirable housekeeper, Mrs. Phoebe McCallaghan who insisted she be called Phoebe. She kept everything in order, would tackle any task, never became flustered and cooked meals so tasty every plate was cleared. Then the domestic angel went home quietly, leaving the evening to the family.

Lucy, a teenage girl, came in thrice a week to help clean. Sophie had not taken to Lucy.

"Why not? She seems okay."

"She thinks we're posh and she resents that."

"But we're not posh."

"To her we are. And Mum and I are black. She thinks we should be cleaning for her."

"How horrible! Why would she think like that?"

"Her parents? I can hear her mother's voice saying, *them blackies should be cleaning for you!*"

The girls both loved Phoebe. She didn't chase them out of their own kitchen like the agency woman had done. She welcomed them home from school with treats and listened to their doubts & fears. She explained Aranport to these Londoners and made delicious cinder toffee. The girls had never met cinder toffee before.

*

The success of Sullivan & Ericksen meant there was often no five o'clock finish to the working day for the partners. Yet they were assured that Phoebe was there to welcome the girls home from school with teatime treats in the kitchen and a comforting ear to every hardship endured in school.

"Well, I'm glad there's no ship caught on the Door tonight," Isla concluded.

"I wonder how often children have watched from this window as the poor sailors drowned. While we're safe behind double glazing in a warm bedroom." They turned away from the window.

Isla said, "I keep thinking of the Tull children. I'd like to talk to them."
She fingered the Ouija board.

"We're not allowed to play with the Ouija board."
"We could tell them about the Toy Gallery. They'd like to know that."
Isla turned off the ceiling lighting and set out the board and planchett. The wind clamoured at the windows. Sophie shivered. The roar of the sea whispered in their ears.
Sophie declared, "I'm not happy about this."
"What harm can it do?"

*

Sam said, "I don't wish to be paid for the portrait. I've enjoyed working on it." "Cut the commercial. Let's see the damned thing!"
Holly protested, "Alan! Please, don't!"
"If I like it, I'll buy it."
"I will refuse your money."
"I have a contract signed by you."
"You can wipe your arse on it!"
"You are under contract to work for me."
"Then I will not work."
Holly began to cry.
"Do you have to ruin everything, Alan?"

Sam felt his anger dissolve into self-disgust. Winterton offered his wife a spotless white handkerchief that she accepted.

"Wipe the tears and let's see the cartoon."

Sam unlocked the storeroom. The large canvas stood on the easel, covered with a clean sheet. Sam removed the cover to display the portrait.

*

There was silence in the car until Tom said, "I don't know what to do."

Emily said nothing. "You said you'd done what was asked of you. Why would they harm you?"

"Let me out of the car. Then get as far away from me as you can."

"I'm not leaving you."

"What do I matter to you?"

Tom Fenwick ignored the question and asked, "What's so important about the people who bought the Harbour Mount apartment?"

"Nothing."

"Tell me again."

"Ms Hannah Ericksen and her daughter, about ten, eleven. And a black woman, Ms Keira Sullivan and her daughter, about the same age. Investment consultants. Northern Counties mortgage. Nothing unusual."

Tom turned into the car park of the Percy Arms. He parked behind the building. They sat in silence to watch a man in kitchen whites throw two black sacks into the waste bin.

"What're we doing here?"

Tom said, "We're taking time out."

"You mean we're hiding?"

"I can't think and drive at the same time."

The kitchen worker brought out two more sacks to the bin.

"He's left-handed," Emily remarked.

"We know the Devil is real. And being human we're terrified. But if the Devil is real, then God is real."

"How do you know?"

"Because where there is darkness will also be light."

"Leave me here and save yourself."

"Yet the best that demon could do was fire the house and murder that poor couple."

"Leave me here and drive as fast as you can from Aran."

"You're not listening, are you?"

Emily unbuckled her seat belt and moved to quit the car. Tom caught her by the wrist and restrained her.

"I got myself into this, Tom. It has nothing to do with you. Just let me go!" Emily struggled but Tom didn't let go.

"How did you get involved?"

"I don't know."

"Then start thinking!"

"That's easy to say."

Tom was silent. Emily gave up the struggle.

"What I recollect was one day you were a sweet girl and the next you were Vinegar Vera. Somewhere about then, you made a pact with the Devil. Or you were trapped. What did you do?"

Emily shook her head.

"Don't know."

"Give me your phone. This has something to do with Harbour Mount. Let's follow that story."

Someone tapped on the window and they both jumped with fright. It was the man in kitchen whites. Reluctantly, Tom wound down the window.

"Yes?"

"Nothing to me like, but we're not open. So the boss says, take your lady friend somewheres else? He's just jealous like. But he wants you to move. Okay?"

"As you have phrased it so delicately, my lady friend and I will comply with your employer's wishes."

The man grinned and Emily laughed. Tom wound up the window and started the engine. The man in kitchen whites wandered back to the pub.

Tom asked, "You are my lady friend, are you not?"

*

Isla said, "This is the planchett. We each put a finger on it and if there's a spirit about, it'll move, spelling out words."
"What words?"
"What the spirit wants to tell us."
Sophie picked up the planchett.
"It looks like it could be a bone from somebody's spine."
"It's made of ivory."
"From an elephant?"
"Yes."
"Poor elephant," and on further thought, "How'd'y'know all this?"
"Phoebe told me."

Sophie put the planchett down.
"How does she know?"
"Phoebe has a board. She talks to her grandmother. She says it's like she's still here."
Sophie said, slowly, "I don't like that. Talking to dead people."
"Even if we did, they can't harm us. They're dead. That's what Phoebe said." "Don't keep telling me what Phoebe said."
They sat in an uneasy silence.

Isla said, "How about if we give it one go? If you don't like it, we'll never do it again."
Reluctantly Sophie agreed. Isla switched off all the lights, but the table lamp. Isla centred the

planchett and placed her index finger on it. Sophie hesitated, but followed suit. An odd feeling ran up her arm.

"Ready?"

Sophie nodded. The planchett moved.

"Don't push it. Let it go where it wants to go."

Sophie was too frightened to speak.

Isla asked, "Is there anyone there?"

*

Tom flicked through the pages on Emily's pad.

"The connection is Harbour Mount. Agreed?"

Emily nodded dumbly.

"My God, you don't hesitate to record an opinion, do you? Every detail. So precise."

He flicked through the pages and stopped.

"The thirteenth? Which fortunately was a Thursday. That would be too spooky. You had a viewing?"

"If you say so."

"It says so. But just name and address. A Mister and Missis Clifford. No catty remarks."

Emily tried to take the pad from him and failed.

"Tom, we're wasting time! Let's get out of here!"

"That day you were really rude to Maria. She couldn't understand what had come over you. That's when it all started. After you'd been to Harbour Mount. The clients were the Cliffords."

"Wha'd'y'remember of the Cliffords?"

331

Emily shook her head.

"They didn't buy the apartment."

"But something happened. You were a really foul person after you met the Cliffords."

Emily said slowly, "They liked the apartment, but the stairs were a no-no." Tom waited, but Emily was silent.

"That's all?"

"Sorry."

Tom switched on the engine.

Emily said, "I just need to grab a few things."

"We're not going to yours."

"Where then?"

"Alston. The Cliffords live there. Or used to."

CHAPTER TWENTY-FIVE

"Aren't you going to say you love me?"

Alan Winterton said, "Don't get too excited, my angel. He's probably depicted you as a Picasso princess, all triangles and bangles."
Sam smiled at Holly and uncovered her portrait. He was watching her and saw the passing emotions in her face. Holly began to cry, tears running unheeded down her cheeks, her hands clutching her tote bag. Sam looked at the portrait and knew she saw what he had intended.

There was the beautiful, abused, unfulfilled child. Not provocative or wistful. A portrait of a lost soul. A linnet in a golden cage with not a glimpse of sky. But in her stance and face there was defiance. For when everything is taken from us, all we have is defiance.

Holly cried, "Oh, Sam, it's magical! I never dreamt."
Winterton asked, "Then why are you blubbing, my poppet?"
"Anyone may cry at this wonderful painting."
Winterton laughed. "Never heard such utter nonsense."

Before Sam could stop him, Winterton drew the blade from his swordstick and began to slash at the portrait, cutting the canvas to ribbons. Holly began to wail and Sam caught Winterton by the shoulder and struck him fiercely in the face. The man fell back snarling, blood pouring from his nose.

"Do you understand what you've done?"

"What someone should've done years ago."

Winterton turned the blade upon Sam who pushed it aside.

"That you treat Holly like this disgusts me."

"Does it, indeed? Do not tempt me to deprive this foolish creature of her head." "If you hurt Holly, I will kill you."

"Is this an art at which you are practised?"

"Yes."

He felt the bonds tighten around him. But relaxing, found them loosening.

"I am considering whether to blind you. Be careful what you say."

"Be careful how close you come to me."

"On second thoughts, I shall keep you unbroken. I have a task for you." "Which I will refuse."

Winterton turned upon the woman and struck at her arm with his stick. Sam heard bone break. Holly screamed and floundered into a chair, holding the failing limb. Sam leapt for Winterton, but found himself chained to the floor. "You will do as I command. Why? Because I will hurt your lady love if you do not." Winterton turned to the distraught young woman in the chair. A white bone stood out from her arm.

"I'm tempted to pluck out an eye, but I will desist. If I ask you nicely, I'm sure you will agree to assist me in some small matter."

Sam shook his head and Winterton laughed.

He declaimed, "Pax vobiscum!"

Everything was as it had been. There were no broken bones, no bloody nose, no chains, no shredded painting.

"The portrait is charming, my dear! Congratulations, my friend!"

To Holly he offered, "Darling, would you wish me to arrange to have your portrait brought to our home? Or would you prefer to leave it here to solace Mister Ericksen in his lonely hours?"

Alan Winterton smiled and winked at Sam.

*

Sophie said, "I don't like this."

"Nothing's happened!"

"It doesn't feel right."

"How'd'y'mean, it doesn't feel right?"

"It feels wrong."

"But nothing's happened!"

Sophie sat back from the little table. Isla fidgeted with the planchett.

Sophie said, "Don't you feel anything?"

Isla shook her head. She handed the planchett to Sophie who took it reluctantly. Isla said, "If I didn't know you better, I'd say you were afraid. You're not a coward, are you?"

She regretted the words as they left her mouth. Sophie hid her hurt and shook her head.

"Give it one more go. Wha'd'y'say?"

Sophie nodded agreement reluctantly.

"But I want you to put the lights on."

Sophie put a cautious finger on the planchett. She felt an electric tremor. The planchett moved under Isla's finger.

"Don't push it," warned Sophie.

Isla said, "Is there anyone there?"

In the silence they stared at the planchett. Isla took a deep breath and repeated the question.

"Is there anyone out there, please?"

The ivory piece slowly began to move. Sophie accused Isla.

"You're pushing it!"

"I am not!"

The planchett stopped on A. From A it moved to B and from B to C. Slowly and hesitantly, it travelled through the alphabet, hesitating at U and V before settling on Z. Sophie knew Isla was not manipulating the planchett. The ivory was still. They waited until impatience overcame them, but the planchett didn't move again.

"That wasn't funny," Sophie complained.

"I didn't push it!"

*

As they drove into Alston, Tom said, "More ups than downs for older people. I can see why the Cliffords wanted to move."

"They may have already gone."

"We can but try. Estate agents are made of sterner stuff."

They found Buttermere Rise and parked. The garden was neatly kept. The windows shone. The notice board by the low wall offered the property *For Sale*. Tom rang the bell.

The door was opened by a middle-aged woman whose welcoming smile switched off abruptly. She screamed, "Dennis! It's that woman!"

She struggled to close the door, but Tom resisted, saying, "Missis Clifford, we only want to talk to you!"

A middle-aged man appeared, pushing aside his wife. He held a large kitchen knife.

"We don't want to talk to you!"

Tom Fenwick apologised, "I'm sorry. I don't know what this is all about." "Then, I'll tell you, son!"

With dramatic gestures, Mr. Clifford related, "That young woman fell down the stairs at a property we were viewing and broke her neck. She was dead."

Emily tried to interrupt, but failed.

His wife chimed in, "My husband knows dead when he sees it. Thirty years on the ambulance."

"So I called the police. When he turned up, this young woman is sitting in her car, large as life. You sort that out! Now bugger off and leave us in peace!"

He slammed the door. Tom and Emily retreated to the car.

*

The Reverend Norman Gillespie shook hands with Sam. A short neat man with silver hair.

"Please take a seat!"

The room was furnished with Victorian furniture. To Sam it appeared they might change the vicar, but never the furniture. He sank into a chair that closed about him.

"You're not one of my parishioners, are you, Mister Ericksen?"

Sam considered the possibility of a bearded man, six feet four, passing unnoticed among a handful of parishioners at prayer.

"No."

Sam refrained from making excuses.

"How can I help you?"

"I've met the Devil."

"Indeed?"

"Yes."

"Does he take a particular form?"

"Immaculately dressed. Not ostentatious. Confident. Articulate. As human in appearance as you or I."

"So how do you know he is the Devil?"

"He kills people. Or has them killed. A good friend of mine. A young girl. My cat. A ceramics collector. And others."

"And you can prove this in a court of law?"

"I don't know how many judges he has corrupted. He is very well connected."

"Forgive me, but have you ever had mental health problems, Mister Ericksen?" "Haven't we all?"

"Do you drink alcohol?"

"Whenever I have the opportunity."

"I respect your honesty."

The clergyman was silent.

"What does this man want from you?"

"He wants me to commit a great evil."

"How will he make you do that?"

"He has threatened to hurt someone I care about if I do not comply."

The vicar was silent for so long, Sam suggested, "I have come to the right shop, haven't I? For help?"

"What do you want me to do?"

"Show me or tell me how to overcome the Devil."

"I will certainly engage in prayer with you. A season of prayer, perhaps, which others may join to strengthen you against such temptation as is brought against you."

"And that's it?"

"What would you expect of me?"

"A blessing? A sprinkling of holy water? A crucifix blessed by the Archbishop? Spells to use against the Devil? A sprig of the Burning Bush? Organic garlic? Something!"

"In the twenty-first century?"

"The Devil's right here in the twenty-first century, sir! Haven't you noticed?"

The clergyman stirred uneasily.

"There is no need to raise your voice, Mister Ericksen!"

Sam stood up. The Reverend Gillespie visibly cringed.

"I'll find my own way out."

From behind the net curtain the cleric watched Sam Ericksen pedal away. Satisfied, he tore away the dog collar and dropped it into the waste bin. He chose a coat from the hallstand and quit the house, walking quickly away. In the study, the Reverend Norman Gillespie lay staring with sightless eyes at the ceiling. His throat had been cut from ear to ear. The outpouring of blood had been such as to suggest he wore a scarlet scarf.

*

The planchett still sat on the Z. Both Isla and Sophie felt disappointed. The girls were sitting on Isla's bed: Sophie was brushing Isla's hair. In almost a whisper, Sophie said, "If you made it move, Isla, tell me now, please. I promise I won't be angry."
Isla shook her head.
"I didn't."
"Something moved it."
Nothing more was said. Both heads of hair brushed to satisfaction, they retired to bed. They left the owl lamp on as a night-light and settled down to sleep. It seemed to Sophie that she woke in the night to hear a young girl's voice reciting the alphabet. She stumbled once and started again. Sophie thought she heard the child say, "Yi see, I knaa me letters."

When she asked Isla in the morning, she had been undisturbed.
"It was a girl, reciting the alphabet."
"Maybe you were dreaming?"
"I suppose so."
But the reality of the voice persisted.

341

*

On the summit of Hartside, Tom stopped the car and they sat in silence, listening to the engine cooling. A couple came from the old transport cafe to their car. They were quarrelling. As they came closer, the bitterness of both was acid to the ears. Both doors slammed. The car moved forward and stalled. The argument raged. Finally, the woman got out, slammed the door and returned to the cafe. The man emerged, went to the cafe and after ten minutes got into the car and drove away.

Emily said, "That's what you must do. I'll get out and you drive away. You'll be safe because I don't know where you've gone."

"I'm trying to come to terms with you being dead."

"Don't laugh, but al my toes have dropped off."

She pushed off her shoe and Tom took her foot. The foot was dry, clean and bereft of toes.

"Have you ever been bitten by a red squirrel?"

"You're kidding?"

"Red squirrels can give you leprosy."

"You made that up."

"It's true. I read about it. Have you been bitten?"

Emily shook her head.

"Did they drop off all at once?"

"One, two at a time. Like leaves falling from a tree."

Tom released the foot and took her wrist. He counted against his watch.

"Good, strong pulse says you're alive. May I see where you were stabbed?" "I'm not that kind of girl."

Emily displayed enough bosom to show no scars. "And they didn't bleed."

For good measure Emily revolved her neck. "As graceful as a swan."

The woman came out from the cafe and surveyed the handful of parked cars. She appeared shocked and returned to the café

"I believe the Cliffords. They saw you die. And the Devil restored you. For his own purposes."

Reading Emily's face, he added, "But you're alive now and we're going to keep you that way. There must be an answer and we'll find it."

Emily kissed him and wept at the same time. They both had tearful faces.

She asked, "Aren't you going to say you love me?"

"I'm an estate agent. I never give direct answers. You must wait for the survey."

Tom started the engine. As they left Hartside, the quarrel car returned and parked. The driver marched to the cafe.

"Where're we going?"

"Edinburgh Airport."

"To fly where?"

"Anywhere. First, we'll stop for your passport. I have enough dirty washing in the boot."

"Isn't that risky?"

"I'll find a launderette somewhere."

"You know what I mean."

"They'd never expect us to go back there."

*

A judge, in all his pomp & circumstance, will, with stern address, imprison a foolish creature who has fallen into temptation, yet release a vicious criminal onto the street when his guilt is apparent, because he is a victim of a neglectful upbringing and toddle off to his private club where the most appalling cruelties are committed upon children with a clear conscience. Yet when we ask him to undertake some simple task on behalf of Our Lord, he will whimper and whine. If he continues to refuse, we settle the matter by having Missis Ridley sit on his face until he expires. It's something the dear lady enjoys.

Then we choose another judge to carry out Our Lord's wishes. The middle classes have even less integrity. When an ambitious executive wished to have a rival removed from his career path, we agreed to do so. The price was that he would need to perform a similar service for Our Lord.

The rival walked into an elevator that wasn't there and fell twenty-three storeys to strike the roof of the elevator in the lobby. When the elevator ascended to the engine house, the dying man was crushed. The elevator was out of action for two days, which was most inconvenient. Our Tom Fool was most grateful. We visited his splendid new office atop the tower to enjoy champagne, served by his mammiferous new secretary. We reminded him of his obligation.

When he received a certain e-mail, he was to shoot the next person to enter his office. We knew, of course, he would clear his appointments and invite the next obstacle to his progress urgently. Unfortunately, his secretary entered the office to introduce his visitor. He refused to shoot her because he was engaged in an affair of the heart with her.

We suggested a compromise. Who should we persuade to fly from the window? The light of his secret life? Or himself? After some thought, he decided it would be best if Michelle were defenestrated. He screamed and wept when Alan and Jonathan forced him out of the window. Michelle broke his grip on the sill with a stiletto heel. She cleaned the cacca from the windowsill and has become a most popular member of our congregation. She's quite a girl! As I am sure you are all aware, we are approaching our Annual Celebration. We are anticipating the appearance of Our Lord Himself. This will be a most momentous occasion for Congregation.

Who would not wish to be present at the Coming of Our Lord?

As   recorded   by   Amanuensis.

CHAPTER TWENTY-SIX

"Sam would like him. He used to have a cat."

They stood in the corridor.
Emily whispered, "I'm not going in."
"How do I find anything?"

They had parked behind the block and entered by
the service door. To Tom it seemed unreal;
furtive feet on the stairs. Tom unlocked the door.
"Stay there."
He slipped into the flat. Everything seemed in
order. Tom checked the kitchen, the bedroom
and the bathroom. He grabbed at the shower
curtain and the rail came down.
"Shit!"
The flat was empty.
"No one here!"
Cautiously, Emily entered the flat.
"Quick as you can."
"Like I won't be?"

Emily vanished into the bedroom. When she
emerged from the bathroom she carried an
overnight bag.
"Someone's torn down the shower curtain."
"That was me."
Relieved, Emily offered, "Let's get out of here."

She opened the door. Jacqueline smiled at her. Emily stepped back into the flat to cry, "Oh, my God!"

Jacqueline embraced her.

"I've been trying to reach you two all day? Don't you ever answer your phones?"

*

Emily begged, "Please let Tom go! I don't care what you do to me! But leave Tom alone! He's done nothing."

"He knows too much."

"Who would believe him?"

"Then I should kill you?"

Tom said, "If you touch Emily."

Jacqueline asked, "What would you do, sweetie?"

Tom pulled Emily behind him.

"We're going away. Now. We'll never speak to anyone about this. Just let us go."

The freckled pixie laughed.

"You're talking as if I were someone who could be reasoned with."

"What would it serve to kill either of us?"

Jacqueline considered for a moment. Tom struggled to open the penknife in his trouser pocket, turning to Emily to hide the movement.

"I would certainly enjoy killing you, Tom. But as your sweetie is already dead, it's not much of a thrill to dismember her."

Emily said, "I'll do anything He wants me to do, if you will let Tom live. Absolutely anything!"

Jacqueline seemed surprised and in the moment of distraction, Tom pulled out his penknife and sprang at Jacqueline. He hit an invisible wall and ended up on his backside. The imp laughed at his helplessness. She was still laughing when Emily embraced her. She hugged Emily, mocking Tom, until Emily's body began to crack and emit a molten lava that engulfed the creature called Jacqueline. She struggled to free herself from this deadly embrace without success. Engulfed in flames, Jacqueline screamed as the women burned. Emily turned one last loving look upon Tom Fenwick before the pyre flared and both women were lost in flaking ashes.

*

The telephone rang and Sam sang, "The bells of Hell go ting-a-ling-a-ling, For you, but not for me!"
The telephone persisted and Sam finally surrendered. He rose from the stool, stretching aching shoulders, to answer the phone.
"Yes?"
"That you, Sam?"
The voice was familiar.
"Bruce! Good to hear you, mate! How's the millionaire lifestyle?"
"Tony's dead."

Sam was smitten speechless.

"Did you hear me?"

"How the hell did that happen?"

"Motorway. Truck ran him into a bridge."

"Aw, God!"

"Came across the central reservation. Crushed the car. Driver swears he blacked out."

"Anybody with Tony?"

"Lucy and the twins. All gone."

The pain was overwhelming. Sam could think of nothing to say.

"They were murdered, Sam. Murdered."

Sam said slowly, "I don't want to believe that. But I know it's the truth." "We're leaving now. We'll never come back to the U.K. But I had to warn you."

"Don't tell me where you're going."

"I won't ring again, Sam."

"God go with you, Bruce."

Where the hell did that come from? I've never said that before.

"You take care, Sam. These people are bloody devils."

Bruce closed the call and Sam stood silent, his being flooded with emotion, sorrow to fear to anger to sorrow.

"You're right, Bruce. They're devils. And I brought them on us. My fault."

From under the sink, he took his pistol and re-united it with a full magazine. He recovered his old shoulder holster, stripped off his teeshirt, and slipped on gun and holster. In the bathroom mirror he checked the bulge under the armpit was not too obtrusive. He found the weight comforting.

*

Tom felt nothing. His mind was numb. He knew Emily was dead, but the reality was meaningless. The image repeated in his head. Emily looked at him again, burning brightly, clutching Jacqueline as the liquid fire leaked from her breaking body. Jacqueline was screaming in terror. He covered his ears to shut out the voice. Emily wasn't screaming. She was smiling at him. Her mouth formed the words, I love you. Tom Fenwick felt nothing.

He took Emily's overnight bag and dropped it into the bottom of her wardrobe. He brought the vacuum cleaner from the kitchen and vacuumed the sitting room floor of the scanty ashes. There was no mark on the carpet. Tom returned the vacuum cleaner to the kitchen. He felt nothing. He emptied Emily's handbag onto the table and sorted through the items. He took the money from her wallet, but left the credit cards. There were two sets of keys. He added the key ring with the Frederick Street label to the cash. There

351

was a pepper spray, a souvenir from a holiday. He was tempted, but decided against. He held the soft leather roll that was Emily's father's lock-picking kit.

One evening they had opened every door, drawer and lock in the office, causing alarm & distress that he regretted, but Emily enjoyed. She was blamed, but denied it. No one suspected local good guy, Thomas Fenwick, apprentice locksmith, was involved. Tom didn't confess. He remembered, but it all happened to someone else. There was a litter of personal oddments, principally cosmetics that Tom lifted back into the handbag, using a clean handkerchief. Momentarily, he was tempted by the photograph of Emily and her cat, Sparky. He cleaned everything with the linen and returned them to the bag. The cash and Emily's Locksmith Guild card he placed in his wallet. The Harbour Mount keys and the lock-pick kit he added to his pockets. He cleaned the handbag with the linen. He was playing a part in a feature film. He knew the script, but he felt nothing. He cleaned his way to the door and spied upon the corridor to ensure no one saw him leave. Only the camera on the service stairs saw him. He parked Emily's Megane on the Terrace car park and removed as much of his presence as any handkerchief might manage. He only made one mistake.

He decided to go to the office and retrieve some personal items. He had stepped into the office before he realised there was a stranger at every monitor. A young Asian man sat at his desk. A middle-aged woman smiled from the first desk. "Can I help you, sir?"

Tom Fenwick turned on his heel.

He awoke from a bloody nightmare screaming. Someone in the next room banged on the wall. Tom Fenwick wept quietly because he loved Emily Harrison and knew now nothing would ever be alright again.

*

The box on Hannah's desk buzzed.

"Yes?"

Angela said, "Oliver's coming through."

"Fine. Buzz Keira, please."

"Will do."

Someone tapped on the office door.

"Come in!"

A smiling Oliver De'ath entered.

"Good morning, Hannah!"

"Nobody knocks more politely than you do, Oliver."

Keira appeared in the doorway.

"Ah, the three musketeers together again!" smiled Oliver.

"Good morning, Oliver," Keira said, "Why so cheery on this dreary Tyneside morning?"

Oliver moved the chairs.

"Because I am full of good cheer!"

Angela opened the office door whilst manoeuvring a tray of coffee, milk jug and crockery. Keira said, thank you and Angela withdrew. While Hannah poured coffee, Oliver recited figures with barely a glance at his tablet.

"Most satisfactory. Are you aware you have enjoyed a turnover of thirty-seven million pounds?"

The partners looked to one another.

"It's frightening when you say it like that!"

"It's satisfying when you know it's your own hard work."

"Largely due to you, Oliver."

The banker ignored the compliment.

"Well, there is a reward for all this hard work."

Hannah hesitated. "We don't take bonuses. We agreed that from the beginning." Oliver laughed, "No, no, nothing like that! Although if you wished to pay yourselves bonuses, I don't see a problem. But I have something better for you."

From his briefcase, he took out two sheets of paper, giving one to each partner. "It's the new stationery I'd like you to use."

Hannah, reading, laughed.

"That's wonderful."

Oliver said, "You are now preferred investment partners of the Northern Counties Bank. You may display the logo and statement."

Keira cried, "Thank you, Oliver! That's wonderful!"

Hannah offered, "I'd hug you, but we have another rule."

"I'll take a rain check on the hug. It's my pleasure to offer you this reward for your hard work. Long may our partnership thrive!"

"Amen to that!"

"One more thing before I go. I'd like you, Hannah, to accompany me to the Northern Hemisphere Economies Conference in Canada. Toronto, that is. All expenses paid."

The partners read the surprise in each other's face.

"I'd have to think on that, Oliver."

"So be it! But perhaps, I may be able to persuade you? It won't all be meetings. There will be a leisure element."

When Oliver De'ath had gone. Keira mimicked. *"I'll take a rain check?* He's been seeing too many old movies. Next, it'll be, *just whistle and I'll come."*

Hannah laughed. "But he is quite sweet."

"And there will be a leisure element? Late night rendezvous in the hotel corridor? Turning door handles at midnight?"

Hannah laughed and tried to slap Keira.

The desk buzzed.

"Yes, Angela?"

"There's a man here who wants to put something on the windows?"

They rose as one.

"We're coming!"

*

"We're home, Phoebe!"

The girls shouted. The front door slammed. They dropped their coats and school bags in the hallway. With the scent of fresh baking in their nostrils, they charged for the kitchen. They burst in upon Phoebe who was sitting in the old chair by the stove.

"There's nee need to bawl. I heard you on the stairs. Besides, ladies is supposed to have decorum. D'y'fancy trying a slice?"

"We're not ladies, we're Aran girls," Isla declared.

Sophie cried, "Oh, golly gumdrops!"

Phoebe was nursing a cat, the colour of bracken, moss, ivy and hawthorn.

"He's got two different eyes!" Isla declared, "Blue and green."

"Where'd he come from?"

Phoebe rose and the cat slipped to the floor to be admired by the girls.

"So nobody's interested in hot buttered scones with real strawberry jam that'll give yi tummy ache, sure as our cat ate the goldfish."

The girls laughed.

"Where'd he come from?" Isla cuddled the cat, defying his belonging to any other apartment.

As she took baking trays from the oven, the housekeeper said, "Was the oddest thing. He followed Lucy up the ladders."

Sophie, who feared the exposed metal staircase outside the kitchen door, offered, "Must be a very brave cat."

Rain was running down the kitchen window.

"When I lets Lucy in, he marches in, bold as brass, sif he owns the place. I says to Lucy let him be, it's raining. When you goes home, take him down with you."

"But she didn't?"

"Could we get him out? Not even with the broom. Finally, I says, pick him up. Then he goes and scratches Lucy. Proper fierce. So he's still here."

Sophie said, "He thinks he belongs here."

"Couldn't we keep him, Phoebe?"

"Please?"

"Not up to me. Yi'll have to ask your Mams. But not if he scratches."

"He's not scratching us."

The cat was lying at ease, enjoying attention from the girls.

"Nor iffy has fleas."

"Sam would like him," Isla said and Sophie agreed.

"Who's Sam?" asked the housekeeper.

"He's our Uncle." "He used to have a cat like this."

CHAPTER TWENTY-SEVEN

"This is not The Thirty-Nine Steps. You're not Richard Hannay."

It was raining heavily into darkness. Tom Fenwick was grateful for the shelter of the barber shop. A bell rang as he entered. The chair was empty. The barber was reading a newspaper. He rose to say cheerily, "Nice weather for ducks, sir?"

Tom said, "If they don't drown."

Civilities observed, Tom hung up his wet coat, grateful for the hood and climbed into the chair. As he did so, the bell rang again. A man entered the shop.

The barber said, "Nice weather for ducks, sir?"

"Indeed," said the incoming customer, "So I am told."

As he hung up his wet mackintosh and hat, Tom caught a glimpse of a balding pate and clerical collar. In the remotest corner of his brain, uncertainty awoke. His mind sought for reason and found; *What's a vicar doing out in this weather for a light trim?*

"You're not from around here, sir."

"No. Does it always rain here?"

"Noted for it, sir."

The barber scanned Tom's head.

"So, what can I do for you today?"

"Shave it clean, please."

The barber was disappointed.

"Skinhead is not going to do you any favours."

Tom said, "I appreciate your advice, but, please, all off!"

The barber regarded the image in his mirror.

"We all have these disappointments in life, sir."

Tom snapped, "Just shave my bloody head!"

The barber worked silently and when he had finished, Tom couldn't recognise himself. When he climbed out of the chair, he apologised.

"I'm sorry. I'm not at my best today. Apology accepted?"

"Apology accepted, sir."

To the plump cleric rising from the chair, he offered, "You, too, sir. My apologies."

"You're a troubled soul, sir. I'm not offended."

Tom refused his change. As he stepped out into the gathering darkness, the barber called, "Good luck, sir!"

*

Tom Fenwick moved no farther than the shadow of the window where he could see into the barber shop. The cleric had decided to postpone his haircut and the barber was helping him on with his coat. Tom wrote the stage direction; *the dedicated minister rushes out to save a troubled soul.*

On the small parade of shops, the only other window illuminated was the charity shop. The cardboard sign said, CLOSED. Two women were feeding the racks, going to and from a rear room. Tom knocked loudly and one woman mouthed CLOSED at him. Tom persisted until the young woman came to the door. Her muffled voice explained,

"Can't you read? We're closed!"

Tom said, "Do I have to push my money through the door?"

The woman signified incomprehension and Tom pushed a twenty-pound note through the letter box. The woman picked up the note and opened the door. She offered him the money, which he refused.

Tom had his story ready. "I'm an actor. I'm desperate for the right gear. Or I'll lose the part. Please? Don't you want my money?"

The woman turned to her colleague who nodded.

"Thank you!"

Tom entered the shop.

"Wha'd'y'need?"

Twenty minutes later, Tom Fenwick stood arrayed in faded combat trousers, manic teeshirt, battered leather jacket, well-worn duck-billed cap and ferocious metal-capped boots. He almost believed his own lie that he was on his way to

Alnwick to join the Northumberland Theatre Company.

The older woman said, "I can't say as I approve. But as it's for the acting." The young woman was much impressed. His suit and apparel were packed neatly in a carrier bag. The manager's parting words were, "Warn your Mam afore she sees yi!" Tom dropped the carrier bag into the Eden.

It was a question of a second night in the motel or to take a train. Tom Fenwick flipped a coin that came up heads, the motel. But a lurking uneasiness rose to the surface. Michael Connolly never slept in the same bed two nights running. But still the bastards found him, a small voice whispered. He walked towards the railway station. Again he flipped a coin. North or South? The coin favoured North. Tom bought a single for London.

In the madding crowd of would-be passengers, Tom thought he saw the clergyman from the barber's shop, but he also recognised paranoia. To still this anxiety, he waited until the very last moment before he boarded.
"You getting on this train or not?"
"She promised she'd be here!"
"They all make promises. Few keeps 'em!"

Tom Fenwick, jilted lover, reluctantly climbed aboard.

"Thank you, sir! Can I go home now?"

*

Helen offered the little plastic cup. Victoria obediently swallowed the capsule. The nurse had expected fuss; Victoria demanding to know what the capsule contained.

"You seem very happy this evening, Vicky?"

"I am."

She smiled to herself.

"Any particular reason?"

"Not from seeing you."

Helen struggled to hide her feelings.

"Why would you say that?"

"Oh, I know what you're up to! I see through your little game, Whitey. Keeping me here while that man abducts my daughter. You will pay for that."

It was so unlike her previous behaviour, Helen was foolish enough to say, "There is no conspiracy to keep you from your daughter. What I've seen of Mister Ericksen, he is very concerned for you."

"You both pretend very well."

Helen tried again. "I thought we were friends, Vicky?"

"Did you indeed? Sit down!"

Helen sat on the bedside chair.

"My name is Victoria Sullivan. Who gave you permission to call me Vicky?" "My apologies, Missis Sullivan. I won't do so again."

Helen rose to leave, but sat again when Victoria asked, "Where are you going? Did I give you permission to leave?"

"No, Missis Sullivan."

"The Angel Oliver."

Helen couldn't prevent herself interrupting.

"He's been here again?"

"The Angel Oliver has warned me. The time is coming. I must prepare myself. I am to be amongst the Highest. You would be wise not to anger me."

Victoria Sullivan smiled upon the nurse. Her smile startled Helen.

"What've you done?"

"I am preparing myself."

Victoria's front teeth had been filed to a point.

"To protect Our Lord."

*

Sam Ericksen and Colin Bridger stood outside Victoria Sullivan's room.

"How is she on the phone with her daughter?"

"Normal. Keira would've said something otherwise. Victoria's told her she's attending the Cadogan for tests."

A nurse excused herself and slipped quietly into the room.

364

"Two matters are of concern. She is losing feeling in her left arm. The virus that destroyed her feet is attacking her mind."

"What can you do?"

"This is a most elusive virus. We have enlisted the best brains in the business." "The nurse said this Guardian Angel told Victoria she's been chosen to be amongst the Highest. To prepare herself for the Second Coming. She's damaged her teeth to do so. That doesn't sit right with me. I think."

Sam stopped. Colin said, "Say what you want to say."

"Would you consider the notion that the Devil has a hand in this?"

Colin Bridger laughed.

"Sam, old mate, don't tell me you've started attending the spooky church?"

*

It was a spiteful rain promoted by a sour wind that nagged Sam as he pedalled home from the Cadogan. The wind tugged at his cape and every passing car seemed intent on homicide. The news of Victoria's condition was depressing. He had funked answering Colin's spooky church gibe. As he unlocked the yard gate, he said aloud, "What if I were to tell you, Colin, that I know the Devil?"

It sounded almost rational.

He pushed the cycle to the rear of the studio and covered it with his cape. When he walked to the studio door he saw a figure huddled on the step. He was surprised how quickly the pistol leapt to his hand.

"Stand up! Keep your hands where I can see them!"

The shadow rose slowly.

"It's me, Sam."

"Holly! What you doing here?"

"Don't say it like that."

"Like what?"

"Like angry."

The pistol vanished. He took her hand.

"You're wet. Freezing."

"See! You're angry. I want you to be pleased to see me. But you're not." "Let's get you inside."

Sam opened the door and the warmth of the studio greeted them. He closed the door and switched on the lights. Holly wore an evening dress of the palest blue that clung to her body. Her hair was tumbled into tangled strands by wind & rain. She blew a rain drop from her nose. Sam thought she had never looked more desirable.

"God, you look like a drowned angel!"

Holly began to weep. He clamoured to retrieve his error, folding her into an embrace that he wished might endure forever.

"A very, very, beautiful drowned angel!"

"You're right, I must look awful!"

"No, no! You look beautiful! An adorable mermaid. Yes, a mermaid! Fresh from the salty sea! Escaping the clutches of a rapacious Poseidon!"

"Really? Do you mean that?"

"A beautiful mermaid princess who has fallen in love with a simple peasant boy."

"Does he have to be simple?"

"A handsome, simple peasant boy who has just won the National Lottery." "How much has he won?"

"You shameless trollop!"

Holly laughed and Sam reluctantly released her.

"Let me fetch you a towel. Two towels! All my towels!"

When Sam returned, Holly was warming herself at the kiln. He left her drying her hair and returned with brush and comb.

"My meagre wardrobe is at your command. If not elegant, my rags are clean and dry."

Holly vanished into the bedroom with towels, brush and comb. Sam went to fill the coffee pot and set the machine to soak expensive rat droppings. He stood looking into the rainy darkness, wondering what catastrophe this beautiful creature had brought upon him now.

*

Tom Fenwick found the train crowded and gave up trying to find a seat. He stood at a door and watched the lights of unknown towns and villages flash by. "This is not The Thirty-Nine Steps," he counselled himself, "You're not Richard Hannay."

A seat-seeker stopped, thinking he had been spoken to, but when Tom looked at him, moved on quickly. His appearance was no longer that of an estate agent. He had no idea where he was heading or what he was going to do. He had simply panicked to get as far away as he could from South Aranport, abandoning car, flat, everything. The speed with which Madison & Major had been neutralised was terrifying. The image of Emily and Jacqueline locked in a furnace of flame would haunt him forever. He was leaning against the wall, half asleep, when the wire noose dropped about his neck.

He turned to find the plump cleric from the barber shop, smiling at him as he pulled the wire tight and tighter. Struggling for breath, Tom kicked at the cleric who laughed and danced. He struggled in vain to get fingers within the wire cutting into his neck. As his sight began to fail, he glimpsed his killer trying to open the door.

His gasping squeaks might've been a protest that you can't do that on a modern train. The blast of cold air contradicted him. The door was open. With the last of his strength, Tom Fenwick clutched the clergyman and they fell from the train together.

*

Quentin Westwater was eight years old and very bored when I met him. He had just finished destroying all the soft toys that belonged to his new baby sister. He had shut his mother's shiatsu puppy in the bedroom to take the blame.

He was hiding in the tree house his father had built for him in the sweet chestnut tree. There were many trees in the expansive garden, but Quentin had insisted on his tree house being built in the chestnut. This was to spite his mother who loved the tree. She had protested, but his father supported Quentin. The silver space ship sat in the centre of the tree from which a number of limbs had been cut away. Every time she looked from the kitchen window, Quentin's mother could see the brutal damage that had been inflicted on her tree.

Quentin's Daddy always did what he wanted since the afternoon Quentin found Daddy and Eloise, the au pair, in the spare bedroom without their clothes. He didn't understand everything, but he recognised power when he saw it. He knew before she left, Eloise had vandalized his radio-controlled Porsche. In return, he boiled his father's smart phone in a pan, having switched it on first.

Quentin's mother spent most of her time with Mary Rose who was almost two now. Quentin hated his little sister, which was why his mother spent so much time with her. She had tried to encourage her son to care for his sister, but had stopped when Mary Rose was ill because Quentin had added bleach to her bottle. When she tried to get his father to punish him, he laughed it off. Quentin's excuse was that Mary Rose smelt so badly he was trying to clean her. His father said, it showed enterprise, mistaken but laudable. But his mother knew what he was trying to do. It was a problem that Quentin shared with me. How to get rid of Mary Rose. It was easily solved.

On the day Quentin's mother was sleeping off a liquid lunch, the boy persuaded his little sister to climb up to the space ship, which was forbidden. It was a great adventure for Mary Rose and she followed her brother eagerly up the ladder. When she reached the space ship, Quentin pushed her and she fell, striking her head on the concrete paving around the tree. In his excitement, Quentin slipped too and died beside his sister.

When the mother found her children, she carried them indoors and sat them on the settee. When her husband came home, he screamed at the sight of his dead children watching television. His wife stabbed him twelve times. They had been married twelve years. She made sure all the doors and windows were shut tight and turned on all the gas appliances in the house. She sat with her husband and her children with a lighted candle in each hand, watching children's television. The explosion destroyed the house completely and body parts were found three gardens away. Fortunately, the silver space ship was untouched. It's surprising what mischief can be made in the suburbs. Never neglect Acacia Avenue.

A Personal Memoir from the Amanuensis.

CHAPTER TWENTY-EIGHT

"Those welfare people they sure do treat you mean,
Give you one can of pork and a dozen can of beans"

The family spent a wonderful afternoon on the beach in unseasonable sunshine for the summer was dying. There were fewer of the coaches that brought visitors to the Aranport beaches. It amused Hannah and Keira to hear the girls describe the visitors as day trippers.

"So you really feel you belong?" Hannah questioned.

"We wouldn't want to be anywhere else." Sophie said, "We're Aran girls now." "And always will be!"

"What is it," queried Keira, "you like most?"

The girls looked to one another.

"Being sisters," Isla said.

"With two mothers!"

They laughed together.

"Couldn't you be so in London?"

"Not and hear the sea at night."

They walked up through the park and bought fish & chips at Notariani's. With the girls running up the stairs ahead of them, Keira said, "Don't you think it odd we never see or hear our neighbours?"

"I hadn't thought about it. I suppose I think of them as being old and retired?" "And now they have two elephant calves thundering up the stairs?"

"I have a phone number for an emergency concierge. Would you want me to phone him? Her."

"We'll wait for the complaints."

They ate at the dining table from plates, despite the girls' protests.

"How is it at school?"

The girls looked to one another.

"It's fine."

"Heaps better than the Academy."

"No problems? With you being new?"

"They were curious at first. But we told them stories about London. Like where we lived."

"Like where we lived where?"

"Buckingham Palace Road."

"We could look into the garden and see the Queen. And all the family."

"We used to wave, but only the Queen and Prince Harry waved back."

Hannah and Keira laughed.

"We've been raising a couple of."

"We tell them stories. We don't tell lies."

"The teachers like us because we do our homework."

"The geeks think we're geeks."

"They should see Sophie at netball. She has a thing going with the net."

"The teacher has to go next door and ask for the ball back when Isla gets the rounders stick."

Sophie mimicked a teacher's voice. "There's no need to hit the ball quite so hard, Isla!"

The girls laughed together.

Hannah said, "Have you ever had to explain our family to the teacher?"

Sophie admitted, "Don't worry! We told them you, Mum, you're Bob Marley's granddaughter."

"You what!" "I'm Bob Marley's Great Granddaughter."

"Sophie gets a lot of respect," Isla admitted.

"I don't believe it!"

"It's okay! You're one of his granddaughters by one of his other baby-mammas. So you have to keep it secret."

"But I've never even been to the West Indies! Your Grandmother is from Los Angeles."

"You had to leave because of the shame."

*

When the girls went to their room, they returned the Ouija board, planchett and box to the little table. A storm raged against the windows and the North Sea pounded the beaches below. They sat at the window in pyjamas, watching the maelstrom.

"God help sailors on a night like this," recited Isla.

"Amen to that."

"People must've said that a hundred, two hundred years ago."

"I'm saying it tonight."

They shared the same bed, two spoons in a drawer, seeking comfort.

Half asleep, in the darkness, they heard a child cry out. They sat up.

"Did you hear that?"

"I think so."

They were silent and when their patience was most stretched, the child spoke again.

"Is neebody there?"

The girls cried out together.

"We're here!"

There was no reply. They waited until the Town Hall clock struck midnight before they lay down to sleep. Sophie thought she was called from sleep to hear a child weeping. She woke Isla and they listened to the silence until Isla began to snore and Sophie laughed into her pillow.

*

Sam said, "I shouldn't be surprised, but I am."

Holly had found shorts and teeshirt. Her feet were bare, but her hair was combed into a pony tail.   Marilyn Monroe would've bitten her thumbs in envy. Holly had transformed herself into the Lollipop Kid and took Sam's breath away.

"Do I look okay?"

"You look fabulous. And cheap to keep."

"That's bad. I have to be expensive to keep."

"Come and sit down."

Sam yielded the only half-decent chair and offered a mug of coffee. He found himself a stool.

"Tell me what exciting scenario your dear hubby has planned for us tonight." Holly looked blank, clutching the aromatic coffee. Sam tried again.

"What's the plot, Scott? Why're you here?"

Holly turned beseeching eyes upon Sam.

"I've left Alan. Before you say anything. I'm never going back."

"Did he say, cheerio, good luck, see you sometime? Look after yourself? Where shall I send your wardrobe? Have you got your credit cards?"

"No."

"It wasn't an amicable parting?"

"He behaved like the pig he is."

Holly's eyes filled with tears and Sam offered a paper towel. Holly blew her nose loudly.

"Tell me what he did."

"We were at this dinner party. Some embassy. I can never tell one from another. They're full of foreigners. I just stand or sit as I'm told."
Sam nodded encouragement.
"You don't understand what they say, but you have to smile and nod when they say something. Laugh when they laugh. Don't drop food on yourself or spill wine. Never get drunk. Alan takes the glass away if I try."

Holly paused and looked to Sam for understanding.
"He gave me away, Sam. He does it sometimes and he's just joking. I pretend to laugh, but it's humiliating! Tonight he was in a bad mood and he meant it. He gave me to this awful man, Egyptian, I think."
She sat silent.
"He meant it. He gave my hand to this fat, slobbering creature. He gave me away."
"What did you do?"
"I threw my wine in his face and ran."
"Good for you, kid!"
"I know Alan is evil and hurtful. But I never thought he would do that to me."

They sat silent, Sam not knowing what to say.
"Are you going to turn me out?"
"Why would you ask that?"
"Alan came after me with the car. I wouldn't get in. He said, I know where you're going. Shall I give you a lift? He'll turn you away. Then you

can come home with me. Are you going to turn me out?"

Sam smiled to say, "I could never do that, Holly."

He avoided her embrace, saying, "And we shouldn't do that."

"But you love me. I want you to love me. Tell me you love me, Sam."

"And now abideth faith, hope, charity, these three; but the greatest of these is charity."

"I don't understand."

"The definition of charity has changed over the centuries. Now abideth faith, hope and love."

"You're playing games. Do you love me?"

"Why else would I do what I'm doing?"

Holly overflowed with happiness.

Is that all it takes?

"Are you hungry?"

"I'm starving."

"Don't they feed you at these embassies?"

"I'm always too nervous to eat."

"Why?"

"I don't want to let Alan down."

"Cowboy dinner okay?"

"Cowboy?"

Holly laughed and all the shadows dropped away.

"Pork and beans. Pork sausages and baked beans."

Sam fried the sausages while Holly stirred the beans. He sang the old depression blues and Holly made him sing it again. Then she sang it with real feeling that left Sam torn by emotion. *Those welfare people they sure do treat you mean, Give you one can of pork and a dozen can of beans.* . . .

Sam gave up the bedroom to Holly and settled into his thinking chair.

*

A Personal Memoir from the Chancellor.

It is to be known to all the faithful of Congregation that the Second Coming of Our Lord is upon us. Our Diocese has been chosen and we are most deeply honoured. We must watch and pray that we may safely conduct the birth of The Child. That He may enter this world among those who will give their lives that He should grow to maturity, unhampered by those who would harm Him in his infancy. If you believe you are worthy to be at the Second Coming, then you may approach the Archbishop, the Bishop interim and the Chancellor that you may be judged. Be assured we will look to what you have wrought in His name. Do not come burdened with gold, myrrh and frankincense. There are those of us who have waited centuries for His return. We will not fail Him.

*

Sam Ericksen was sleeping soundly in his thinking chair when he was awakened to find Holly at his elbow. His hand grasped the pistol.

"What's wrong?"

"Come to bed."

Sam suppressed his irritation to say, "Thank you for the invitation, but the answer is no, thank you."

"Don't you want to be with me?"

"I am with you. Right here."

Finally, he chased her back to bed.

Later in the night he was awoken again.

"Go back to bed, Holly!"

"As ever the impeccable gentleman."

Sam shot upright to find Alan Winterton by his chair. He reached for a gun that wasn't there.

"I removed the pistol. We wouldn't want any unfortunate accidents, would we?"

The bedroom door opened and Holly cried out in terror.

"Don't be alarmed, my dearest! 'Tis only I, your loving husband! I will not harm your paramour. I was concerned for your reputation. The fabled Holly Winterton sleeping with a pot maker? How sad! Thankfully, friend Sam-uel, is a gentleman. Alas, so few and far between these days!"

Holly wailed in despair.

"I'm never coming back to you."

Sam said, "Wha'd'y'want, Winterton?"

With a sickening lurch, Sam was aboard the Lynx, casting its fleeting shadow over the desolate slopes below. Geordie was at the controls. The new kid in the seat beside him. The gunner hugged his machine gun in the open doorway. The stink of cordite and hot oil stung the lungs. The clatter of the ship was deafening. Frog was dozing beside Sam. Gobber and the interpreter, Salim, arguing, in front of them. Behind were Taff and Tipper. Geordie turned to grin at Sam and raise a hand. Three minutes. Sam relaxed. Mission accomplished. No problems. No casualties. Home.

Then Holly became the new kid, looking to Sam, helpless and afraid. Frog became Winterton who said, "Here's an idea to chew on, old chum, give me your promise to undertake a small task for me and the helicopter will land safely.   With everyone alive. Wha'd'y'say, old chum? Small favour for me? Everybody lives happily ever after?"

Everything froze. It seemed to Sam they were all looking at him, expectant faces smiling, the people who meant most to him in the entire world.
Sam said, "No."

The Stinger came in the open door, decapitating the gunner and exploded. The helicopter fell like a stone.

Winterton said, "You do surprise me."

Holly had vanished into the bedroom. Sam said nothing. The pain was unbearable.

"Why did you let them die?"

"Correction. They are dead. They have been dead for years."

His heart ached with regret. Winterton laid the pistol down.

"Holly! Time for us to go, sweetling! Say thank you to Mister Ericksen for having you. Although he didn't."

Holly came like a whipped dog.

Winterton said, "You look ridiculous!"

"You said you were never going back to him."

The broken child asked, "What else can I do?"

"Stay with me."

Holly shook her head, "He would have you killed."

"He's tried already and failed."

"It was just a dream, Sam."

"Just say no."

"Thank you for my cowboy supper."

Winterton laughed out loud.

"I really should record this. It's priceless!"

Holly followed Winterton out of the studio. At the door she hesitated. "Do you hate me?"

"No."

"But you do love me?"

Holly vanished before Sam could reply.

CHAPTER TWENTY-NINE

"All you have to do, is accept my hand in friendship."

Isla woke first when the voice called. "I hear yi breathe, but I has no sight of ye."
She switched on the owl lamp and shook Sophie awake. Both girls gasped. At the foot of Sophie's bed, in the limited light of the owl, stood a girl of their own age. She was dressed in a cut-down shirt and old tartan skirt that reached to her dirty bare feet. Her belt was of leather and adorned with tassels. Her hair was tangled and ear-length; blue eyes and dirty blonde hair above a red and white kerchief. When she saw the girls, she hesitated and dipped her head in acknowledgement. Isla and Sophie copied her.

The child said, "It's been see lang a coming. Dark see lang. I called oot, but neebody answered. Cud not find our father. Nor our mother. Dost thee know where they is? And Jacob? Adam? Do yi knaa me sisters?"
The girls shook their heads.
Isla persuaded, "Come and sit with us."
She patted the bed and the child came hesitantly to join them. She smelt strongly of fish.
The child announced, "I knaas me letters. An' me numbers. I's been to scuel afore."

She stopped and Sophie said, "We're new here. Strangers really."

The child nodded to say, "I knaa yi was. But I seen blackies afore. Yi dain't frit me."

Sophie smiled, "I should hope not. We're just people."

The child nodded.

"I seen a dead blackie."

"How horrid!"

"A floater. Angus poked him with his oar, but he were long dead."

"How sad!"

"Seen ginger people too."

Isla said, "But you know people like me?"

"Oh, aye! But me sister Greta's prettier than ye. An' she has three combs."

She seemed to expect appreciation and was disappointed.

"Thodren give them to her. One he brought from a fair. One he bought from a pedlar and one he won gamblin'. But that don't say, Greta's promised. Father made that clear. But she is past ten and four."

"Perhaps we might meet her?"

"We'd like that."

"Then yis shall, cause they's comin. But don't yis look too lang at Thodren." "How'd'y'know?"

"Because Greta'll tear off ya face, she thinks yi lucks at Thodren too lang."

"No! I mean, how do you know your people are coming?"

"Cos I knaas."

The bedroom door opened to Hannah.

"What on earth is going on, girls?"

"Nothing."

"Have you any idea what time it is?"

The girls shook their heads.

"School tomorrow."

"Sorry!"

"I don't want to hear another word. Lights out!"

The door closed and the girls waited until they were assured Hannah had gone back to bed before they switched on the light. Their visitor had gone.

"We never got to tell her our names. Or learn hers," Sophie complained.

"But we learned not to moon over superstar Thodren."

They laughed, but quietly, being good girls.

They slept soundly and were visited by no night terrors.

*

Tom Fenwick was awoken by a passing train. He was lying on a dead man. As he recovered his wits, he realised the corpse had been dead many years. The face was mummified. The eyes were sunken and dry. Repulsed, he rolled off the corpse. In the dawn light, he recognised the clerical collar of his would-be murderer. Tom freed the wire noose from about his neck. He rolled & tucked it into a pocket. Then he turned his attention to the desiccated corpse.

The wallet contained the cleric's train ticket and two hundred and thirty pounds in cash. There was no debit or credit card. All the suit pockets were empty. The corpse had no identity.
"This creature was given money and dispatched on a mission. To kill Thomas McKinley Fenwick."

He scoured the ground where they had fallen from the train and found his cap and the black homburg. Tom took the ticket, cash and wallet. He pulled away the clerical collar. There was a neglected ditch beyond the field fence. He steeled himself and picked up the mummified corpse. He dropped it into the ditch where it vanished beneath the tangled grasses. He decided to lose the hat a good distance from the corpse.
"Wha'd'we know now, Thomas? That we didn't know before? One, there is no place to hide. Two, these creatures are not living beings. They can be killed. Three, I owe my life to Emily."
He looked over the fields to the far horizon. As another train thundered past on the embankment, Tom Fenwick began to walk in the direction from which it had come.

*

Victoria drank from the glass of water Sam offered. When she returned the glass, Sam tried again. "We must tell Keira something. Whatever you want to tell her."

"Did you know there were black angels, Sam? I never even saw a picture before. Only white angels."

"But we can't keep her in the dark forever with viruses and tests."

"It's a secret."

Sam kept patience with difficulty.

"Keira's your daughter. She needs to know."

"And she will, in due course. She has been chosen. She is one of the Blessed. We are to be at the Coming of Our Lord. Pray with me, Sam!"

He waited until the slight tremor of the lips ceased and her eyes opened.

"When will this be?"

"When all is as it should be. When are met together, the Believers who will open the Path for His Coming."

"This would be the Messiah, we're talking about?"

"At His Coming, the world will be under His benign governance forever." Victoria smiled, assured of certain certainties.

"And how will you know when he is coming?"

"I will know and I will go to await His Coming."

"And we gather together on some mountain top in the freezing rain?"
"You mock me? Oh, ye of little faith!"
"No, I believe every word. What concerns me most, Victoria, is who is coming? Is it the true Messiah? Or is it the Devil come to seize this sad, disordered world?"
"So if the angel is black?"
Victoria laughed and Sam saw again the mutilated teeth.

"Vicky, will you tell me when it's time to go? I will see you safely to wherever you're meant to be."
Victoria smiled and stroked his hand.
"How kind, Sam! However, I am secure in the hands of the Angel Oliver. I await his command."

*

It was a very ordinary house, no different from any other on the terrace. Sam checked his notebook. Edith Street. Mrs. Bosenquette. He padlocked his bicycle to the iron drainpipe and knocked on the door of number nineteen. He heard someone approaching in the passageway.

When she opened the door, he was surprised how small she was. A wisp of an elderly woman in what might be a faded kimono.

"Missis Bosenquette? Sam Ericksen."

The old woman ignored him.

"No, no! That won't do! They'll have your bike away and the drain pipe down!" "I'm sorry. I didn't think."

Sam retrieved the chain & padlock. He stood chastened, holding the bicycle. "Don't stand there like a turnip! Bring it in the passage!"

Sam bumbled the bicycle into the narrow passage and leaned it carefully against a wall. When he looked up, the old woman had vanished, but a door stood open. Sam tapped on the door frame and stepped in. Mrs. Bosenquette was sitting in a chair by an empty fireplace.

"Do come in!"

Sam was humbled, being so big and Mrs. Bosenquette so small. The room was little larger than a matchbox; the unused, smartest room kept for visitors only. The old lady said, "Are you slow-witted by nature?"

"Not particularly."

"Then sit down. You're floundering like a landed fish."

She regarded him carefully.

"Your mother must have fed you well."

Sam sat in the chair across the fireplace from the elfin lady.

"Would you like coffee or tea?"

"No."

"Good. Because I won't be serving any. This isn't a social visit."

"I came for help."

"Have you got money?"

Sam took out the folded notes.

"Is that all you have?"

"Don't know what I'm paying for yet."

"I wasn't asking for more. If that was all you had, I'd've given you something back."

Sam smiled and added a further note.

"Why have you come to me?"

"The Devil is pressing me to carry out a task for him. I think it is something truly horrendous. Blowing up Parliament? Killing the Queen? Said aloud that sounds silly."

"He is, of course, offering you rewards?"

"Everything I don't want."

"Would I know this devil?"

"Alan Winterton. Mixes with the great and the greedy. Immensely rich. But he's the Devil incarnate."

"What do you want to know?"

"I want to know how to kill him."

The old woman was silent.

"He can be defeated because he and his kind don't yet rule the world."

"Are you a virtuous man?"

"I wouldn't have thought so."

"Virtue is the weapon that may overcome a Devil."

Sam sat silent, struggling with a rising tide of despair.

"To oppose him, you place all whom you love in mortal danger."

"My parents are dead. I have no wife or children. Only my sister, her daughter. Her friend and daughter. And a woman I've met."

"Would you risk them?"

"Have you met the Devil, Missis Bosenquette?"

"Yes."

Sam looked for further explanation.

The old woman hesitated to say, "I refused to do what he wanted. He tortured and killed everyone I loved. Leaving me alive as punishment."

The old woman took his hands. Her fingers were cold

"You were in an explosion?"

Sam nodded.

"Everyone but you died."

It was a statement, not a question.

"So you know what a punishment it is to survive."

"Tell me what will help me."

"They fear fire. Fire will kill them, but they must be restrained."

"A sort of kamikaze? Hugged to death?"

"Unfortunately, yes. A tactic of last resort."

The old woman plucked something from the air and placed it on his palm. Sam examined the gold disc.

"It is a soul coin."

Impressed on one side was a ferryman, holding his sweep, standing in his reed boat. On the reverse was the profile of a god or king.

"A soul coin?"

"Pay the ferryman and he will bring you a human soul."

"I can raise the dead with this?"

"I didn't say that."

Abruptly, he rode within the clattering Lynx again. Geordie grinned and signalled three minutes. Then Death entered to kill his blood brothers and he was alone.

"Are you alright, Mister Ericksen?"

As the room came back into focus, Sam nodded at the old woman. For the briefest moment, it had seemed she had burned with the purest flame. Then Mrs. Bosenquette rose to say, "Now, let's have your contraption out of my passage! I didn't invite you to tea!"

The good lady had no sooner seen Sam off her doorstep and retired to her chair, before someone knocked on the front door. Mrs. Bosenquette opened the door, saying, "My lavatory is not for common usage, Mister Ericksen."

It wasn't her previous visitor, but a stranger who threw her the length of the passage. She was dead at the kitchen door before he started stamping on her head.

*

Sam worried he would lose the coin all the way home. He stopped twice to reassure himself it was still in his wallet. In his haste, he locked the bicycle safety chain around the handle bar so any thief had only to lift the chain to free the bicycle.

Within the security of the studio, he sat down at the computer to search for classical coins. He could find no coin that featured a ferryman. He searched for and found a small leather pouch that once held two wedding rings. He hung the pouch & coin with a leather lace about his neck. It seemed a satisfying end to the day. Sipping his toxic tincture, he said aloud, "If it's nothing more than a baby's comforter, it's still a comfort."

*

The girls were sitting at the kitchen table watching Phoebe prepare supper. It was a time they enjoyed; a comforting time. When things went wrong at school, it was to Phoebe they turned. Mountains became molehills. The wisest words she had spoken had been when they first bumped heads with classmates. "Yis has to change ya spots. Yis cannot be London lasses in Aran. They don't like it. They won't like it. You has to join their team. You're good as them, no doubt. But you're not better. Don't tell them. Listen to them."

The cat was sitting in Sophie's lap while Isla stroked his head. He seemed to be listening intently.
"While we're not on the subject. One thing yi hasn't done is name that cat. We can't go on calling him That Cat forever. Though that's what he is. That Cat." The trio regarded the cat that seemed unconcerned.
"Why ya Mams let him stay, I don't know."
Sophie looked to Isla.

"Now, don't just come out with somethin daft. Yous has to be careful with cats. They's not always what they seem to be."
"He's a very good cat."
"Yous know nowt about him. Is he someat Eno's circus left behind? Has he come off a boat? Has he been stealing from the cafee bins in Ocean Road? Has he done something bad and been turned out? Has he got worms?"

Phoebe closed the oven door. She sat down, fanning a flushed face with a tea towel.

"Well?"

Isla announced, "We're waiting."

"What for? A name's a name."

Sophie offered, "We don't know. So we're waiting."

The kitchen door opened and Lucy entered. She started to say, "I've done the," when the cat snarled from Sophie's lap. She struggled to hold him.

"Sorry, Lucy!"

"Well, I don't know what I done to upset him. I like cats."

"Well, he don't like you," stated Phoebe.

Lucy edged around the table as the girls tried to soothe the snarling, spitting cat. She gathered her coat and opened the kitchen door onto the fire escape. Sophie tried again.

"I'm very sorry, Lucy."

She was ignored as Lucy vanished, saying, "Wednesday, then, Missis Em!" They listened to Lucy's feet descending.

The cat relaxed and slipped from Isla's lap.

"Sorry!" Sophie said again.

"Nowt ti do with you, lass," chimed Phoebe.

"I'm not keen on Lucy," Isla said, "But she's not afraid of the fire escape."

Isla opened the kitchen door and bravely stepped onto the steel landing. She could see across Aranport to the Western horizon bathed in myriad colour as the sun sank into darkness. She realised she had never looked West; always East to the sea.

"Sophie, come and see the sunset! It's so beautiful!"

Sophie joined her, warily, closing the door behind her.

"Should we tell Phoebe about seeing that girl?"

*

There were a couple about to buy a frog jug and a dealer surveying Sam's work in the studio when the lorry arrived with the skip. Sam excused himself and went out to the driver who dropped the skip and prepared to leave.

"Hang on! I didn't order a skip."

"Nothing to do with me, mate! Collection tomorrow."

Sam accepted a delivery sheet and the driver swung up into his cab.

He went to lift the corner of the tarpaulin cover. All the Exhibition work lay shattered in the skip. Sam felt sick and then angry. When he returned to the studio, his prospective customers had gone. Alan Winterton was sitting on a stool, examining the work in progress.

"My God, but I envy the talent!"

The young soldier was holding a metal detector. The companion figure of a boy, shadowing his movements, was working with a hoe.

"Why did you do that?"
"I became bored with it."
Sam controlled his anger with difficulty.
"All you have to do is accept my hand in friendship."
"I would rather eat shite."
"What if I were to give you Holly?"
In Sam's body language, Winterton caught the fleeting images.
"Of course, how remiss of me! Your sister's friend! Keira? You hope to develop a relationship? Might you not enjoy her and a spare?"
Sam fought for control, saying nothing.

"We shouldn't be enemies, old chum. We have so much in common. I truly admire your talent. You're now a much-admired potter. But I could do so much more for you."
Sam snorted disbelief.
"In good faith. Without obligation, I'll restore your work. I'm not a vengeful creature. Let's part without bad feeling."
When the limousine had departed Sam went out to the skip. The Exhibition was securely packed

in boxes bound in bubble wrap. The temptation to retrieve the work was almost overwhelming. The pigeons returned to reclaim the yard as Sam stood at the skip.

He remembered the painful creation of every item from tree jug to hedgehog; from individual figure to unique vase; from clay to creation; from cold hands to aching shoulders. Then he pulled the tarpaulin over the skip, frightening the pigeons and returned to the studio.

He washed the floor with mop and bucket, ran all stray clay through the pug mill, loaded the kiln from the drying shelves, rearranged every item on his display shelves, replaced the odd errant light bulb, scrubbed every bench top and cleaned the wheels. Then he settled into his thinking chair and tried not to think. He almost rose to fetch his Highly Toxic bottle, but resisted the temptation.

CHAPTER THIRTY

"It'll stop hurting, if you take my hand."

Hannah answered the phone.
"You rang me, Hannah?"
"Oliver! Thanks for getting back to me so quickly."
"That's what I'm here for. How can I help?"
"I'm looking at a document arrived by hand this morning."
"It's on my screen."
"It says *Sullivan and Ericksen are investing two hundred and thirty-five million pounds in the Bright Star programme in Venezuela?*"
She waited for his response.

"Indeed you are! Congratulations!"
"Oliver, this is the first I've heard of it."
"Mea culpa! It's very simple. You have been chosen as the principal partner of Northern Counties in this new programme."
"We have?"
"It's all politicking really. We get more credit for involving a local finance consultancy."
"But two hundred and thirty-five million pounds?"
She heard Oliver's reassuring laugh.

"Don't worry, Hannah! The money doesn't go anywhere. It's all smoke and mirrors. All you have to do is check the progress sheets that will start coming through to you and sign them off when you're satisfied they're correct. And collect your commission."

"I see," Hannah said, doubtfully.

She was surprised when Oliver said, "You must take great care of this document, Hannah. In the most unlikely circumstance that anything goes awry, the shareholders bear the liability."

"I don't know what you mean?"

"How is Isla? Is she on the mend?"

"She's envying Sophie going to school."

"And is Keira envious of you running S&E single-handed?"

Hannah was left with nagging doubts when the conversation ended. She read the document again. It was, as Oliver had said, endorsed by Northern Counties and approved by Real Aid South America. She wondered whether to phone Keira and decided not to do so. Yet the nagging doubt was difficult to dispel. From the first day of opening the office, everything had gone so smoothly. Business was a succession of projects launched by Sullivan & Ericksen as an associate of the Northern Counties Bank. She buzzed Angela to cancel appointments. They spent the day going through every project the partnership had been engaged in. Angela asked as they began, "What are we looking for, Hannah?"

"You'll recognise it when you see it."

When Angela looked confused, Hannah said, "Think of it as an internal audit."

Despite intense scrutiny, they could find nothing amiss. It was late when they finished, eyes and shoulders aching. The office staff had gone home.

"Thank you, Angela. Couldn't have done it on my own."

"Did you think there was something wrong?"

Angela was now Secretary to the partners and proud of her advancement.

"I don't know. Just a feeling. We're too successful."

Angela laughed.

"Isn't that what we're trying to be?"

*

Tom Fenwick parked the hire car on South Street and walked up to where he could watch Harbour Mount from the park. He pretended to read until he realised a man struggling with a newspaper in a North Sea breeze was more obviously "wrong" than a man sitting on a park bench. In an hour no one came from or entered the house. No one walked by and he could count passing traffic on one hand.

Tom retired to the car and struggled into his overalls. He drove up Mount Road and parked outside Harbour Mount. He sat for twenty minutes, apparently studying his clipboard. When Tom stepped out and locked the car, his heart was beating as a marching drum. The pedestrian gate opened smoothly, without a squeak.

Come into my parlour, said the spider to the fly.

He stood for some minutes, inspecting the roof and consulting his clipboard. There were no cameras visible. His legs were trembling. Tom said aloud, "You're acting like an estate agent, jerk. A workman just does his stuff."
He was absurdly grateful for the sound of a human voice. Tom crossed the gravel to the front steps and walked up to the front door. Looking back to the car, it seemed a world away.

The door furniture shone gold. *Where is the housemaid who polishes this every day?* Tom put down his workbox and found the keys. He took comfort from the image of Emily speaking from the flames and inserted the key. The Yale key opened the door. The deadlock was free. The hallway was silent and empty. The ocean of mosaic tiles stretched before him to the dark staircase. Left and right of him were the doors to the first two apartments, B & C. Tom was surprised to find excitement overcoming fear.

He pressed the doorbell of apartment B and heard it ring within. Nothing disturbed the silence. Tom rang again briskly, once, twice. Nothing stirred within the apartment. He listened to the silence of the house. Tom knelt to open the lock-pick pack on his workbox. He remembered the evening Emily and he opened every door and drawer at Madison & Major. He chose two probes. "Here goes nothing, Emily!"
To his surprise, it only took him ten minutes to open the door. He braced himself.

I'm sorry, madam, but we had a report of a gas leak and when you didn't respond.

Tom opened the door and there was no apartment.

*

Sam was glazing a series of vases when the telephone rang. They had been exceedingly tricky to create. Sam ignored the summons, but it persisted in ringing. A young woman who was watching him work, said, "Shall I answer it. Tell them you're busy?"
Sam shook his head. "It'll stop."
But the ringing didn't.

The young woman said, "They really need to speak to you. Shall I?"
Sam nodded. The young woman answered the phone.
"It's a Doctor Bridger? Victoria has gone?"

Sam stopped, frozen, one hand in the glaze bucket.
"Ask him what he means. Gone."
The young woman turned from the telephone.
"As in a-wol?"
"I'm coming."
"He's coming," the young woman echoed.
Rinsing his hands at the sink, pulling off his apron, grabbing his jacket, heading for the door, Sam said, "You're in charge."
The young woman looked around the handful of possible customers.
"I've no idea of the prices."
"Whatever they're willing to pay."

*

Colin was waiting in Reception.
"I'm terribly sorry. This has never happened before."
"You can't lock them up, Colin."
"You need to talk to Helen."
The nurse was waiting for them.
"I'm so sorry, Mister Ericksen. I should've believed what Missis Sullivan said." "Which was?"

405

"When I brought her lunch, she was in very good spirits. I asked her why she was so happy. She said today her Guardian Angel Oliver would be coming to take her to the Hall of Eibor where she would be prepared for the Coming of Our Lord. I'm so sorry I didn't take her seriously."

Colin stated, "No young black man, as Victoria describes her Angel, came to her room today. The CCTV says no young man entered or left the hospital. Neither did Missis Sullivan leave the hospital."
Sam said, "Would she have access to her clothes?"
The wardrobe was empty.
"Is there any possibility she left by a service entry? That a staff member would smuggle her out?"
Sam regretted the words as they left his mouth.
Colin said, "All exits & entrances of the hospital are covered by CCTV."

"Her Guardian Angel Oliver flew in and carried her off. Do you believe that?" Neither the doctor nor the nurse made any response.
"Then I stand in a minority of one."
"You're not serious, Sam?"
"Absolutely! And I know where they're heading."
"Which is?"

"Newcastle upon Tyne. Not Newcastle-under-Lyme or Newcastle, Newry, Northern Ireland. Newcastle upon Tyne."

*

Tom Fenwick found he was standing in a public cloakroom, bristling with racks of coat hooks. Curiosity drove him to the double doors. Opening a door cautiously, he stepped into an assembly hall, complete with rows of chairs. No one challenged him. The hall was empty. It smelt of stale humanity. At the farther end of the hall, on a raised dais stood an enormous chair; an elaborately carved ebony throne. Tom was irresistibly drawn forward as if the chair beckoned him. Yet when he moved to step onto the dais, life stirred within the chair. The surface rippled and flowed menacingly. Tom could hear his own heart in the silence of the hall.

He retreated slowly and the beast within the chair subsided. But something continued to watch him. He backed into what appeared to be two large tables, surfaces well-scrubbed, that had the solidity of butchers' benches. Fear overwhelmed curiosity. He knew here was a terrible place that neighboured on Hell, where pain & torment reigned.

On trembling legs, Tom went to the near door and opened it. He entered a washroom complete with toilets and showers. The room had a sweet smell that Tom found disturbing. Catching sight of himself in a mirror startled him.

"If I met you in a dark alley."

The words echoed, driving Tom to the farther door. He stepped out onto the mosaic tiles of the hallway from the front door of apartment C, looking at the front door of apartment B.

"Even for an estate agent that was some viewing, Emily."

*

When Sam Ericksen arrived back at the studio, there were people still at the shelves and the young woman was sitting on a stool by his work bench.

She jumped up to say, "I've rather enjoyed myself. We've taken just short of four hundred pounds."

Sam apologised, saying, "Thank you. Thank you very much. But I have to go now. Sorry, but I'm in more than a hurry. Emergency! Would you like to choose a piece for your kindness? Anything you like!"

Reality shivered and he was talking to Alan Winterton.

"I might have known. Stupid me!"

"No need to worry about our dear Victoria. She's in safe hands."

"If anything happens to her."

"Dear chum, she has gone willingly to attend the coming of Our Lord. Please feel free to attend yourself. You will, of course, receive an invitation."

The image fluttered between Winterton and the young lady so helpful to Sam.
"I thought I was rather good. Naive young woman, attracted to husky potter. Dreams of becoming his soul mate, never to be parted. Living a romantic, gypsy life in an old tin hut. Watching breathlessly, as you slop goo on your miserable, misshapen pots."

Sam let him ramble on as his soul flooded with horror. They were all gathered by the shelves. Blakey, Geordie, Gobber, Salim, Frog, Taff, Tipper. As they had been lifted out of the wrecked Lynx. He tried not to look at the headless gunner. Sam wanted to scream as other figures began to form, crowding the studio; troopers, Afghanis, Iraqis, all dead, all dead. Before them stood the girl-child who haunted his dreams. Dead, all dead.
Then he was on his knees by the dying child. The girl died in his arms, lingeringly, smiling, looking at him wonderingly, reluctant to leave him.
"God's sake, I'm not responsible for everyone!"
No one answered.

Winterton laughed. "I can put all this right, old chum, in the blink of an eye. Just take my hand in friendship."

Sam stared at smiling Winterton, the outstretched hand.

"It'll stop hurting if you take my hand. No more pain, Sam. No more regret."

It was a clean hand, a friendly hand, a comforting hand.

Sam screamed, "No!"

He stuck out his tongue and began to bite savagely, again and again. He choked on his own blood, struggling to breathe. The pain was excruciating, but only a morsel of the price paid by others. Sam staggered to the bathroom. When he returned, Winterton was gone and all Sam's ghosts had returned to whatever darkness they inhabited.

*

Rain spattered the sitting room windows. The wind tore at the park trees, stripped of leaves. The sea pounded the beach below. Sophie and Isla stood at the sitting room window watching the havoc of the day. Hannah and Keira were in Newcastle attending a Saturday seminar. They had tired of the jigsaw in their bedroom and come hunting entertainment. The first storm of the winter fascinated them.

"I think sometimes London isn't real."

"Wha'd'y'mean?"

"You must've done what I did. I got up in the morning, had my breakfast. Got ready for school. Got in a car with Eileen and Zoe and went to school. The Mums took turns."

"Had a dreary morning in school. Ate my packed lunch. Put up with school in the afternoon. Came home."

"Did my homework. Had supper. Went to bed. Got up."

"And the roundabout started again."

They laughed together.

"But here, the world is real."

"And frightening."

"Real stuff was going on all the time and we never knew."

They stared at the distant lighthouses.

The girl child said, "Weren't like this, our time."

Isla and Sophie were startled. The child stood at the other window.

"How long you been there?"

"Heard yis talking so I come."

She approached the girls cautiously and they smelt fish.

"We're glad to see you again. I'm Isla."

"And I'm Sophie."

"Pretty names."

A wistful tone.

"And you are?"

411

"Lizzie. Skinny Lizzie."
The girls laughed and Lizzie laughed too.

Isla asked, "You said, it wasn't like this?"
"No, weren't. Nee geat stone sea walls like you has. No towers with lights. No light on the Midden."
"The midden?"
Sophie guessed, "The reef? The Door."
"Bad night, old Jacob's son Tom died on the Midden. Nearly took our father with him."
The girls stared uncomprehending.
"Cobles. We has cobles. When the tide catches yi, no matter how strong yous row, yi can broach on the Midden. D'yi understand?"
"That's so sad."
"Weren't meaning to happen, but it does. But there weren't no storm when they come."
"When who came?"

The sitting room door opened and Lucy appeared.
"I've done what was needed, so I'll be off."
Isla asked, "Have you got a waterproof?"
"Eddie's meeting me with his car."
I have a boyfriend with a car.
The door closed.
Lizzie remarked, "Don't like her."
The door reopened. Lucy said, "Near forgets. Locked that cat in the cleaner's cupboard so's I could get on."

Lucy vanished and the door closed.

Sophie turned to Lizzie, saying, "Why don't you like?"

Only to discover their visitor had gone too. When they went to release the cat from the cupboard, they found Lizzie among the mops & brooms, nursing the cat.

"But I likes your cat. I has a cat then. Called Sir Thieving Tull after the landlord."

Sophie and Isla settled down with Lizzie. It was snug in the cupboard. Wreathed in lavender and bleach, the smell of fish was lost.

Sophie asked, "You said when they came. Who came?"

"Strangers. Neebody knaad them. But they set us shielings on fire. Granda died. Then they killed Molly and her babby. Then's when I died."

The girls knew not what to say.

"When they come. If you don't want to die, find somewheres to hide."

Sophie looked to Isla.

"Who   is   it   that's   coming?"

CHAPTER THIRTY-ONE

"The Taliban must've pissed themselves when you appeared."

Tom Fenwick put one foot on the staircase and the darkness dissolved. He stepped back startled and darkness returned. He stood listening to the silence of the house. Nothing stirred. Taking a deep breath, he climbed the illuminated stairs as quietly as he could. He stood half a dozen steps below the next landing and waited, listening to the house. The landing was empty. With a last look behind him, Tom mounted to the landing and surveyed the two apartment doors. He approached apartment D and rang the bell. There was no response. He rang again. No one answered.

Tom knelt to begin work on the lock. He was absorbed in his task when a voice spoke behind him.
"What the hell d'y'think you're doing?"
A black woman was standing on the upper staircase. Tom stood up slowly. The woman countered by showing him the mobile phone in her hand.
"One press and I'm talking to the police."
"It's not what you think."
"You don't know what I think."

"You're either Ms Ericksen or Ms Sullivan from Apartment F. There are two children."

"I'm Keira Sullivan."

"Despite appearances, I am Tom Fenwick and I work for Madison and Major. We met briefly when your posse set me the impossible task of finding you a home. My colleague, Emily Harrison, found you Harbour Mount."

He saw the hand holding the mobile relax.

"Then what're you doing, breaking into this apartment?"

"To see if it's as empty as downstairs."

"I don't know what you mean."

"The ground floor is not two apartments. It's a meeting hall."

Keira shook her head.

"No, that's not true."

"I believe you are all are in the gravest danger."

The woman came down two stairs. "How?"

"Emily Harrison is dead. As is a friend and a colleague of mine. They have tried to kill me. I don't doubt there are many others."

"The Mafia, no doubt!"

"The Devil. You're living in the Devil's house."

"I don't believe in the Devil." "Believe me, neither did I before I met him. Take the children and get out of here."

The woman considered what he said. "If that were true, why?"

"Something diabolical is happening. Something very terrible. And it all has to do with this house."

Two photographs a hundred and twenty years apart. And a ring on a man's finger.

"Let me open this door. If there is a normal apartment."
Keira nodded.

*

Sam Ericksen sat on the studio steps, watching the surveyors wandering about the yard with sight poles and loud voices. They grumbled about the six or seven parked cars that interfered with their important work. His tongue was healing, but slowly. He was called inside to agree a price with a patron for a simple bowl. The woman said delightedly, to her husband, "If someone mistook this for a Bernard Leach, I wouldn't be surprised."
Sam gathered the words and spoke precisely as he could.
"I'd be happier if they recognised an Ericksen."
They smiled at his odd accent, agreed his price readily and Sam bubble-wrapped & boxed the bowl.

He said good-bye and turned to find Alan Winterton counting the money in the box. Holly, all but eyes hidden in an Islamic scarf, stood behind him. Sam hissed, "Wha'd'y'think you're doing?"

His tongue hurt. He was aware of other patrons browsing. The studio had become oddly fashionable.

"You'll never get rich like this, old chum. Let me help you."

Fifty-pound notes began to flow into the box, overflowing onto the bench and from the bench to the floor, a veritable waterfall.

"God's sake!"

Winterton mocked him, "Goths shake," and laughed.

The money vanished.

Holly stood silent.

"Holly?" Sam enquired.

She didn't respond. Sam turned to Winterton.

"What've you done?"

"I didn't quite catch that?"

Sam reached for Holly who stepped away, shaking her head. Winterton dragged a reluctant Holly before Sam.

"I'm sick of her talking. Yack, yack, yack! Please let me go to Sam! You're a cruel monster! You don't love me. I love Sam. Please, let me go!"

Winterton pulled away the scarf.

"I've done no more than the scold's bridle would do."

Sam struggled to believe what he saw.
"You utter bastard!"

Sam felt his possible customers melt away. He reached for Holly, but Winterton pulled her away. Sam stared at the crude stitches that sealed the swollen lips. Tears ran unhindered down Holly's face. Sam was consumed with anger.
"It's not difficult to do, old chum. A bare bodkin. Fuse wire. The screaming stops very quickly. Result silence. No more whining on about her lover man."

Sam launched himself at Winterton, but achieved nothing, but to bring Holly to her knees with Winterton's hand grasping her hair.
"Undo this barbarity!"
"Nothing I'd like better. In return, there's a minor task I need you to undertake." "Get someone else."
"No one else will do, I'm afraid. You're the chappy for the job. It's not a difficult task and my Master will be eternally grateful to you. You will be exalted among mankind."

Sam hesitated, looking down at forlorn Holly on her hands and knees. The brutal hand forced her to look up at him. He was overwhelmed by the love that looked upon him. Sam hesitated, uncertain, the grasping hand relaxed and Holly shook her head. Sam struck a distracted

Winterton with a marble rolling pin, battering him to the floor until he surrendered and vanished.

Patiently, slowly, Sam cut the wire stitches from Holly's swollen mouth. She murmured at the pain. He washed and cleaned the ravaged lips. Then Sam applied the only pain relief he knew: sipping from his Toxic Tincture. Holly struggled to speak and Sam kissed her tortured lips to silence. He struggled to frame the words clearly. "You are going to rest in the bedroom. He's not going to hurt you again. And no! Tonight, I will sleep in my chair. Understood, monkey-face?"

*

The apartment was empty. Tom Fenwick and Keira walked through the vacant rooms together, footsteps echoing.

"We were given a list of our neighbours when we moved in. All retired. I can't think of a name offhand. An oil industry executive. A doctor and his wife. Two sisters."

"Have you ever met any of your neighbours?"

Keira shook her head.

"Heard them? Voices? Music? Noise on the stairs?"

"No, it's been as silent as the."

Keira stopped. "Can we get out of here, please?"

Tom locked the door. They stood on the landing, listening to the seagulls mourning over the park.

"It's true then, isn't it?"

"Haven't you ever had an inkling that something was wrong?"

Keira nodded.

"Yes. But you ignore it. For the children."

"Do you want to see the meeting hall?"

*

Keira backed away from the ebony throne as it surged as an ocean, drowning faces of despair, appearing and vanishing.

"Oh, my God! Why us?"

Tom was silent, struggling with his own fear, trying to think of words to soften the frightful truth. He found none.

"You're here because the Devil wants you here."

"But we're just ordinary people."

"We should go up to your apartment. I think you need to sit down."

On the stairs, Keira said, "Of course! How stupid of me! Why would old people wish to live in a house with so many stairs?"

"The Devil isn't very bright. That's what gives me hope."

When they reached the apartment, Keira locked the door and went straight to the telephone.

"What're you doing?"

"Calling my partner."

"Don't!"

He took the receiver from her hand and replaced it.

"We must get you safely out of here. When would you expect your partner home?"

"Half five. Six."

"The children?"

"At school."

Tom stopped at a noise from the kitchen.

"Who's that?"

"The housekeeper."

"Does she live in?"

Keira shook her head.

"She's gone by eight."

"Everything is normal. Not a word. I'll be back when the housekeeper has gone. Then we'll get out of here. Okay?"

Keira nodded.

"Don't trust the housekeeper. These creatures won't hesitate to kill you and the children."

*

"Can I help you, sir?"

The young woman in the white overall smiled upon Sam. The ambience of the chemist's shop with its complement of sure cures he had found most comforting.

"My girlfriend has bitten her lip very badly. What would help, d'y'think?" "What do I think?" the young lady smiled, "I think you're a liar,

Sam. Your girlfriend's bitten her lip? Liar, liar, pants on fire!"

Sam found himself staring at Alan Winterton. No one else in the shop seemed to have noticed.

Sam tried to turn away, but Winterton took his arm.

"Come into the druggies' den. You look as if you need a fix."

Sam allowed himself to be taken into the airless box.

"I think I did that rather well? Young maiden leads desperate druggie into booth for his fix at the public expense?"

"You don't amuse me."

"But you admit my dear wife is your girlfriend? Oh, calamity! I am the cuckolded husband. I shall weep on my lonely pillow tonight."

"What do you want?"

"What do I want? I want us to be friends, old chum. Time is running out. I make a last appeal to you. Promise to undertake one simple task and I will never trouble you again. Scout's honour!"

Winterton gravely saluted Sam.

"Tell me what you want."

With breath-snatching speed, Sam found himself sitting with Winterton on the dome of St. Paul's. He cried out in alarm. Winterton laughed.

"I'm not very good with heights."

"You're safer with me than in a helicopter."

The Lynx began to form about Sam, but Winterton waved it away. Sam clutched at the dome and tried not to look down.

Winterton said, "My Master took your chappy up onto the highest height to show what he could have, all the kingdoms of the Earth, if only they became chums. And the ungrateful wretch said, Retro me, Satane! If I'd been behind him, I would've pushed the rotter off the highest height."

"I hate heights."

"Wonderful view, what?"

"Tell me what you want."

Sam felt the dome shift abruptly. He hadn't time to cry out.

They were sitting in a coffee house in Piccadilly. Winterton was sipping his coffee.

"Isn't it to your liking?"

"I'm waiting 'til my hands stop shaking."

No one seemed to have noticed their arrival.

"I'm putting together a little do at Windsor."

"You mean the Castle?"

Winterton ignored the question.

"We're giving the Chinese their pots back."

"I don't disagree with that."

"The President of China, Her Majesty, all the VVIPs will be there. And the television cameras.

The pieces will be on display and I want you to front for me."

Sam looked into the honest eyes and gentle smile of the creature before him. "You want me to 'front' for you?"
"I'll say a few words of welcome in Mandarin to the President. Introducing you as the famous potter you are."
Light dawned upon Sam.
"Now I understand. You need a potter."
Winterton ignored the interruption.
"Then you will tell the President how wonderful the pieces are. You will explain each piece to him."

"I don't know any Chinese."
"You will speak directly to the President. Which is a very great honour. He may give you a gift."
"He doesn't have to bother."
"Accept gratefully. You'll be on Chinese television."
"I don't want to be on television."
"There are whispers you'll be invited to visit China? An exhibition of your work?"
"I gave it to salvage."
"And I rescued it for you, ungrateful man."

Fresh coffee arrived at the table. Winterton charmed the young woman. Sam sat pondering upon Winterton's words.

"Well, old chum, I expect you're quite overwhelmed."

"I can't find anything devilish in what you've said. Tell me the worst."

"You must shoot the President of China and break every piece of porcelain. Try to avoid shooting our dear Queen."

The nightmare played out for Sam. The throne room in bloody confusion. Screaming women blind with terror. Men and women in elaborate costumes, falling over chairs in panic to escape. On the long table the Chinese porcelain was smashed to smithereens. The President of China lay dead on the floor amongst other dead and dying. Sam held Blakey's pistol. He fired again at the retreating backs. Someone cried out in pain, falling down in the doorway. Security had been overwhelmed by cowardly popinjays and hysterical women.

From the corner of his eye, Sam had seen Her Majesty rise from the throne to walk calmly from the Throne Room with her accompanying ladies and shielding security. A terrible silence fell, broken by the gathering wail of alarms. Sam took aim when one body stirred. Winterton rose from the dead and brushed himself down.

"Capital show, old chum! The Taliban must've pissed themselves when you appeared. You're a top murdering bastard!"

Sam put the pistol to his head and pulled the trigger. The magazine was empty.

The Throne Room shivered and the coffee house returned. Sam sat silent, struggling to come to terms with what he had witnessed.

Winterton asked, "Would you like a Danish pastry? I understand they're a speciality here."

"You don't smash the original Chinese porcelain. You destroy my copies." "Bright boy! That would be an act of sheer vandalism."

"Then what?"

"You have murdered the President of China. You have destroyed their precious porcelain. You have started World War Three. Congratulations!"

CHAPTER THIRTY-TWO

"We're going to mix with the common people."

Hannah had just returned to her office, after supervising the transfer of the last cash stored in the Pilgrim Street vault. She had signed the papers with a flourish.

"I won't hide my relief at seeing this money go, Oliver. I've always been uneasy about it being here."

Oliver laughed.

"And here you see it leave, Hannah, surrounded by burly security men. Nary a penny short!"

"Not a penny short, Oliver!"

She sat down in her chair and read the release document again. Oliver had taught her to read all documents twice. The second time to find the errors & omissions. It was impeccable. Sullivan & Ericksen held no further responsibility for the listed valuables & documents given into the custody of representatives of the Northern Counties Bank. The telephone rang and Hannah placed the release documents in her out tray.

She picked up the receiver.

"Katherine? What a wonderful surprise! How is the city surviving without me?" She heard Katherine Lucas laugh; once familiar when they sat at screens together in the august offices of Prentiss & Poplar.

"You sound happy, Hannah."

"I am. Newcastle is wonderful. Here's where you should be."

"How's Isla?"

"She's fine. Loves it here. An Aranport brat."

"And that great hulking brother of yours?"

"Sam? As badly behaved as ever. Didn't you once have a thing about him?" "Dennis is more tameable. Useful to take me places. He always knows somebody."

"Katherine, you didn't ring me just to check on my health."

"There's a whisper Northern Counties are in trouble."

"Today I signed off three million plus. Does that sound like trouble?"

The call ended with a flurry of promises that would never be kept.

Hannah rang Oliver De'ath, but he couldn't be reached. Friday. It could wait until Monday.

*

The familiar walls of the studio rose around Sam Ericksen and Alan Winterton. Sam, struck by vertigo, grabbed the edge of the bench to stop himself falling. Winterton was perched mockingly on a stool, sipping coffee.

"A due reminder. You're no Spring chicken, old chum."

"And when I blow up the world, what then?"

"Fear not! You and everyone you care about will be perfectly safe. You will be a hero and Our Lord will take you to His bosom. You will be honoured among the nations."

"Do I get a medal?"

"You can have anything your heart desires."

"In all seriousness, how d'y'propose to persuade me to carry out this atrocity?"

Before Sam could take a breath they stood by the bed where Holly lay sleeping peacefully.

"This simple child loves you, old chum. She has never met kindness before, only trickery. Whatever I do, the silly creature gladly suffers any torment to save you harm. Have you never questioned why you still have two eyes?"

Winterton smiled at Sam.

"You've never given it a thought, have you?"

Sam shook his head.

"Men are naturally selfish, I suppose."

Winterton patted Sam on the shoulder consolingly.

"This innocent will gladly die for you. She would think the price well paid. Wouldn't you undertake a simple task for me to save her?"

Sam could find no answer.

"For example, I could whistle up a couple of Komodo dragons."

A startled Sam leapt back from the bed as the creatures appeared, crowding the room.

"On a word from me, they will attack the poor girl, dragging her intestines to the floor while she screams loud enough to break our ear drums."

The dragons waited, watching Winterton.

"Don't do this."

"Why not? You won't help me."

Sam drew his pistol and fired at the restless beasts. The pistol said click, click and the dragons turned their heads to Sam.

Winterton laughed.

"You didn't reload after killing the President."

"That was fantasy."

"This is fantasy."

The dragons vanished and Holly slept undisturbed.

"You need a drink, old chum."

Sam sat in his thinking chair and Winterton offered him his Toxic Tincture. He took it gladly and drank heavily.

"I'm going to leave you now, Samu-el."

"Don't hurry back."

"There will be someone who means so much to you that you will obey me. I will find him or her. But time is running out for us both."

Winterton smiled and closed the studio door behind him.

*

The security lights illuminated the frontage of
Harbour Mount, but nothing could dispel the
baleful presence of the house. Tom Fenwick ate
fish and chips on a park bench watching the
gates. In the gathering darkness, he was startled
when someone spoke to him. The constable was
middle-aged with grey showing beneath his cap.
He shone his torch into Tom's face.

"What you doing here?"
"Could you shine that torch somewhere else?"
The torch was lowered, but remained on Tom.
"Having my supper."
"Where'd yi get it?"
"Ocean Road.""
Then you walked all the way up here to eat?"
"I like watching the sea."
"In the time I've been here, yi haven't looked
once."
The torch rose to study Tom's face.
"Is it illegal to sit here and eat my supper?"
"Not unless you drop litter."
"Then I'd like you to leave me in peace, please."
The torch was lowered.

"One last thing, sir."
"Yes?"
"Despite you being dressed for a part in Train
Spotters."

Tom interrupted, saying, "How I dress is my business!"

"Can I confirm you are Thomas Fenwick, estate agent, Madison and Major?" "Yes, I am, but what's that to you?"

"Just checking. We've made too many mistakes recently."

As Tom grasped his meaning, the wire noose settled around his neck. His killer braced a boot against the bench to tighten the wire, cutting off both breath and speech. His supper fell to the ground, spilling chips and fish fragments. Tom Fenwick died, trying fruitlessly to loosen the wire about his neck.

"We could've had him for littering."

The older constable went through Tom's pockets. The bank notes he split roughly into two halves and handed one to his colleague.

"Unexpected bonus, Mickey!"

He opened the locksmith's pack.

"Just what I wanted for Christmas."

The two policemen walked the drunken man to his car, chatting cheerfully with him. No one noticed his dragging toe caps. They drove his car into the park, set the corpse in the driving seat, tuned the radio to Magic, started the engine and set fire to the car. They waited patiently until the car was nigh consumed before they rang it in.

*

Sam checked the pistol. It contained a full magazine and a cartridge in the breach. Taking the First Aid box, he went to the bedroom and gently shook Holly awake. She awoke startled and he shushed her to silence. He washed her swollen mouth.

"Listen to me, Holly. It's important."

She nodded obediently.

"It's not safe here. We have to leave."

Holly stirred to rise.

"But you cannot go anywhere in that dress. Play the tom boy again."

Holly nodded.

"I'll be waiting for you."

Sam retired to the studio and found a warm gansey to fit under his windcheater and laid out a duffel coat for Holly. He raided his piggy bank. Holly appeared to ask silently how she looked. Sam raised eyes to Heaven.

"My God, but you're a heart-breaker!"

Holly laughed and her mouth cried out. Sam offered the duffel coat. Obediently, Holly slipped it on. Sam fastened the toggles.

"What are these things?"

"They're called toggles."

"I don't like them."

Sam pulled up the hood.

"We're going to walk some distance before we take a cab. Safer. Okay?"

Holly took his hand.

Sam kissed her hand, saying, "Ah, mais oui, nous sommes Jules et Jim!"

Holly looked puzzled. Sam turned out the lights in the studio.

They slipped out and Sam locked the door. They stood in darkness on the wet gravel. The nearest lights were on the main road.

"Haven't you ever seen the film? Jules et Jim? Non? We are Jules et Jim! You can be Jules or Jim. Whichever you wish."

Sam quietly opened the gate and re-locked it. A car swept by. They stood in the shadow of the unkempt shrubbery until he was sure there was no one in sight. "Forgive me. It will be necessary."

Sam placed an arm about Holly's shoulders and began to walk.

"We are a courting couple. I am returning you to your father's care unsullied. So we walk in this weird fashion."

Holly chuckled.

"I didn't know girls chuckled. What a delightful sound!"

Holly pressed into him closely and when Sam looked down upon her he saw, to his surprise, she was happy.

"We're going to walk as far as we can before taking a cab. We are disappearing, Jules! Vanishing with your faithful Jim! And I will tell you the story of the film as we walk."

Sam narrated the story as they walked. Whatever he couldn't remember he invented. When she stumbled, he realised she was almost asleep. Sam picked up Holly and carried her. He waved off the first cab. The second cab was parked. He walked past, despite the invitation. He accepted the third cab that drove past and then stopped to wait for Sam to approach.
"You need a cab, guvnor."
"Kind of you! She's all in, poor kid."

*

Keira waited in the hallway for Hannah's return. She pretended to be sketching the Victorian tiling. On another page, Keira had written a précis of all that Tom Fenwick had told her. She had added reminders of Ronald Whitley and photographs of a man a hundred and twenty years old. Her notes explained that Tom Fenwick would return after Phoebe had departed and they would leave the house. Her heart was beating hard enough to break her ribs as she heard Hannah's key in the lock. Hannah was surprised to find Keira in the hallway. They embraced and kissed.

Keira whispered, "Play along with me."

"I've been considering the tiles."

"Oh, yes?"

"They could be very valuable. I've made some notes. Please read them." Keira's eyes were insistent. Hannah read the notes steadily as Keira struggled not to interrupt. She saw Hannah's hand shaking as she read.

"You're sure?"

Keira noticed that Phoebe had joined them in the hallway.

"Good evening, Missis Ericksen."

"Good evening, Phoebe. You've come to tell us supper is burning?"

Phoebe laughed.

"Thought I heard voices, so I come to see. Can't help being nosy."

Keira explained, "We're discussing the tiles."

"Oh, aye?"

"Some of the old tiles are worth a load of money."

"That so?"

"Depends who made ours."

Phoebe offered, "Supper will be served when you're ready, ladies," and vanished.

"D'y'think she was fooled?"

"I hope so. I was trying not to pee myself."

*

The cab dropped Sam and Holly at Victoria Coach Station. Sam was relieved to find the station so busy. Holly was confused by the bustling crowds.

"Have I been to this airport before? I don't recognise it."

In the Babel of noise, Sam drew her off to a quieter bench.

"This isn't an airport, Holly."

"Then why isn't there someone to meet us? Travelling by train, we normally have a private carriage."

Sam smiled and kissed her on the forehead.

"Holly, I want you to be very brave."

"You're going to leave me, aren't you?"

The child pleaded, clutching at his hands.

"Never. But we're going to mix with the common people."

"You're making fun of me! Common people!"

She laughed aloud.

"This is a coach station. We're going to get on a bus with thirty or more common people. And we're going to travel with them until tomorrow morning." "I've seen buses, but I've never been on one. It sounds exciting."

"It's not. It's boring. Sometimes smelly. But this is how we escape your husband's attention."

"Then, let's get on the bus, please."

"You mustn't say a word. Don't speak to anyone. I'll be sitting beside you. Do you need to go to the toilet?"

Holly shook her head.

"Sit here while I buy our tickets."

Holly clutched his arm.

"You won't leave me, will you?"

Sam reassured her.

"Do you see that man over there? He's buying tickets from the machine. I'm going to buy our tickets from that machine."

"Do you have to?"

"You'll be able to see me all the time. If anything worries you, shout!"

Sam kissed her brow and Holly smiled. This seemed to reassure her. Sam went to the machine and bought the tickets. Walking back towards Holly, he saw her relax.

She expects to be made use of and tricked. Abandoned. That's what life has taught her.

They found Stand Fourteen and joined the queue. Holly clung to Sam and he wrapped an arm about her. Coaches came and went. To Sam's relief, the queue began to shuffle forward. Being without luggage was an advantage. Holly obediently followed Sam to the mid-rear of the coach where they settled into their seats.

"Where are we going, Sam?"

"Newcastle."

"Is it nice?"

"It's a long way from London."

As the coach filled, Sam said, "This not how I want it to be for us."

The sweet face hidden in the hood agreed.

"This is a field of stones. Not a meadow."

"But we will cross the field, Sam?"

He kissed her brow.

"There's an old riddle."

"I love riddles."

"This girl says to her uncertain lover. Imagine we live in a field of stones. Would you still love me?"

"I would love you more dearly."

"And the girl says, 'Wrong answer."

"I don't understand."

Sam kissed Holly on the mouth.

Holly was asleep, snuggled up to Sam, before they reached the motorway.

CHAPTER THIRTY-THREE

"He can't imagine loving someone."

When supper was finished, the girls rose to go to the sitting room to watch television when Hannah stopped them.

"I want you to go to your room, girls, please."

"But we were going to watch."

"Go to your room, please. Keira and I have some serious talking to do."

"Is something wrong?"

"Are you upset with each other?"

"Is it something we've done?"

Keira laughed and Hannah answered, "Never! We're too old for spits and spats."

"We just need to talk."

"We'll come and get you when we're done."

"And tell us what you're talking about?"

"Yes. Now go!"

Skinny Lizzie standing at the rainy window silenced their wondering.

"Come, see!"

They joined Lizzie at the window to stare into the darkness.

"Can yi stop the lights?"

Darkness blinded them. The lighthouses, North & South, blinked rhythmically green and red through the wind-driven rain.

"What're we looking at?"
"Ayont the sea walls. Watch the lights."

Green and red flashes completed their circuit and began again.
"I can't see anything."
"Cobles is lying off. Waiting."
Isla said, "I can't see anything. Can you, Sophie?"
"Whether yi see, don't matter. All will be as shud be."
"How'd'y'know?"

The child's body was suddenly consumed by light too brilliant for sight, growing until the radiance filled the room. Great white wings encompassed the children and they were filled with an enduring comfort driving out all doubt and fear. Then the darkness returned and Skinny Lizzie stood before them, dirty feet and dirty hair.
"I just knaa."

*

"I don't want to believe."
Keira twisted on the sofa to watch Hannah's restless pacing.
"What Fenwick said makes sense. Everything was made too easy for us. The offices. The amount of business provided by Oliver. Who might be older than Methuselah."

441

Hannah wished to interrupt, but didn't.

"They've killed Emily Harrison. She was a pest, but perhaps she meant to warn us? Fenwick said her job was to make sure the right people moved into the apartment. Us! Remember Ronald Whitley and the Vicar? The Vicar and the girls? The same creature tried to kill Fenwick."

"I don't want to believe."

"Believe me, Hannah, no one else is living in this house. The apartments are a sham. The ground floor is a meeting hall, laid out with chairs. There are two butcher blocks. Worse is a black throne. Hannah, this is a house of devils." Hannah came to sit beside Keira.

"I have to stop believing in everything I know."

"I attended a Catholic High School in L.A. Perhaps it's easier for me. We're here because the Devil brought us here. From what Fenwick said, people have been murdered to ensure we are here. Why I don't know. And I would hesitate to ask."

Hannah made up her mind.

"Then we must get the children out of here. But we don't wait for Fenwick. We go now."

"What do we say?"

Hannah guessed, "Special treat. Boldon Cinerama?"

"We take nothing with us. We go and we don't come back?"

"What about Phoebe?"

"We're taking the girls to the cinema."

Someone tapped at the door.

Hannah called, "Come in!"

Phoebe entered carrying a tray with two cups of coffee.

"Yous were all in a rush from the table tonight. Were supper that bad?"

The partners essayed a laugh.

"Supper was perfect, Phoebe. It's just we're taking the girls to the Cinerama as a treat."

"That would be nice, if 'twere true."

"What did you say, Phoebe?"

Phoebe sat down in a chair.

"When I come first, I were happy enough to be paid a bit extra for keeping an eye on yous for Mister De'ath. Didn't see no harm in it. But I've grown fond of the lasses and I knows you're good people."

"You're part of the family, Phoebe. The girls worship you."

"Well, I tell you somethin in this house is wrong."

*

Hannah, Keira, Phoebe and the girls walked quietly down to the front door. When the trio had walked in on Isla and Sophie, the girls had chorused, "You don't have to tell us. We've just seen an angel!"

Hannah turned the Yale knob, but the door didn't open.

"Sorry. Nerves."

She made to unlock the dead lock, but it was free.

Again the Yale failed to yield.

"Let iss have a go?" Phoebe suggested.

Even at risk of breaking the key, the door wouldn't open. In the silence of the hallway the adults tried not to convey anxiety.

Sophie said, "We're locked in."

"The kitchen door?"

Once they were into the apartment, Hannah said, "Let's not scare ourselves." They walked through the apartment following Phoebe. Sophie held Isla's hand tightly. At the kitchen door they stopped. Phoebe looked to Hannah who nodded. Phoebe turned the handle and the door opened to a scattering of starlings and a nocturnal view of Aranport. Everyone gave a sigh of relief. "There y'are!" rejoiced Phoebe.

She stepped out onto the steel platform of the fire escape. Smiling, she held out a hand to Sophie who hesitated.

"You're safe with me, pet!"

Sophie stepped onto the steel framework and the fire escape fell away from the House.

Sophie screamed and Phoebe threw the girl back into the kitchen. As the steelwork fell, Phoebe didn't cry out. There was a metallic clatter and then silence. Hannah locked the door on the abyss. The girls began to weep.

Tom Fenwick never came to lead them to safety. They slept four in the one bed for comfort.

*

Holly and Sam stepped uncertainly into a grey morning from the dismal coach station. They stood on the pavement, drained of energy, as other passengers vanished into their private lives.
"Where are we?"
"Aranport. My sister lives here."
"Are we going to meet her?"
"Soon."
This seemed to satisfy Holly.

"I'm hungry."
"Snap!"
"Snap what?"
"You didn't play card games with your Grandmother, did you?"
"Billie taught me to play poker."
"She was Norwegian and won every game of Snap."
Holly smiled and said, "Snap!"
She pointed at the McDonald's sign at the street corner.

There were only two teenagers and an old man in the restaurant. Sam sought a table from where he could watch the door. Most of Holly's burger and fries vanished before Sam unwrapped his. He was watching the old man. He discounted the teenagers, boy & girl. They were far too interested in each other to be aware of the fugitives. The old man was eating a packet of fries very slowly. Holly had finished her food and was watching Sam eat.

"You eat very. Delicately."
"Cautiously. I expect to find something nasty."
"That old man is watching us, Sam."
"Would you like anything else?"
"The same again, please."
"You're joking?"
"I told you I was hungry."

When he returned with a second tray of burger and fries, Sam complained, "You'll get fat."
"No, I won't."
"You will, if you keep eating junk food."
"Then you must buy me better."
"I can't afford better."
"Then I will find someone who will."
Holly looked into Sam's face and cried, "No, I won't. A joke to make you laugh. I wish I never said that. I love you. More than anyone ever. It was a joke. I'll love you forever."

446

Without thought, Sam said, "I don't know I'd want to live without you, Holly. And I shouldn't have said that."

For a moment they weren't within peril of their souls, but teenagers in a burger bar with only eyes for each other. Sam watched Holly eat her second helping of burger and fries while the old man pretended to eat fries from an empty packet.
"Why is he spying on us?"
"Winterton knows by now we aren't at the studio. Where would we go? To my sister? Perhaps. We don't have a car. Train? Coach? Not by air. He knows I don't like flying."
"But he is the Devil."
"He's not all powerful. He's very good at causing fear, pain, torment. But he can't imagine dying to save someone. He can't imagine loving someone."
Sam stopped, overwhelmed by Holly's eyes.

"So, an old man is watching us and soon he'll tell Winterton where we are." "Then you must stop him."
"We're both going to the toilet now."
"We are?"
"Soon the old man will start worrying about us. Have we climbed through a window? When you hear him go into the gents, walk to the newsstand in the coach station. Don't hurry. Wait there for me."

447

By Sam's watch it was nine minutes, before the old man decided to investigate. He was almost on hands and knees looking under the second toilet door when Sam stepped out of the third cubicle and kicked him in the face. He dragged him into the cubicle. When he broke the old man's neck, the creature began to crumble into fragments and dust. He had been dead centuries. Sam fed the mess into the toilet bowl and flushed the old man away. He rescued the mobile, broke it and dropped it into the floor drain. The clothes, he stuffed into a waste bin.

At the newsstand, a solitary figure in an old duffle coat came to life and waved frantically.
"Why were you waving?"
"So you could see me."
"Holly, we're trying to pass unnoticed. Waving wildly isn't the way to do it." "Sorry, Sam. I won't do it again."
"God, when you look at me like that, I could forgive you anything!"
"That's why I do it."

*

There was very little conversation at the breakfast table. Hannah had made breakfast. The girls were quiet, lacking appetite. Sophie asked, "What's going to happen today?"
"Let's wait and see, shall we?"

Hannah added, "We're together. Whatever happens, nobody's going to hurt you. I promise."

"Who's going to stop them?"

"We will!" came the determined answer.

When the intercom buzzed, they all jumped. Keira said, "Go to your room, girls, please!"

"Who d'y'think it is?"

"There's only one way to find out."

Hannah pressed the button.

"Yes?"

"It's Oliver. May I come up?"

They waited in the hallway. The bell rang and Hannah opened the door. A smiling Oliver De'ath stood before them, bald head shining as a peeled onion. "Good morning, Hannah, Keira!"

When they hesitated, Oliver asked, "May I come in?"

They stood in the hallway.

Oliver smiled, saying, "Shall we withdraw to the sitting room?"

He waited until the partners were seated before he began.

"Tomorrow is a very important occasion for our association. Miss Ross and the Gilbeys have generously offered their apartments for the ceremony."

"Then we'll meet them at last?"

"I'm afraid not. Too old for such excitement. We've booked them into Dormey's for the week."
"How kind!"

"The 'top brass' has been somewhat demanding on security. The house is presently in lock-down. I believe that is the current phrase?"
"Why?"
"Tomorrow we inaugurate a new President of our association."
"Which is?"
"Known simply as The Congregation. Something like the Masons. A private association devoted to human welfare. We don't seek publicity."

The cat jumped down from the windowsill distracting Oliver De'ath. He crossed the floor to jump up into Hannah's lap.
"We have been most impressed by your progress and tomorrow, you will be invited to join our Congregation. I assure you, it is a most sought after honour." Keira said, "We both feel most honoured."
The irony was wasted.
"So you see, everything is subject to security. There are those who would wish to impede our progress."
"And poor Phoebe McCallaghan?"

"A lamentable tragedy. Her family are our principal concern. We shall see they want for nothing. The fire escape will be replaced."

"Changing the subject? How are the girls?"
"They're very upset. Phoebe saved Sophie's life. Pushing her back into the kitchen when the fire escape fell."
"A most remarkable woman! Is there anything you need? Groceries? Videos?" "No, thank you."
"Then I shall leave you in peace. We shall meet tomorrow, as I leave you, in trust and friendship."
He smiled upon Hannah. They shook Oliver's cold hand and endured his empty smile. When the apartment door closed, they shuddered: then embarrassed, they laughed and embraced.
"I'm so glad we found each other."

*

Keira was lost in the big sofa when Hannah entered the sitting room. She hesitated to say, "Would you like me to leave you in peace?"
"No. I was just thinking about this."
She raised a familiar photograph frame. Hannah joined Keira on the sofa.
"Aren't you becoming a little obsessive?"
"We've been looking at the wrong person."
Keira gave the frame to Hannah.

451

"Look at the three girls. Recognise anyone?"
Hannah studied the photograph.
"The girl in the middle looks somewhat like me?"
"A younger you. Who is she looking at?"
"Oh, yes! I see! Oliver! And he's looking at her! How remarkable!"
"I believe before Oliver De'ath became whatever he is now, he was a perfectly decent young man."

CHAPTER THIRTY-FOUR

"What's in soldier sandwiches?"

"Why don't we ask someone where Harbour Mount is? When I ask, they always take me where I want to go."
The angel eyes looked upon him reprovingly. Sam tried not to laugh.
"Holly, what's most important right now?"
"Getting out of this coat. It's beastly."
"Noooo! We're trying to stay clear of your husband. If we start asking for directions."
"I absolutely hate it. I am trapped by these tiggles."
"Toggles."
"Whatever."

Sam realised Holly wasn't listening.
"You don't believe anything nasty can happen to us, do you?"
"Not while you're with me."
They were standing at the crossroads of Aranport's principal streets awakening to a busy Saturday's trading.
"I know they can look out of the windows at the sea. I know it's a big house on a hill overlooking the harbour."
"Why don't we take the bus?"

Holly pointed to where a bus displaying MOUNT ROAD had drawn in across the street. As they crossed to join the short queue, Holly held Sam's hand. "We're like real people. We ride on coaches and buses now."

*

There were seven cars outside the row of garages. Standing on the gravel drive of Harbour Mount were a black Bentley and an old people carrier.

Sam said, "The green car is Hannah's."

They were watching from the park. They had stayed on the bus and walked back from River Drive. On first sight Holly had rejoiced.

"That is a wonderful house! You didn't tell me your sister was rich."

"She's not. She has an apartment on the third floor."

Holly hugged Sam's arm.

"But I would live in a stable with you."

"How about a studio with a tin roof?"

"A stable would be better. We could keep a donkey. The children could ride the donkey. Or, perhaps, you would make the children a little cart?"

A man came out of the front door. His bald head shone in the morning sun. A man emerged from the rear door of the Bentley. He held the door open for the bald-headed man. Then he went to the people carrier and climbed into the driver's seat. The limousine moved towards the gates. The people carrier followed. The gates opened automatically. When the cars passed through, the gates closed again.

"He stole your sister's car!"
Sam was silent in thought.
"It was her car, wasn't it?"
"Winterton's latched onto Hannah."
"Then we should go now."
Sam looked at the innocent face, buried in the duffel hood.
"I can't leave my sister. You should go. Somewhere he wouldn't expect you to be?"
Holly shook her head.
"I'll never leave you."
"I'd be with you once this is over. I promise."
"I can't leave you, Sam."
"Why not?"
"I can't open these toggles."
"Will you never take anything seriously?"
"Why should I? No one takes me seriously."

*

When the intercom buzzed, they stood frozen. In a calm tone, Hannah said, "A little early for Father Christmas." The girls tried to laugh.
Keira offered, "If it's the Mormons, invite them up."
The girls weren't sure who the Mormons were.

"Yes?"

"It's me!"

"Who's me?"

"Great steaming puddens, Hannah! It's me! Sam!"

The girls danced with delight. Keira felt a great sense of relief and almost joined the dance. Hannah shushed them to silence.

"Where were you born?"

"What?"

"Where were you born?"

"Cinema car park. Ullevalseter. Norway."

"Come up."

"Our mother was mad for Michael Douglas. She wanted to see the end of Coma. Sam was lucky not to be born in the cinema."

The girls laughed, forgetting for a moment.

In a tense hallway, they heard feet and voices. Hannah put an eye to the spy hole.

"Who's that with you?"

"A friend."

A female voice said something inaudible. Hannah opened the door. She fell into her brother's arms.

"Oh, my God, am I glad to see you, Sam!"

The girls flung themselves at him. Holly pulled off her hood and looked to Keira. They smiled uncertainly.

"I'm Keira. Sophie's mother?"

"I'm Holly. Nobody's mother."

She called out in surprise when That Cat entwined himself about her ankles. "Oh, you have a cat?"

Holly bent down and gathered the cat to herself. When she looked at him, she was shocked.

"Look, Sam, it's."

But no one was listening.

When Sam was freed, he struggled to introduce Holly.

"This is Holly. Alan Winterton's wife."

He was interrupted by Holly.

"Alan is the Devil. Sam rescued me. And I love him more than anyone in the whole world. We're going to live in his tin hut. We'll have a donkey for the children. Sam will make them a cart."

Sam turned to Keira, apologising.

"I can explain. This isn't what it seems. I'm escorting Holly because Winterton will kill her."

Keira was regarding Sam with wry amusement.

Hannah said, "Don't you know Keira and I are an item?"

"An item? You mean?"

Sam hoped the floor would open to swallow him up. The floor refused to assist.

Hannah apologised.

"I'm sorry I just assumed."

"That I wasn't as stupid as I appeared."

Keira said, "I'm sorry, Sam. Of the men we've known, you're the best."

Isla declared, "We're a family, Sam. You too. You're our uncle."

"Sisters with two mothers and the best uncle in the world. Isn't it wonderful?" Holly asked, "Does anyone know how to undo toggles?"

*

Hannah had brought Sam up to date when Keira and Holly returned with the girls.

"Isn't she beautiful?" Sophie demanded.

Holly was dressed in a simple black teeshirt and trousers. Her hair shone as pale gold.

"I'm really, very, very jealous. Whatever I do with my hair, doesn't work," Hannah admitted.

Keira said, "Teeshirt and trousers? And who remembers Marilyn Monroe? You are totally gorgeous, Holly!"

"Thank you."

To stir in a little mischief, Keira added, "Captain Birdseye, is fortunate to be 'escorting' you. Wha'd'y'say, Cap'n?"

"She looks very nice."

The girls laughed at Sam who was suitably embarrassed.

Isla offered, "Look what Holly gave me, Mum!"

She displayed a chain about her neck carrying a silver cross.

"How very kind!"

"She gave me this," commented Sophie.

To the admiring adults, she displayed a bracelet above her elbow, carrying a gold cross.

"Are you sure, Holly?" Keira asked.

"If it may help, why not?"

"But what about you?"

Holly shrugged.

Sam said, "Hannah says tomorrow, they elect the next top devil. And we're invited to the party."

Holly was looking at him with such love and trust. *We're all going to die and she looks at me with utter belief that I can save us.*

He was suddenly frozen with shock when he looked at the cat nestled in Holly's lap.

"Wha'd'y'call your cat?"

Hannah apologised, saying, "He hasn't really got a name. He just turned up." "His name is Glaze," Holly assured them, "We've met before."

For no reason, Sam felt light of heart.

"Glaze?" Sophie questioned.

"He's a potter's cat," Sam explained.

*

"I have two phosphorus grenades. Very nasty things. If I use them, you may be blinded momentarily. They burn ferociously down to the bone. If I use them, seize the moment and get the girls out."

Hannah and Keira nodded agreement.

"These creatures are not all powerful. They've become flabby and careless. They are vulnerable. Particularly to flame."

"What're we going to do?" Isla asked uncertainly.

"Have we any board games?"

They settled to play Monopoly, another game Holly had never played before. Sam was bankrupted and Holly won the game. The girls were hungry and they retired to the kitchen where Sam offered to make soldier sandwiches. Holly begged to be allowed to butter bread. She had never done so before. The girls found this odd, but Sophie taught her how not to overdo it. Hannah filled a big jug with orange squash.

"What's in soldier sandwiches?"

With his head in the refrigerator, Sam announced, "Soldier sandwiches are made of anything to hand. Worms, love letters, hair clippings, lizards, old boots." Which was greeted with horror.

"Rubber bands, leaves, caterpillars, old cake, floor polish, dogs."

Keira interrupted. "Dogs?"

"Hot dogs. Americans always have cans of hot dogs. And in the last resort, beetles, Christmas cards, bottle tops, socks and sand."

"Sand?"

"Have you never heard of a sandwich?"

The girls fed Glaze while the adults created a pile of sandwiches.

"Dig in!"

They began to eat. As silence fell, the shadows drew in.

Holly said, "Tell them a story, Sam. He tells such stories, it is hard not to believe them."

Isla, puzzled, asked. "Wha'd'y'mean? Hard not to believe?"

"She's means he's a natural-born liar," Hannah responded.

Sam looked hurt.

"Not too grisly," Hannah warned.

"A true story," begged Sophie, the cat in her lap.

"One day we were sitting in the big canvas cafeteria, the team and our operational boss, Blakey. We were committed that night and we'd finished briefing."

As he talked Sam saw them gather around to listen, all the familiar faces, Blakey, Geordie, Newbie, Gobber, Salim, Frog, Tipper and Taff. Geordie had the most infectious grin Sam had ever known. He would have them all smiling at a funeral. The sandwich-chewing faces were riveted upon the hairy historian.

"We were pretty scruff, beards, scarves, woolly hats, brown as over-baked buns."

Holly said, "We said a true story! I've been to Buck House, Gatcombe Park, heaps of places. The soldiers are always totally dishy!"
Sam smiled, "Chocolate soldiers."

"We had to pass among our enemy. Blakey, as ever, was the most unsoldierly. Dressed like an Afghan toilet cleaner on a bad Monday morning."
The girls spluttered sandwiches.
"In the army when you eat, an officer comes to the table and says, 'Any complaints?' To which the senior man will stand up to say, 'No complaints, sir.'"
"You never complain?"
"It's wiser not to."
The team agreed.
"This major we'd never seen before, a chocolate soldier, totally dishy." Everyone laughed and Holly punched Sam.

"This major comes to our table. We were laughing at something Gobber had said. Officers never get to share with squaddies and they hate that."
Gobber nodded agreement.
"I was ready to recite no complaints, sir, but instead, he tore into Blakey."
The team shot to attention.
"The state of him, deplorable. When did he wash last? No soap and water? Accept a certain laxity

of dress in a combat zone. But a Mickey Mouse teeshirt! Beyond any reasonable laxity. An absolute disgrace. Fifteen minutes, my office! I want to see a soldier. Not a button out of place.' Off he pranced."

Sam picked a sandwich and chewed steadily. He wanted to say Blakey died in that teeshirt, but he didn't. His audience was impatient.
"Well?"
"We have to wait while Blakey changes."
"No, we don't!"
"We accompanied Blakey to the office of Major Bumptious. Blakey taps and a voice commands, Come!"
Sam took a further bite from the sandwich.

"You're just doing that to annoy us!"
Sam finished his sandwich, shook off any lingering crumbs from his beard and continued. "We heard the Major start off and then it went quiet. It was alarming. Geordie banged on the door saying, 'Yi hasn't killed him, has yi, ya mad bastard?'"
Hannah moved the sandwich plate away from her brother.
"Get on with it, Sam! Without the bad language!"

"The door opened and Blakey led the Major out. The Major wasn't the man he'd been at the table.

He was totally cringing. Blakey was in full dress uniform as Colonel, U.S. Special Forces. His medals were blinding."

The girls clapped wildly. Holly hugged Sam. Hannah and Keira were most impressed.

"Are you going to let me finish?"

A delighted silence fell.

"Blakey said, 'Major, I want to introduce you to some real soldiers.'"

He announced our names and ranks. We came to attention and saluted the Major.

"These are the men, Major, who go out into darkness, dawn or dusk and fight our battles for us. When you prepare for bed tonight, they'll be jumping down from a helicopter. In the nastiest place our Command can find for us. We'll do our job and hopefully all come home. Would you like to ride along with us, Major?"

"What did he say?"

"He looked as if he was going to blub. Then he ran into the office and shut the door."

"What did you do?"

"We laughed."

As Team Red Fox faded away, Sam saw the last to leave was Blakey who saluted him.

"Is it a true story?" Sophie asked, with the cat nestled in her lap.

"Would I tell you lies?"

Glaze reassured Sophie, perhaps this time he was telling the truth.

They returned to the sitting room and played Monopoly. Sophie won the first game and Isla the second. Sam was bankrupted in both games.

"Take warning, Holly. He's absolutely useless with money."

"I will be in charge. He sells his lovely pots for pennies. I will stop that."

"He gives them to us," chorused the girls.

Sam offered, "Why don't we have a video?"

Solaced by the softest sofas, they watched the girls' favourite film, *Pete's Dragon,* which they insisted on replaying. Sam thought he heard a noise from the kitchen. Looking to Hannah he saw she too had heard something. They rose to investigate, leaving Keira and Holly singing along with the girls. There were voices in the kitchen. Sam opened the door to find Lucy on hands and knees clearing a broken baking dish, supervised by Phoebe. Sam heard Hannah cry out and seized her hand.

"Now ya done it, Lucy! Yous gone and disturbed Missis Ericksen! Me apologies! Swear this lass has butter fingers!"

Sam couldn't stop Hannah asking, "What're you doing here, Phoebe?"

The housekeeper looked confused.

"Cooking supper. Won't yis be eating?"

Sam intervened to say, "Of course, we are! I should introduce myself. I'm Missis Ericksen's brother, Sam."

Phoebe wiped a strong hand on her apron to shake Sam's hand.

"By, yarra big un! I can see the likeness. 'Part from the beard, that is. But that's all the fashion now."

"So there'll be two extra for supper tonight, Phoebe. Sam and his girlfriend, Holly."

"That don't faze iss. Unless we runs out of dishes with Lucy breaking up the happy home."

Lucy had retired to the bin with the broken glassware.

"Ya cannot just tip it in the bin, lass. Gerra carrier bag. Bin man won't thank yi if he gets a nasty cut."

"I'm sure she didn't mean it," Sam offered, smiling at the sulky teenager.

Hannah said, "How did you come in, Phoebe?"

"Come up the back as usual."

She nodded towards the kitchen door. Sam hastened to offer, "We'll leave you in peace, Missis McCallaghan. I've heard a lot about your cooking. I look forward to supper."

Phoebe fluttered with pleasure and they withdrew.

Sam stopped Hannah opening the sitting room door.

"You've been very brave, kiddo, but you're in shock. You cannot just waltz in and say a dead woman is making supper for us."

"She is dead. There are no back stairs. I saw the fire escape fall away. Almost taking Sophie with Phoebe."

"Let me do the talking."

Hannah nodded. Sam opened the door.

*

Sam halted the video and the girls looked expectantly at him.

"I need you to be very grown up. Okay?"

The girls nodded agreement. Hannah sat down with Keira and Holly.

"Phoebe and Lucy are in the kitchen making supper."

Sam waited for the reaction.

Keira cried, "No!"

Hannah put an arm about her.

Sophie said slowly, "But Phoebe's dead."

"These evil creatures have brought her back to frighten us. But we mustn't let them."

Isla declared, "I don't want to eat anything cooked by a dead person."

Sophie said, "Phoebe saved my life!"

"The poor woman doesn't know she's dead. She's the same kindly Phoebe you know. She's warm and friendly as ever. She doesn't know what a wicked thing they've done to her. Please, help Phoebe and help us."

The children were silent.

"Let us remember the Phoebe whose last thought was to save Sophie. We owe it to her to show these evil creatures we're not easily frightened."

The silence was too long.

Sam crouched before the girls, taking a hand from each.

"The enemy does this all the time to our soldiers. In the darkest night, the enemy prowls, making noises. Silence is even more frightening. Squaddies are alone in the darkness. But we're together, as you said, a family. Are we going to let them scare us? Or enjoy a little extra time with Phoebe who was very fond of you?"

Holly couldn't contain herself.

"Don't worry, girls! Sam is here. All will be well. He's very brave. He'll shoot my husband if he comes."

Isla asked, "Can we go and see Phoebe?"

Hannah agreed, "Of course, you can!"

Keira looked doubtful, but Sophie said, "Don't worry! We'll be fine."

When the girls departed, Sam said, admiringly, "Wow! Where did you get those girls?"

*

468

The girls entered, carrying smaller bowls, escorting Phoebe who was burdened with two heavy dishes.

"Whoa! Yi'll have iss dropping these. Then that Lucy'll have the laugh on iss." They put down their dishes. Hannah and Keira hugged Phoebe.

"What've I done for this?"

"Fed us like Royalty?" suggested Hannah.

Sophie kissed Phoebe and said, "Thank you. Thank you very much, Phoebe!" "You're welcome, pet!"

It was an oddly happy supper.

When Phoebe and Lucy came to say goodnight, the adults restrained themselves, but the girls clung to Phoebe. When they heard the kitchen door close, Sophie and Isla burst into tears, clinging to their mothers. Holly was very quiet. Sam opened the kitchen door. He stood on the edge of a cliff. There was no fire escape. When he returned to the dining room, the girls were quieter. "Well done, girls! We'll make soldiers of you yet."

"No, you won't!" Hannah declared. Keira, cuddling Sophie, agreed.

Holly offered, "Do you know how to play poker? I'm very good at poker." Hannah was about to say, "I don't think," but changed her mind.

Holly suggested, "When you're older, you can win loads of money from stupid men."

While the girls, Keira and Holly played poker, Sam and Hannah made up a bed for Holly in the master bedroom. They laid a mattress outside the door for Sam. "Thank you, Sam."

"Nothing to it."

"I mean, you've held us together today."

She kissed her brother who wiped it off, saying, "What do you stick on your face?"

Goodnights were exchanged through the door. Sam had barely fallen asleep when Holly opened a creaking bedroom door and slipped under the duvet.

CHAPTER THIRTY-FIVE

"It's going very well, don't you think?"

Sam was sharpening the kitchen knives.
Holly was watching.
"Would you stick that knife into somebody?"
"If necessary, yes."
"Have you done it before?"
"Heaps of times," Sam lied.
"Then I will do it too. I will shut my eyes."
Sam stopped to look at Holly, eyes shut, waving
a phantom knife.
He sang, *"You have put such a spell on me."*
Holly punched him, saying, "Please don't sing. It
hurts my ears."
Sam began to sharpen another knife. Holly
kissed his stinging ear.

"I should've found you a long time ago. Why
didn't you come looking for me, Sam?"
"I didn't have your address."
"That's no excuse. We would've run away
together."
"You wouldn't have liked where we ran to."
"Why has it got to end here?"
Sam stopped sharpening the sharp knife.
"Don't think like that. We'll survive today, I
promise you."

Holly smiled to say, "It's all too late, Sam. Thank you for my Saturday."

The door opened and the family arrived in the kitchen. Hannah kissed Sam good morning. The girls hugged him and Keira started breakfast. Isla said, "What're you doing, Sam?"
Sam looked to the innocent faces.
"If the worst comes to the worst, we need to be prepared."
Hannah complained, "You're not suggesting the girls should have knives?" "We don't need knives," Sophie declared.
"We have hat pins. Found lots of them in the bottom of the wardrobe." "Victorian girls used them to keep the boys away."
Holly asked, "Did it work?"

From their hair, Isla and Sophie pulled out long pins with glass heads.
"They're very old, but they're sharp."
Hannah said, "Keep the hat pins. Just don't stick them in anybody."
She turned to her brother.
"What're you expecting?"
"I've no idea. They have us trapped here, but we're not helpless. Many of their Congregation are walking dead. All have sold their souls. They're not heroes." "Neither are we," Hannah confessed.
"But we will fight for the children."

472

Sam tested the last knife on his thumb nail.

"They showed us Phoebe to frighten us. Well, they got that wrong. We should thank them for the extra time we had with Phoebe. So we go along with the charade that we're 'invited' to this Congregation."

Surprisingly, they ate well at breakfast. Sam told them the story of the cook who bought the same goat three times before he realised he'd been cheated. Surprisingly, they laughed together.

"In the end did you eat the goat?"

"No, we ate the cook. And very tasty he was too! His apron had marinated for thirty years in Army cookhouses."

"Ugh!"

"Another story, please!"

Sam told another story.

When Oliver De'ath walked in, he was annoyed to find them laughing. The adults noted this and were heartened. He ignored the arrival of Holly and Sam.

"I've come to escort you to the Assembly Hall. Members of Congregation are filling the seats now, but chairs are reserved for you, as honoured guests, in the front row."

Isla asked, "What about Glaze?"

"What about him?"

"We haven't seen him this morning."

"We don't want him locked in the apartment."
Sam said, "I'll check he's not here."

They waited in the hallway until Sam returned to shake his head.
"Glaze has skedaddled."
He produced a candle and standing it on the hall table, lit the wick. The flame burnt clean and true.
Sophie asked, "What's that for?"
"To ensure we will return."
Oliver De'ath smiled.

*

It was noisy in the Assembly Hall. Most of the seats were filled. At their entry Congregation applauded. Oliver led them to a row of empty chairs. They stood before sitting, looking over the clamorous assembly. Congregation was naked apart from plastic aprons. Everyone had bottles from which they drank.
Sam said, "These are the people you don't want to grow up to be, girls. Cruel, soulless, greedy, cowardly creatures. They don't understand love or loyalty." When they sat down they became aware of a faint scent of decay.
Sophie said, "We're not going to be afraid."
Isla agreed, "But I might be sick. They stink."

Oliver came forward to clap his hands and announce, "Be upstanding for his Unholiness, the Lord Bishop of Congregation."

Behind them the chairs rattled as Congregation rose.

Sam rose, saying, "Wrong time to say no."

The family rose, controlling trembling legs. Across the liquid surface of the ebony throne, thousands of despairing faces drifted, mouths open in endless agony. Isla shuddered, her arm about Sophie.

Hannah said, "It's all a show to scare us."

"Silence!" cried Oliver.

The double doors behind the throne opened. There emerged a little old man on two sticks, dragging failing legs, supported by two Oliver clones. They struggled to mount the ancient creature onto the throne. Once seated, with bad-tempered reproofs to his helpers, the Lord Bishop of Congregation farted loudly.

The head was hairless and the eyes were those of a ferret. The face was skull-like and the creature breathed through the mouth of a rapacious catfish. It wore a parody of a Bishop's garments. The mitre was a dunce's cap. The cross upon its scrawny breast was reversed. With a movement of a bony hand, the Bishop signalled his Congregation to sit. Sam calculated how long it would take to reach the creature. He noted no bodyguard by the throne.

Oliver stepped forward.
"My dear Lord Bishop, it is a particular honour to me that I have served as your Amanuensis for a hundred and twenty years."
Congregation dutifully applauded. Keira and Hannah exchanged glances. Holly clung to Sam.

"But on this unique occasion, we have an immensely greater honour placed upon us. Today we will bear witness to the Renewal of our Immaculate Lord. Today we shall welcome the Second Coming of Our Lord Lucifer, Bearer of Light. All the kingdoms of the earth shall bow down and worship his Name." Oliver paused to catch his breath. Congregation applauded and the Lord Bishop farted to display approval.
"However, are we all worthy to be here on this momentous occasion? A question we must ask ourselves. Are you worthy to be present at His Coming?" Oliver paraded solemnly before Congregation studying faces. His clones prowled the aisles.

A hysterical voice broke the silence.
"I sabotaged the school bus to kill Aaron Probart. Twenty-seven children died and three teachers. One of the children was my own son. I was following the bus. I didn't phone for help. I set

fire to the bus. All this, I have done in service to Our Lord."

Many voices began to cry out, proclaiming the foulest of deeds. Holly began to weep silently at the atrocities performed upon the innocent. Suddenly, at a gesture from Oliver, his clones began to drag out men and women from the assembly. They protested, screaming their worthiness.

In a voice of thunder, Oliver shouted, "I do not believe you! Dispatch them!"

To the horror of the family the clones began to cut and stab at the unfortunates. The girls hid their heads within their mothers' arms, Men and women screamed hysterically as their murderers chased them around the Assembly Hall. Congregation roared with laughter. When a woman would beg for mercy, Congregation jeered and laughed. At the end of a frantic five minutes, all the chosen were dead. The clones dragged them to the marble slabs where butchers awaited them.
"That's got us off to a lively start! Show your appreciation, please! Give the lads a round of applause!"

The grinning, bloody clones pranced before the altar, stabbing and slashing the air in mindless mimicry. Congregation stamped its collective feet, whistled, cheered and applauded their heroes. As the din faded, Sam said to the girls, "Being afraid is okay. But keep your head."

Oliver caught the words and scowled at Sam. He dismissed his clones, turning to the creature on the throne.

"My Lord, an unworthy sacrifice in His name, but no one will go hungry today."

The assembly howled again.

"Later, you may enjoy yourself and each other. From the hour of his Coming discord will reign."

The beasts howled longer and louder. Oliver came to speak to Sam.

"Foolish words, my friend, foolish words."

Again taking centre stage, Oliver declaimed, "My Lord Bishop, let me record my small part in celebrating the Coming of Our Lord. Tomorrow morning, the banking world will learn the Northern and Counties Bank."

He stopped to smile at Hannah and Keira.

"The Northern and Counties Bank has collapsed."

Hannah tried to struggle to her feet, but Keira urged her down. "All four hundred and twenty-seven branches. Not a penny in the till of any of them. Not a diamond in any safety deposit box. The mortgages are worthless." Congregation applauded.

"Dear friends, when you're feeling a little blue, think of all those hundreds of thousands of people who thought their savings were safe in the bank."

The Assembly Hall shook with waves of laughter.

"It has been the work of many hands, but I'm sure you will wish to congratulate Hannah Ericksen and Keira Sullivan who are here with us today."

A trickle of applause.

"They contrived to steal almost four hundred and sixty-seven million pounds by bogus investments."

The partners stared at one another in disbelief, mirrored in the children's faces.

"That's not true!" shouted Isla.

Holly whispered to Sam, "Did they?"

Sam shook his head.

"I've no idea."

"A round of applause, please! For Hannah and Keira!"

The applause was deafening.

"Stand up, stand up! They wish to see you!"

Sam nodded to them and the partners rose, holding hands.

"It has been a wonderful experience, working with you both. Thank you, ladies!"

They sank to their chairs, bewildered.

"Patience," said Sam, "Wait for them to make a mistake."

Sophie became aware Glaze was sitting under her chair. She nudged Isla who almost cried out on seeing the cat. The girls shared a smile. Oliver went to consult with the Bishop.

"There will be a short intermission to our programme. Refreshments are available. The cloakroom is open. If your interest is buggery, please, remember, there will be others who wish to use the toilets after you."

Almost before Oliver had finished speaking, there was a rush to the butchery blocks where the crowd hid the vile behaviour. Happy, bloody faces turned from the crush, chewing choice morsels of offal, grasping paper cups of blood. A clone came to offer paper cups to the girls who politely refused. Sam was surprised how calm the children were.

Holly said, "I wish these were our children, Sam."

"Whoa! Who said anything about children?"

Above the clatter, Oliver's voice could be heard calming the uproar.

"My apologies, ladies and gentlemen, for the paper cups. But what does our opposition offer? A stale wafer biscuit and a sip of sour wine."

It was obviously an old joke as a large minority joined in the telling. Congregation applauded.

A member chased a woman around the hall, waving a decapitated head. He cried, "Give iss a kiss, love!" and Congregation exploded in laughter when she relented and kissed the bloody head. Oliver De'ath called for silence.

The double doors behind the throne opened. A hospital trolley, dressed in scarlet, was led into the hall by a figure in surgical blues. A nurse carried a drip stand. The trolley came to rest before the altar. Under a scarlet sheet, a woman's body was discernible. She moved a feeble arm.

A horrified Hannah whispered, "My God! They're going to induce the birth here!"

Oliver declaimed, "Kneel in the presence of Our Lord. His entry into his Kingdom is imminent. We are honoured beyond measure."

Everyone knelt, blooded faces solemnly chewing steadily. Sam sensed Congregation was barely in order. He had seen it before in troops who were over-inflated with success, careless of discipline, slack and disorderly. Even as they knelt, Sam turned to watch two men exchange blows while a woman fought with the clone who came to intervene. It took three clones to quieten them. Glaze moved cautiously below the chair.

Isla whispered, "The Bishop! He's nodding off!!"

The girls watched the Bishop, eyes closing, head nodding. A group of women began catcalling another group. The obscenity on the throne opened an eye for a moment and nodded off again.

Oliver declaimed, "You may rise! Those who are chosen may pass about the Blessed Mother, whose honour it has been to carry our Lord safely to the moment of His birth."

Clones were busy among Congregation as to who would be chosen to pass about the birthing bed, causing further dissension.

Sam said quietly, "This is close to disruption. Be ready."

A queue began to form of the privileged and a clone pressed pilgrims to offer gold and jewellery to a church platen. Those who were reluctant to donate had jewellery taken from them. The fool who promised a cheque was kicked repeatedly to his seat.

Oliver De'ath approached Sam smiling.

"It's going very well, don't you think? Congregation's somewhat excited, but how can one blame them on such an occasion?"

Sam said, "Why don't you let Hannah, Keira and the children go?"

Oliver smiled.

"I wonder if you recognise the doctor. He's an old friend."
Sam stared at the figure in hospital blues.

"Colin?"

The unshakable Sam Ericksen was shaken to his boots. The image rose as fresh as ever. Sam was running with Colin Bridger across his back, leaving the doctor's left leg behind in the dust. The endlessly repeated crude joke. *You say you never left a man behind, Sam? What about Doc's leg?*

"The nurse in happier circumstances might've been your mother-in-law."

CHAPTER THIRTY-SIX

"Who told you that fairy story?"

Before Hannah and Keira could stop them, the girls ran to join the line attending the hospital trolley. Sam said, "Let them go." The mothers fought not to panic. Congregation applauded the children. Oliver came smiling to whisper to the girls. They appeared not to be afraid. He mouthed theatrically to the front row. "Wonderful children!" Sam kept a tight hold on Holly who was straining to fly at Oliver. Isla and Sophie promenaded about the bed and returned to their chairs. The silence ended.

A man in the mould of a politician, ignorant and greedy, rose to deliver the most boring speech ever copied from the Guardian. Congregation members wandered to the butchery blocks to return with paper cups and delicacies to share with friends. At moments the disorder among the audience rendered the speaker inaudible. Sam realised the assembly sought to be normal. It might've been a Party Political Conference or a parents' evening at any large school. Evil is banal. Killing six million Jews was simply a matter of good bookkeeping.

Holly grumbled, "This is really very boring, Sam. If they're going to kill us, why don't they just get on with it?"

"You're not frightened?"

"'Course, I am, but you can only be scared so long and then it wears off. Look at the girls."

The girls were explaining what they had seen.

"She's like us, Mum."

"Wha'd'y'mean? Like us?"

"She has a brown skin." Isla explained, "Milk chocolate like Sophie."

"Got the biggest tummy we've ever seen. You'd think she'd burst."

"Not much older than us."

"She said, 'I want my Mammy.'"

"She wouldn't let go my hand."

The girls looked to one another.

"Should we?"

"Should you what?"

Sophie said, "We think the nurse is Grandma. But that can't be right, can it?"

Hannah and Keira turned to Sam who said, "I'm afraid it's true."

"My mother? How'd'you know?"

"The doctor is Doctor Colin Bridger. He was my friend. Rather, I thought he was my friend. That poor woman has been hidden away at his hospital."

"My mother is with the Devil?"

485

The speech ended and the applause dribbled to silence. Sam stood up and shouted, "Why have you betrayed us, Colin?"
Congregation stirred with interest.

Oliver De'ath responded, "Ho, ho! We have debate! How I miss the Oxford Union! Shall we permit them to debate?"
Congregation approved.
"I would like to know how they corrupted you. You were gold brick, Colin. You risked your life for strangers. Lost your leg trying to save an Afghan policeman. What went wrong?"

Colin pulled down the surgical mask.
"Nothing went wrong, Sam. No more than I might have expected. There are those who do not favour ex-Army medics with one leg. They regard us as being somewhat basic. What Alan Winterton."
Sam interrupted, "Ah, yes! The ubiquitous Alan Winterton, friend of all the world."
"Do not mock our Chancellor!"
Sam blew a raspberry of disgust.
"Carry on, doctor."
"Alan Winterton gave me a hospital. All I've had to do, is treat the patients who come to me. Many ex-servicemen ignored by authority. When the Army'd finished with you, Sam, what did they give you? A pottery course. Alan Winterton offered you fame and fortune."

Keira cried, "What about you, Mum?"

The doctor offered, "Let me say this, Keira. Your mother was a highly skilled clinical psychiatrist in the USA. Yet patients would ask to see a colleague. Why? Because of the colour of her skin. It hasn't been any easier for her in London."

"I want to hear my mother! What did they give you?"

Victoria cried, "They gave me belief."

"I don't understand, Mum."

"What I was taught about justice and equality was all lies. Behind their slogans and smiles, Whitey hates and fears us! I am to be the Guardian of the Child Lucifer who cares not what colour my skin is. Come to us, Keira! You will be the exalted Chosen Mother of the Prince Lucifer. Sophie will be His handmaiden. We will fry their white arses!"

"No way!" cried Sophie.

Congregation exploded in applause and Keira was desolated.

"Did someone mention my name? Nothing disparaging, I trust?"

Immaculately turned out, Alan Winterton, swordstick in hand, manifested himself in obeisance before the dozing Bishop.

Oliver De'ath demanded, "Be upstanding for our Lord Chancellor!" Congregation rose.

An oaf of a man in a rear row mocked Winterton's swagger and speech. With surprising speed, Winterton had him out of his chair in front of Congregation with the swordstick blade at his throat.

"We have not met before, have we, my friend?"

"No, sir! I was only having a laugh, sir."

"Then it's my turn now."

"Yes, sir, sorry, sir."

"I used the word disparaging. Did I not?"

"I think so, sir?"

"Did I or did I not?"

"Yes, sir."

"If you wish to use a word, you must be able to spell it. Yes, or no?"

"Yes, sir." "Then spell it for me. I'll give you a start. Dee!"

The feckless creature stood silent.

"Can't you spell disparaging?"

"No, sir."

"Then I'll help you. Dee!"

The blade moved so swiftly the right ear seemed to fly from his head. The victim cried out as his left ear vanished. At every letter the blade struck. Instinctively he put hands to his bleeding head. He began to moan with increasing volume as fingers and hands were cut away. Hannah and Keira pulled the children to themselves, hiding their eyes. The pitiful creature screamed as his genitals were sliced away. He fell to his knees, wailing in such a fashion as chilled the blood. He screamed at eagle pitch as the blade removed his eyes. The woman, into whose lap the left eye fell, screeched hysterically. There was silence in the hall when the man's head hit the floor. Winterton kicked it away.

In the arctic silence, the decapitated head rolled across the floor, leaving skeins of blood. It stopped in front of Holly who covered her eyes. No one moved. No one breathed.
"Clear away this garbage!
The corpse was dragged away as a slaughtered bull from the ring. A clone dribbled out the head to the inevitable accompaniment of 'On me 'ead, son! On me 'ead!' The tension faltered and Congregation laughed.

Winterton took centre stage and the assembly fell silent.
"Do you understand that you are living in the singular hour of this millennium? Today will be born the Child that we have waited for through long lifetimes. Today is the birth day of Our Lord Incarnate."

He was silent for a moment and no one breathed. Every eye was upon him. "But are we ready to receive the beneficence of His Presence? Will he look upon us as the true guardians of His childhood and youth? When he accepts Ultimate Power, will he look to us as his vanguard? Think upon this. Look into yourselves. Are we worthy?"

He left the question unanswered.

"There must be change! We must be awake and aware!"

Winterton stepped onto the dais and seizing the dozing Bishop by the arm, threw the old man to the floor. Congregation cried out in surprise and shock. "This mindless creature has long outlived any worth he may once have had."

The old man on the floor whimpered and raised a feeble arm. Winterton began to stamp on the old man's skull. Hannah and Keira clutched their children. Sam held Holly, one hand to her left ear, his lips to its twin. The breaking of the carapace echoed in the hall as the skull splintered. He began to dance on the fragile corpse. A mouth organ struck up an Irish jig. Dancers stepped out in imitation in the aisles and Congregation applauded. Winterton held up an arm and they fell silent.

He picked up the dunce's cap and set it on his head. Oliver De'ath screamed hysterically, "Rise to acclaim our Lord Bishop!"

The Congregation rose to chorus, "We acclaim our Lord Bishop!"

The family sat silent in their chairs.

As the shouting died, Winterton cried, "Then we are of one purpose! We dedicate our lives to the Baby Lucifer, Prince of Light, Master of Mankind!" They cheered again and again until his hand silenced them.

"Do we have a broom?"

A broom was hastened from the cloakroom. The Lord Bishop began to sweep the remnants of his predecessor from the hall. The assembly roared. A man eagerly seized the broom from his Bishop. Other brooms appeared and more volunteers hastened to accept the honour of sweeping fragments from the old man's corpse from the hall.

When the housework was completed, Winterton called, "Is there not someone here who can entertain us with a jolly story? Do I have to provide all the entertainment myself?"

A fat man wearing three balloon breasts and a metre-long rubber penis came forward to narrate a humorous story of rape, buggery, murder, abuse, mutilation and humiliation that soon had Congregation in fits of laughter, lowering the emotional temperature. Alan Winterton approached the guests.

"Hannah, Keira, welcome! I've heard so much about you. Oliver had quite a thing about you, Hannah. Holly! My faithless wife! As beautiful as ever! I wonder how much my dear old chum, Sam, would lust after you, if I removed your left breast or your right eye?"

Holly sat still, eyes closed, holding Sam's hand tightly. Winterton jerked her head up.

"Your lips are healing well. Next time I'll cut them off."

"Have you an answer for me, Sam old chum? I grow irritable if ignored."

"Do you remember the old riddle? Will you lie with me in a field of stone?"

"Charming, most charming! But irrelevant."

Holly said, "You never told me the right answer.

Sam replied, "I would die with you in a field of stone."

Holly smiled and kissed him. They stared at a furious Winterton until he turned away to address the girls.

"And the children! Such delightful girls! So pretty! Which is which? Isla? Sophie?"

The girls refused to acknowledge the names.

"Are your titties beginning to blossom? Are you going to be chummy mummies if you grow up?"

Before Isla could stop Sophie.

"You should be ashamed of yourself, to speak like that to children. Is that all you do? Frighten people, threaten them, hurt them, kill them. Go ahead, kill me!"

Keira cried out. For a moment, it seemed Winterton would strike the child, then he relaxed.

"And if I did kill you?"

"You would have nothing."

"But you would be dead?"

"If you exist, then God exists. And I am his child."

Winterton stopped to look closely at Sophie.

"Who told you that fairy story?"

"It's the truth. There can be no darkness without light."

Winterton walked away.

To the girls' surprise, Skinny Lizzie appeared before them to say, "Don't get frit! They's coming!"

As they turned to introduce her to their mothers, Skinny Lizzie vanished.

The comedian ended his performance with a remarkable display of projectile vomiting. Victims in the second row proudly displayed his prowess on arms, legs and aprons. Congregation applauded. Alan Winterton waved the applause to silence.

"On this momentous day in the history of the world, I have not come empty-handed to honour my Lord and Master."

The pregnant child on the trolley began to whimper. The doctor silenced her. Oliver moved to talk to the doctor. Alan Winterton continued. He indicated Sam Ericksen.
"Stand up, Sam! Let Congregation see you."
In an undertone, he snarled, "Get up, damn you! Or I'll kill that child, I promise."
Sam stood up.
"My dear friend, Sam Ericksen!"
Congregation applauded politely. Sam gave the finger to Congregation. They found this most amusing and reciprocated. Winterton's face was taut with anger.
"Sit down!"
"You wanted me to stand up."
Sam sat down. Holly kissed his cheek.
"That was very naughty!"

Winterton threatened, "Any more shit like that and I'll blind that child."
"Why that child?"
Winterton didn't respond.
"Some months ago, I found a hoard of ancient Chinese porcelain in a storeroom in Windsor Castle. Incredibly valuable."
Congregation was impressed.

"We have arranged to return this treasure tomorrow afternoon to the People's Republic of China. My dear friend, Sam, being a renowned potter, will present the porcelain."

Congregation was silent.

"He will shoot the President and destroy the porcelain."

He was forced to cease as the volume of applause overwhelmed him.

Sam noted that De'ath wasn't pleased by this triomphe de theatre.

"If you have a hole, go hide in it. The rockets will be flying!"

Congregation roared with laughter.

"This is my humble offering upon the birth of Our Lord Lucifer! But first I must encourage Sam to do what I wish. One of these people is the person whom he loves most. All we have to do is find who it is!"

Congregation relished the notion of such entertainment.

"Stand up!"

Oliver De'ath urged the family to rise.

"Turn to face Congregation."

Holly, Hannah, Keira, Isla and Sophie stood up, holding hands, to face the ravening, lustful, greedy faces.

"Who shall it be?"

Strictly off cue, the girl on the trolley began to scream, tearing at her grotesque belly. Colin Bridger cut open the black girl's abdomen and hoisted out the baby. The girl screamed again and died.

Colin Bridger cried, "I couldn't hold back any longer. The baby would die!"

He was a big strong boy with a melanin-shaded skin. He croaked like a carrion crow and struggled in Bridger's arms, dark eyes glistening, questing. Victoria Sullivan cut the cord. The Congregation roared in triumph. Winterton and De'ath fell to their knees in worship.

Sam Ericksen shot the baby twice, his head exploding like a melon. He killed Colin Bridger and Victoria Sullivan as they turned to flee. Glaze sprang at his old enemy, Winterton, tearing at his eyes, as he moved to kill Sam. Blinded, he struggled to pull the cat away, finally freeing himself to slash at Sam. Holly flung herself into Winterton's arms, breaking the phosphorus grenade against his mid-spine.

The hall was lit by a blinding light and Winterton began to scream. The pair, consumed in deadly flame, burned bright as a funeral pyre. Eyes could not face their overwhelming agony.

"Now!" cried Sam.

Hannah and Keira, grabbing the girls, struggled to reach the door to freedom. Oliver grabbed Hannah by the wrist, forestalling their escape. Isla drove a hat pin through his right hand as Sophie speared his left wrist. Oliver fell back, shocked, screaming, staring at the hat pins.

Into the onrushing Congregation Sam emptied the pistol and calmly changed magazines. He killed the nearest of the Congregation and threw the second grenade into the mob where it exploded in a deadly snowstorm. Where the bright phosphorus fell, soulless & undead began to tear at their bodies.

Then caved in the floor. Men and women armed with filleting knives, eel spears, gaffs and clubs clambered out from the prison of their grave to attack the Congregation. The front doors of the House burst open to admit the men and women from the cobles that had returned to claim their own. As the people of the shielings overran the living and undead, Sam turned away.

Oliver De'ath drove the swordstick blade through his body. Sam fell down in shock, clutching the raw blade. Before his sight failed, Sam saw Hannah, Keira, Isla and Sophie were no longer in the hall. The last thing he heard was the cataclysmic explosion when the gas found the candle in Apartment F. The ancient timbers and brickwork of the ancient House collapsed, burning fiercely. A column of black smoke began to flow across the town on the wings of the North Sea wind.

The creature called Oliver De'ath was hacked to pieces on the steps of the House by Thodren, much beloved of Greta who has three combs. Skinny Lizzie and Glaze led the family from the melee to safety in the park. The fire engines were baulked by the automatic gates from tackling the inferno. All the fire fighters could do was watch the House burn. The family, Hannah, Keira, Isla, Sophie and Glaze, watched what no one else saw: the cobles of the people of the shielings leave the Aranport shore forever.

*

Sam Ericksen was clearing the compound that had turned out to be a school. The presence of the children was a surprise to the patrol. The Taliban were retreating, herding the girls with them as a shield. Driven into the open, the madmen pointed their weapons at the helpless children. The leader shouted to the patrol to go away or. Blakcy opened fire without hesitation. A young girl was shot as a Taliban fell, discharging his weapon.

The girl died in Sam's arms, lingeringly, smiling, looking at him wonderingly, reluctant to leave him. Samuel Ericksen pressed the soul coin into the girl's forehead. Her eyes opened and she smiled at him. Sam stood up and offered his hand. They walked together and then, the child shook herself free from the big man to run across the field of stones to join her friends and the Afghan militia. Sam trotted to where his team was boarding the helicopter.

The Ministry of Defence has confirmed that yesterday a helicopter carrying British servicemen crashed near Sangin, Helmand. There were no survivors. The next of kin have been informed.

THE END

© Alex Ferguson
September 2017

Printed in Great Britain
by Amazon